Sommerhjem Journeys Series:

Journey's Middle: Winner of the Midwest Independent Publishing Association (MIPA) 2012 Midwest Book Award for Young Adult Fiction and finalist in the Fiction: Fantasy and Science Fiction category.

Journey's Lost and Found: Finalist of the MIPA 2013 Midwest Book Awards in both the Young Adult Fiction and the Fiction: Fantasy and Science Fiction categories.

Journey's Seekers: Winner of the MIPA 2014 Midwest Book Awards in both the Young Adult Fiction and the Fiction: Fantasy and Science Fiction categories.

Journey's Crossroads: Finalist of the MIPA 2015 Midwest Book Awards in the Young Adult Fiction category.

Journey's Chosen

B. K. PARENT

JOURNEY'S CHOSEN

iUniverse books may be ordered through booksellers or by contacting:

iUniverse
1663 Liberty Drive
Bloomington, IN 47403
www.iuniverse.com
1-800-Authors (1-800-288-4677)

Because of the dynamic nature of the Internet, any web addresses or links contained in this book may have changed since publication and may no longer be valid. The views expressed in this work are solely those of the author and do not necessarily reflect the views of the publisher, and the publisher hereby disclaims any responsibility for them.

Any people depicted in stock imagery provided by Thinkstock are models, and such images are being used for illustrative purposes only.
Certain stock imagery © Thinkstock.

ISBN: 978-1-5320-1781-0 (sc)
ISBN: 978-1-5320-1960-9 (hc)
ISBN: 978-1-5320-1780-3 (e)

Library of Congress Control Number: 2017902660

Print information available on the last page.

iUniverse rev. date: 03/14/2017

Acknowledgments

Many thanks to the Chapter of the Week Group members who have been my main readers, critics, suppliers of ideas and support, and have kept me on track; to Celeste Klein who encouraged me daily; to my sister Patti Callaway, Flika Gardner, and Joni Amundson who insisted on their chapter every week and let me know if the cliff hanger at the end of the chapter worked; to Aimee Brown, René Carlberg, Cathy Carlson, Sarah Charleston, Glennis Cohen, Sarah Huelskoetter, Beth and Josh Irish, Vickie Keating, Jenni Meyer, niece Anna Perkins, Connie Stirling, and Robin Villwock for also being members of the Chapter of the Week Group and reading the story.

Once again, many thanks to my niece Katherine M. Parent for her cover art and interior art. I can only hope the inside of the book is as good as the cover she has designed.

A special thanks to Steven Freund, who took copious notes on all of the books, and created a detailed map of the country of Sommerhjem. The map contained in this book is a simplified version of the map Steven created, redrawn by Katherine M. Parent.

Special thanks goes to Linne Jensen for surviving editing yet another book with me. I am extremely grateful for her knowledge of grammar and punctuation, and her ability to make sure the stories have consistency. Thanks also to Mary Sturm for finding the errors we missed.

To Gail (Flika) Gardner: Someone once wrote it takes a long time to grow an old friend. That is certainly true for us. Thank you for years of fond memories. Thanks for demanding your chapter each week and keeping me writing.

To CEK, always.

Introduction

Journey's Chosen was written as a serial. The chapters were each approximately four plus pages long and sent via e-mail to friends and relations once a week. A cliffhanger was written into the end of each chapter in order to build anticipation for the next chapter or, in some cases, merely to irritate the reader. You, as a new reader, have choices. You can read a chapter, walk away, and then later pick up the book and read the next chapter to get the serial experience. Another choice is to just read *Journey's Chosen* as a conventional book and "one more chapter" yourself to three o'clock in the morning on a work or school night.

PROLOGUE

Well of Speaking, three quarters of a year past.

Lord Cedric Klingflug, who had been appointed regent to rule Sommerhjem until Princess Esmeralda came of age, had tried to convince all who would listen for the past several weeks, and repeated now to the crowd assembled in the Well of Speaking, that Princess Esmeralda was gravely ill.

"Under usual circumstances and during usual times, a call to the Well of Speaking by the Crown would be to welcome you to the fair, or for some type of ceremony to honor someone. Today, Princess Esmeralda should have been stepping forward here in the Well of Speaking to claim her rightful place as the next queen of Sommerhjem. This fair should have been a week-long celebration of the coming of age of our fair Princess Esmeralda and her rise to the leadership role she has been trained for all her life. I regret that is not possible, for as we gather here this day, and as I am sure many of you have already heard, our beloved Princess is gravely ill. Despite all of the combined knowledge of our best healers and herbalists, her condition does not seem to be improving. Due to the fact that we do not know when the Princess will be healthy enough to assume her duties, and to prevent chaos from reigning, I have consulted with the royal advisors, and I am prepared to continue to act as regent until such time as the Princess is well enough to rule."

Standing, rising to his considerable height, and straightening his formal blue seeker's cloak around himself with an air of authority, Seeker Eshana addressed the Regent. "Will you step down when the Princess is well enough to rule?"

The Regent confirmed he would.

"I suggest that you are now relieved of your duties as regent," stated Seeker Eshana.

"Oh, for goodness sakes, did you not hear what I just said? The Princess is gravely ill, and keeping everything the same as to how Sommerhjem is governed is only common sense," the Regent said, running a hand through his thinning gray hair in frustration.

The hunched figure who had been standing quietly beside Seeker Eshana slowly straightened up, removed her hat, and handed it to Seeker Eshana with great dignity. One of the royal guards stepped forward and removed her light cloak, revealing a young woman with light brown hair and flashing green eyes.

"The rumors about my grave illness have been blown greatly out of proportion," stated the Princess, in a voice that carried conviction and the weight of command behind it.

A very loud murmur ran through the crowd.

"What are you trying to pull, Seeker?" the Regent demanded. "Why would you try to put an imposter before the crowd assembled here?"

A hush came over the crowd and hung in the air when Regent Klingflug declared Princess Esmeralda was an imposter. In truth, a number of folks loyal to the Crown had helped the Princess escape from impending harm and kept her safe. Only a very few folks knew that she had traveled for several weeks disguised as a rover. Though Regent Klingflug questioned her identity, it quickly became obvious that she was indeed the real Princess Esmeralda.

The silence in the Well of Speaking was intense as the crowd held its collective breath, waiting to see what would happen next in the confrontation between Regent Klingflug and Princess Esmeralda.

"It would seem we are at an impasse," the Princess said, aiming her remark at the Regent. "Many of the folk are loath to have you continue on as ruler and …," she held her hand up to stop the Regent from interrupting, "… and, in my recent travels, I have come to understand that many are equally not thrilled to have me take the throne. There is a solution, however."

"And just what do you think that might be?" the Regent asked, with a sneer in his voice, implying he would have the upper hand no matter what she would propose.

"It does this land we both love no good if we divide it in a power struggle over who is to rule," the Princess said calmly. "One solution, of course, is for me to abdicate, but …," the Princess held up her hand once again, indicating she wanted all to remain quiet, "… I am not going to do that. You could arrange for me to be seated on the throne right now, this very day, but I am thinking you are not willing to do that, based on everything you have done to maintain control, so …," the Princess paused, turned to face those assembled, and declared, "… I call the Gylden Sirklene challenge."

By calling the Gylden Sirklene challenge, the Princess forced the Regent, Lord Klingflug, to step down. To end any quarreling or further discussion, Master Clarisse stood, and her voice rang out clearly over the noise of the crowd. The assembled folks fell silent to listen. "The Gylden Sirklene challenge has been called by Princess Esmeralda to choose a new ruler of our land. Do you, Princess Esmeralda, relinquish your right to the throne at this time?"

"As I understand it, I never really had a right to the throne, so I cannot give up what I did not have. But to answer your question, I will honor the rules of the challenge and, if I have the right, vie for the throne."

"According to the Book of Rules, anyone, no matter their station, has both the right to call and to participate in the Gylden Sirklene challenge, so, Lady Esmeralda, you have just as much right as anyone else to take the challenge. Until the challenge is completed, the rule of Sommerhjem will be carried out by an interim ruling council made up of members chosen from the various clans, classes, and guilds. Lady Esmeralda, will you take a place on the interim ruling council for the next year?" Master Clarisse asked. There was a loud gasp from those assembled at the moment that Master Clarisse addressed her as a noble and not as a princess.

"A double demotion, all in one day. First, no longer the heir to the throne and now, no longer a princess," she noted with a gentle smile. "To answer your question, I, Lady Esmeralda, would be honored to serve on the interim ruling council for the next year," she answered graciously.

Master Clarisse nodded in approval and turned back to face the crowd. "Before we adjourn this assembly, let word go out across the land that the Gylden Sirklene challenge has been called. Know that, according to the Book of Rules, the remaining seven rings of the nine rings that make up the oppgave ringe need to be placed in the vessteboks here before one year's time passes. Anyone trying to prevent a ring carrier from making the journey here does so at his or her own risk. In addition, no harm should befall seekers, whose task it is to search out the ring carriers."

Before those in the crowd could begin to talk once again, Master Clarisse held up her hand for continued silence. "In addition, the individual, or individuals, who are living keys during the Gylden Sirklene challenge, are also protected. Should any try to harm them, harm will come back to them threefold."

When Master Clarisse made that statement, it was easy to believe every word she was saying, as her voice carried a conviction and authority that was hard to deny. "What Lady Esmeralda has called into being is now started. Let those who feel called to be our next king or queen assemble here one year from this day to face the Gylden Sirklene challenge. This assembly is dismissed."

CHAPTER ONE

"There is some irony that I am packing my homewagon, preparing to leave Mumblesey in the dark of night once again, one year from the day I left the last time. This year, however, I will not be sneaking out of town the back way," I said to Thomas, the pub keeper, and his eldest son, Padget.

Thomas had come out to my father's cottage, Journey's End, to help Padget move in. Thomas' son was going to be the caretaker of Da's place until the summer fair season was over, and Thorval and Nana, my Da and grandmother, returned.

"Just like last year, Da is not here," I said, "but, unlike last year, when I came home from gathering herbs in the hills east of here to find him missing and needed your help, this year I know where he is. He and Nana left three days ago and intend to go down the coast. They will head toward the capital moving from summer fair to summer fair. I intend to take the same route I took last year and go inland a bit. I got so behind with last minute things to do with my new homewagon that if I hope to get to Treebles on time, I need to leave this night."

"Well, Nissa, lass, at least it's not rainin' this year, and I don't have to help you sneak out the back way either," Thomas remarked. "Would be a shame to have all that new paint scratched and scraped goin' down that narrow path off of my Aunt Heddy's farm again. Sure 'tis a beautiful homewagon you and your Da built."

I was pleased to hear Thomas admire the work my Da and I had so recently finished. It had been a joy to work with Da to build my new homewagon over the last few months. He had done all of the metal work, and I had done the woodwork. I had spent hours in the evening planning just how to use the designs the Huntress had given me, using them in both the carvings I was doing on the cabinetry and the painted designs on the outside of the homewagon and the small cart I would pull behind. I painted the designs on the outside of the homewagon in a deep forest green, which contrasted nicely with the natural wood color and looked good.

My new homewagon was smaller than Da's, the one I had driven the entire summer before. His was a family-sized homewagon, built to house at least four comfortably. Mine was more compact, yet very comfortable for one or two, and held all that Carz and I would need to live in it. The homewagon had a stove for heating, cubby for firewood, wash basin, water jug, table, seating, and storage. I had made the bed large enough to fit both Carz and me. Carz, a silver-hued, medium-haired hunting cat, was slightly bigger than a large herding dog and took up much more room on a bed than, say, a house cat.

I surveyed my homewagon and commented, "I really like the look of the dip in the middle of the roof. Also, I like the look of the way the side windows stick out just a bit, the tops being rounded. What do you think of the cedar shake roof?"

"Makes the homewagon look like a wee cottage on wheels," Thomas replied.

Every nook and cranny of my new homewagon was packed. All of the goods I had made over the long cold months, after I had come back to Mumblesey from my last errand for the Crown, were packed in the cart along with my wood working tools. Gifts for the Neebings were tucked away over my bed, and the small Neebing room hidden in the homewagon's base moved up and down smoothly, so that I could easily lower it when camped overnight and raise it before moving on.

Built into the cupboard beneath my bed was a panel that had a design that looked like a door. If one knew the secret, the door actually opened to reveal a tiny door that opened to a small room. When a plain panel next to the door panel was pressed a certain way, it swung open to reveal a hollow that had a small crank inside. If one turned the crank, it let down a telescoping rectangular tube of wood that reached the ground and allowed access to this wee room. I had been taught to place a gift for the Neebings in this small room whenever I was camped.

Neebings are bit difficult to either describe or explain, since I have never actually seen one. It has been suggested that they are so very hard to see because they blend so very well into their environment. They are said to be small, furry, wily, elusive, mischievous, but basically tenderhearted. Frequent tales told by elder rovers suggest that Neebings prefer to live in woods, quirrelit tree groves, and near water. They are said to be mischievous, especially when neglected. Truth be told, when I was packing the homewagon last year and Nana had brought out gifts for the Neebings for me to pack, I thought she was just perpetuating an elaborate joke that adults played on susceptible younglings. I no longer think that way and had packed away plenty of Neebing gifts for my journey.

It was almost time to leave. I had topped off the water barrel, latched the window shutters, and filled the outside lamps with oil. I had greased the wheels, and not with bacon fat as I had needed to do when I snuck away a year ago. I started chuckling at the thought of driving through town with all of the village dogs smelling the bacon fat and nipping at my wheels if I had done that on the new homewagon. Thomas and his son gave me odd looks, so I told them about greasing the wheels with bacon fat the previous year.

"I'll be havin' a hard time tryin' to get that picture out of my head," Thomas said, laughing.

Padget laughed in agreement. "I sure would've liked to see you with your Da's homewagon heading down the narrow path on Great-Aunt Heddy's farm when you sneaked away at this time last summer. I've heard my father tell that tale many times by the fire at night."

Now all that was left to do was to hitch up the horses. "How my friend Journeyman Evan managed to wrangle me a pair of O'Gara's horses at a price I could afford remains an unsolved mystery. He said they were twins. Though very good horses, they are smaller than what Farmer O'Gara is breeding for. Fortunately, they are just the right size for my homewagon," I said.

"Can I help with the horses?" Padget asked eagerly. "They sure are a fine-looking pair of dappled grays."

"I would welcome your help." I knew the horses were in good hands, since Padget was in charge of the stables at Thomas' family's pub, the Leeward Inn.

"So, why didn't you head off with your Da and Nana?" asked Thomas.

Turning my attention back to Thomas, I answered, "We talked about it. Da thought that, while much has changed since last year at this time, there might still be some danger for us if we traveled together. Only a few know that the same Thorval Pedersen, whom the former regent was looking for most of last summer, is my Da. We don't want to give those who are loyal to the former regent a chance to get at both of us at the same time. When we meet up at the first fair in Tverdal, we should also meet up with others that we know and trust. We will follow the fair route with them, giving us safety in numbers."

I knew traveling from summer fair to summer fair would not be the same as the year before. Many of those folks I had traveled with the previous summer would not be traveling the same fair route this year. Master Clarisse, who had been just a journeywoman in the Glassmakers Guild when I met her the summer before, most probably would not be at Master Nadag's glassmaking shop, for she had important duties for the Crown in the capital. Missing also would be Journeyman Evan, Master Clarisse's former apprentice, who was now serving under the Glassmakers Guild Master of the Horse. And then there was Beezle, Lord Hadrack's nephew, who was off on mysterious assignments for the Crown and would not be traveling the fair route to promote his family's highly regarded cheeses. With all of these friends missing from the fair route, it was comforting to know I would meet up with Da and Nana at the Tverdal Fair, along with the other rovers I had traveled with last summer: Oscar, Bertram, and their families, and Shueller and Tannar.

"Besides, I want to get back to Treebles to see if old Farmer Josh is all right. I want to let him know that his friend Farmer Ned Fairwalker is doing well. Truth be told, I also had some of the best berry tarts of the entire summer in Treebles last year," I stated, with a hint of laughter in my voice. "I'm hoping that Trader Jalcones and his wife, whom I met there last year, will be in Treebles this year also. If not, I'm hoping they have kept to their annual schedule and I can catch up with them at the village where Master Nadag lives. It would be nice to travel with the Jalcones again from fair to fair."

"Looks like you're all set to go. I think your travelin' companion is gettin' a bit impatient," said Thomas.

I looked up to see that Carz was sitting in the driver's seat and looking my way. He did have an air of impatience about him as he twitched his silvery ears slightly.

"Thank you for everything. I had best get going before Carz decides to take up the reins and leave without me."

"Ah, lass, wouldn't that be a sight to see? Now, don't you worry none. My lad will take good care of things here. Safe travel."

I thanked Thomas and Padget once again and climbed aboard the homewagon. Flicking the reins lightly, I started off on what I hoped would be an easy and profitable summer traveling from fair to fair. After a few hours on the road, I felt better than I had in months. Not that I did not like spending time with Da and Nana at the cottage Journey's End on Rumblesea Cove, near Mumblesey, but I had missed being on the road.

"Well, Carz, we're off once again. You going to stay up here with me or go inside? Here with me then? The homewagon rides pretty nice, doesn't it, Carz?"

Carz lifted his head and gave me a disgusted look.

"So sorry to bother you while you are trying to nap, your royalness." *Some things never change*, I thought, *which, considering all that has changed in the last year, is comforting.*

After hours of travel, when I jerked awake for the umpteenth time, I decided it was time to find a place to pull over for the rest of the night.

The next day, around the noon hour, as I traveled down a narrow lane, I heard horses pounding up behind me at a fast pace. I was beginning to feel like I was reliving what had happened to me a year ago all over again. Last year at dusk, around this very area, I had heard riders approaching. They had ridden by then, much to my relief. As the sounds of fast-approaching horses grew closer, I opened the top half of the door into the homewagon and asked Carz to get inside, but stay alert. I moved my shoulders about, trying to ease the tightness I could feel in them. When I could clearly see the three riders coming toward me, I pulled the homewagon over to the edge of the roadway to let them pass, raising my hand in greeting, as was the custom, hoping as I had last year that they would pass by. Such, however, was not to be the case, for they slowed down and halted.

"You, rover, we are looking for Thorval Pedersen. Do you know him?"

"I know of him," I said, for I was not getting a good feeling about this meeting. I thought, *This cannot be happening, not again.* "I have heard he is quite a good metalsmith. Do you have need of him?" I inquired. The man did not answer my question.

"You have not seen him pass this way?"

"No, sir, I have not," I answered truthfully.

After I finished speaking, the man in charge signaled they were done with me, and they began to move on. Once they were past, one of the riders slowed and looked as if she were going to turn around and head back, but the lead rider signaled that they should all continue ahead. I hoped they would not change their minds and urged the horses forward at a steady pace. Something about that trio made me nervous. I had left home last year because folks were looking for my Da, and he had felt that the search for him put me in danger. I had worried all summer that he had been harmed or worse. I had hoped not to have to worry so much about him this summer. I had hoped our parts were done and we would not be involved in the events that were to unfold at the capital during the great summer fair.

I wondered if the woman rider who had turned around had thought she recognized me. Until the great summer fair in the capital last summer, few in Sommerhjem would have known of me, much less known what I looked like. I am of average height, and no one would ever accuse me of being slender or willowy. I do not glide gracefully into a room on any occasion. I remember my mother always commented that I had the stride of a rover, long and ground-eating. I am of light complexion, and Nana told me I was fair of face, but truthfully, I think I am rather plain. I feel my best feature is my hair, long and deep auburn with red highlights. I wear it in a thick braid down my back, not so much for fashion, but to keep it out of the way.

The rest of the day's journey passed without incident. Upon finally arriving at the high gate entrance to Treebles, I realized much had stayed the same, even though so much had happened since I was here last year. The same gatekeeper was at his post to greet me. He even directed me to set up my booth by the really big maple tree on the village green, the same spot he had directed me to the year before. I knew I could try for a better spot, but did not. The spot under the big maple tree had been the first place I had set up as an independent rover, and I was feeling a bit nostalgic about it.

I was glad when the gatekeeper told me that Farmer Josh was allowing travelers to camp on his land again. Once I had my cart set up, Carz and I headed out of the village toward Farmer Josh's land. After pulling the homewagon in close to the pines, just a little way away from several tents and wagons, I looked at those camped there and was disappointed to see that the Jalcones were not among them.

I unhitched the horses, fed and watered them, and got them settled. With the setting up chores done, I called to Carz, told him I was heading up to Farmer Josh's cottage, and asked if he wanted to come along. We walked up the well-worn path to the cottage and stopped at the front gate. Farmer Josh, an older man whose kindly face was weatherworn from spending all of his life out-of-doors, was sitting on the porch, rocking gently back and forth, petting the cat on his lap.

"So, have you not moved from that rocking chair since I was here last year? Looks like the same cat on your lap, too," I commented. "Asking your permission to camp below again, if you please."

"Ah, rover lass, you've come back. Welcome you are," Farmer Josh said. "Of course you can camp below. Your fee is the same as last year. Come sit a spell with an old man and have a talk. You're still only one of a few that follow the old ways and offer payment for camping on my land. A few more did this year though, which gives a hope to an ol' body that times are a-changing, and for the better."

"Before I forget," I said, "I have greetings from Farmer Ned Fairwalker. When I saw him last summer, he was well."

"Good to know my old friend is well. Now tell me, what has happened to you over the last year? Some word has trickled back, but I want to hear it from you."

Where do I begin? "After I left Treebles, I traveled with the Jalcones to several small villages and then on to Tverdal. I left home last year because my Da, Thorval Pedersen, had disappeared. He left me a note stating I should disguise myself and my homewagon and take to the road, for I was in danger. Seems the former regent and his agents were trying to find and capture my Da."

"Your Da all right?"

"Yes, he is well, thank you. He and my Nana have taken the family homewagon and headed down the coast. I hope to meet up with them in Tverdal."

"So, go on with your tale, lass."

"Anyway, the summer was an adventure, to say the least. I was terribly worried about Da on and off for most of it. In addition, it seems the former regent was not very happy with rovers, and he and others tried a number of ways to create problems for us. Someone started snatching rovers off the streets in Tverdal. I, unfortunately, was one of them. Fortunately, Carz here came to the rescue. Then some folks put some items in some of our homewagons that, if we had been caught with them, would have caused us a great deal of trouble. If it hadn't been for Master Clarisse from the Glassmakers Guild intervening at a roadblock on the royal road as we headed toward Glendalen, I could well be still languishing in a deep, dark dungeon."

"Not a good place to spend the summer months, those deep, dark dungeons," said Farmer Josh with a grin. "Or the fall, winter, or spring months, for that matter."

"No, indeed. After that, I got involved in rescuing the Princess, now Lady Esmeralda."

"We heard a little about that, even way out here. So you were part of that, were you? Were you at the Well of Speaking when Regent Cedric Klingflug was made to step down? When the challenge was called?"

"Yes, Carz and I were there. Along the way to the capital last summer, I acquired two pieces of the oppgave ringe and placed them in the vessteboks. Of course, when I first acquired the pieces of the oppgave ringe, I did not know what they were or that they were as important as they turned out to be. They just looked like misshapen gold rings with random scratches."

"Well, I'll be. When we first heard about what had happened, we really thought it was a tall tale. You know, the former regent stepping down, a challenge being called to choose a new king or queen. Stuff of legends. Then there have been the lights. Saw that first one myself. Must have been something, seeing it close up like you did."

I could only nod my head as I thought back to when I had placed the two rings in the vessteboks. I certainly had not expected the column of light, carrying all of the colors of the rainbow, to rise up out of the box in a steady stream. The column of light had risen until it almost touched the clouds, and then it had arced out in all directions until it had formed a canopy in the sky. The light had pulsed out of the box for several minutes and then, as abruptly as it had started, it had just stopped.

"I've seen more lights since," stated Farmer Josh. "Each time they have appeared in the sky, they have been different."

Farmer Josh was right. All six times that pieces of the oppgave ringe had been placed in the vessteboks, different patterns of light had risen out of the gold box set in the sea wall in the Well of Speaking. More importantly, each time a ring had been placed in the gold box, the more the folks of Sommerhjem came to believe that the Gylden Sirklene challenge was real, and not just some ploy by the Crown to wrest control away from the former regent.

"How are folks around here feeling about what is happening?" I asked.

"At first, there were very mixed feelings. Most of us around here weren't much pleased with the former regent's rule. Gotten hard for an honest farmer to make ends meet, to keep the family farm. When word came that the former regent was made to step down and there was a new type of rule, most of us just held our breaths for a bit, waiting to see what was going to happen. Didn't think much about a challenge being called. We were just grateful that there was some relief from the taxes and licenses that the former regent had placed on us," said Farmer Josh.

"And now?" I asked.

"And now, hearing what's been happening in the capital with the coming of the rings and seeing the lights in the sky, well, folks are beginning to talk. Folks around here have been turning to the elders, asking for any old tales they can remember. Seems we have forgotten much, but not all. A lot of us are thinking that choosing a new ruler by way of the challenge is the right thing to do."

Before I could comment, Farmer Josh stopped rocking and looked down the path leading up to his cottage. "Looks like we are about to have company, and they don't look like they're rovers."

CHAPTER TWO

I looked down the path from Farmer Josh's cottage and saw that he was indeed right. Two folks of middle years, whose dress clearly showed that they were not rovers, were coming up the path. They wore colorful waist sashes clearly marking them as long distance traders. As they grew closer, the smile on my face grew large, for coming up the path were the Jalcones. I jumped up, excused myself from Farmer Josh, and ran down the path to greet the two.

"Now, there's a sight for these eyes," exclaimed Trader Jalcones. "We had hoped you might be here. We were disappointed when we didn't see your homewagon."

"That's because I have a new homewagon. Da and Nana are in the one I drove last summer. I'm so glad to see you both. I was hoping I would catch up with you folks here. Are you traveling your same route this summer?"

"Aye, lass, we are indeed, and glad we would be of your company, if you've a mind to travel with us again," said Trader Jalcones' wife, Hannelore, as the three of us walked up to Farmer Josh's porch.

"Permission to camp on your land?" Trader Jalcones asked Farmer Josh. When Farmer Josh nodded consent, Trader Jalcones asked what help the farmer could use as payment for being allowed to camp on the land.

"Might I suggest something?" I asked. The three others nodded yes. "I have been waiting a long time to taste Mistress Jalcones' cooking again. Perhaps fair payment for camping here would be a home-cooked meal."

"I certainly would not object to that," commented Farmer Josh.

A good meal and good conversation followed. It was well past dusk when the Jalcones, Carz, and I headed back to the campsite.

"Much as we would love to stay up and catch up, it's been a very long day and both of us are weary. You will travel with us after Treebles then?" asked Trader Jalcones.

"I would like to. I'm hoping to catch up with Da and Nana at Tverdal."

"It will be good to see your Da again. Will Oscar, Bertram, and their families be there too?"

"As far as I know. I also hope to catch up with Shueller and Tannar."

"I'm looking forward to having the group back together, though some will be missing. Well, lass, sleep well, and we'll see you in the morning."

After the market day at Treebles, the days went by smoothly traveling with the Jalcones. While I enjoyed the smaller villages, as the days passed, I grew more and more anxious to reach Tverdal. I needed to know that Da and Nana were all right. Even though many of the problems the former regent had caused had been, or were being, addressed by the interim ruling council, the land of Sommerhjem was still unsettled. Just because the former regent had been forced to step down did not mean he and his followers had quietly slunk off.

I had found Tverdal to be an interesting place. Tverdal was originally built as a walled town, but, with time and prosperity, it had expanded outside the original walls. The old town was perched atop a hill with newer parts sprawled at its base. Built a short distance from the deep-channeled Travers River, the town was an ideal location to be a crossroads for land and river travel and trade. The Travers River was very navigable to the port of Willing on the coast and provided an easy way to move goods from the sea to the interior and back. Many merchants and guilds had headquarters in Tverdal.

The town itself was built mostly of local stone of a light gray color. Most of the dwellings were one story and similar in design. The whole town would have looked quite dingy on a gloomy day were it not for the colorful doors and shutters, each different from its neighbors, and the window boxes filled with a profusion of flowers and green plants.

Close to the noon hour on the day before the Tverdal fair was to open, the Jalcones, Carz, and I reached the place where we had camped last year, about a half hour walk from town. The fairgrounds, with the noise, dust, smells, and crowds, was a less desirable camping place than the spot we had stayed last summer.

"So, Carz, I hope Da and Nana have arrived before us and have claimed several camping spots."

Turning my homewagon down the lane that led to a large clearing among very tall trees, I was relieved when I spotted my Da's homewagon parked where I had camped the year before, and my Da waving me over.

"Ah, daughter, so very glad you made it here safely. Did you have any trouble?"

"No, Da, the way here was fairly uneventful." *Well, unless you count the three folks looking for you who made me a tad nervous, but now is not the time to talk about that.* "You?"

"Also fairly uneventful. Let's hope our travels continue to be so. We saved a place for you and your friends, the Jalcones. Oscar, Bertram, Shueller, and Tannar are here also," said my Da. "The fair in Tverdal is set up differently this year. Apparently, word has gotten back on how successful the fair in Glendalen was, so we will be spread out, crafts, trades, food, and entertainment, all mixed together. I got us spaces next to each other. I hope that's all right with you. I picked up fair badges for you and Carz, so you are all set."

I thanked Da, and told him I was glad to have my booth next to his. Climbing down and stretching my legs, I greeted Nana, who was tending a cook fire. Setting up camp was quick work with Da helping.

After we settled the horses, I glanced around and noticed that Carz was nowhere in sight. I always feel a niggling of worry when Carz disappears. I'm not quite sure what I would do without him. In my heart of hearts, I know he is a wild hunting cat, and I do not own him. He could decide to leave at any time, and there is nothing I could or would do to prevent that. I just hope I will never have to face the loss of Carz.

While I had been setting up, I noticed that Mistress Jalcones and Nana had taken an instant liking to each other. By the time I had topped the water barrel off with cool water from the clear stream that ran through the woods behind the campsite, Mistress Jalcones and Nana had a hearty noon meal ready.

After the meal, the other rovers, Oscar, Bertram, and their families, Shueller, and Tannar joined the group around the cook fire. Once greetings were exchanged, the group settled in to talk.

"So much has happened since we were here last, it is hard to know where to start," I said. "I'm glad to see you are all safe. There were times during the last year that I worried about all of you."

"Our troubles are not over yet," stated Shueller quietly. "We know that seven of the nine rings are in the capital, but two are still out. That is worrisome, considering that in a few short weeks the great fair at the capital will begin."

"As we traveled about Sommerhjem during the cold months, I heard much talk about what is supposed to happen this summer," said Trader Jalcones. "Folks' spirits were up by late fall when they saw the lights in the sky and knew that the seventh ring was in the capital. With the darker and harder days of the cold months, it has been hard for folks to hold on to those hopeful feelings. I have heard much worry and grumbling lately."

"There has also been much talk about what happened to the land under the former regent's rule," stated Oscar.

"The land began to change long before the former regent began to control the country," said Shueller quietly.

The others sitting around the cook fire turned to look at the short Günnary man.

"What do you mean?" I asked.

"It has been a slow decline, to be sure, since the death of King Griswold. Almost unnoticeable. If you listen to any of the elders talk about the old days, really listen, you can hear those voices speak of longing and loss. We have lost so much knowledge, so much of the old ways. You are an example of what I am talking about, Nissa."

"I don't understand."

"One only has to look at your homewagon and the carvings you do on the items you sell at the fairs to see what I am talking about. You have brought back an old art that was once found everywhere in Sommerhjem. But that is not all that has changed over time. If you really listen to what the farmers talk about, you will hear tales of the past about more abundant crops, longer growing seasons, more plentiful fruits and berries, more wild game. The foresters will tell you of slower growth in the forests now. The fishers tell of less abundant catches of fish and crabs. The changes have been very slow, and not all that has gone wrong in Sommerhjem can be blamed on the former regent."

All sitting around the cook fire were very quiet for a long time, clearly thinking over what Shueller had said. Finally, Oscar spoke up.

"A number of times since the Gylden Sirklene challenge was called, I have heard that change will come to Sommerhjem because the Neebing blessed once again walk the land."

I was just about to ask what that meant when a horse and rider came swiftly down the lane, stopping at Thorval's homewagon. I looked up and a wide smile spread across my face.

"Journeyman Evan, what are you doing here?" I asked. I noticed he had filled out a bit since I had seen him last. No longer did he look like a gangly boy. The flop of brown hair that fell over his forehead remained the same, as did his boyish grin.

"Looking for you. I had hoped you were following the same route you took last year."

"Is something wrong?"

"Not exactly. I have a message for you. I asked to be the one to tell you, so you would know it is not just a rumor."

"Now you get your body off of that horse, young man," Mistress Jalcones demanded. "You get right down here, and we'll have a hot meal ready for you in no time. Don't they feed you in the capital?"

Journeyman Evan and I just looked at each other and shrugged. What he had ridden from the capital to tell me was just going to have to wait while Mistress Jalcones fussed over him. I suspected she had a very soft spot in her heart for the young man. Once Journeyman Evan had a plate of food in his hands and everyone was settled, I again asked what had brought him to Tverdal.

"Word has reached us in the capital that the former regent and his allies have noticed that all of you who have placed one of the pieces of the oppgave ringe in the vessteboks arrived at the capital accompanied by an uncommon animal. You arrived with Carz. Greer was accompanied by Kasa, the border dog with the old colorings. Meryl came with Tashi, the griff falcon. Yara was with Toki, the bog fox. Piper had the mountain cat, Jing, with her, and Seeker Chance had the oddest animal of all, the halekrets, Ashu. Word has gone out to be on the lookout for folks traveling with uncommon animals. Lady Esmeralda and others on the interim ruling council are concerned for your safety. They have sent word out to all of you who have carried pieces of the oppgave ringe into the capital."

I sat back with a sigh. I knew now that this summer was not going to be any more typical a summer than last summer had been. I had been holding out hope, however, that at least the smaller fairs before the great summer fair at the capital might be uneventful. All I really wanted was to travel from fair to fair, selling my wooden items. I wanted to travel this summer with my Da and Nana, like we had in the times before my mother died and Da had stopped traveling. I wanted so much to travel without feeling like I needed to be on alert, always looking over my shoulder, always being careful.

"It was good of you to come to let me know. I will certainly be more vigilant," I told Journeyman Evan.

"Lady Esmeralda and the interim ruling council have several offers for you. You are welcome to come to the capital and stay at the royal palace until the time of the great fair. If that doesn't suit you, they have formed a special unit of the royal guard and are willing to have one or more accompany you as you travel from fair to fair to give you some measure of protection. They are also making this offer to everyone who has carried a piece of the oppgave ringe to the capital," said Journeyman Evan.

"I'll need some time to think on it. Are you going to stay the night?"

"I will be here for several days, staying at the Glassmakers Guildhall. On another note, I do have a question for Mistress Jalcones. Will you be making any of those berry tarts or maybe griddle cakes with hot berries on top?" Journeyman Evan asked, putting as much wistfulness in his voice as he could.

"Ack, you may be a year older and a journeyman now to boot, but you are still a rascal," Mistress Jalcones remarked. "You'll be welcome here for breakfast, and don't you be late."

The banter between the two was enough to break the tension Journeyman Evan's news had brought. A short while later the group broke up. I called to Carz, who was napping by the fire, and invited him to join me in the homewagon, for it was time to turn in for the night. Just before I headed back to my homewagon, Da drew me aside.

"What do you think you want to do, lass?" he asked.

"I don't know." I noted the worried look on my Da's face as we said our goodnights.

Morning came way too early, as it always seemed to on the first day of a fair. I still had not decided what I wanted to do with the offers Journeyman Evan had told me about the night before. I had ruled out going to the capital right away. In the short term, it would probably be the safest choice. The problem with going to the capital now was the fact that I would be unable to earn the coin or commissions I would need to carry me through the cold months. It was all fine and good to be safe now, and no good not to be able to feed myself later. Like many other rovers, I depended on what I sold during the fair season to provide for myself during the long cold season.

Walking into the Tverdal fair I thought about the other choice Journeyman Evan had suggested. It might be nice having someone who was a skilled guard to watch over me, and yet again, that might not be very good for trade. I worried that folks might be reluctant to come to my booth if there were royal guards hovering close by. Many folks were still distrustful of anyone representing the Crown, despite all the good the interim ruling council had tried to do over the past year. By the time I had reached my booth at the fairgrounds, I had made my decision.

Chapter Three

So far I was comfortable with the choice I had made to continue moving from fair to fair not accompanied by one of the special royal guards. My time at the fair in Tverdal had been profitable, and uneventful. My whimsies were very popular. Whimsies are small carvings combining two animals like a squirrel and a goose, which would make it either a gouirrel or a squoose. My puzzle boxes had also sold well, especially if a whimsy was hidden inside. I was gaining a good reputation for my carving. My other wood products, such as turned bowls and small carved chests, sold less frequently, but I did manage to sell a few.

I was glad to have been able to set up my booth next to Da and Nana. It gladdened my heart to see how my Da had been welcomed back on the fair circuit. His reputation for knife making had not diminished during the time he had been off the road. The addition to his knives of my handles, carved in the old patterns, had added to their value and had certainly put a healthy amount of coin in both of our pockets.

It had been good to reconnect with Shyla, Bertram's young daughter, whom I had begun to teach woodcraft the summer before. She had progressed quite well over the cold months, and I was glad to welcome her back to my booth. She was good with customers, and also eager to learn more.

The fair at Glendalen also went well, though it was more tiring due to late night meetings with Lord Hadrack and his nephew, Beezle. It was only few short weeks before the great summer fair at the capital. All were concerned that time was drawing short, yet two pieces of the oppgave ringe were still out. By the third day of the fair at the capital, all nine pieces of the oppgave ringe needed to be in the vessteboks. So far, there had been no word that anyone had either discovered one of the last two rings, or even knew where to look. All the clues folks had found had been followed up. Those who were searching had uncovered no new information. There had also been no word that the former regent, Lord Cedric Klingflug, or his followers had discovered one or both of the missing rings.

It had been good to see Beezle and catch up on what he had been doing during the cold months. Over the past year, he had become my friend. I had first met him in Glendalen a year ago, and since then, our paths had crossed a number of times. He had changed. His strawberry blond hair was a bit longer and wind tossed. Tall with wide shoulders, he seemed taller than when I first met him, but perhaps that was because of the way he held himself now. More telling of what he had been through this last year were the lines now etched in his face.

When the former regent and his followers had decided Lady Esmeralda, the then-heir to the throne, was expendable, Beezle had been involved with helping me keep her safe until the great summer fair at the capital. In late fall, he had been captured and held in the Raven's tower when the former regent's agents thought he either had, or knew where to find, one of the pieces of the oppgave ringe. I would have liked to have spent more time in Glendalen catching up, but all too soon, the fair was over, and we once again parted ways.

Traveling the road to the Crestbury fair had been uneventful. Once again Da, Nana, and I had booths together. The first day of the fair went well. Just after dinner was finished and the chores were done, the sky, which had been threatening rain all day, delivered a deluge. I took shelter in Da's homewagon.

"The saying 'no news is good news' is not all that comforting," I said to Da and Nana. "We only know that the last two rings have not been placed in the vessteboks. We really don't know if someone who sides with the former regent has one or both of them."

"We don't know if either of the two rings that are still not at the capital have been found. We don't know if someone else, someone who is neither loyal to the Crown nor loyal to the former regent, has one or both," suggested Da. "For that matter, we don't know if someone loyal to the Crown has one or both. What we do know is that time is running short, and folks are getting very nervous. Did you feel it this day at the fair too, Nissa?"

"Yes. At times there were more folks gathered in clumps talking, rather than wandering the fair looking at wares. Folks are very uneasy. I had hoped that folks would feel better because the former regent no longer rules and a lot of good has come from him stepping down. This not knowing what is going to happen in a few short weeks has many folks on edge."

It was on the second day of the fair in Crestbury that the atmosphere changed. Midmorning, I was sitting at my turning lathe, working with a beautiful piece of spalted maple. A bowl was taking shape. Wood curls littered the ground. I was concentrating so hard, I did not notice a hush had come over the fairgrounds until Nana called over from their booth.

"Nissa. Nissa!"

Pulling my carving tool away from the bowl, I looked up at Nana to see what she wanted. "What?"

"Look up," was all Nana said.

I did as she asked, and a small sigh escaped my lips. The sky was filled with green light in the shape of vines and leaves. I reached down and placed a hand on Carz' shoulder, when I became aware of him leaning against me. I kept my head turned upward, watching the sky long after the lights had faded and disappeared. Slowly, the sounds returned to the fair as folks gathered in small groups to talk about what they had just seen.

"Nissa," Da called quietly from his booth next to mine.

"That's number eight. At least, I suspect the lights in the sky are signaling that the eighth piece of the oppgave ringe has been placed in the vessteboks this day. Only one more to go. All of this is getting very, very real, isn't it?" I asked Da.

"It has always been very, very real to some of us, you included," Da replied. "To others, with the placing of each ring, it becomes less of a granny tale and more real. Even the land itself feels different. I don't quite know how to explain it."

"I know what you mean. This spring the greens seemed greener, the sunlight on the meadows just a bit brighter. The spring rains, while steady, were not filled with howling winds and torrents of ice cold rain. Would it sound silly if I said the land itself seems happier?"

"Not silly at all," answered Da. "Of course, some of that happy feeling might be coming from the folks of Sommerhjem. Being no longer under the rule of the former regent has helped immensely. The foresters have been returned to their home forests, and folks have been given back lands that were wrongfully taken from them. With the higher taxes and the special licenses done away with, folks have a better chance of making ends meet. The small fishers aren't being forced off their fishing grounds, and the small merchants aren't being forced to close their shops. While folks are still leery, and somewhat mistrustful as to the future, there is hope."

"You have the right of it. Now, if we are going to take advantage of all those good feelings, we had best tend to our booths," scolded the ever-practical Nana.

I realized Nana was right. The small groups that had gathered to talk about the lights in the sky were breaking up, and folks were beginning to wander the fair again. The rest of the day was very busy, so, when the end of the fair day horn blew, I was quite happy to close my booth up and head back to my homewagon.

There was much talk around the cook fires that night concerning the lights that had been seen in the sky earlier that day. Groups of folks stayed up much later than usual talking about what the lights meant.

Several days later, just as I was getting ready to get up from the cook fire and head to bed, a hand was placed on my shoulder. Looking over my shoulder, I was surprised to see who was standing behind me.

"A quiet word with you, if I could," said Beezle.

"Of course. Should I get Da and Nana?"

"That would be a good idea."

I went to the homewagon next to mine and quietly knocked on the door. Da opened it.

"Could we come in?" I asked. "Beezle is here."

Da motioned for us to enter and called over his shoulder to alert Nana that they had visitors. Once all of us were settled, Beezle began to speak in a quiet voice, not wanting to be overheard by anyone outside the homewagon.

"I am sure you saw the lights in the sky the other day. My uncle, Lord Hadrack, has since received several messenger birds from the capital. As we all suspected, the green vine lights signaled the placing of the eighth ring in the vessteboks. Now only one is not there. Those who would oppose the

Crown are getting more desperate. They are looking even harder to detain anyone traveling with an uncommon animal. You and Carz obviously fit that description. The interim ruling council is worried about your safety, and that of the other ring carriers. Master Clarisse sent a message out to all of you who have carried rings that you need to head to the capital immediately. She did not explain in her brief message, but it had something to do with something revealed in the Book of Rules."

When I did not respond right away, Beezle went on. "I know this is a great deal to ask of all of you, and you in particular, Nissa. If you head to the capital now, you miss out on a number of fairs, and the chance to earn a living."

I reached down and stroked Carz' head before speaking. "I will pack up this night and move out at dawn."

"If you are sure, daughter, that that is what you want to do, Nana and I will pack up and go with you."

"No, Da, thank you for the offer, but I think this is something Carz and I need to do on our own. No need for you and Nana to lose coin by not going on to the next several fairs."

"Perhaps you need not lose any coin either," suggested Nana, speaking up for the first time.

"Thank you for caring …." I started to say, before Nana cut me off.

"Hush now, gel, I'm not talking about you not doing your duty and going to the capital. No, I was about to suggest that you leave some of your wares with me. After all, I owe you from last year when you sold my herbs and salves. I'll just return the favor. You leave me some of those beautiful inlaid puzzle boxes and a number of those whimsies."

"Thanks, Nana. That is a kind offer."

"Oh pish-posh. It's what families do."

"If the former regent's followers are looking for folks who are traveling with uncommon animals, what is going to be done to keep Nissa safe?" Da asked.

"My uncle asked his head of the Glendalen guard, Captain Gwen, to put together a patrol to escort Nissa and Carz to the capital. That patrol rode here with me. I will also be riding to the capital with Nissa," Beezle replied.

"Good, that will be good." Turning to me, Da said, "Before we lose the light, why don't you and Nana go sort out what you want to leave with us? Beezle, will you check over the horses and tack while I check over Nissa's homewagon?"

Once Nissa and Nana were out of hearing range, Thorval turned to Beezle. "Just how much danger is Nissa in?"

"We are not really sure."

"And yet, there must be very strong reasons for sending you after her."

"All I know is there has been an increased presence of folks loyal to the former regent or his followers in the out country seeking to find and detain folks who travel with uncommon animals. As you know, each folk who has carried a piece of the oppgave ringe to the capital has been accompanied by an animal not often seen, much less choosing to travel with folks. I know some might think the border dog Kasa who travels with Greer is just an ordinary border dog with rarer coloring," stated Beezle.

"But you think otherwise."

"After talking to Journeyman Evan, why yes, I do."

"Why would those opposing the Crown be interested in Nissa at this point? She already placed the two rings she carried into the vessteboks. She is traveling the fair circuit as would be expected, not off somewhere looking for a piece of the oppgave ringe," Thorval said.

"Again, I do not have a clear answer for you. It is worrisome in its own right that she might be targeted just because she is accompanied by Carz."

"You think it's more than that."

"I do. One thing I know is that, after Master Clarisse sent her messages out, all of the other ring carriers have either requested an escort to the capital, or are already there. Something is in the wind, but we are not quite sure what."

"After what you have just told me, I think I will begin to pack too and head to the capital with Nissa," Thorval stated, beginning to turn away.

"Sir, I do not think that would be a good idea."

At Beezle's words, Thorval pulled up short.

"I appreciate that you want to protect your daughter," Beezle continued.

"I hear a 'however' in your words," Thorval said.

"You are correct. I think this is a journey she needs to take by herself.

Something is drawing all of those who have carried rings to the capital to go back there now. In addition, Uncle also received a letter from Lady Celik, which arrived at Glendalen just after you left. Included in the letter was a message with a request for you."

"Perhaps we had best take this conversation into my homewagon. You never know who might be listening," suggested Thorval.

CHAPTER FOUR

It was hard for me to say goodbye to Da and Nana. I had hoped that this summer would be a more normal one than last summer. Not even in the wildest imagination of the most accomplished of storytellers would the tale of what happened to me last summer be believable. And obviously, that tale had not ended in the happily ever after way that many tales do when the heroine gets the job done, and then the tale ends. *Not that I think I am a heroine. Far from it. I am just someone who got caught up in a series of happenings. And perhaps the job is not yet done.*

The ride to the capital was without incident. No would-be snatchers of folks traveling with uncommon animals sprang out of the woods. No agents of the former regent tried to snatch Carz and me in the middle of the night. Truth be told, it would have been a pretty boring ride had Beezle not taken the opportunity to ride at times with us in the homewagon.

As we approached the main gate to the capital, Beezle directed me to drive my homewagon to the royal palace. When we reached the front of the royal palace, we were greeted by Master Clarisse. She is quite a tall woman, and is six to eight years older than me. She has a presence that seems more than that of a master of her craft, but I never could quite put my finger on what it is about her that does not match.

"I suspect you would be more comfortable camping at the capital fairgrounds, especially since there are a number of other rovers camped there. However, we think you might be safer here on the palace grounds. All of the rest of those who carried pieces of the oppgave ringe to the capital are here. Beezle, your aunt, Lady Hadrack, asked that you find her immediately upon your arrival, if you would."

Once Beezle had said his goodbyes to us and assured me he would catch up with me later, Master Clarisse climbed aboard my homewagon and gave me directions.

I was not familiar with the royal palace or the royal palace grounds, so I was surprised by the large size of the area behind the palace. In addition to the gardens, there were ponds and fountains, and small groves of trees scattered about the landscape. Stone paths and lanes crisscrossed the grounds. It was clear that the area closest to the royal palace had been well-tended for a long time. As we moved farther through the grounds, I saw that the section we were heading for had only been groomed recently. I also saw that the bottom of the royal palace grounds was still a tangle of greenery, but some work had recently been done to begin to clear the area.

Master Clarisse directed me to follow a stone lane to the back side of one of the groves of trees. I was surprised to see what I had thought was a grove was really a circle of trees and trimmed bushes with an opening wide enough to allow my homewagon to enter. Once inside, several things struck me at once. There was a wagon already within the circle of trees, plus several tents and, to my surprise, another homewagon. At least, it looked like a homewagon, but I could not imagine any rover driving a homewagon that plain. In addition, there was a central well and a number of established fire rings placed about the area. Though the area looked recently raked and trimmed, from the looks of the weathering on the well and fire rings, this was quite an old site, and I realized that this circle of trees had been set up as a campsite long ago.

I had just stepped down from my homewagon after Master Clarisse when I saw two of the most unusual men I had ever seen walk into the grove of trees. One was tall and thin and of middle years. The other was a slim, fit, young man. That is not what made either of them unusual. It was the fact that the tall man was twined in vines, which started out of the tops of his boots and extended upward until they threaded through his beard and hair. The young man had a single vine, growing up out of his shirt pocket and twining in his beard. What was even more unusual was that the young man was accompanied by a large black wolf. Before I could even begin to react to the new arrivals, Carz jumped down out of the homewagon and headed toward the wolf. I stood frozen, afraid of what might happen between the hunting cat and the wolf.

Master Clarisse did not seem at all concerned. "Oh, good, you are here," Master Clarisse said, addressing the two men. "Nissa, these gentlemen are responsible for your current camping spot. I would like you to meet Ealdred," indicating the tall man, "and Lom, who carried the eighth piece of the oppgave ringe to the capital. The night wolf with Lom is Taarig."

While Master Clarisse was speaking, Carz approached the night wolf. Once he was within five feet of the night wolf, he stopped. The two animals studied each other, nodded their heads, and then Carz returned to stand next to me. Both Lom and I let out deep breaths that neither of us probably knew we had been holding.

In a slightly shaky voice, I said, "You did say night wolf?"

"Yes," Master Clarisse answered, as if night wolves were an everyday occurrence rather than the stuff of legend.

Before I could say anything else, another night wolf entered the grove of trees, followed by a fit young woman in a royal guard uniform with neatly tied back, long, dark hair. On closer inspection, I realized that the uniform was not exactly like the royal guard uniforms I was familiar with, though it was clear that she was a royal guard by her stride and her bearing.

"Good, you're here too, so I can get the introductions done all at once. Nissa, this is Theora and her night wolf, Tala. She is one of the special royal guards and is assigned to Lom. Well, that is not quite correct, but will do for now. Theora, this is Nissa and her hunting cat, Carz. Nissa, Theora is the owner of the wagon with the canvas top camped here. The other wagon belongs to the finder, Meryl, and the tent next to it belongs to the finder, Finn. I will let Lom or Ealdred, who are staying in the larger tent next to Theora's wagon, explain about your campsite. I need to get back to the royal palace. Get settled in, and then, at dinner time, wander up. We will all gather for the evening meal."

While Master Clarisse did the introductions, Carz and Tala took each other's measure, and then Carz again returned to stand next to me.

"Well met, Nissa," Ealdred said. "Lom here, as you might suspect, is responsible for the lights in the sky a while back. Carried in the eighth ring. Since the great summer fair at the capital was not that far off, we were requested to remain in the capital. But Lom, you tell them about this campsite, for it is your story to tell."

"I worked here in the royal garden before, well, before my life took a different direction. After carrying the eighth piece of the oppgave ringe to the capital, I was offered an assistant royal gardener position. That would have been a dream come true for me, even half a year ago," Lom stated.

"But not now," I said sympathetically, for I well knew how being a ring carrier could affect one's life. "Somehow carrying one of the rings changes the path one's life takes."

"Yes," Lom answered, giving me a grateful look for my understanding. "In the course of my travels, I met Ealdred, who has offered me a chance to learn more about my particular skills and talents with plants. I wish to return to his home, if we are able, after the summer fair here. Sorry, I got sidetracked. Neither Ealdred nor I do very well being idle," he continued. "About this campsite, you might have noticed when you came around the back of the royal palace that the grounds are very large, extending way, way back to the cliff behind them."

"Yes, I was surprised at the extent of the royal palace grounds," I replied.

"You may also have noticed that the groomed part of the grounds does not extend very far back from the royal palace. While beautiful, much of the grounds was let to go wild long before the former regent took control."

"Although he did not help the situation," said Ealdred. "Staff was severely reduced, like many other things. Lord Klingflug neglected the care of the grounds, due to not wanting to have coin leave his coffers. The royal palace garden was maintained out front where folks could see it, but much of it behind the royal palace was left to grow wild. As Lom stated, Lord Klingflug was not the first to neglect the grounds behind the royal palace. King Griswold had other concerns during his reign, as did his descendants. Our most recent queen, Queen Octavia, also had other concerns, and so not much coin was allotted to maintaining such extensive grounds. In other words, a great many years have gone by since anything has been done to the royal palace garden's back area. We think at one time these campsites might have been here for rovers to camp in while attending to affairs of the country. They were also likely available for use by foresters and others who prefer to stay in the out-of-doors. We have discovered that, early in King Griswold's reign, he had a council made up of folks from varying clans and groups similar to our present interim ruling council. That fell by the wayside toward the latter part of his reign."

"When I worked here," Lom said, taking up the narrative once again. "I was often assigned to work at the bottom of the groomed part of the garden, along the edge of the wild and neglected back area. I liked cleaning up a small area and finding what was hidden under the dead branches and leaves. Sometimes many of the original plantings were still there. They just needed to be given space to grow."

"And that led you to finding this campsite? From the looks of the well and the fire pits, I would guess this area was built a long time ago. I agree this could have been a space where rovers and others could bring their wagons or tents and camp," I stated. "I can see, however, that the brush and foliage surrounding the grove has been recently trimmed, as has the ground cover."

"Being idle, as I said, is not something Ealdred, Theora, or I are very good at. We got curious about the grounds. With the help of Yara, a librarian-at-large from the royal library and also one of the ring carriers, we have found out a great deal about the history of these grounds in the last few weeks," said Lom.

"Yes," said Ealdred, picking up the tale. "In the royal palace archives, there were original plans for the grounds. They are fascinating and intriguing."

"How so?" I asked.

"There is a whole section at the very back of the grounds next to the cliff wall that is blank on all of the plans," said Lom. "We have looked and looked through the archives here, and Yara has looked throughout the royal library, to no avail. Finding our way through a dense tangle of foliage to satisfy our curiosity as to what is there near the cliff wall has not been a priority. It was more important to us to get several of the campsites that were marked on the original plans cleaned up so there would be places for Theora, you, and others to camp on the royal palace grounds."

"For which I thank you, for this seems to be a lovely place to camp," I said gracefully. "I had thought I would camp at the fairgrounds, or perhaps at the Glassmakers Guildhall where I camped last year."

"It would not be as safe as here," Theora commented, speaking up for the first time. "There is much fear that those of you who carried pieces of the oppgave ringe into the capital are still in danger. It will be much more difficult to get to you here where the tall walls guard the royal palace on the west, the sheer drop to the river prevents anyone coming from the north or south, and the sheer cliff rising to the plateau in the back does the same. The six other folks who carried pieces of the oppgave ringe to the capital are here, and some are staying in the royal palace. You could do that also, if you choose. It's just that Master Clarisse and Lady Esmeralda thought you might be more comfortable in your own home, so to speak."

"They were correct."

"The night wolves did not find the royal palace to their liking and, quite frankly, neither did we. All of us would rather be outdoors," said Lom.

"Now, enough of this talk. What can we do to help you get settled?" Ealdred asked.

"You can direct me to where the horses are pastured."

"Ah, that's easy. Just behind Theora's wagon is a narrow passage that leads into a second ring of trees. Good grazing there," said Lom.

Once I unharnessed the horses, leveled and set up the homewagon, put a gift in the Neebing room, and lowered it to the ground, I pulled out a camp chair and settled in to whittle. It was a while until dinner and, even though I was no longer tending a booth at a fair, there was no reason not to continue to make more stock. Ealdred and Lom had gone back to working on a way to get to the far back part of the garden to discover what might be there. Theora and the two night wolves had gone with them. They said they would return when it was time to head up to the royal palace for dinner. Carz settled in next to me for an afternoon nap.

I had been enjoying the quiet within the circle of trees, with just the sounds of insects buzzing and birds singing. If I had not been alert, I would have missed the sound of wings, and then the slight rustle of branches in the tree I was sitting closest to. When I looked up, I was only partly surprised to see that Tashi, the griff falcon that accompanied Meryl, had flown in. That meant Meryl was probably not far behind. A very short while later, Meryl and her friend, Finn, entered the campsite clearing.

The pair was very recognizable, even without a griff falcon accompanying them, flashing gold and red in the sun. Meryl had a climber's build and grace. She was slender, which belied the obvious strength within her. Her eyes were her most arresting feature, sea blue with lines that spoke of hours in the sun looking out over sea or land. Finn was mostly varying shades of gray. His hair was a wispy silver gray and stuck up every which way on his head. His face was covered by a scraggly gray beard and lined with age. His clothing had gray splotches of varying shades across its very wrinkled surface. Even his deep sunken eyes were gray.

"Well met, Meryl, Finn."

"Ah, Nissa, we heard you had arrived. I hope your trip to the capital was uneventful," said Meryl.

"Very, and yours?"

"Also uneventful. We were most reluctant to leave our summer search area to come here. I imagine you were equally reluctant to leave the fair circuit."

"Yes. Beezle, however, had some convincing arguments, and I have not lost all sales, for my Da and Nana offered to sell some of my wares at the fairs I will be missing."

Fortunately, I thought, *I am also fairly far along on the piece I want to enter in the judging at the capital fair. With all that is going on, I might be hard-pressed to finish the piece now. A shame, for I won a medal last year and hoped to gain more recognition this year.*

Bringing my attention back to Finn, I said, "It must be hard on you also, for is this not the time you do some traveling to find things?"

"All is not lost, no not lost," said Finn. "This back garden and the royal palace walls are worth a second look, oh my yes, a second look. Found a few things, yes indeed, found a few things."

The rest of the afternoon passed swiftly by, as time always does in good company. True to their word, Ealdred, Lom, Theora, and the two night wolves returned by late afternoon. They were covered with leafy debris, and their hands and boots were dirty with mud and grime. All of them bore scratches.

"Who won?" I asked.

Looking down at himself and then at the others, Lom smiled. "Ah, I can see how you might think that. We were working on finding a way through the brush and tangled vegetation to the place that does not show on the plans of the royal garden, if that makes any sense. The tangle is quite overgrown."

"Aye, and the plants are particularly resistant to any polite requests," commented Ealdred.

When I raised an eyebrow in inquiry concerning Ealdred's last remark, Theora spoke up.

"Seems these two can ask green living things to move. I know that sounds impossible, but believe me when I tell you it is true. I would love to tell you tales, however, the hour grows late, and we still need to wash up for dinner. We are heading up to the bath house. Do you want to come?"

I decided that I would join them. After all, we were to dine with Lady Esmeralda, Master Clarisse, and other folks on the interim ruling council, plus all of the other folks who had carried pieces of the oppgave ringe into the capital. It would not do to gather with all of those folks still covered in road dust and wood shavings.

Once cleaned up and dressed in one of my better sets of clothes, nothing could have prepared me for the odd assembly that was gathered on the first back terrace of the royal palace.

Chapter Five

Walking up from my homewagon, I was glad I had taken the time to wash and change. There were a great many folks gathered on the terrace and, as I drew closer, I recognized many of the faces. There were, however, a number of folks I did not recognize.

"Nissa, hurry on up, lass. It's good you are finally here," stated Master Rollag, coming forward to greet me. "You are the last to arrive of those who carried a piece, or in your case two pieces, of the oppgave ringe into the capital. Come greet or meet the others. I'll let Master Clarisse do the honors."

I was not so much concerned about meeting or greeting the other folks. Rather, I was concerned about Carz and the other animal companions. I need not have been worried. Some of the folks and their animal companions Carz and I had already met: Meryl and Tashi, the griff falcon, Seeker Chance and Ashu, the halekrets, Piper and Jing, the mountain cat, and Lom and Theora and their night wolves, Taarig and Tala. Master Clarisse introduced me to Greer and his border dog, Kasa, and Yara and her red bog fox, Toki. I also noticed a small green light glowing just off Yara's left shoulder. I was about to inquire about it when we were asked to sit down at the tables.

Once everyone was settled in comfortable chairs with cool drinks in hand, I had a chance to observe those around me, especially the animal companions. I was struck by a sense that the companion animals respected each other. They gave an impression of both great dignity and familiarity, despite the fact that they had all made themselves comfortable. Carz and Jing had settled in the sun on the warm paving stones of the terrace and were each grooming. The two night wolves were stretched out in the shade of the wall surrounding the terrace, napping. Kasa and Toki were chasing each other in a playful romp, and Tashi had taken herself to a nearby tree to preen.

Ashu was sitting in his customary spot on Seeker Chance's shoulder, worrying open a nut. He was a cute, small animal not even a foot high, covered in reddish fur. He had golden eyes with a mask of black around them, a black and white ringed tail, and paws that were more like hands.

My attention was drawn away from the animals when Master Clarisse began to speak. "We have been gathering out here for our meals when the weather is good. Everyone seems more comfortable out here, as opposed to being inside, even in an informal dining room within the royal palace. Let us partake of the fine spread of food that has been provided, and then put our heads together to share information and plan what we can for the coming weeks."

While we were gathering plates of food and settling down to eat, several more folks joined us on the terrace. Lady Celik arrived with her son, Elek. Journeyman Evan joined the group, as did the head royal librarian, Eluta. Seeker Eshana stepped onto the terrace shortly after them, accompanied by the rover elder, Zeroun, and his granddaughter, Gersemi.

The conversation flowed around the gathering. One of the main topics was whether any of them had had any difficulty getting to the capital. I listened while the others told of their journeys here.

"I was surprised when Elek showed up with a patrol of royal guards," Yara said. "I was surprised he even found me. Toki and I were in the forest where Elder Nelda resides. She sends her fond greetings, Seeker Chance. Anyway, I was there, for I wanted to try to make a copy of the book she had about animals, including the halekrets. I was partway done when Elek showed up. I hope I can return …." Yara's voice trailed off.

I knew that those of us gathered, no matter how nice it was to be sitting around on the terrace with old friends and new acquaintances, were all feeling uneasy as to what could happen or not happen in a few short weeks.

"Tell me, lad," Master Rollag said, addressing Greer. "Besides getting into general mischief, did you and Journeyman Evan have any difficulty getting to the capital this time?"

"No, sir. Not many folks are willing to confront a whole patrol of royal guard. The journey was quite comfortable, for we traveled by coach. Lambing season was long over, so my father, Lord Avital, decided to travel with us, for he wanted to be here to meet with the interim ruling council. Since his journey across Sommerhjem late last summer, he has become very active in our region, gaining support for the Crown and for the Gylden Sirklene challenge. He, like many, is aware that, once the challenge is fulfilled, it does not necessarily mean there will be acceptance by all, or a smooth transition."

"And you, Meryl?" Lady Esmeralda inquired.

"Most folks don't pay much a mind to us, so we passed through the countryside fairly overlooked. We are just simple finders, off on our annual summer trek. Tashi can be quite undetected when she wishes to be. Having the wagon also helps, for she can ride inside."

"You were one of the ones we really worried about finding in time, since you do not follow the fairs like Nissa, or live on a land holding like Greer," Lady Celik said.

"You can thank Tashi for us being here now. One day she just became very insistent that we follow her, and she led us here."

"We did not have any trouble getting here, either," Seeker Chance stated. "Not a lot of folks are foolish enough to attempt to detain seekers. The old ways, thankfully, still hold in that respect, for most folks."

"And Piper, how was your journey here?" asked Master Clarisse.

"Much easier than the last time I headed here," Piper replied, with great good humor. "When your messenger bird arrived, I was home, so I set off immediately. My mother and a small patrol of border guards accompanied me. Quite frankly, if I were intent on stopping someone accompanied by an uncommon animal, I would not want to face my mother. She is a highly skilled defender and could hold off a whole passel of ruffians by herself."

When all had settled in after dinner, Lady Esmeralda addressed the group. The year had added a maturity to her face. She certainly was not the wan girl I had first seen in the Günnary caves, nor did she look or act like she had when disguised as a rover. Now she had a regal bearing and faced all of us with hard-won confidence.

"I am glad all of you are here. I am sure that you all are as concerned as I am that the ninth ring is still not here in the capital. Time is growing extremely short. Have any of you heard anything from any of your sources that might give us a clue as to where to look for the ninth piece of the oppgave ringe?"

Murmuring went through the group as we looked from one to another. In the end, we all shook our heads in the negative.

"Lady Celik, Elek?" inquired Lady Esmeralda, directing her question to them.

"Nothing. Absolutely nothing is in the wind about the last piece of the oppgave ringe," stated Lady Celik. "Both my son and I have tapped into all of the grapevines, rumor mongers, and our informants, and nothing. If the ninth piece does not show up by the third day of the fair here, we are going to need a plan."

I could feel the tension rising among the group gathered on the terrace. The future of Sommerhjem had come down to the ninth ring. How amazing that in a few short weeks chaos could reign if a misshapen gold band with random markings was not placed in the vessteboks. If the ninth ring did not appear, all that a number of folks, plus eight very uncommon animals, had endured in the last year to make sure eight of the needed rings had been delivered to the capital on time might be for naught.

"I, for one, think better when I'm busy," stated Ealdred. "Lom and I could use help on the morrow from any or all of you who are not running the country, or figuring out ways to keep the former regent, his followers, or others from taking over the country, should the ninth ring not appear. Lom …."

All eyes turned toward Lom. Clearing his throat, he said, "Something is pulling me toward the bottom of the royal palace grounds. I really can't explain it. The pull has grown more and more urgent with each passing day. We could use your help clearing a pathway to the area that is not described on any of the plans we have found of the royal palace grounds."

"I would suggest you come prepared to get dirty, scratched, and tired. The plants at the bottom of the grounds have been left to grow into a tangled mess for a long time," contributed Ealdred.

"Why not hire more labor for the job?" I asked. "Not that I mind hard work."

"You ask a valid question," answered Lady Esmeralda. "Part of the answer is due to the safety of all of you. Hiring on day laborers to help untangle the tangled parts of the royal palace grounds appears harmless enough on the surface. Letting folks we are unfamiliar with onto the grounds opens up the possibility that we could inadvertently hire someone who means one of you harm. It is a chance none of us wants to take."

"Also," Master Clarisse said, "I think this pull of Lom's, and other hints gathered from the Book of Rules, suggest that this is a task for the eight of you who companion the animals. I really cannot explain it further, but I think that is the right of it."

After more discussion, it was agreed the folks gathered would split into two groups and assemble the next morning. One group would continue to try to find out more about how to find the last ring, in addition to trying to find out more about what those who were opposed to the Crown were doing. Those of us in the other group would try to get through the tangle at the bottom of the garden.

After the discussion broke up, I was glad to be heading back to my homewagon. It had been a long few days traveling to the capital, plus I had much to think about. I wondered what we might find beyond the tangle of foliage toward the cliff at the back of the royal palace grounds. Ealdred, Lom, and Yara had said that many of the plans they had looked at, from the oldest to the most recent, were very detailed, down to what plant to plant where and how many would be needed for the planting. Ealdred had told me that he and the head royal gardener were especially interested in the oldest of the plans, for they showed plantings of plants that neither of them had ever heard of. The head royal gardener had pleaded with Ealdred and Lom to be especially careful when uprooting or cutting plants to make a way into the area they wanted to explore, and to take care not to damage any of these long-lost types of plants by accident, should any still survive.

It is interesting, I thought, *that none of the plans of the royal palace grounds that Lom, Ealdred, and Yara had found, have any details about that one area.*

The next morning, I gathered with the others. Looking at the tangle of greenery ahead of me, I knew we were facing a long day of hard labor.

"As you can see," Lom stated, "it is hard to know where to start. Ealdred, Theora, and I have tested different places to see if there might be a natural opening. So far we have found none. We ...."

"Ah, folks, you might want to look to your left," I suggested, interrupting Lom.

Tashi was perched on a branch of a tree opposite a tree in which Ashu was sitting. The two cats, Carz and Jing, were each sitting at the base of one of those two trees, facing out, as if guarding the trees. Taarig, Tala, Kasa, and Toki were side by side, digging in the ground between the two trees.

"They seem to have no problem deciding where to start," I said dryly.

"I think you have the right of it," said Ealdred. "Perhaps we should go check out what they have found so fascinating about that spot."

As we approached, the two night wolves, the border dog, and the red bog fox ceased their digging and moved away. Both Lom and Ealdred walked to where the animals had been digging. The rest of us stood a little behind.

"Look, Ealdred, they have uncovered stones, paving stones, I think," said Lom.

"Well, lad, the only way to find out is to get our shovels and put our backs to the task. Grab your shovels and the other tools we will need, folks. I know that Master Clarisse said this job is for you seven who carried the pieces of the oppgave ringe in, but …."

"But you have been a part of looking at plans and helping me try to move the plants which have resisted the effort from each of us individually, and the two of us combined. Give it a try and let's see what happens. I, for one, would welcome you at my side, digging," said Lom.

Grabbing a shovel from the pile of tools they had brought down, Ealdred stepped forward with Lom at his side. None of the animals stopped him when he pushed the shovel into the soft earth. However, when I tried to dig to the left of where the animals had dug, Taarig blocked my way. The same thing happened to Meryl on the other side of the dug-up spot.

"It would seem that the night wolves are quiet insistent. They either want you two to do all the digging," I suggested to Lom and Ealdred, "or they do not want us to dig outside where they have dug."

"I think it is the latter," Lom said. He was now down on his knees taking a closer look at the area he had cleared. "There is clearly a stone path here under the dirt and ground cover. Unlike the other paths on the grounds, this one has a distinct raised edge. At least on my side. What have you found, Ealdred?"

"The same. Let's divide up the work. Two of us shovel the dirt and debris into the wheelbarrows, and the rest of you haul it away. We will trade off jobs as the day progresses. I just tried to put the dirt from my shovel off the edge of the path, and Taarig pushed it right back on."

"Glad I am that there is a paved path that runs along the edge of this tangle," Meryl said, joining the conversation for the first time. "Finn was a little miffed at the thought of being left out of this fun project. He will be happy he can contribute now."

"What do you have in mind?" I asked.

"I, for one, don't look forward to pushing a wheelbarrow all the way to the compost piles. I think we could ask for a wagon and horse. This path bisects a lane not too far from here that a wagon could come down. We could put the wheelbarrow loads in the wagon, and Finn could drive the wagon to the compost piles. I imagine the head royal gardener could arrange for some of his folks to unload the wagon."

"Great idea," said Seeker Chance. "Why do I think we will all need a good soak and liniment for our aching muscles by the end of this day?"

"Not to mention something for blisters," Yara suggested. "I know my hands, for one, are not accustomed to shoveling and hauling."

"Though I did not directly bring a piece of the oppgave ringe to the capital, I will make sure you are able to work undisturbed. In other words, my job is to keep away anyone who is showing too much interest in what you folks are doing," said Theora.

After several hours of pushing a wheelbarrow loaded with dirt, leaf mulch, and debris, I would have gladly traded places with Theora. I think chasing off a nosey parker or two would have been a relief. While the work of clearing the path was tedious, we were making fairly quick headway. The ground cover, leaf mulch, and dirt that covered the path we were working on was not very thick. Due to a rain this last week, and the fact that the path was fairly shaded, the ground cover and dirt was soft and easy to remove.

Once the first portion of the path was fairly clear, the tangle hanging over either side of the path began to draw back. I did not quite understand what was happening. It surprised me when Theora thanked Ealdred and Lom for saving us the work of having to cut it down. Seeing the confused look on my face, she explained that both Ealdred and Lom had the ability to request actions from living plants and had asked the tangle to draw back.

The farther we cleared the path, the clearer it became that the path did not run in a straight line toward the back cliff wall and the area we wanted to get to. In fact, the path meandered its way through the tangle of greenery. At one point, the group had a serious discussion as to whether they should continue to clear the path, or look for some other way to reach the unmarked area on the royal ground's plans. We were quickly disabused of that notion when the animals blocked our way back. At that point, someone was heard to mutter something about wondering who really was in charge, folks or animals?

It was well after the noon hour when Theora walked back to where we were digging and suggested we might want to halt, take a rest, and get something to drink and eat.

"You might want to suggest that to the animals, then," I told her, setting the wheelbarrow down. "They have been quite insistent that we keep working, or at least that we keep working on this path."

Fortunately, none of the animals objected to us taking time for rest and a meal. After the break, there was a bit of moaning and groaning, not to mention some grumbling, when we got up and moved back to work. It was late afternoon when Seeker Chance and Lom looked up from their shoveling and realized they had finally cleared their way through the tangle of foliage.

"Is this what you were expecting to find, Lom?" Seeker Chance asked.

CHAPTER SIX

"I don't know what I expected, really," said Lom. "I do know I didn't expect what I'm looking at. Although the plans for this area showed no plantings, flower beds, groves of trees, or scattered trees and shrubs, I still expected something. I guess, when the plans showed us there was nothing here, we should have trusted the plan makers, for there is nothing here, except a wide open space covered in grass with a single, and from the looks of it, very old quirrelit tree in the center."

I took a good hard look at the open space ahead of me. It was roughly circular in shape, surrounded by the tangle we had been working our way through all day. The single quirrelit tree did indeed look like an old tree. It struck me as odd that there was only a single quirrelit tree in the center of the space. I had never seen a quirrelit tree which was not part of a grove. Taking a close look at the grass surrounding the quirrelit tree, I saw no sign that this tree had ever been part of a grove. There were no stumps of trees, or mounds where stumps might have been and were now grown over by grass.

As I continued to survey the open area, I noticed something else. Since it was later in the day, shadows were cast over much of the open area, making it hard to read the terrain. However, I was fairly sure of what I was seeing. Squatting down and pulling the brim of my hat lower, I stared at the grassy area for a time before saying anything.

"I think the path we have been clearing continues on into this open area. If you look closely, you can see a slight indentation in the earth," I said.

The others took time to follow where I was pointing and agreed with me.

"I think the indentation we are looking at around the quirrelit tree is a labyrinth," said Seeker Chance. "Seeker Eshana and I have seen one in our travels, albeit a small one. It was back behind an herbalist's cottage in a small village in the northern mountains. Unlike mazes, which are puzzles often made of hedges or walls, and difficult to find your way out of, a labyrinth has only a single path to the center and back, and is not difficult to navigate. The herbalist told us that, when she walks along the turnings, she loses track of direction and the world around her. It helps quiet her mind. Also, if she is seeking an answer to a question, she tries to empty her mind of everything but that question. She suggested that walking the labyrinth helps her find pathways to answers. Both Seeker Eshana and I tried her labyrinth, and found what she said about it to be true. Hers was made of stones lined up to mark the path. If what we are seeing before us is indeed a labyrinth, then it is certainly much bigger and more elaborate than the one she had. I would like to take a closer look."

Before Seeker Chance could even place one foot on the grass in front of him, Tashi flew straight at him, veering off at the last minute. Seeker Chance abruptly stepped back.

"Interesting," Seeker Chance said, "It would seem Tashi does not want me to enter the open area."

"That may not be it," suggested Meryl, who was now soothing the feathers on the griff falcon's head. "Look at where you tried to step."

"Ah, I see what you are suggesting. The path we have been working on continues into this open area. I tried to enter not on the path."

"What I see is a very long day of cutting turf and clearing the path to the quirrelit tree," stated Yara wearily. "I suggest we follow the example of our companions who are even now wiser than we are, for they are all resting. I, for one, have an aching back and a nice set of blisters from this day. I could do with a hot soak and a warm meal."

All of us were in full agreement with Yara, so we left all of the tools in the wheelbarrow and headed out of the tangle. As we walked back toward the royal palace, I had a chance to talk to Lom.

"Do you think the area we discovered this day is what has been drawing you?" I asked.

"Partly. The urgency I have felt these last few days lessened when we got through the tangle. The pull is still there," said Lom. "I think clearing the way to the quirrelit tree is important, though I can't explain why."

The evening meal was a quiet one. The two groups who had gathered the night before talked about the day. No progress had been made in finding any more information concerning the final piece of the oppgave ringe. No one had an explanation as to why there might be a labyrinth in the clearing, nor why a single quirrelit tree grew there. There was a discussion about how a number of known supporters of the former regent had come into the capital in the last few days, and what that might mean. We were a discouraged and weary group of folks as we headed off to our quarters after the evening meal.

The next day, I rose early to a gray and threatening sky. Dark storm clouds loomed overhead. "Too bad we can't command where the rain should fall, eh Carz? If we could direct the rain to fall where we need to dig and shovel this day, and get it to wash the sod and dirt away, that would make our job easier."

Carz gave me a look over his shoulder that seemed to suggest that my idea was ridiculous, and went back to grooming his ears.

"I know, wishful thinking. I'm not looking forward to digging to begin with, much less digging in the rain and mud. Oh well, we had best go," I said, grabbing my rain gear in anticipation of the storm.

The impending storm hit while we were eating breakfast. The rain poured down in torrents for a surprisingly short time, and then moved inland. The upshot of the brief storm was it washed any remaining dirt and debris off the path we had already cleared through the tangle, and it softened up the turf we now needed to clear.

"When I saw those storm clouds this morning, I thought they would severely hamper our progress this day," Ealdred said. "It seems I was wrong. The removal of the turf off the path to the quirrelit tree has gone much faster than I anticipated. Your idea of cutting the edges, and then putting a flat shovel underneath to loosen the turf from the stone path, has worked well, Lom. We have been able to roll the turf right up."

"The head royal palace gardener has been happy too, for he has use for the rolls of grass turf," Lom said in reply. "He has never seen grass so thick and green. I did not tell him about your pasture, Ealdred, for he seemed so happy with this grass. I didn't want to see him weep, if he discovered there was even better grass somewhere else."

"My, aren't you getting cheeky now that you are a famous ring carrier and a night wolf's companion?" responded Ealdred, with great good humor.

I noticed that the mood of our group working on clearing the path to the quirrelit tree was much lighter this day than it had been in the previous several days, even though the worries about finding the ninth piece of the oppgave ringe had not diminished. There was a rising tension concerning what might happen on the third day of the great fair at the capital whether the ninth piece arrived in time or not. And yet, here in this grassy opening in the tangle, there was a sense of peace.

"Do you folks notice it too, the sense of peace here?" asked Yara, after Meryl and I placed another roll of sod on the wheelbarrow.

"It is striking," replied Meryl. "I can feel the difference as soon as I step out of the tangle and into this grassy area. I also notice, the closer we get to the quirrelit tree, the stronger that sense of peace becomes. It will be interesting to learn if that's what everyone feels."

Piper and Seeker Chance arrived with another roll of sod and overheard what Meryl was saying.

Piper told Nissa, "When I was hiding in a quirrelit tree trying to stay out of the hands of the folks who had captured Beezle, I overheard the forester Bradwr mention how Quirrelit groves were normally quite peaceful and welcoming. He said the one we were in was no longer that. He told the other man to trust him that the grove no longer welcomed them, and it was time to leave. I, however, did not find the quirrelit grove unwelcoming. Quite the opposite. Nissa, it's time for you and me to take up cutting and rolling sod."

By the time it was time to quit, we had cleared half of the labyrinth, up to the quirrelit tree. I do not think it was just the shade of the quirrelit tree that made me want to stay close to the trunk. There was something so soothing about being near it. I also thought the firestar gem in my ring warmed when I was working under the quirrelit tree, similar to how it warms when I am near another firestar gem or an object of power. It was such a hot summer day, I could not be sure. On the morrow, we would come back and clear the other half of the labyrinth path, and maybe I would be able to tell then.

The next day, like most mornings, dawn arrived too quickly, but I found I did not mind the early hour. I thought perhaps I would go and start cutting and rolling sod for a few hours before breakfast. When I stepped out of the tangle into the clearing, I was surprised I was not the only one who had had that idea. Ealdred and Lom were already there and hard at work.

"Ah, Nissa, you are just in time to wheel the first load of sod out," called Ealdred.

As I stepped on the path at the beginning of the labyrinth, I thought to just cut across the grass between the circular path to get to where Ealdred and Lom were. Carz blocked my path.

"So, I guess that taking a shortcut in a labyrinth is not allowed. All right, Carz, I will follow the path."

When I reached the wheelbarrow, I noticed it was facing out, for which I was thankful. I was not sure how I would have gotten it turned around on the narrow path without stepping out onto the grass.

"Thanks for having the wheelbarrow facing out," I told Ealdred and Lom.

"You're welcome" said Lom. "We learned to do that the hard way. We had the wheelbarrow facing in for the first load. Taarig was quite emphatic that we were to stay on the path, so we had to unload the rolls of sod, lift up and turn the wheelbarrow around, and then reload the sod. That took longer than we planned. Fortunately, with our early start, and if everyone who was here yesterday is here this day, we should have the labyrinth path completely cleared by the end of the day."

While I was waiting for Lom and Ealdred to fill the wheelbarrow again, I noticed Carz pawing at the top of the edge that ran along both sides of the path. Wandering over, I noticed he was brushing away the dirt left behind from when we had peeled the sod back. Those of us cutting and rolling sod the day before had not taken the time to clear the raised edge of the path. I hunkered down and began to brush away the dirt where Carz had been pawing, and discovered embedded in the top of the edging of the path was a cabochon of stone or glass. I could not tell which.

"I'm going back out to get a hand broom, some rags, and some water," I told Ealdred and Lom. "Carz uncovered something, and I want to look at it further, if that's all right."

"Fine with us," said Lom. "Another early bird has come to take your place anyway."

I looked over my shoulder and saw that Lom spoke the truth, for Seeker Chance was walking toward us. We exchanged greetings as we passed by each other. I walked back through the tangle and back to my homewagon to gather what I needed. When I returned, I gently swept away the dirt surrounding a half-globe of glass or stone. Then I poured a bit of water on it and wiped away the remaining dirt. When I sat back, I could see the object embedded in the raised path edge shone a vibrant clear bright blue in the sunlight. When I looked up to say something to the others, I noticed that Carz was pawing at a place about nine feet down from where I was, and Ashu, Seeker Chance's companion was helping. I walked over to where they were working.

"Have you found another one?" I asked Carz and Ashu.

Carz and Ashu both moved back, and I could see they had uncovered another blue object shaped like a half-globe embedded in the raised path edge. I called over to Ealdred, Lom, and Seeker Chance.

"You folks might want to stop for a moment and come look at what Carz and Ashu have uncovered."

"Interesting," said Seeker Chance. "I wonder if they are on both sides of the path?"

I shifted over to the other side of the path directly across from where I had cleaned off the first blue half-globe. Again sweeping the dirt away from the top of the raised path edge, I did not find another blue half-globe in the path border. Seeker Chance had crossed over from the second one Carz and Ashu had uncovered and gently brushed away the dirt with his gloved hand. He too uncovered nothing but the edge of the path. I did notice Ashu was tugging on Seeker Chance's sleeve and pointing farther up the path. Taking a clue from Ashu, I too moved farther up the path, sweeping the dirt away. In about four feet, or a little more, I uncovered another blue half-globe embedded in the path edge, identical to the one I had found on the other side.

"There is another one here, too," Seeker Chance stated.

Ealdred had moved out of the labyrinth and was brushing away dirt from the path edge near the entrance to the tangle. He stood up and walked back to us.

"I uncovered one of the blue half-globes out there also. Looks just like the ones you all have uncovered," said Ealdred.

"At least here on the path in the labyrinth, the blue half-globes, I guess you could call them stones, or maybe they are gems, anyway, they seem to be offset," said Seeker Chance. "I wonder if they continue to be offset all along the path?"

"The only way to find out will be to clear the raised path edge. It looks like we have more work to do here besides removing the sod. Why don't I keep working on clearing the top of the edge of the path while the rest of you keep clearing sod?" I suggested. "Or I could help with the sod clearing and one of the other of you folks could do the sweeping and cleaning."

Greer returned with an empty wheelbarrow and joined the group. After we showed him what we had found, he suggested, "How about I take the other side? Even looks like I could sit down on the job," he stated with self-deprecating good humor.

"I would welcome the help. Well, perhaps only your help" I told him. I then began to chuckle, for Kasa, Greer's border dog, looking for all the world like he was ready for a nap, had flopped down beside Greer. "Doesn't look like he's going to be much help."

"No more than Carz. Guess it is just up to us," Greer said, as he started clearing off the edge of the pathway.

The others were content to go back to peeling and hauling sod, so I went back to my sweeping and cleaning. I decided I would work my way back to the labyrinth from the tangle down one side of the path, content to let Greer clear the other side. I do not know how long I had been working when Seeker Eshana called to me from the edge of the tangle.

"Nissa, would you mind going and getting Seeker Chance. I have an urgent message for him."

CHAPTER SEVEN

Seeker Chance could not imagine who would be sending him an urgent message. His family, having made a new life for themselves in the Havkoller Islands, had chosen not to return to Sommerhjem after the former regent stepped down. There was no one left in the town he had grown up in who would be contacting him. He could not imagine another seeker seeking him out, for he was so new to the Order of Seekers. Handing his shovel to Lom, he walked swiftly down the path toward Seeker Eshana, with Ashu riding on his shoulder, firmly gripping his hair.

When Seeker Chance got to the entrance of the tangle, Seeker Eshana said, "We will talk when we are in a more secure area. Follow me, please."

Seeker Eshana led them over to a bench situated by a flowing fountain. From where they sat, in the more formal gardens behind the royal palace, they could see all around them.

"It does not appear that there is anyone close enough to overhear. A message from Keeper Odette arrived at the royal palace a short while ago."

"Keeper Odette?" Seeker Chance questioned.

"Yes. It would seem she is on Captain Nereo's ship anchored in the capital harbor, and urgently needs to see both you and Ashu. She also asked you to bring a wagon with a cover and a number of wooden crates. I do not know any more than that. As I was heading for a meeting with those of us in the other group, Master Rollag and Journeyman Evan arrived at the royal palace. I asked Master Rollag where I might acquire a wagon and wooden crates without being asked a lot of questions or arousing suspicion. He sent Journeyman Evan off to get what you will need. He should be here to meet you shortly."

"Were you expecting Keep ... Seeker Odette I should say, since those who have met her here in Sommerhjem know her as a seeker." Looking around to once again make sure no one was in listening range, Seeker Chance went on. "I will have to work hard not to call her Keeper Odette. I don't want anyone questioning why I would do so. I wouldn't be able to explain without giving away the secret of the Shadow Islands and that the three of us call them home. Anyway, were you expecting Seeker Odette here at the capital? Also, do you know why she wants a wagon and crates?" Seeker Chance asked.

"I had an inkling she might arrive prior to the capital fair. I have no idea why she wants a wagon and wooden crates. I think you are missing an important point here, however. She did not send a message for me to come to the harbor. She sent a message for you and Ashu to come to the harbor. You had best be off. Journeyman Evan will meet you near the head gardener's cottage. Do you know where that is?"

"Yes." Seeker Chance could not imagine what Keeper Odette could want with both Ashu and him. Getting up, he asked Seeker Eshana if he was going to come also.

"No, lad, I think it should be just you and Journeyman Evan. I appreciate that this is risky, but Keeper Odette asked for discretion when coming down to the harbor. She suggested strongly that you not draw attention to yourself. Go just as you are. You have the look of a day laborer right now, and that might serve you well. Leave your staff behind. I might also suggest you grab your pack and see if Ashu will tuck into it. Riding through the capital with a halekrets on your shoulder would make you very noticeable."

Seeker Chance quickly went by his quarters and grabbed a backpack and a slouchy hat. Slapping the hat on his head, he asked Ashu to please climb into the backpack and remain hidden. The little halekrets did as asked, and soon Seeker Chance was swiftly running down the back stairs of the royal palace. He arrived at the head royal gardener's cottage just moments before Journeyman Evan arrived with a wagon.

"I didn't know what size wooden boxes to get, so I got a variety. They're tucked in back. Climb on up. Where is Ashu?"

At the mention of his name, Ashu poked his head up out of the backpack and snatched Journeyman Evan's hat off his head.

"Ah, so there you are. I brought you a treat." Journeyman Evan reached into his pocket and pulled out several nuts. "Hope that's all right, that I brought the nuts," Journeyman Evan said to Seeker Chance.

"You never need to ask my permission, for Ashu makes his own choices," Seeker Chance reminded Journeyman Evan, handing him back his hat.

"Ah, you are right. Sorry. Nissa's Carz, your Ashu, and the other animals who have accompanied those of you who carried rings into the capital are more like companions. However, for the most part, they are, in truth, wild animals and not pets."

"It always worries me that Ashu could at any time leave me. I try not to think about that possibility very often."

The three rode in silence the rest of the way to the capital harbor.

"Do you know where we are to go?" asked Journeyman Evan.

"Yes. Captain Nereo usually anchors out in the harbor and brings his cargo in by dory to the northern docks, about midway down. I have been there several times, so I should be able to find it again."

"This would be easier if we were using Lady Celik's dock," Journeyman Evan stated. "Too many folks might be watching there though."

Seeker Chance was glad that Journeyman Evan did not question him as to how he knew about a specific ship and its captain. Certainly one advantage of being a seeker was that he was rarely questioned on where he had been, or how he knew things.

Both Seeker Chance and Journeyman Evan had been watching all around as they traveled through the capital streets to the docks. They arrived at the docks without incident. Seeker Chance felt a bit of the tension he had been feeling ease. He knew that those who opposed the Crown had folks scattered all over the capital. It was a risk for him to be outside the safety of the royal palace. That could not be helped. He was surprised to find Captain Nereo himself waiting for him on the dock.

After being introduced to Journeyman Evan, Captain Nereo said, "Good, you have brought someone to help you offload the dory, and then we will put your wooden boxes in the dory and head back out to my boat."

Seeker Chance and Journeyman Evan made quick work of unloading the dory. Once the dory was unloaded, the three approached the wagon.

Journeyman Evan eased back the canvas covering. "I didn't know what size wooden boxes you wanted, so I brought several different sizes."

"Let me take a look. Ah, good choices. Those four medium-sized boxes will do nicely. Let's get them aboard the dory, shall we? I think, Journeyman Evan, it would be best if you stay here with the horse, wagon, and the boxes we just unloaded from the dory. Seeker Chance and I will be back shortly," Captain Nereo told Journeyman Evan.

Once they were away from the dock and rowing toward Captain Nereo's ship, Seeker Chance asked why the urgent message.

"I had best let Keeper Odette tell you. Aye, it would be better to hear it from her."

Now Seeker Chance was worried. He wondered if something had happened on the Shadow Islands, his adoptive home. He wondered if something had happened to one of the folks he knew there. He was particularly worried that something might have happened to the halekrets, some of whom were Ashu's family.

When they arrived at Captain Nereo's ship, they quickly handed the boxes up and climbed aboard. Keeper Odette was waiting on deck.

"Glad I am to see you," Keeper Odette said, a warm welcome on her face. "Please, follow me. I assume you brought Ashu."

At the sound of his name, Ashu quickly climbed out of Seeker Chance's backpack. Rather than climbing onto Seeker Chance's shoulder, he immediately dropped down onto the deck, scampered over, and dropped down into the hold. Before Seeker Chance had an opportunity to say anything, Keeper Odette suggested they follow Ashu's example and move on down into the hold.

"We might wish to take a more traditional route getting down into the hold. Not being as nimble as Ashu, I would suggest the ladder," said Keeper Odette.

Seeker Chance could hear the amusement in Keeper Odette's voice and was now more confused than ever. Had he misinterpreted the message from Keeper Odette? He did not feel she was acting like anything was urgent. Before he could ask what was going on, he stepped into the hold.

"Oh my."

"Oh my, indeed," Keeper Odette remarked.

"How did this happen?" Seeker Chance asked.

"How indeed."

"Is it all of them?"

"We are not sure, for we never knew just how many halekrets lived in the quirrelit grove back home. It could be."

Seeker Chance looked around for someplace to sit down, for his legs felt a little wobbly. The scene before him took a little time to adjust to. In one corner of the hold, tucked between crates, wooden barrels, and wooden boxes, small hammocks had been hung. Sitting on the various crates, barrels, and boxes, or lying in the hammocks, were at least a dozen halekrets, the reddish-brown, furred, black-masked, ring-tailed animals he had first encountered in a quirrelit grove on the Shadow Islands. Ashu was sitting between two of them, his small hand on the face of the shorter of the two.

"How, how did this come about?" Seeker Chance asked.

"With very little fuss on their part, I can assure you," Keeper Odette replied. "I was at the archives working on something. At this moment, I cannot recall what it was. I am sure it was important at the time. Anyway, as I was saying, I was working at the archives when I heard several folks running toward me, shouting my name. They told me I had to come quickly. They turned around and were racing back the way they had come, without telling me what the fuss was about. You can only imagine what went through my head at that moment."

Knowing that Keeper Odette was one of those who was held in high esteem in the Shadow Islands, and was looked to for both her wisdom and leadership, Seeker Chance could only begin to guess what had gone through her head on that occasion.

"I hurried after them, and when I reached the dock, I did not know if I should grab onto something to keep from falling down because I was so astonished, or because of the laughter bubbling up, due to what I saw before me."

"What did you see?" Seeker Chance asked.

"There on the deck of Captain Nereo's ship were the halekrets you see before you, sitting just as patiently as could be, as if they were accustomed to gathering on ship decks all of the time. There they were, in a group, all facing the dock, just sitting. They were quite a sight. Can you imagine the shock of the folks on the island, who had lived with knowing that halekrets lived in the quirrelit grove, but had rarely, if ever, seen one, and there were at least a dozen, just sitting on the deck? The halekrets also did not look as if they were going to get up anytime soon."

"What did you do?" Seeker Chance asked.

"I boarded the ship and approached them. I was not sure if they would understand me. We looked at each other for a time, and then I asked what they wanted. One of them got up and walked to the bow of the boat and climbed out on the bowsprit. Several more scampered up the mast and began tugging on the lines that held the sails."

"I figured they wanted to sail somewhere," stated Captain Nereo, who spoke up for the first time. "I was happy to oblige, for the only other choice would have been to try to convince them to leave the ship, and that did not seem the right thing to do. Can't really explain why. That was the way of it, though. 'Twas funny what happened next."

Seeker Chance looked back and forth between the two of them. "So, what happened next?"

"After Captain Nereo told the halekrets they were welcome to ride along, I tried to get off the ship. Two of the halekrets got up and blocked my way. I asked if they wanted me to sail with them. I had planned to leave for Sommerhjem fairly soon at any rate, so that was not a problem. I just had not intended to leave immediately. It also occurred to me that they might not want to go where I wished to go. That, however, was a moot point, since they were not letting me off the ship. When I said I would sail on the ship with them, but there were things I needed to take care of before I could leave the Islands, one of the halekrets who was blocking my way climbed up onto my shoulder, and the other one moved aside."

"So, did you leave right away?" Seeker Chance asked.

"No. I explained to the halekrets it would take a while to gather all we needed for the voyage. Food and places for them on the ship needed to be arranged, and I needed to gather what I would need for my time away from the Shadow Islands. I was allowed to leave the ship. Lots of folks helped gather what was needed. I went back to my sleep quarters to pack, and that was another interesting time. Seems the halekrets who accompanied me was more than willing to pull things out of my clothes trunk and put them in my pack to help me. I would then take the items back out, put them on the bed, and turn away to get something I really wanted. I would turn back and find the halekrets stuffing my pack with those things I had already discarded. You would have been down on the floor holding your sides laughing, if you had been there. Finally, I sat the halekrets on the bed with a bowl of fruit and asked politely if he would please just let me pack. I finally managed to finish packing, returned the discarded items back to their proper places, and headed down to the dock. The other halekrets were still waiting patiently on the deck. We set sail the next morning."

"How did you know to come here?" Seeker Chance inquired, once he had stopped chuckling over Keeper Odette's dilemma when trying to pack.

"Once we hit the open seas, I set course for Sommerhjem," said Captain Nereo. "To make sure I was heading the way the halekrets wanted to go, for I suspected they were not just on my ship for a sea cruise, I veered ninety degrees off course. The halekrets all moved to the side of the ship facing the direction of Sommerhjem. I turned back toward Sommerhjem, and they all returned either to where they had been on the deck or in the rigging. I tried that trick several more times with the same results. When we got to the coast of Sommerhjem, they again indicated which direction to go. That brought us here. The why of it is the mystery."

"They seem to want to get off the ship here," said Keeper Odette. "I felt it prudent that we disembark discreetly. Hoping you were in the capital, I had a message for you sent to the Order of Seekers quarters."

"So that is why you asked me to bring a wagon, a cover for the wagon, and the wooden boxes. It will look like we are just unloading cargo. No one will know what the cargo is. I think the best place to take them is to the royal palace," said Seeker Chance.

Keeper Odette raised one eyebrow. "I am not sure how they will fare inside the royal palace."

"Oh, no, you misunderstand. The grounds behind the royal palace are huge, and I think the halekrets would be comfortable there. We are going to have to come up with a story as to just where they came from."

"You are right. I have had the sea voyage to think about that. We will tell anyone who asks that we found them adrift. If I remember right, that worked well for you explaining Ashu. Well then, we had best see if they are willing to go along with our plans."

Chapter Eight

Shortly after Seeker Chance left, the others arrived in the clearing. I showed them what Ashu and Carz had uncovered. We divided the group up, with half working on removing the remaining sod, and the other half working on cleaning off the raised edge of the path. We continued uncovering the blue half-globes all along the path, from the tangle all the way through the labyrinth.

I was working one side of the path, and Yara was working the other side, when I finally reached within three feet of the entrance to the labyrinth. It was then that I could find no more of the raised edge of the path. I thought that perhaps, over time, a fitted stone or two might have been broken or removed. When I scraped away the grass and dirt all the way to the entrance of the labyrinth, I found that was not the case.

Taking a chance that Carz or one of the other animals would not come swiftly over to stop me, I dug into the sod on the outside of the path. I had noticed that that area was slightly lower. After I had peeled away a bit of the sod, I dug into the dirt beneath. About six inches down, my trowel hit something solid. Clearing more dirt away, I discovered paving stones.

"Yara, come take a look at what I found. It looks like the path that enters and exits the labyrinth branches off here. Does it do the same on the side you have been working on?"

Yara came over to look and then went back to her side and cleared sod and dirt away. After a few moments she replied, "Yes, it does."

"You folks might want to come take a look at this," I called to the others. When they gathered, I showed them what we had discovered. "It looks like the path you enter and exit the labyrinth on branches off to the right and left just before you enter."

"And here I thought we were almost done," said Piper. "I guess we had best get to it."

Yara and I traded off with the others clearing away the sod, cleaning off the raised sides of the two new paths, and cleaning the blue half-globes. Once we got behind the labyrinth, the two paths ran parallel for a short distance before they began to curve toward each other. After a bit they came together and formed one path heading straight toward the back cliff wall. We took a break for lunch on the royal palace terrace right after we had uncovered the place where the two paths merged.

I, for one, was glad to have a chance to stretch out my back muscles and give my knees a rest. As I reached for the pitcher of cool water, I glanced over and noticed Lom was looking very distracted, his noon meal barely touched.

"Lom, is everything all right?" I asked.

"What? Sorry. What did you ask?" Lom replied, having been pulled out of wherever his thoughts had taken him.

"You seem distracted. I asked if everything was all right."

"Yes, fine. Well, no."

"Ah, that clears it up nicely."

"My apologies again. I must seem muddleheaded to you right now. I'm just feeling a strong urge to get back to clearing the rest of the path. At first, clearing the path and finding the labyrinth was a way to be useful and pass the time. I felt a pull toward that part of the grounds, sure, but it was not strong. Enough to make me curious, but …." Lom fell silent.

I waited patiently for him to go on. In the short time I had known Lom that was one of the longer speeches I had heard him make. Finally, I prompted him to continue. "Go on."

"Something is back there at the cliff's edge. Ever since we started to uncover the path, I have felt a stronger and stronger pull. I thought it was the labyrinth that had caused the pull, and that may be part of it. Once you discovered that the path continues, and we started uncovering it, the pull became stronger and stronger. It makes it hard to take a break."

"We're almost ready to head back. It's going to be a long afternoon, and you need to eat. We can't have you unable to do your share because you are faint with hunger," I suggested.

It turned out our return to clearing the rest of the path was delayed due to Journeyman Evan arriving just as we were about to get up and head back.

"I'm sorry to disturb your noon meal. Would all of you mind joining me at the campsite where some of you are camped?" Journeyman Evan asked, addressing the group.

"All of us, of us?" asked Finn.

"Yes, if you would. I have sent someone to ask Seeker Eshana to join us also," stated Journeyman Evan.

"Has something happened to Seeker Chance?" I asked, concerned, for Journeyman Evan looked so serious.

"No, he's fine, as is Ashu."

As I stood up to head toward my campsite, it occurred to me that Carz was no longer on the terrace. Upon taking a closer look, I noticed that none of the animal companions were with us. When had they left the terrace and, more importantly, why? Then I felt ashamed that I had not noticed Carz leaving. When had I become so complacent, or so accustomed to having him around, that I ceased to notice?

All the while I walked from the terrace across the wide expanse of the formal garden to the grove I was camped in, I looked for Carz. I was concentrating so hard, trying to spot Carz, that I did not notice if others were as concerned as I was with the missing animals. I cannot begin to describe the high level of my relief upon entering the campsite and finding Carz lying in his favorite spot in the shade of the homewagon. The other folks must have thought I was a bit balmy when I rushed over and bent down to hug him.

"I am so glad you are here," I whispered to Carz. "I'm sorry if I have been taking you for granted. It won't happen again."

"Nissa, I think you might want to come over and meet our new guests," Seeker Chance called from the other side of the campsite.

I looked up to see another wagon had been pulled into the campsite. It was a wagon of the design that was typically used for hauling hay or cargo. I noticed there was a tarp lashed to the top, and there was a woman I did not know standing next to the wagon. She and Seeker Eshana were having a serious conversation. I was hesitant to interrupt. Seeker Chance was not and did the introductions.

"Nissa, this is Seeker Odette," said Seeker Chance. "Seeker Odette, this is the rover, Nissa."

"I am glad to be able to finally meet you. I have heard about both you and your hunting cat, Carz. It is nice to be able to put a face to the name," Seeker Odette said.

It took me a moment to respond, for Seeker Odette had one of the most melodic voices I have ever heard. For a brief moment, I just wanted her to keep on talking. I might not remember Seeker Odette's looks and might pass her by on the street without recognizing her, but I would never forget her voice. "Will you be camping with us?" I inquired.

"No, but thank you for the offer. I will be staying in town. I am just the, um, go-between, I guess you could say, delivering a very special cargo. Seeker Chance, perhaps you will do the honors, and then we will both try to explain."

"Ah, yes. It would be prudent for us to first make sure we are the only ones in the campsite. Piper and Theora, would you be so kind as to check the perimeter? Seeker Odette, if you wouldn't mind, would you help me unlash the tarp?"

Once the tarp was unlashed and rolled back, I could see the wagon contained a number of boxes, including four closed wooden boxes of medium size near the back. Ashu, who had been sitting on Seeker Chance's shoulder as usual, quickly jumped onto one of the boxes and tried to lift the lid.

"Ashu, we will help with the lids just as soon as Theora and Piper say it's all right," said Seeker Chance. "I know you are anxious, but please wait."

Ashu settled on a box with an air of impatience. Piper and Theora entered back into the campsite and stated they saw no one close. Finn volunteered to take up a position just outside the grove where he could see if anyone approached. Seeker Eshana said he would join Finn. Once the two were gone, Seeker Chance climbed up on the wagon and began removing box lids.

With all that had gone on in the last year, I should not have been surprised when at least a dozen halekrets climbed out of the wooden boxes. However, I must admit, I was very surprised. I was about to open my mouth and ask where they had come from when Finn rushed back into the campsite. He came to an abrupt stop and seemed to be having trouble trying to speak.

"Oh my, oh my, halekrets. Not just one. Oh no, not just one."

"Finn, what is it? Why did you rush back?" asked Meryl.

"Sorry, sorry. Folks are coming, coming they are. Number of folks, yes, number of folks. Seeker Eshana is trying to stall them, stall them."

"Nissa, could some of the halekrets hide in your homewagon? Theora, could the rest hide in your wagon?" asked Seeker Chance. "I don't think anyone would be so rude as to want to go into your homes without permission."

"They would be welcome in my homewagon, and I will ask Carz if he will guard against unwanted visitors," I told Seeker Chance.

"They are also welcome in my wagon," stated Theora. "I am sure two night wolves blocking the entrance will be a good deterrent to folks who might be overly curious."

"Ashu, there may be danger coming. Would you invite your friends to follow Nissa and Theora?" asked Seeker Chance.

I moved quickly over to my homewagon, went up the steps, and opened the door. I did not see what Ashu did, and I did not hear him make any noise, but soon all of the halekrets had followed me up the stairs and were making themselves quite comfortable in my homewagon. I would like to have stayed. I was not reluctant to leave them in my homewagon. I just wished I could spend some time with them.

"Sorry, Theora, I guess they may be rovers at heart," I said.

"Or they knew you have a basket of fruit on your table and I do not," Theora said.

It was not long after I climbed back out of my homewagon, and asked Carz to guard the door, that about eight folks arrived at the campsite. From their dress and manner, I thought they were young nobles. Fortunately, they did not stay very long. They told us they were out for a walk and wanted to see the formal royal palace gardens. They said they had heard about the campsite being discovered and wanted to see it. One thought she might take a peek into my homewagon, but Carz discouraged her. After a very short time, they wandered back out of the campsite.

"What was that all about?" Theora asked.

"It is not unusual for the children of some nobles visiting the royal palace to wander the royal palace gardens, often with little regard for the paths, plants, or folks working there. I have seen their type before," suggested Lom.

"I wonder if it was just an innocent stroll on one or all of their parts," questioned Seeker Odette.

"I was concerned about the same thing. There are eyes and ears everywhere. Could someone have been curious about what you folks might have been carrying in the wagon and sent word to folks not loyal to the Crown to check things out?" I asked. *How safe here are we really?* I wondered.

"There has been a great debate going on about whether or not the royal palace grounds should be off limits to one and all until the third day of the fair, since all of those who carried the pieces of the oppgave ringe are staying here for their protection. While the number of royal and special guards has been increased, and the royal palace and grounds are closed at dusk, I have questioned whether the choice to keep the grounds open during the day has been a wise one," said Seeker Eshana.

"Also, should one of us go and make sure our recent visitors do not wander to the bottom of the grounds and into the tangle where we have been working?" I asked.

"When we left to come up for our noon meal, I did not want to leave," said Lom. "Also, I had the feeling I should not leave. Since I could not figure out just what was causing that feeling, I took the precaution of asking the plants of the tangle to hide the entrance to the path. I don't think our visitors will find it. Once they have left the grounds, we can go back."

"What of the halekrets? Where did they come from, and why did you bring them here?" I asked.

"Actually, I did not bring them here. They brought me," suggested Seeker Odette.

We all looked at her in surprise.

"The ship I was on was on a course to come to the capital. We were several days out from Sommerhjem when we spied a large piece of floating flotsam. Imagine our surprise when we drew close and saw the halekrets. I knew what they were since I was acquainted with Ashu. We drew alongside, and the halekrets came aboard. After that, it became very clear that they were indicating which way they wished to go. As long as we were heading toward the capital, they were content to rest and relax on the deck or in the hold. If we veered off course, they would sit on the rail, looking in the direction they wanted to go. Once we arrived in the capital harbor, I sent a message to Seeker Chance. I do not know where they want to go now, but I think they will not hesitate to tell us."

"We certainly can't hide them in this campsite for long. Maybe they would be safe in the area where we have been working, since Lom could hide the entrance each night, and Theora has certainly managed to keep folks out during the day. Besides, other than locking them up somewhere, they really can go where they wish," I said.

CHAPTER NINE

Those who opposed the Crown had been stealthily moving across the capital under cover of darkness toward a meeting place they hoped was not known by the Crown. Lady Farcroft headed down an alley, walked fifty paces, turned left, and slipped through a narrow opening between two buildings. Fifteen paces in, she turned right through an archway, stepped up to the door recessed in the wall, and knocked. Lady Farcroft heard the sound of a small panel being slid back, and a voice questioned "Who goes there?"

"So, Yarrow, you have taken Dubhlainn's place, have you? You well know who I am, so open the door. This alley is dank and rank smelling, and I wish to be out of it. Bode is following close behind me, so be prepared to let him in."

"Yes, m'lady," Yarrow answered, as he opened the door and let Lady Farcroft slip inside. Holding the door open and moving out into the archway, he looked both ways to see if he could spot any movement. He could not, so went back inside.

Lady Farcroft walked down the dimly-lit stone corridor, down several flights of stairs, and down another hallway, until she came to a doorway. She knew all of the folks gathered in the room ahead of her. Even before entering, she could feel waves of tension pouring out of the room. As she stepped in, the men seated around the long table rose.

"Gentlemen and ladies, well met," said Lady Farcroft, addressing those assembled. "Lord Klingflug," Lady Farcroft acknowledged the man sitting at the head of the table. "Is this everyone, then?"

"Other than a few stragglers, yes, unfortunately, this is everyone who has chosen to come to the capital at this time. All too many of those who have been our loyal followers have either had a change of heart, or are hanging back to see which way the wind blows over the next few weeks," said Lord Klingflug.

"Perhaps that could be expected, considering what has happened since that third day of the capital fair last summer," replied Lady Farcroft. "All the scheming and planning, all the effort to prevent the princess taking the throne should have worked, and it did, but not in the way we expected. All the scheming and effort to prevent the Gylden Sirklene challenge from being called should also have worked, and yet, it happened anyway. Preventing the former princess, now Lady Esmeralda, from gaining any popularity was also a goal. Unfortunately, again, that did not quite work out in the way you had planned, Lord Klingflug. Lady Esmeralda has gained quite a good reputation since calling the challenge. Shown herself to be a strong leader," stated Lady Farcroft. "Has there been any good news of late?"

"No," stated Lord Klingflug, "and the time grows short. Eight of the rings are here in the capital. So far there has been no news, not even a hint, as to whether the ninth ring has been found by the Crown. Certainly it has not been found by anyone loyal to this group assembled here, or by anyone else, for that matter."

"I've been thinking about that day, thinking back over what happened, and what was said. Something Master Clarisse said just before the assembly ended did not mean much to me at the time. However, it may be important now," suggested Lady Farcroft.

"What?" one of the others assembled in the room asked impatiently.

"Master Clarisse said the individual or individuals who are living keys in the Gylden Sirklene challenge are also protected. That upstart rover lass, Nissa, is a living key, so to speak, since she could turn the key and open the vessteboks. That accounts for one living key. Please recall that Master Clarisse suggested that there could be more than one. The question, then, becomes: just who are the others who are living keys? Also, if we could prevent them from doing whatever it is they are supposed to do, would that prevent the challenge?"

"You are forgetting the part where Master Clarisse suggested if anyone were to try to harm the living keys, that harm would come back to them threefold," said Lady Henrietta Green.

"She also said that seekers should not be interfered with, and the sky did not fall in when those folks loyal to us crossed paths with them," Lady Farcroft stated.

"It did not go well either," Lady Henrietta Green muttered quietly.

A discussion about who, if any, the other living keys might be ensued. No conclusion was reached. Most agreed that the logical ones who might be living keys were those folks who had carried pieces of the oppgave ringe into the capital. Some suggested that Thorval Pedersen might also qualify, since he had been the one to bring in the vessteboks. Also, possibly Seeker Eshana, since he had brought the Book of Rules to the capital, which in very cryptic terms laid out the rules for the Gylden Sirklene challenge.

A number of plans were proposed. One member of the group suggested that, if they could get their hands on one of the companion animals, they could perhaps lure one of the ring carriers away from the safety of the royal palace. That idea was immediately quashed, since the animals were just as protected on the royal palace grounds as the folks they accompanied, and were not likely to leave the royal palace grounds without their companion folks. They then discussed the fact that the rover Nissa was the daughter of Thorval Pedersen, a fact they had not been aware of the previous summer.

"If we could get a message to one of them suggesting we had the other one captive, which might open up an opportunity to get one or both," suggested Lady Farcroft. The group seemed to warm to her idea. Before the discussion could continue further on the subject of Nissa and Thorval Pedersen, Lord Klingflug interrupted.

"On to another matter. It is too bad we were not alerted soon enough to intercept Seeker Chance when he made a trip to the docks with some journeyman from the Glassmakers Guild. Does anyone have any more information about that?" asked Lord Klingflug, trying to take back command of the meeting before it slipped away from him.

"I thought you had spies everywhere," said Lady Farcroft.

Ignoring the jab from Lady Farcroft, Lord Klingflug indicated that one of his men should give a report.

"Seeker Chance went by wagon to the docks with one Journeyman Evan of the Glassmakers Guild. There they were met by the captain of a ship anchored in the harbor. The two lads helped the captain unload boxes from a dory and load four wooden boxes into it. Journeyman Evan stayed with the cargo on the dock, and Seeker Chance went out to the ship. Our observers said he was met on deck by a woman, went into the hold, and was there briefly. He then returned to the dock with the woman and four closed wooden boxes. It was reported that the wooden boxes appeared to be heavier when they were again loaded on the wagon. The pair returned to the royal palace. Our informants there said they drove the wagon to the grove where several of those being protected are camping. When our informants made their way to the campsite, the tarp had been rolled back on the wagon which contained a number of boxes. Four of the boxes were open. One of our informants tried to get into the rover Nissa's homewagon, but was prevented. It is unclear what, if anything, was transported to the campsite. Oh, one more thing. It was reported that Seeker Chance traveled to and from the harbor not accompanied by that animal that usually sits on his shoulder."

"Do any of you have anything else to add?" asked Lord Klingflug.

"My contact within the royal palace has informed me that those who carried the pieces of the oppgave ring into the capital, along with several others, have been doing something at the bottom of the royal palace garden," said Lady Farcroft. "They have been hauling out wheelbarrow loads of dirt and sod. The lass, Theora, and the two night wolves have prevented anyone from getting near the place where they have been working. Seems like a very odd thing for those folks to be doing."

"Dekle, you have been studying the plans for the royal palace garden. What might be of interest in the area that Lady Farcroft's informant noted?" asked Lord Klingflug.

A fussy-looking man, who looked like he would be more comfortable in the royal library among dusty tomes than in this gathering, answered. "Ahem, well, as near as I can recollect, and if I understand the correct area Lady Farcroft alluded to, well, ah, there is nothing there."

"What do you mean, there is nothing there?" Lord Klingflug asked impatiently.

"Yes, yes, precisely. The area the group who are associated with carrying pieces of the oppgave ringe into the capital are working on shows up on all the plans I have been able to peruse as an empty space. All of the rest of the royal palace grounds are shown in great detail on all of the plans I have looked at. As I said, the space they seem to be interested in shows on all the plans as an empty space."

"Have any of those who are loyal to us and working at the royal palace been able to find out any more?" Lord Klingflug asked.

"As I mentioned, my contacts say that, during the day, one of the special royal guards, a lass named Theora, keeps all who would be interested in the area away. At night, none of the contacts have been able to find the entrance," said Lady Farcroft.

"Cannot find the entrance. Bah, what is wrong with these folks?" remarked Lord Klingflug.

"I think it is not a matter of my contacts not being able, but rather who we are dealing with," suggested Lady Farcroft. "There have always been rumors about folks being able to get foliage to do their bidding. This Ealdred, who has befriended that garden laborer lad, Lom, may be able to do so. There is also some suggestion that the lad, Lom, might also have the ability. If the rumors are true, each night they may be hiding the entrance to where they are working."

"It is also suspected that the lad, Lom, is a sensitive, that he has the ability to identify, or is drawn to, objects of power. I wonder if that is what is causing them to be interested in that particular area of the royal grounds?" said Lord Klingflug.

"None of this speculation brings us any closer to stopping the challenge," Lady Farcroft stated emphatically. *That is the trouble with groups working together on a project,* she thought. *Everyone comes with their own agendas. Too many folks want to take the lead. Too many add their opinions. We waste time going over the same thing, or go over too many ideas, and nothing gets done. Well, I am certainly not going to let this group know what I have planned.*

CHAPTER TEN

Once the unwelcome visitors had left our campsite, I went to my homewagon, which now held over a dozen halekrets. I suspected there was more to the story of how they had gotten to Sommerhjem, but that was not my immediate concern. After all, over a dozen halekrets were now making themselves at home in my home.

"Are those folks gone?" I asked Seeker Chance. Given the affirmative that the visitors were indeed gone, I opened the door to my homewagon, not knowing what I would find inside. What greeted me was indeed a surprise. The halekrets had made themselves at home, and were curled up on the bed and sitting about on other flat surfaces. As I opened the door and stepped in, they all turned toward me and looked at me intently.

"Would you like to come out?" I inquired. None of them moved. "Well then, I will just leave the door open, in case you change your minds."

Later that evening, after all of the others, except Seeker Chance, had gone to bed, I found myself, while tired, still not ready to turn in, nor able to. Earlier, after realizing the halekrets were content for the moment to stay in my homewagon, I had returned to the clearing where we had been working. It had been another afternoon of digging and clearing, hauling and lifting. We had been determined to clear the path that ran on either side of the labyrinth to the cliff wall, which was itself covered with very thick vines. Surprisingly, the path we had been clearing widened out about fifteen feet from the cliff wall, so it had taken longer than we had anticipated to clear the final portion of the path.

Finally, the task was done. Both Ealdred and Lom tried to get the thick vines to move, for Lom had felt a very strong pull of something behind the vines. The vines had remained determinedly stubborn, and would not even budge a leaf. Lom was reluctant to leave, telling us that the pull at that spot was almost overwhelming. After a time, tired, sore, with many blisters, cuts, and scratches to show for the several days of labor, we had all agreed to head back.

I, for one, was curious to discover if Seeker Chance had any luck coaxing the halekrets out of my homewagon, for he had stayed behind with Ashu. He had not. The halekrets had not moved in the hours we had been away from the campsite. Seeker Chance and I were now sitting, long after night had fallen, waiting, when I saw movement at the door of my homewagon.

"Ah, it seems your houseguests are on the move," Seeker Chance whispered quietly out of the darkness.

I looked up to see the halekrets move one by one down the back stairs of the homewagon. Forming a loose group, they began to walk out of the campsite. Ashu climbed down from Seeker Chance's shoulder and joined them. Seeker Chance, Carz, and I followed at a discreet distance. Without hesitation, the halekrets walked to the edge of the tangle at the bottom of the royal palace grounds, and followed the tangle edge to where the opening to the pathway we had been clearing was located. A three-quarter moon gave us enough light to see that when they arrived at the opening, the foliage that hid it pulled back. Seeker Chance and I followed them, keeping well back.

Even before we reached the entrance to the open area, we could see a faint blue light filtering through the trees and brush. When we turned the last bend in the path, both Seeker Chance and I were drawn up short in surprise. As the halekrets passed each of the blue half-globes we had uncovered on the edges of the pathway, the half-globes sent a shaft of blue light several feet upwards. Once the halekrets were past, the light dimmed and faded. I was the first of the two of us to step onto the pathway, and was surprised when the first blue half-globe lit up as I passed it.

Seeker Chance and I walked about halfway down the pathway, close enough to see where the halekrets went, but far enough back not to disturb them. I was curious about whether they would turn right or left on the side path that headed toward the back cliff wall, whether they would follow the labyrinth path, or whether they would just wander onto the open grass. I found myself surprised once again when they followed the cleared pathway to the labyrinth, followed the pathway through the labyrinth, and climbed up into the quirrelit tree, settling themselves on various branches. Seeker Chance and I just stood there in silence as the blue light from the half–globes dimmed and faded, leaving the area bathed in moonlight.

We stood there for a long time before Seeker Chance reluctantly suggested that we should probably head back to the campsite. I could hear the sadness in his voice, for Ashu had gone with the other halekrets up into the quirrelit tree and had not come back down. I could well imagine what he might be feeling. I could not imagine being without Carz. I knew it was unrealistic to think there would not come a time when Carz would go back to the wild. In my heart of hearts, however, I hoped against hope that would not happen. Ashu staying in the quirrelit tree with the other halekrets brought those fears of Carz leaving me rushing in. It was all I could do not to abandon Seeker Chance and rush back to my homewagon to make sure Carz was still there.

I stayed with Seeker Chance as we slowly walked back to the campsite. It was a quiet walk with neither of us talking, both lost in our own thoughts. We parted at the entrance to the campsite. Though I was relieved when I spotted Carz sitting on the back steps of my homewagon, I was sure neither of us would get much sleep this night.

I was up well before dawn. Carz and I slipped out of the campsite and headed toward the open area and the quirrelit tree. I hoped the tangle was open. I do not know what I expected to accomplish there. I just knew I felt great sorrow for Seeker Chance. Maybe I thought to stand beneath the quirrelit tree and try to talk to Ashu. I will never know if that would have worked, since Carz and I were met at the entrance of the pathway through the tangle by one of the halekrets. He or she, I was not sure which, since there was only the slightest hint of light in the sky, took my hand and began to gently pull me down the path. Again, as we walked toward the quirrelit tree, the blue half-globes lit up as we passed them. When I arrived at the base of the quirrelit tree, I was relieved I no longer needed to worry, for I could see Seeker Chance asleep, his back to the quirrelit tree, and Ashu curled in his lap.

Since I did not want to disturb him, I motioned to Carz that we should complete the labyrinth and head back to the campground. I was hoping I could get a little sleep before it was time for breakfast. That was not to be. Just before Carz and I would have emerged from the tangle, Carz halted, blocking my way. A low growl issued from his throat, and then he stilled. I listened as hard as I could to try to figure out what had caused his hackles to rise. It was then that I heard it, the sound of folks walking stealthily on the path leading to the tangle. Then I heard their whispered voices.

"Ya sure the opening is near here?" a male voice asked.

"Yes, yes. Do yah see that crooked branch there hangin' down. Broke that branch off meself to mark the area I saw 'em comin' out of. Theys must draw brush over the openin' or sumthin' so as to cover the path up each night."

"I don't think theys covered it this night, for I can sees an opening."

As the men drew nearer, I crouched down and whispered to Carz, "Can you give them a good scare, yet not harm them?" I had hardly said the last word when Carz charged down the path, let out a fierce growl, and sprang toward the two men. They went down in a tangle of arms and legs for, as they tried to get away from Carz, they had run into each other. At that point, I walked out of the tangle and approached them.

"Gentlemen, is there a problem here? It seems to be either a little early in the morning, or a little late in the night, to be wandering the royal palace grounds. I would suggest you unwrap yourselves. Carz and I will escort you out."

At breakfast, I told the others of the two men who were skulking about the royal palace grounds in the wee hours of the morning. Lady Esmeralda told us she would confer with the head of the royal palace guards and ask her to increase the night patrol.

After breakfast, those of us who had been working on the labyrinth area walked down together and entered the tangle. Seeker Chance had not been to breakfast. I had told the others what had transpired when the halekrets had left my homewagon. When we came out from the tangle, I was surprised to see Seeker Chance and all of the halekrets by the vine-covered back cliff wall. As we all walked down the path to join them, the blue half-globes lit up. I had not warned the others beforehand about the blue half-globes, so they were as surprised as Seeker Chance and I had been the evening before.

It occurred to me, as we headed toward the cliff wall, that the halekrets appeared unconcerned about any of the animals who accompanied us. The halekrets sat with seeming patience as we approached the cliff wall. We slowed when we got close, and Greer asked Seeker Chance if he knew what was going on.

"I do not," said Seeker Chance. "When I awoke this morning, the halekrets climbed down out of the quirrelit tree and walked back here. They have been quietly sitting here ever since."

Seeker Chance had barely finished speaking when the oldest looking halekrets stood up and moved away from the cliff wall. He walked slowly toward the gathered group, looking at each one in turn. He passed by Seeker Chance, Greer, Meryl, Yara, Piper, Lom, Finn, Ealdred, and Theora and stopped in front of me. He looked at me for a long time, and then reached out a hand and took hold of mine.

Lady Farcroft was pacing back and forth in the parlor of her town home and was extremely agitated. Turning to Lady Henrietta Green, she began to vent. "I am beginning to question why we ever put any faith in Lord Klingflug. For all of his planning and plotting to try to prevent the princess from assuming the rule, he has not succeeded. What he has done since the Gylden Sirklene challenge was called almost a year ago has been one bungle after another."

"But …." Lady Green began, only to be cut off by Lady Farcroft's continued rant.

"Lord Klingflug's agents have missed or bungled several opportunities to detain one or more of the folks who carried pieces of the oppgave ringe to the capital. He could not even manage to stop one lone rover from bringing the vessteboks here. He is supposed to have loyal folks all over Sommerhjem on watch for opportunities to get ahold of one of those folks who travel with an uncommon animal, and has not accomplished that," Lady Farcroft said in disgust.

"But …." Lady Green tried again.

"The biggest bungle was when his folks had that lass Piper in their sights and let her slip away. Thought that whelp of a nephew of Lord and Lady Hadrack either had information about a piece of the oppgave ringe or had a piece. Turned out the lass did, and they just let her get away. Then, because Lord Klingflug's agents could not seem to keep Aaron Beecroft contained within the Raven's tower at Waldron Keep, not to mention that lad, Lom, who was a mere day laborer, we lost Waldron Keep, and a number of loyal followers who hold land in that area."

Lady Farcroft halted her pacing at the far end of the parlor, looked out the window, drew a deep breath, and then continued, with her back to Lady Green, whom she once again cut off. "With the placing of each successive ring, more and more of those who were loyal to Lord Klingflug have been pulling back. Now many are sitting back waiting to see what happens at the capital summer fair."

"But …."

"But what?" Lady Farcroft said, turning away from the window.

"But I have some good news."

"Well, why did you not say so?"

"I …." Thinking better of trying to explain that she had been trying to tell Lady Farcroft something for the last few minutes, Lady Green cleared her throat and began. "My second floor maid is very grateful to me for giving her husband a job as a groomsman. Her sister is a serving maid in the royal palace. I have hinted to my maid that there might be a better position for her sister with me, should her sister be willing to gather information for me. Her sister has agreed."

"And?" Lady Farcroft asked impatiently.

"And, well, you know that the servants do talk. They are quite the little gossips, if you ask me. Why, if I thought one of those folks who work for me was talking about me and mine down below in the kitchen, why I just do not …."

"Did your upstairs maid's sister find out anything important?" Lady Farcroft snapped, her patience now gone.

"Well, yes. That is what I have been trying to tell you."

Before Lady Green could explain, there was a light knock on the parlor door.

CHAPTER ELEVEN

I stood frozen, not knowing what to do when the halekrets reached out and took hold of my hand. When he tugged, I found myself moving forward. As we approached the vine-covered cliff wall, I caught movement out of the corner of my left eye. I turned my head slightly and saw Lom was also being led by a halekrets toward the cliff wall. The halekrets leading me stopped just short of the vines. The halekrets leading Lom reached up and tugged on what I assumed was a knife sheath on Lom's belt.

"I think the halekrets wants your knife," I told Lom.

"Billhook."

"What?" I asked.

"She is tugging on the sheath of my billhook."

When I looked at him with a confused look on my face, Lom told me a billhook was used for cutting vines.

"Maybe she wants you to cut the vines away from the cliff here," I suggested.

Lom took the billhook out of its sheath and looked at the halekrets who had led him to the cliff wall. The halekrets reached out and yanked on one of the thick vines that grew there.

"Would you like me to cut the vine?" Lom asked.

The halekrets yanked on the vine again.

"Do you want me to go ask the head royal gardener for some axes?" Piper asked Lom. "That vine is as thick as a small tree trunk."

"Let me see how this billhook fares first," Lom suggested, as he motioned the halekrets back. It took only two cuts at the base of the vine for it to be cut through.

I overheard Meryl tell Finn that they needed to buy some billhooks like that one, for they would come in mighty handy in their travels. I turned back from their conversation to see the halekrets directing Lom to cut another vine at its base. The halekrets then climbed up to Lom's shoulder and began pulling at one of the vines.

"Here, if I may," Ealdred said to the halekrets on Lom's shoulder, pulling out a billhook that was in a sheath on his belt. "I'll cut away above you, while you, Lom, cut below. The rest of you might wish to haul away the vines."

Once the halekrets saw that Ealdred was going to cut the vine she had been tugging at, she climbed back down and rejoined the other halekrets who were sitting patiently along the edge of the path. The one holding my hand remained with me.

As the vines began to come down, it became apparent to all of us that there was an opening behind the vines, a good twelve to fifteen feet wide and about as high. As more vines came down, it was clear the archway over the opening was carved, and beyond the archway was a large wooden door.

"Look at the carvings on the archway and the door," Yara said.

I do not know why I was surprised that the carvings on both were in the same style as the patterns in the book the Huntress had given me. I knew I needed to tuck this thought away for another time. I hoped someday, assuming all went well in a couple of weeks, I could go back to the Huntress' woods and talk to her. I had tried to locate her when I had been at the Crestbury fair recently. I could not find either her or her dwelling, and did not want to call, for I was not in great need. I only had to glance at my hand and see the ring with the firestar gem in it to know the night I had spent in the Huntress' woods had been real, not some elaborate fanciful dream, and yet, when I tried just recently, I could not find my way within her woods to her home in a quirrelit tree.

I was pulled out of my musings when the halekrets who was still holding my hand began to pull me toward the opening. When we reached the door, he let go of my hand. The carvings on the door were what I could only aspire to achieve in my lifetime as a woodworker. I do not know how long I would have stood there transfixed by the carvings and designs had not the halekrets tugged on my hand, distracting me. He climbed up to my shoulder, reached out and pushed against the door. He seemed to want me to open it.

As I examined the door further, I discovered there was neither a latch nor a knob by which to open the door. I pushed against the door. It did not move and was as solid as the rock cliff it was set into. Seeker Chance, with Ashu on his shoulder, moved to stand beside me and look at the door also.

"The door is split down the middle, so it is actually two doors," I told him. "I can't really tell if it swings inward or outward, for there are no visible hinges. Something about the design carved into the doors looks familiar, but I just can't quite seem to put my finger on it."

Seeker Chance and I examined the doors for a while longer and then stepped back to let the others look. None of us were any more successful with trying to get the doors open.

"I am sorry we can't get the doors open," I said, addressing the halekrets, who was still sitting on my shoulder.

It was then the halekrets did the strangest thing of all. He climbed down and gathered all of the other halekrets to him, including Ashu. The entire group of halekrets looked up toward the top of the cliff where the halekrets who had been on my shoulder was pointing. Three of the halekrets separated themselves from the others. One of them was Ashu. He patted the face of each of the two halekrets in turn, then scampered back to Seeker Chance and climbed up to his shoulder. The two returned to the group and all of the halekrets, minus Ashu, climbed very swiftly up the vines covering the cliff wall and disappeared over the top. I noticed Seeker Chance swiped a hand at his eye.

"Must have gotten a bit of fur in my eye," Seeker Chance said, as he reached in his pocket, searching for a handkerchief.

I saw Lom also reach in his pocket, I assumed for a handkerchief. The look of concern on his face swiftly turned to dismay. I saw him begin to turn out his pockets one by one as if searching for something.

"Is something wrong, lad?" Ealdred asked, for he too had noticed how frantic Lom had become.

"The rings, they're gone."

"Are you sure?" Theora asked, moving swiftly to Lom's side. "Perhaps you left them back at the camp."

"No, I always keep them with me. As a matter of fact, I'm in the habit of checking my pocket quite frequently, for I'm always worried I will lose them. I remember checking my pocket just before we started cutting down the vines. I wanted to make sure they were secure before I started cutting and tugging on the vines."

"What rings?" I asked. "Just what is missing?"

Lom looked to Theora and Ealdred, who both nodded their heads in the affirmative. "When I found the eighth piece of the oppgave ringe, along with it were nine more golden pine spider silk pouches. Each pouch was a different color. Some were the color of quirrelit leaves from the early spring colors to the fall colors. Others were the color of the bark of the quirrelit tree from early growth to that of a very mature tree. Each of the nine pouches held a ring. They are all made of the same material, I think, as the billhook. The designs on the rings are similar to the designs on the billhook, Theora's bow, and the ring I wear. Each ring is just a little bit different. I think they are important, and now they are gone."

"I suggest we take a look around and see if they are near where you were cutting, or in the pile of vines we pulled down," Ealdred suggested calmly.

We all spread out, being careful to stay on the path, and looked for the pouches. Several of us went through the pile of vines, vine by vine. We did not find the pouches. After we had exhausted every possible place the pouches could be, to no avail, Lom was asked again if he was sure he had had them in his pocket just before he had started cutting the vines. He was sure.

"Ashu?" Seeker Chance was heard to say.

I turned around to see Ashu quickly climbing up the vines just as his fellow halekrets had done earlier.

"I had hoped he would stay with me," Seeker Chance remarked.

I could hear the sadness in his voice. It was hard to watch Ashu climb up the vines and disappear over the top of the cliff wall. All of us who were companioned by uncommon animals feared that at some point, they would leave us.

"We had best get back to finishing our task here, then," Ealdred said gently. "We'll clean up the vines and other debris. Nissa, maybe you might like to spend some time looking over the door and arch here with Seeker

Chance while the rest of us finish up. Two heads will be better than one, trying to figure out how to open the doors."

I appreciated what Ealdred was trying to do. Maybe if Seeker Chance was occupied with a task, the loss of Ashu would not be so hard on him. I sincerely doubted that would be the case, however, for I know I would be distraught if Carz suddenly left me.

"Let's take another look at the doors," I suggested to Seeker Chance. Once we were under the archway and away from the others, I said, "Has he left you before?"

"No, but up until now, he has been the only halekrets that I know of in Sommerhjem. Now there are others of his kind here. They could even be his family. I worry that, now that they are here, he will not be content to stay with me."

"You are his family, too, I think," I said, hoping that what I was saying was the truth. "While we wait, let's use this time to see what we can figure out about these doors. So far I cannot find a way to open them."

I had been concentrating so hard, trying to find a pattern or a hidden handle, that at first I did not hear the rustling of the vines above me. Finally, I looked up to see Ashu climbing down the vine-covered cliff wall. When he jumped from the vines onto Seeker Chance's shoulder, I could see he was wearing golden pine spider silk pouches around his neck.

"Well, there's one mystery solved. It would seem the halekrets took the pouches from Lom," I said. "I'm sure he will be relieved that he did not carelessly lose them." *But not as relieved as Chance is that Ashu is back on his shoulder,* I surmised.

Seeker Chance called Lom to come over to us. While I waited for him to walk up, I glanced at what the others were doing. The last of the vines were being hauled away by Meryl. The rest of the folks were sweeping and picking up the last of the debris. Theora was nowhere to be seen. Carz and Jing were napping on wide branches of the quirrelit tree. Taarig and Tala, the night wolves, were sitting alert at the edge of the tangle, almost as if they were on guard. Toki, the red bog fox, was lying in the shade of the quirrelit tree with the border dog, Kasa. As a shadow flew over me, I glanced up to see the griff falcon, Tashi, riding the thermals above me. I had to pull my attention away from the peaceful scene when Lom reached us.

"Where did Ashu find them?" Lom asked, as he lifted the pouches over Ashu's head.

"I'm not sure," Seeker Chance replied. "He climbed up the cliff wall and disappeared over the top. Later, he returned with the pouches around his neck. One guess is that one of the halekrets either simply found them and took them, or one of the halekrets is a pickpocket."

"Or one of the halekrets took them for some reason we do not yet know," I suggested.

"I, for one, am just glad …. Wait, the pouches are empty," exclaimed Lom.

"All nine pouches are empty?" I asked.

"Yes."

"You don't think Ashu just emptied them out up there on the top of the cliff, do you?" Lom asked reluctantly, for he did not want to say anything bad about the little halekrets sitting on Seeker Chance's shoulder.

"I can think of no reason why he might do that," said Seeker Chance. "If you want my opinion, I think he went and got the pouches to return them to you so you would know that you had not carelessly lost them."

"You know, for some reason, I think you are right. Thank you, Ashu," Lom said.

Theora approached me, accompanied by both Taarig and Tala. "Nissa, there is a message for you from the elder rover, Zeroun. He asks that you meet with him at your earliest convenience," said Theora.

I wonder what that is all about? Well, maybe it is good timing, for I had already thought about seeking him out and asking him to come and look at the carvings on this door with me. I wish Shueller were here now, I thought.

"His message concerned nine missing firestar gems," stated Theora.

Chapter Twelve

Piper, who had been sweeping the path close to the uncovered doors, when Theora had given Nissa the message, quickly walked over to join the group. "I couldn't help overhearing you mention nine missing firestar gems to Nissa. You said the message was from an elder rover?"

"Yes, the rover Zeroun. He is a gem cutter by trade, a very well respected one. Why?"

"In my travels this year, I met a young Günnary man who gave me my bracelet that is inset with a firestar gem. How that came about is a story for another time. However, he was in possession of nine uncut firestar gems, something I think is quite rare, both uncut gems and the amount. He was concerned that he would be hard-pressed to find someone who was skilled enough to cut them. I wonder if these are the same gems?" questioned Piper.

"Nine pieces of the oppgave ringe, the nine rings in golden pine spider silk pouches that Lom found when he found the eighth piece of the oppgave ringe, nine firestar gems found by your Günnary man and, so far, nine of us are companioned by uncommon animals …." I mused.

"Nine animals, yes, but I did not bring a piece of the oppgave ringe here, and the ninth ring is still out. Whoever might have that, if anyone does, might also be accompanied by an uncommon animal, and that would bring the number up to ten," suggested Theora.

"Well, all of this speculating about things coming in nines does not get me over to the fair campground and meeting with Zeroun. I had best go. So Carz, are you interested in a change of scenery?"

"You don't intend to go alone, do you?" Piper asked, concern evident in her voice.

"Oh, you're right. I wasn't thinking. I can't begin to tell you how very much I wish I was back on the summer fair route plying my trade where my main concern might be whether Mistress Jalcones was making some type of fruit crumble for dessert for the evening meal, or whether it was my night for cleanup. Instead, I now need to go figure out how to get across the capital to the fairgrounds safely."

I said my goodbyes to the others, and Carz and I walked up toward the royal palace. Theora had wanted to accompany me, taking her role as our protector seriously. I had pointed out that she really could not be in two places at once. She could not guard me so I would get to the fair campground safely and also watch over Lom, the others, and the place where we had been working, all at the same time. She had reluctantly agreed. Just as I was about to enter the tangle, Greer and Kasa caught up with us.

"We would go with you, if you would like company," Greer said. "It would be nice to get off the royal palace grounds for a while."

"We would welcome your company," I told him.

When we neared the royal palace, one of the royal palace servants approached us and said a carriage had been arranged to take me to the fair campground. She looked a little disconcerted and stammered that she had not expected there to be someone with me. She recovered quickly and asked that we follow her. I remembered her name was Domana. I was familiar with Domana, for she had been one of the servers at all of our meals, and I did not think much of her slight reaction upon seeing Greer and Kasa.

"Is the carriage that has been arranged large enough to carry the four of us?" I inquired.

"Yes, ma'am."

I was surprised when we arrived at the drive, where carriages pulled up to the royal palace, to see not one of the royal palace carriages, but rather a carriage-for-hire. Even more curious was the fact that none of the royal guard were present. Even before I could ask, Domana explained.

"It was thought you might draw too much attention traveling in one of the royal palace carriages. Your driver is very loyal, will take you safely where you need to go, and return you here."

The first part of the ride was humdrum. Greer and I chatted about what we had found this day back at the clearing, and speculated on what might be behind the door we found in the cliff wall. I was not paying too much attention to our route. One moment bright sunlight was shining in the carriage windows, and the next, it was dark, for we had turned down an alley between buildings. I looked out just in time to see a black hooded figure rush toward the carriage and slam the outside shutters shut. I also heard something hit the door on my side. As I jumped up and lunged toward the door, I could feel movement behind me as Greer moved toward the carriage door on his side. I tried to open the door on my side to no avail.

"My door won't budge. Yours?"

"No, doesn't give an inch. This is not good," Greer remarked quietly.

"How about the window?" I asked, after trying mine to no avail.

"Locked tight." Greer leaned down and put a calming hand on Kasa's shoulder. "Hold. Wait," he told the border dog.

I looked at Carz who was sitting, alert. I turned back to Greer and said, "I thought Domana looked startled when I arrived at the royal palace with you, but I thought it was because they had a small carriage or wagon waiting. Now I think it has more to do with the fact that whatever plans she was in on did not include someone being with me. I wonder if we can use that to our advantage."

"We'll need to be ready. Right now, we still seem to be in the city, and I think we are heading downward toward the harbor." observed Greer.

The farther we traveled, the more I concluded Greer's observation that we were heading toward the harbor was correct. *Were we being taken to the harbor to be put on a ship?* We talked quietly about what we might be able to do once we arrived wherever the carriage was taking us. We needed to be ready for anything.

Unfortunately, being ready did nothing to help us. The carriage we were in slowed, turned a sharp corner, and then bumped over something, throwing us about. When the carriage stopped, I could hear the low murmur of voices, the sound of horses' tack, and finally the sound of horses being led away. Shortly thereafter, a sharp rap sounded on the door.

"Now that I have your attention, listen carefully. We will not harm you or the animals, if you cooperate. Know we will not hesitate to eliminate the hunting cat or the border dog if they appear threatening."

"Carz, stay with me, please. I don't want you to come to harm." I recommended to Greer we do as the folks on the other side of the carriage suggested. "I don't know if I trust whoever is on the other side of the carriage door. Be ready. Don't risk your life, or that of Kasa," I said in a whisper.

"Right."

I did not see what Greer did to cause Kasa to sit patiently beside him. He must have given the border dog some type of hand signal. I wondered what other signals Kasa was trained to respond to. That was something best left to ask about at another time.

I heard something happening to the outside of the door. Slowly, the door opened. Very little light entered the carriage.

"Step down slowly. No harm if you do as I say."

I stepped slowly out of the carriage, hoping that Carz would stay at my side. I did not wish harm to come to any of us. Thankfully, he followed me out of the carriage and stayed close. I could hear Greer and Kasa moving behind us. I tried to take in as much as I could in the dim light. Besides the folk who had directed us to step out of the carriage, there were about six more hooded folks standing behind him. I thought the one who spoke was a man based on the voice, but it was hard to tell, since his face was difficult to make out, shadowed as it was by the hood of his cloak. We were in some large open building. I could see stacks of crates scattered here and there in the shadowy corners. The smell of the sea was strong. I concluded that we were in a warehouse on or near the docks of the capital harbor. Faced with not one but seven cloaked figures, rushing out of the carriage and trying to make a break for it did not seem like a wise idea.

"Follow me," the man in charge said, as the others parted, formed a corridor for us to pass through, and then, surrounded us. They were eerily silent. We proceeded to the back left corner of the warehouse, where a small group of crates were stacked. Several of the cloaked folks went ahead of us and moved the crates aside. The one who was in charge stepped forward, bent down, and grabbed hold of a metal ring anchored in the floor. He pulled upward on the ring, opening a trapdoor.

I could feel Carz tense beside me, and I put a calming hand on his shoulder, though I was feeling anything but calm.

Again we were told to follow the man in charge. He led us down a short flight of stairs into a small area that held only a single barred door on the opposite side of the stairs. Smells of salty sea air, rotting seaweed, and fish were very strong here. One of the others who had followed us down stepped around us and unlocked the barred door.

"If you would be so kind as to step inside your temporary quarters. As I have stated, no harm will come to you or your animals if you cooperate. We merely want you out of the way until after the fair. As you can see, there are all the comforts of home, but, alas, there will be no maid service," he said sarcastically. "You can just throw your waste down that grate in the corner. The tide will take it out. Now if you would be so kind as to hand your cloaks over to my man there, and empty your pockets. We will return your cloaks once we have divested them of anything that might help you leave here. Once we are gone, please feel free to yell and holler for help all you wish. With the crashing of the waves on the rocks below, and no one using the building above, you will not be heard."

The cloaked figures who had brought us here tossed our cloaks back to us, withdrew, and closed the barred door. I heard the lock click shut.

It was late afternoon when Lom straightened up from cleaning off the last of the blue half-globes, arched his back to try to work the soreness out, and called over to Ealdred.

"I think that is the last of them." Glancing around, he saw the others were gathering up shovels, rakes, and brooms and putting them in the several wheelbarrows.

Soon all of those who had been working on clearing the path to the labyrinth, and beyond to the door in the cliff wall, were gathered together.

"I have to tell you that I have a whole new respect for those who work with plants and earth, who toil in the soil," stated Yara, placing her hand on the small of her back and giving a wee moan. "Hunching over repairing old and tattered books never gave me as much of a backache as these last few days of lugging, hauling, bending, lifting, and sweeping has. Even Toki looks just plum tuckered out, though I do not know why, since his new friend Kasa has been gone ...." Yara's voice trailed off. "Speaking of Kasa, Greer, Nissa, and Carz, they have been gone for a very long time."

"They're probably just lingering in the rover camp over a second or third cup of tea, stalling so they don't have to return here to join us and finish up lugging and hauling. Now that the tasks are over, they will undoubtedly show up," groused Seeker Chance. "I trust we will give them a really hard time at the evening meal."

"I think that's a good possibility," Piper declared, as she looked around at the tired group covered in dirt and plant debris.

"Now that we are finished, I would like to suggest that it is time to ask a few others to join us here," Seeker Chance suggested.

"Who do you have in mind, lad?" Ealdred asked.

"I would like to invite Seeker Eshana and Seeker Odette."

"I might also add the head royal librarian, Eluta, to the list," suggested Yara, "and the head royal historian."

"Why don't we send messages out to those you suggested and invite them to breakfast on the morrow?" Piper proposed. "Meanwhile, I don't know about the rest of you, but I'm going to take advantage of the bathhouse and get cleaned up."

When all had finally reassembled on the terrace where they had been taking their meals, Theora expressed concern that Nissa, Greer, Carz, and Kasa were still absent. "I may just be a worrywart …."

"No, I don't think so," said Piper. "You would think they would have been back by now."

"If you will excuse me, I will go check with the captain of the royal guard and see if she has any information," said Theora. A short while later, Theora returned, a very concerned look on her face.

"Something is wrong, isn't it?" Seeker Chance asked.

"The captain of the royal guard told me that she was not aware that any of the royal guards were called upon to escort Nissa, Greer, Carz, and Kasa anywhere."

"Who gave you the message that Zeroun wanted to see Nissa?" Seeker Chance asked.

"It was the serving lass, Domana. She said a message had arrived from Zeroun requesting Nissa come to the rover camp to discuss the missing firestar gems."

"Perhaps we need to find Domana and find out what she might know," proposed Yara.

Theora left the group once again to seek out Domana. When she returned, the group gathered could tell by her face that the news was not good.

"When I talked to the housekeeper in charge of the serving staff, she was quite put out, for it seems that she is short one serving lass this evening."

"Let me guess. Domana?" said Piper.

"That is correct. This is not looking good," said Theora.

Chapter Thirteen

I was glad when the door swung closed and was locked that we were not in complete darkness. A dim light seeped in through the cracks between the wall boards, and reflected up from the water through a grate in the floor near the far wall. Our captor's remark about all the comforts of home had certainly been a jest, since the room was bare.

I was concerned, for the wooden walls showed signs of having been in water. I hoped the water marks were from high waves crashing during a storm, rather than ones caused by high tide.

From the sounds of retreating footsteps, I thought Greer, Carz, Kasa, and I were now alone. "My best guess is we are in a warehouse built out over the harbor," I said.

"I think you are right. I don't think the room we are in is usual. More like something that you might attach to a warehouse if you wanted to sneak something or someone in or out by water. I imagine at night you could pull a small skiff in quite easily and on-load or off-load folks or small cargo, with none the wiser. I wonder if that is what they intend to do with us?" asked Greer.

"I'm hoping we are long gone from here before we have to find that out. Let's take a look and see if we can discover a way out."

Both Greer and I took a look at the grate in the floor. It did not budge when we pulled on it, nor did the grate budge when we pushed or stomped on it.

"You can see by the hasp that the grate can be locked from the inside. However, I would guess in this case, it's locked from the outside."

I watched as Greer lay down on the floor and reached through the grate looking for what was holding the grate in place.

"They really do not want anyone to get out or in. The grate is held in place with metal bars and locks. I can barely reach the locks. There is another problem with trying to get out of here, even if we could get the grate open."

"What is that?" I asked.

"I, for one, can't swim. Can you?"

"Ah, I can see where that could be a problem. Even though I can swim, I'm not sure I could keep both of us afloat. I also know swimming is not going to be Carz' first choice. Let's take a look at the door."

The barred door was too sturdy for us to kick open, and was designed in such a way that we could not reach the hinges. Without a key, it seemed getting out of the small room was going to be impossible. We would have to wait until our captors returned, and hope for a break that would allow us to get away. I was just about to mention this to Greer when I noticed he was examining the door lock very closely.

"It's too bad they made us clean out our pockets, not that I had a key or two in mine that would have helped," I said. "We should put our heads together and try to figure out a plan for when our captors come back."

"Hold that thought for a moment," suggested Greer, who sat down and began to take off one of his boots.

I could not imagine why, at this moment, Greer would choose to remove his boot, and yet that was just what he was doing, calmly sitting on the floor, removing his boot. I was surprised when he reached into his boot and pulled the insole out of it. Very matter-of-factly, he explained to me what he was doing.

"I'm not aware if you know that one of my legs is shorter than the other. My boots are designed in such a way so as to allow me to stand even and walk without leaning or limping. I thought the extra space in the boot should not go to waste, thinking it would be a good place to carry small valuables and other useful items. What seems like a long time ago, but was less than a year ago, I lived on the streets of Høyhauger. I learned a lot of useful skills which allowed me to survive. I can only hope I haven't lost my touch."

"Lost your touch?"

Greer did not answer, for he had drawn two slender pieces of metal out of his boot and had inserted them into the keyhole of the barred door. I could see his deep concentration, the tip of his tongue sticking out, as he maneuvered the thin pieces of metal in the lock. Both Carz and Kasa stood behind us, alert.

"Almost there," Greer mumbled. "Sorry this is taking so long. I'm a bit rusty."

I heard a click, and then Greer cracked the door open a sliver. Lock picking was an unusual talent, and it had me wondering about Greer's past. I would have to ask him about it another time. Right now we needed to move.

"Not a problem," I told Greer. "Getting out of this room is only the first step. Once we leave the warehouse above, assuming no guards were left behind, we still need to get back to the royal palace safely. Since we are in work clothes rather than any finery, we will not look out of place in the warehouse district. The same cannot be said about Carz, or even Kasa. Both will stand out."

Carz gave me a look that had me revising my statement. "I beg your pardon, Carz." Turning to Greer I said, "Carz is very capable of blending in and remaining hidden. Maybe if we could find some rope in the warehouse above and dirty Kasa up a bit, so he looks like a mongrel, we could just walk out of here and back to the royal palace."

"It's as good a plan as any. Just let me put things away, get my boot back on, and we can be on our way."

Very cautiously, I eased the door open a wee bit. Finding the area beyond the barred door empty, we moved out toward the stairs. Once we reached the top of the short stairs, I tried to open the trapdoor. It moved up about an inch, which was good, for I had feared it would be locked. However, our captors must have replaced some or all of the crates they had covering the trapdoor.

"I was afraid of that. They must have restacked the crates back on top of the trapdoor. We can hope they did not restack all of them. Perhaps the two of us working together can get them to move," I said.

"We can also hope that they did not leave a guard or guards behind, for there is no way we can move the crates above us without making noise. If there is anyone up there, they are going to notice. Let's hope we get lucky, and can both move the crates and move them unnoticed by anyone," Greer replied.

Fortune favored us, for not only was the warehouse empty when we opened the trapdoor, but our captors had not restacked all of the crates, making getting the trapdoor open a lot easier that we had expected. Scrounging around, we found some discarded twine that Greer braided into a collar and leash for Kasa.

"Kasa doesn't really need a leash, for he will stick with me and follow my hand signals or whistles. For appearance sake, however, it might be best if it looks like I'm walking my dog," said Greer, as he was scooping dirt and dust off the floor of the warehouse and rubbing it into Kasa's fur.

Kasa looked less than pleased with Greer's efforts, took matters into his own paws, moved away, and rolled in the dirt. Meanwhile, Greer added more dirt to his clothing, face, and hands. As disguises go, he probably could pass once again as a street lad, having worn his oldest clothes this day, since he knew he would be digging, hauling, and cleaning the path we had been working on.

While his disguise would probably work for him, even though I had worn the oldest and most worn of my rover clothing, which was now looking much the worse for wear, I still looked like a rover. In addition, no amount of dust or dirt would disguise Carz.

"On second thought, I think you need to go on without me. You will have a pretty good chance to get back to the royal palace without being picked up again. Carz and I, no matter how much dust and dirt we roll in, are still going to stand out."

"While you are right, and Kasa and I could most probably make our way back to the royal palace, I think we should stick together. What we need is to find someplace where we can hide until dark."

"Come," Lady Farcroft said, when she heard the light knock on the door. One of the serving maids entered the room.

"Beggin' yer ladyship's pardon. There's a messenger here for Lady Green. Says 'tis urgent."

"Well, do not just stand there, send the messenger in," stated Lady

Farcroft, almost snarling at the serving maid. "Lady Green, why would a messenger be looking for you here?"

"That's what I have been trying to tell you. I left word at my home that if any messages arrived from the royal palace, they should be brought to me immediately. Ah, Sherwin, what news do you have for me?"

Swiftly doffing his hat and bowing slightly to the two noblewomen, Sherwin said, "Just received word a few minutes ago that the rover Nissa got a message asking her to go to the fairgrounds to talk to an elder rover. Domana took the message, and will wait half an hour to deliver it. Says she wouldn't alert the royal guards and would direct them to the carriage you mentioned, if it arrives on time."

"Thank you, Sherwin. Quickly run and make sure that carriage-for-hire is in place in the next fifteen minutes."

When Sherwin had left, Lady Farcroft closed the door, turned, and asked what all that had been about.

"I know you have not thought much of me in the past, thinking I am just a meddling fool. I have learned from my earlier attempts to support Lord Klingflug and you in your efforts to not have the rule of Sommerhjem change hands. You were right at our last meeting with Lord Klingflug that we may be able to stop the challenge by removing one or more of the ring carriers, for they may be living keys. To that end, I have been prepared to try to capture one or more, if the situation arose, as it just did. Let me tell you about my plan."

A great deal of discussion swirled around the dinner table as the folks gathered on the terrace of the royal palace debated the best way to find Nissa, Carz, Greer, and Kasa. Lady Celik and her son Elek were sent for, for they had a network of informants. Yet nothing came of their inquiries.

"No one seems to have seen or heard a thing, which is odd in and of itself," suggested Lady Celik. "No rumblings through the grapevines, either above or underground.

"I have had Cook question her folks, the steward his, and the housekeeper hers. Elek checked in with the marshal, since he is in charge of the farriers, grooms, carters, smiths, and clerks. No one saw anything unusual, nothing that might point us in the right direction," stated Lady Esmeralda.

Just then, the royal palace marshal stepped onto the terrace, accompanied by a footman. "Begging your pardon your High…, er, Lady Esmeralda, but this footman just returned from his half day. He has some information that might be helpful. Go ahead, lad, tell the folks here what you told me."

The footman stood frozen in place, looking too nervous to speak. Finally, in a voice that started out rather high, he told his tale.

"This day was a busy one, as carriages came and went quite often. It's not unusual for both private carriages and carriages-for-hire to draw up in front of the royal palace, either picking folks up or dropping them off. When I was helping her ladyship, Lady Pirkete, I noticed a carriage-for-hire arrive, but stay way back from her ladyship's carriage. I canna tell you who took the carriage, but I thought at the time it looked strange."

"Go on lad, tell these folks what you told me about the carriage," the marshal encouraged.

"It was clearly a carriage-for-hire. Two odd things about it, however. I'ms not familiar with the driver. Now minds you, I don't knows all of the carriage-for-hire drivers in the capital, but I knows most of them."

"What else seemed odd to you?" Lady Celik asked.

"The shutters." When everyone looked at him expectantly, he went on. "I don' know hows to explain it, other than they looked heavier than you'd expect. You would be hard-pressed to open them if theys was locked in place."

"Thank you, lad." Lady Celik told him. Once the marshal and the footman had left, she turned to the others. "I will send word out to see if we can get any information on an odd carriage-for-hire. I'll let all of you know if I find out anything. Elek, will you please get our carriage? We can work better from our town home."

After Lady Celik and her son left, the group lingered on the terrace for a short while, and then the group began to break up.

"I feel like we should be doing something to try to find Nissa, Carz, Greer, and Kasa. I can't help but feel if they were all right, they would be back by now. I'm going to take a stroll around the grounds, for I think better when I'm moving," Theora said to Piper and Yara, the only others still remaining on the terrace. "Would you folks, and Jing and Toki, care to join Tala and me? Safety in numbers …."

Theora stopped in midsentence, for she noticed that the small green light she had gotten used to hovering just off Yara's left shoulder had been joined by another, and then another.

"Ah, Yara, I think we have company," Theora said, slightly less than calm, since she had always found the small green light hovering close to Yara a bit disconcerting, and now there were more, except they were blue.

Chapter Fourteen

It did not take either Greer or me very long to figure out that there was no place to hide in the waterfront warehouse we had been brought to. We had briefly considered hiding in the carriage-for-hire that had been left behind. We quickly thought better of that idea.

"I can't imagine that we won't be missed, if we don't return in time for the evening meal," Greer stated.

"You're right. If we aren't back by the evening meal, our friends will begin to inquire about what happened to us. If they find out we left by a carriage-for-hire and get a description, they are certainly not going to have an easy time locating it, since it is hidden here with us," I suggested to Greer.

"Unfortunately, you have the right of it. Let's take a peek out the front doors and see if we can leave here without being seen."

I cautiously cracked open the wicket gate, the small door built into the larger warehouse door, and looked out. From the looks of the buildings that lined the lane, we were not in the section of the docks that was used by the more prosperous merchants.

"Let me slip out and at least check out this block," proposed Greer. "My disguise should hold. I will look just like a street lad. No one will really pay much attention to me, if I am lucky. I will look for any place where we might hide out until dark. You and Carz should not wait overly long for my return. If Kasa and I get detained or caught, you need to get back to the royal palace, if you can. Stay safe. Hopefully, I won't be gone long."

I was torn about staying behind. I knew it was a wise decision, and yet, being separated from Greer and Kasa did not feel like the best option. With my back pressed against the wall next to the door, I waited, ears straining to catch any sounds of movement near my hiding place. Several minutes passed before I heard the sounds of stealthy footsteps pass by where I was hiding. I was just about to let out the breath I was holding when I heard the footsteps heading back. Very slowly, the small door to the warehouse began to open.

"Hey, Merak, come on, lass. Don't you go even stickin' yer nose in that door. Youse don't want thems folks who use that buildin' to even know yer face. Put that door back just the way ya found it. Do it now!"

I watched the door ease back to the position it was in when Greer and Kasa had left. I could only hope the two who were on the other side of the door had not noticed them. Time passed slowly after the two folks left. Again, I strained my ears, trying to catch any sound. Everything was quiet. I was just debating with myself as to whether I should move on and not wait any longer for Greer, when the door once again began to slowly open. I had not heard anyone approaching. Kasa poked a nose in the opening.

"Nissa?"

"Greer?"

"Yes," answered Greer. Following Kasa, Greer slipped through the door.

"Some watch cat you are, Carz. You could have given me some warning."

Carz just looked at me with a look that might have suggested that there was no need to give me any warning, since he knew who was approaching, and why had I not.

"I'm ashamed to admit I didn't hear either of you approach."

"Nice to know I haven't lost my skills from my time on the streets," Greer said with a smile. "I've kept in practice, because it is so much fun to sneak up on my sisters."

I was sorry to see Greer's smile fade and his face take on a serious look once again. "Did you have any luck finding someplace where we can wait until dark?"

"I did indeed. It was actually thanks to a street lad and lass. I heard them talking, and Kasa and I ducked behind some crates. From there I had a fairly good view of them. They have quite a clever bolt-hole that they stashed something into and moved on. I think we should move to there."

"If it is a bolt-hole, what's to say they won't be back soon?"

"I overheard them talking. They have something planned for this night. Someone is paying them to watch a certain house to see who's coming and going. I don't know who they're supposed to watch, or for whom. They didn't say. What I do know is their bolt-hole is large enough for the four of us to wait in until dark. While it'll be a little cramped, it'll be safer than staying here."

"Lead on."

We reached the bolt-hole without incident, and hopefully, with no one noticing us. Greer had certainly been right about the hiding place being very cramped. It was just a large, abandoned crate that was piled high with, and surrounded by, broken crab traps. In addition, it had several large fishing nets in various stages of rot and disrepair draped over it. Several buoys, which had long past been afloat, were also leaning against the crate. The entrance into the crate was cleverly hidden behind a really odiferous piece of netting, smelling of rotting fish.

It was almost unbearably hot inside the crate with the four of us practically sitting on top of each other. Normally, it is fairly cool by the harbor, with a breeze off the water. Unfortunately, the place where we were hiding did not have any openings to allow those cooling breezes in.

Time ticked by at an agonizingly slow rate while we waited for darkness. We did not dare talk to each other, for fear of being discovered. While this was a rundown part of the docks, it certainly was not deserted, for we could hear activity off and on during the long wait. When it had been quiet outside our hiding place for a very long time, Greer broke our silence.

"I'm going to poke my nose out, for I think it should be full dark by now," Greer whispered.

Greer moved a board and squeezed through the narrow exit. I waited. Soon he returned.

"I have worried that there might be more activity at these warehouses once darkness fell than we heard during the day. Nature seems to be giving us a hand. A very, very thick fog has come in from the sea this night. The fog would be especially helpful, if we knew the capital well."

"We are just going to have to chance it. Too bad Piper is not with us. It's my understanding she has an uncanny sense of direction," I told Greer.

"Um, Nissa, I think we are no longer alone here."

I stuck my head out. Greer had not understated the thickness of the fog surrounding us. The old saying that the fog was so thick you could cut it with a knife would not do for this fog. I think you would need a really large sword or a huge double-bladed ax. He was indeed correct. We were no longer alone.

"Ah, Yara, um, do you think these little blue glowing lights are friends of your blek …. What do you call your green light? Ah yes, your blekbrann?" Piper asked.

"I have no idea. The one that has chosen to stick with me doesn't seem to be winking out," said Yara. "Curious."

"What is curious?" asked Theora.

"The blue blekbrann, now that we are noticing them, are spreading out. The three are lining up just about far enough in this fog so you can barely see the farthest one," suggested Yara. "They are acting just like the green blekbrann did when Eluta and I followed them in the salt marsh. Let's try something," suggested Yara.

"What do you have in mind?" Theora asked.

"Let's try to go in their direction."

"Why would you wish to do that?" Piper questioned.

"Because on other occasions when I followed one or more blekbrann, they have led me to where I needed to go. Perhaps these blue ones are pointing the way to where we need to go this night. Besides, our animal friends have already set out without us, doing just that."

The three watched as Toki approached the first of the blue blekbrann. It winked out. Toki, Jing, and Tala approached the second blekbrann only to have it too wink out at the same time another blekbrann appeared beyond the third.

"I think your idea is correct, Yara. Do you think we can trust these blue lights?" asked Theora.

"Again, I have no idea. I only know that the green blekbrann who has chosen to travel with me since I left the southern marshes does not seem to be showing any reaction to the blue blekbrann ...."

That proved to be untrue when the green blekbrann suddenly winked out and, a scant time later, appeared ahead of the farthest blue light.

"It would seem that the green blekbrann has joined with the blue blekbrann, if that's what they are," said Piper. "I think you are right, Yara, about following them."

"They look like they are heading us off the royal palace grounds," Theora said. "I have mixed feelings about leaving the safety of the royal palace grounds, and yet Tala, Jing, and Toki have no such misgivings."

When Theora stopped, undecided as to what to do, Tala came back, took Theora's hand gently between her teeth, and tugged. "I guess that settles it. Now we just have to get by the royal guard posted at the nearest gate without causing a problem. Let me go first. Stay far enough back so the guard or guards do not see you."

Theora headed toward a guarded gate with Tala by her side. Even though she was not wearing her special royal guard uniform, since she had not been wearing it while working in the far reaches of the royal palace gardens, she hoped the guard on duty would recognize her. To her surprise, she ran into a guard much sooner than she expected, for he was standing next to a row of tall shrubs that grew along the wall. Piper, Jing, Yara, and Toki were not too far behind her.

"Halt, who goes there?" the guard questioned.

"Do folks really say that, other than in stories?" Yara whispered to Piper.

"Hush, now," Piper whispered back, trying not to laugh, for the guard's question really was rather ridiculous. "It's not as if the three of us are not known or recognizable, since we are accompanied by a night wolf, a mountain cat, and a red bog fox. Plus, we are now surrounded by at least four blekbrann, who are shining bright enough to give enough light so the guard can get a fairly good look at us."

Theora drew herself up and took on the air of a commanding officer. "Guard, have you left your post?"

"No, ma'am, I'm right where I was assigned."

"Ah, that is good then, that you are minding your post, Dabbah," Theora said. Before she could speak further, Piper stepped forward and spoke up.

"It's good that the captain of the royal guard knows the royal palace grounds so well, and had the foresight to have you guard one of the hidden entrances to the royal palace grounds. These are troubling times, and it is better to be cautious. We have need this night to leave the royal palace grounds undetected, which is why we are here."

The guard Dabbah shifted uneasily from one foot to the other and looked at these three folks who were at the royal palace because they had carried pieces of the oppgave ringe to the capital. Looking very uncomfortable he said, "Begging your pardon, my orders are to not let anyone leave the palace grounds after dark."

Theora, once she had recovered from her surprise as to what Piper had just said about there possibly being a hidden exit behind the tall shrubs, took back the conversation. "As a member of the special royal guard, I will take full responsibility for our leaving. You will not be held responsible. As you can see, we are dressed is a manner so as not to draw attention to ourselves on the streets. Also, we hope to use the fog that has rolled in this night to conceal where we are going and what we hope to do. I will need to trust that you will tell no one we have left, for our very lives depend on it. Are you posted here all night, or will there be a change of guard?"

"I'm here 'til dawn."

"Then we will need to hurry, if we want to get done what we need to do this night, and still make it back before you go off duty. I trust you will make sure no one knows we left this way, that no one follows, and that you will await our return. If we are not back by dawn, alert your captain. Do you understand?"

"Yes ma'am."

"Good. Carry on," said Theora, as she followed Yara through a break in the shrubbery.

Once the six of them had slipped through the concealed opening in the wall and were safely off the royal palace grounds, Theora called a halt and turned to Piper.

"How did you know Dabbah was guarding a way off the royal palace grounds?"

"Well, actually, I didn't. It was going to be either a really good guess or a great bluff on my part. Our new blue companions winked out once you had the guard's attention. Yara's green light also left, as did Jing, Toki, and

Tala. They all headed into the shrubs. While I knew Jing might be able to climb or jump over the wall, I did not think either Tala or Toki had that ability, so I concluded they must all know something we didn't know, like maybe there was a way out through the shrubs."

"Well, now that we are off the royal palace grounds, now what?" Theora asked.

"If you will note, the blekbrann have lined up again. They are closer together, which is good, for the fog seems to be getting thicker by the minute," said Yara. "The question is, where are they leading us, and why?"

CHAPTER FIFTEEN

"Lady Farcroft, I have news, good news," declared Lady Green, when Lady Farcroft entered the guest parlor.

"If that is the case, then let us take your good news to my study where we will not be disturbed. Come along," Lady Farcroft directed, turning smartly on her heel and walking out of the guest parlor before Lady Green could say another word. Once they were seated in the study with the door closed, Lady Farcroft directed Lady Green to tell her good news.

"I just received word that the plan I told you about worked. My agents have captured not one, but two of the folks who carried pieces of the oppgave ringe to the capital. Not only that, but they have also captured their animals," Lady Green stated, unable to keep the smugness out of her voice.

"Go on."

"It worked like clockwork. The serving maid was given a message to give to the rover gal, Nissa. The serving maid sent a message to my agents, and delayed thirty minutes before delivering the message to the rover. She then met Nissa, who was accompanied by Greer, and directed them both to our carriage-for-hire. All went as planned after that. The two and their animals are now safely locked up. This night they will be picked up and removed from the capital until after the third day of the great summer fair."

"There is no possible way they can escape?" Lady Farcroft asked.

"The carriage-for-hire is hidden. Nissa and Greer's clothing was searched, and anything that might have helped them was removed. The room they are in is locked up tight. The room is bare, so, while it will be an uncomfortable wait for them, there is nothing in the room that will help them escape. They are in a place where no one is going to hear them if they yell. I really cannot see how they could escape before my agents return to get them this night."

"It would seem for once you have planned well," Lady Farcroft stated grudgingly. "Now, we can only hope the removal of those two will somehow prevent the challenge. They will be gone by night's end?"

"Um, well, there is some concern about the possibility of a very heavy fog this night ...."

Greer was absolutely right. We were no longer alone in the fog. As we stepped out of our hiding place, we were surrounded by dozens of very small blue lights.

"I have seen the small green light that often hovers off Yara's left shoulder. It seems benign. Yara has told me that is not always the case. Twice a group of what I would call will-o'-wisps...." I said.

"And where I grew up, we called them hinkypunks," interrupted Greer softly.

"Yes, well, whatever they may be called, they came to Yara's rescue. Yara calls them blekbrann. The question here is: are blue will-o'-wisps, if that is what these are, here to help us like the green will-o'-wisps helped Yara, or are they just here to light up the area and give our position away?"

Just as I finished talking, I thought I heard very muffled footsteps. I felt Carz, Greer, Kasa, and I were now very exposed with the blue will-o'-wisps lighting up the area.

"Quick, let's go back into the hidey-hole and hope whoever is out there does not arrive before we are hidden once again," I suggested.

I tried to edge my way back to the opening of the hidey-hole only to find my way blocked by the blue will-o'-wisps. The closer I tried to get to the opening of the hidey-hole, the more blue will-o'-wisps gathered in front of it, and the brighter they became.

"So, going back into the hidey-hole is not an option," I said.

"I might suggest we back away from them and see if they might dim just a bit. We certainly don't need to attract any more attention to ourselves by causing the hinkypunks to glow brighter," said Greer.

I certainly agreed with him, and so, slowly and cautiously, I stepped back. The blue will-o'-wisps once again surrounded us, glowing softly now. When I stepped forward, they became brighter. I had a fleeting thought of just stepping through them and heading out, then I thought better of the idea.

Minutes passed. As I watched the blue will-o'-wisps in front of me, I noticed they once again began to move, parting just slightly. Unfortunately, the opening they made was certainly not wide enough for Greer, Carz, Kasa, or me to slip through, not to mention that the opening was about four to five feet off the ground. Carz might have been able to jump through, if it had been wide enough, but I certainly would not have been able to.

As I watched the slight opening in the blue will-o'-wisps, I saw a single will-o'-wisp slip through. It took me a moment to realize that the new will-o'-wisp was green.

"Greer, does that single will-o'-wisp hovering inside with us look green to you?"

"Yes. Do you think it might be Yara's? If it is, might it be able to understand us? Could we could ask it to go get help?" Greer whispered, for we still did not know who might be out in the fog.

I was about to answer Greer when several things happened at once. Carz moved to stand and lean against me, Kasa got up and stood next to Greer, and the green will-o'-wisp suddenly winked out.

"Do you think the green hinkypunk understood me and has gone for help?" Greer whispered.

"Listen," I whispered back. "There is someone or something out there in the fog, and whatever or whoever it is, it is getting close. Be ready!"

I was certainly not ready for what happened next. The green will-o'-wisp returned, followed by three blue will-o'-wisps. The blue will-o'-wisps who had been surrounding us parted in front of us, Toki emerged out of the fog, followed closely by Jing, Tala, and to my surprise, Piper, Yara, and Theora.

"Fancy meeting you here," Piper quipped. "Seriously, we are very glad to see all of you. You have had us worried. How did you end up here so far from the rover camp at the fairgrounds?"

"For that matter, why are you here in this rather rundown, unsavory part of the docks?" asked Yara.

"Perhaps there is a more immediate and more important question right now," suggested Theora. "Do you wish to stay here?"

"No, we don't wish to stay here. We are certainly not here by our own choosing. Greer, Kasa, Carz, and I have just been waiting until full dark to leave here and try to get back to the royal palace. How did you even find us?" I asked.

"I think answering everyone's questions needs to wait. The one thing I'm very sure of is we should not linger here surrounded by an amazing number of softly glowing blue blekbrann," stated Theora.

The minute Theora mentioned we should leave, all of the blue will-o'-wisps winked out, leaving us in darkness. I was just about to speak, when Theora whispered that we should stand very still and be quiet.

Was it coincidence that all of the blue will-o'-wisps had winked out just as it was mentioned that we needed to leave, or did they know something we did not? I wondered.

As I stood frozen in place, I felt Carz lean against me. When I reached down and placed a hand on his shoulder, I could feel the tension in his muscles. Running my hand up to caress his head, I could feel his ears were tipped forward. He was listening very hard. Taking a cue from Carz, I strained my ears. Sound is so muffled by heavy fog that I worried I would not hear anyone approaching until they were almost upon us.

"Yer can't see more 'n a foot in front of yer face in this fog, even wit' both of our lanterns turned full up. Can'ts sees why m'lady didn' understand that. We left thems two locked up tight. No need ta send us out in fog heavier than sheep's wool in the spring. 'Sides, this damp 'tis causin' me bones ta ache."

"Quit yer bellyaching. The sooner we check on thems two that's locked up, the sooner we can get back, sit back by the fire, an' have a spot of warm brew."

Once the two passed by, and I judged they were far enough away that I could whisper, I suggested to Theora, Piper, and Yara that we needed to get away quickly, for Greer and I were the folks those two were sent to check up on. "When they find us missing, I am sure a hue and cry will arise."

"Yara?" Piper asked.

"Yes."

"Do you think the blekbrann are gone for good, or will they continue to be our guides?" questioned Piper.

"I have no idea. No, wait, look."

I had no notion what they were talking about. In addition, I was becoming more and more anxious that we were not moving. "What are we looking at?" I asked. It was difficult to keep the anxiety out of my voice.

"The blekbrann, or at least four of them. See the one that is usually with me?" Yara said.

In the almost total darkness, I had trouble seeing my hand in front of my face, so I really did not know which way to look to see the green will-o'-wisp. Suddenly, I felt Carz, at least I hoped it was Carz, take my hand in his teeth and pull me around a bit to the left. Once situated the way Carz had aimed me, I could see the soft green glow ahead of me.

"Now look beyond my blekbrann. You can just make out the blue one ahead. We got here by following them. I hope they will lead us back. Having Piper with us, who I declare must be able to see even in the dark, does not hurt either. She, thankfully, has an uncanny sense of direction. She follows the blekbrann, we follow her, and we hope the blekbrann are leading us where we need to go," said Yara. "Piper will try her best not to run us into or over anything. She will warn us if we need to go up or down stairs, cross gaps, and about other hazards we are not going to be able to see along the way due to the heavy dense fog."

I was not so sure of this leading and following business. Having no better plan, however, I got in line behind Yara. Greer got behind me, and Theora brought up the rear. All of the animals had gone on ahead.

I was glad when we left the warehouse area of the harbor and began moving through the area of the capital that held small shops, eateries, boarding houses, and inns that catered to the needs of those who worked in or near the harbor. Though still not the best part of the capital, it was an improvement over the warehouse area.

I was getting tired. It had been a long day. I had been hungry while waiting for full dark to arrive, since I had not eaten since breakfast. At several points during the time we were hidden in the hidey-hole, I worried we would be discovered by the noise made by my rumbling stomach. In all the books I have read, folks in trouble of being discovered never seem to have rumbling stomachs. My rumbling stomach brought me back to my musings about being hungry, and I wondered if we dared try to find an eatery that might still be open at this time of night so I might get a bite to eat. I quickly threw that idea out.

As we continued on, there were times that we walked single file, each with an arm stretched out in front, with a hand on the folk ahead of us. There were times, as we moved higher and farther away from the harbor, that the fog was not quite as dense and walking became easier. We continued to follow the will-o'-wisps. As near as I could tell, they were leading us back toward the royal palace.

We finally reached a level of the capital where the street lamps were both mostly lit and closer together. In addition, the fog was beginning to thin a bit, though there were still patches and swirls of the thicker fog. Though the thinning fog made walking easier and allowed us to walk faster, we also became more visible to others who were out on the streets.

The continuing thinning of the fog was becoming worrisome. As a group, we were a bit hard to miss. I imagine it is not ordinary to run into five folks out for a stroll accompanied by a hunting cat, a mountain cat, a night wolf, a bog fox, and a border dog of rare coloring.

I could see a bit farther ahead as we left a patch of very dense fog when I noticed that the animals we had been following, with the exception of Kasa, suddenly were not in front of us any longer. In addition, the will-o'-wisps had winked out. I wondered if Carz and the other animals were sticking to the shadows so as to not be quite so noticeable. I wondered if we should also be more cautious and follow their lead.

We had just turned a corner when we were confronted by a group of six or seven men and women. They did not look like a very savory lot.

"Well, looky here. I think this night is about to become much better for us," said the apparent leader of the group, blocking our way.

CHAPTER SIXTEEN

The odds did not look good. After all, there were seven of them, and they loomed big and were tough looking. However, there were ten of us, though the folks standing in our way were probably not aware of at least four of us, not counting the will-o'-wisps. Because I knew what to look for, I caught a glimpse of Carz moving silently in and out of patches of fog. Since he was silver-hued, he was difficult to spot in the fog. He was moving to circle around the seven in front of us. I imagine Tala, the night wolf, was also equally difficult to spot, with a coat as black as midnight tipped with silver. Toki's and Jing's coats were more in the red or rust range, and yet, I could not spot them moving through the fog.

"Do street thugs go through some sort of training to learn what to say when approaching their prey?" I asked Greer in a whisper. "I mean, who really says 'well, looky here'?"

"Hush," Greer said, trying to hold back a snicker. "Let me distract them."

Greer stepped forward and addressed the seven blocking our way. When he started to speak, I was surprised in his change of demeanor. There was a swagger to him I had not ever seen before. Even his speech changed.

"Hey now, no poachin'. These here folks are my coin, not yers," Greer said.

"I'm thinkin' they be our coin now. We's be takin' 'em," said the leader of the seven. "It's our seven to yer five. Oh, and a dog that ya don't even 'ave trained since ya gotta 'ave it tied up. Bet if'n ya was to let go of that rope, he'd jus' run off. Now jus' step aside, laddy."

"I'm thinking ya 'ave miscounted the number ya're up against. We's be countin' ten. Actually, eleven," Greer said.

I could tell Greer was having a good time facing the seven blocking our way. I also realized how clever he was by engaging the leader of the seven, for he was giving the animals a chance to get in position. I could hardly wait until those seven realized just who the rest of our party was.

"Has the fog gotten to yer noggin, lad, er canna ya count? I'm still seein' only five of youse, not countin' the dog," the leader of the seven said, as he and his followers began to advance.

While the fog had certainly not gotten to Greer's noggin, it had crept in thicker, all around us, obscuring the fronts of the buildings on either side of the lane, leaving the lane visible between our two groups and just a little beyond. It might have been better if the fog had filled the lane, for then we might have been able to slip away.

When I saw one of the seven beginning to turn around, having been alerted, I suspect, by a sound behind her, I stepped forward to get her attention.

"Wait," I shouted. "Just what do you think you're doing? We have nothing of value, no coin to line your pockets this night. We're just laborers."

"Some of ya may be laborers, but some of ya are too fancy dressed, makin' what ya're sayin' a pretty tall tale."

Once she finished speaking, several things happened at once. The group of seven began rushing toward our group. Suddenly, I found myself surrounded by dozens and dozens of brightly glowing blue lights, blinding me from seeing what was going on. I could hear snarls, growls, barking, and the noises of folks panicking. I was afraid to move.

As quickly as the blue will-o'-wisps had swarmed around me, they winked out. It took a few moments for me to be able to see clearly. Once I could, I looked around me. Greer, Piper, Yara, and Theora were all standing a few feet from me. Coming out of the fog ahead of me were Carz, Kasa, Jing, Toki, and Tala. For a moment, it seemed I saw a fox the color of fog at the very edge of the heavy fog. I blinked my eyes, trying to clear them of some of the spots caused by the bright blue lights. When I looked again, all I saw was fog, and it was getting thicker by the second.

"I think we should move on, and quickly," Theora stated with urgency. "No telling who those folks were, or if they will gather more folks and come back."

"Oh, I don't think they will be back. Between our animal companions and the display the hinkypunks put on, they will probably not stop running until they reach the river," said Greer. "I agree, though, that we should move on. Dense fog nights are never good nights to be out on the streets, and we may not be so lucky next time."

"I agree. Look, our guides are back," said Yara, pointing ahead at the three blue and one green blekbrann lined up at equal intervals. "Piper, would you take the lead again?"

"Be glad to. Stay close."

Ingo sat in the pub huddled over a full tankard of hot brew, trying not to spill any, which was proving difficult since he could not stop his hands from shaking.

"What happened to youse and yer gang," the pub keeper asked. "Ya look like youse all were attacked by a pack of wolves."

"Only one," Ingo muttered under his breath.

"What was that you said?"

"It was only one wolf, a night wolf. Not to mention a hunting cat, a mountain cat, a border dog, and two foxes."

Before the pub keeper could ask for more information, an argument broke out among the members of Ingo's gang as to whether there had been one fox or two.

"I seen a red fox, that's all," said one.

"I seen a gray fox, the same color as the fog," said another.

"Enough," Ingo said sharply. "There was two foxes, one red and one gray, all right. But that weren't all. It were all of thems blue lights that come out of nowhere. Surrounded that one lass, blazin' bright as'n the sun. Between them blue lights and all thems animals clawin' an' nippin' at our heels, ya can betja we's left real quick."

The pub keeper, shaking his head in disbelief, picked up a rag that had seen clean water in the far distant past, and resumed wiping down tables.

"It's the truth, I tells ya," said Ingo. "Strange things be happ'in' in the capital. Strange things …," he muttered.

Time dragged as we moved very slowly up the lanes heading, we hoped, toward the royal palace. The higher we moved, the thinner the fog became, allowing us see more than a few feet ahead of us. Finally, we came to the royal palace wall, and Piper led us to the hidden gate they had passed through hours earlier. Before we began to slip through the gate, the three blue will-o'-wisps winked out. I said a very quiet thanks, and was not really surprised when I heard Yara echo my words.

Once we slipped through the gate, the guard greeted us. Theora let him know that all had gone well, and thanked him for keeping guard. Once we were away from the hidden gate, I did not know whether my bed was calling me or whether my stomach was more demanding. Even in the fog, I could see that the sky was beginning to lighten, so my stomach won. As the others were heading off to get some well-needed rest, I headed toward the royal palace bakery, hoping to throw myself on the mercy of Clare, a journeywoman baker whom I had first met at the Snoddleton fair a little over a year ago.

I needed some time to think about what had happened this night. I could not help but wonder why the blue will-o'-wisps had led the others to Greer, Kasa, Carz, and me. I also wondered why they had surrounded me and not all of us. In addition, I wondered why they were blue and not green like the one who was with Yara. I had never heard of blue will-o'-wisps, but then, before meeting Yara, I had never heard them called blekbrann, so that did not say much.

By the time I had lingered on a bench in the garden, eating the incredibly delicious pastries Journeywoman Clare had provided, and walked back to my homewagon, the fog had almost dissipated. It was full dawn, and folks were moving about the royal palace grounds on their early morning tasks. When I entered the camping area, I was not surprised to see Meryl, Finn, Seeker Eshana, Seeker Chance, and Yara in quiet conversation. Yara waved me over.

"Did you get any sleep?" I asked Yara.

"No. I spent the rest of the night in the extensive archives in the royal palace trying to find some reference to blekbrann in general, and blue blekbrann in particular."

"Did you have any success?" I asked.

"No. I wandered down here with the seekers, hoping Meryl and Finn might be up. Between the four of them, they have traveled to the far reaches of Sommerhjem and might have learned something in their travels about blekbrann. They, too, know little or nothing about them," Yara said.

"Nowhere in all of my travels have I heard even a whisper about blue blekbrann. I had heard a very wee bit about the green ones, in that what I would call will-o'-wisps might be found in the southern salt marshes," stated Seeker Eshana.

"After I get a short nap, I intend to go to the royal library and consult with the head librarian, Eluta, and anyone else there who might steer me toward a book or scroll that could give us more information," said Yara, trying to stifle a yawn while she talked. "Oh, dear, sorry. If you will excuse me, I think I will head up to the royal palace."

"Thank you for coming to find Greer and me last night. You all took quite a risk," I told Yara.

"You would have done the same. I'll be off now. See all of you later," Yara said through another yawn.

"Are you going to get some rest now, Nissa?" Seeker Eshana inquired.

"A hot cup of tea right now would hit the spot. I think I have a wee spark of energy left before I need to get some sleep. Carz, on the other hand, is probably smarter than I am, for he headed for the homewagon the minute we entered the campsite."

"We were all so worried when you, Carz, Greer, and Kasa were not back by dinner time," said Seeker Chance. "We checked with Zeroun, and he is indeed missing nine firestar gems."

"I'm sorry I didn't get to talk to Zeroun, for I was curious about the nine firestar gems he had," I said.

"I can answer that," said Piper. "They are the ones found by the young Günnary man, Collier, whom I met in the southern mountains. Where they came from is, perhaps, not as important as the fact that we found out Zeroun did not send the note asking you to come and meet with him at the fairgrounds."

"We are not sure if the same folk who found out about the missing firestar gems and sent you the note, is the same folk or folks who kidnapped you and Greer," said Seeker Eshana. "I realize the possibility that more than one group is trying to kidnap you is a disturbing thought. We are aware that Lord Cedric Klingflug, the former regent, has many loyal followers still, despite his poor showing in trying to prevent the challenge from being called and in his plotting to stop any of the rings making it to the capital. Then again, we are also aware of the machinations of Lady Farcroft. Those two stand out as possibly being behind the kidnapping. If there are other parties getting involved with trying to stop the challenge from happening, we have even more to worry about."

"I think from now on, if any of us need to leave the royal palace grounds, we should always check in with the captain of the royal guard and have her arrange an escort," stated Meryl, speaking up for the first time. "Especially you, Nissa."

"Why me?"

"So far as we know, you are the only one of us who can handle more than one of the pieces of the oppgave ringe," said Meryl. "Before you got here, the rest of us went down to the Well of Speaking to look at the vesteboks. As you well know, on the day one places one of the rings into the vesteboks, there is a great deal going on. There is no time to reflect on what is happening, or has just happened. All too soon, after the light rising out of the vesteboks dims and fades, you get swept up in the entire goings on. So one day during the noon meal, we all got to talking about what had happened and decided we wanted to go to the Well of Speaking. Greer opened the vesteboks easily. I don't remember who it was who wondered since we had carried the rings to the capital, whether we would be able to remove them, if that was what was going to be needed. When each one of us tried to remove the ring we had placed in the vesteboks, none of us even got our hand in that little golden box."

"What happened?" I asked.

"I'm really not sure. All I'm sure of is I did not want to touch any of the rings, much less the one I placed there," stated Meryl emphatically.

"And you, Seeker Chance?"

"The same."

"So you see, as near as we can tell, you are the only one who has ever been able to touch more than one," said Meryl.

"Perhaps that is why the blue will-o'-wisps chose to protect you this night," suggested Seeker Eshana.

And isn't that a frightening idea, I thought to myself, after bidding the others a belated goodnight, or good dawn, as was more the case.

CHAPTER SEVENTEEN

I allowed myself the luxury of sleeping late, since I had not gotten to bed until long after dawn broke. I had thought I would probably not fall asleep easily, since I had so much on my mind. That was not the case at all. As soon as my head hit the pillow, I was out like a light. I must have had a lot of disturbing dreams, however, for when I moved to get up, I found myself tangled in my covers. I think I am glad I could not remember the dreams.

Carz was also not in his customary spot on the bed. When I finally wrangled myself out of my covers, I spotted him lying on the floor of the homewagon near the door. He gave me a disgruntled look as I swung my legs over the edge of the bed.

"Sorry, my friend. I must have been really restless."

As I stood up and stretched, I decided to beg off working with the others this day. I had chores I had neglected that needed to be done. Besides putting my homewagon in order, I wanted some time to myself to put my thoughts in order.

In addition, I needed to work on my entry to the Woodworkers Guild contest that was being held soon here at the great summer fair. Working at my craft gave me a feeling of normalcy. By working, I might be able to block out all the worries, at least for a little while. Who knew what was going to happen at the great summer fair, or after? When I stepped outside my homewagon, I saw others had gathered around the cook fire and were talking quietly.

"Ah, good morn to you, Nissa," Ealdred called out as I climbed down the steps of my homewagon. "Or perhaps good noon might be more correct since it is past the middle of the morning. Hope you are well recovered from the adventures of last night. The seekers and Yara left a short while ago, heading to the royal library to see if they could find out anything about the blue lights. I have never seen or heard of them in the eastern hill country, so was of no help."

"Never seen or heard of them in the southern mountains. I had not seen or heard of green ones either, until I was in the southern salt marsh. The blue ones certainly seemed to like you best," said Piper, with humor in her voice. "What about you, Meryl? Finn?"

"Neither in my travels for my family's messenger bird business, nor in my travels with Finn, have I either seen or heard about these blekbrann," stated Meryl. "Finn?"

"Heard about will-o'-wisps, I have. Heard about them. Never saw one, no never saw one. Just stories you know, just tall tales," said Finn.

"We were just talking about what would be best to do for the rest of the day," Piper said, changing the subject. "Ealdred, Lom, Theora, and I are going to go back to the clearing to finish up. Greer is meeting with his father on family business. Meryl and Finn have asked to be let off clearing duty, for they have some areas of the royal palace grounds they wish to explore. What about you, Nissa?"

"With all of you going about different tasks, it makes it easier for me to beg off helping with the clearing. I need some time to catch up on chores too long neglected, and I need to get some things finished before the great capital fair. We don't know what is going to happen on or after the third day of the fair …." I paused to gather my thoughts. "We can hope all goes well, that the ninth piece of the oppgave ringe is found in time, and the challenge is successful. I really don't want to think about what might happen if the ninth piece of the oppgave ringe is not found. No matter what happens, I still will need to earn a living, if a living is to be had."

I really do not want to think about what might happen if the ninth ring is not found or the challenge does not happen. I really, really do not want to think about what might happen to me, or to other rovers, should Lord Klingflug regain power. I am also worried about what might happen to the others who carried rings into the capital, should the challenge not happen, I thought.

Everyone helped with general cleanup around the campsite, and with the care and feeding of the horses. After the others left, I sat down and began doing the finishing carving on a set of shutters I was working on. After a few hours, I got up to stretch. It was then I remembered that I had planned the day before to check what I had come to call the Neebing room, but had forgotten. So far in my stay on the royal palace grounds, the Neebings had not taken the gift I had left in the small room.

Since there was no time like the present, and no one was around, I decided to just duck under my homewagon and check out the Neebing room. Carz got up from the tree he had been napping under and wandered over to join me. He probably was wondering why I was lying down on the ground. Just as I was about to open the door to the Neebing room, he plopped down next to me.

"Ah, Carz, I hate to disappoint you, but I'm not down here to nap. You are also blocking what little light I have here, so do you think you can move?"

With a huge yawn, Carz stood up, stretched out first his back legs, then his front legs, and finally moved over enough to give me some light. I opened the door to the Neebing room and looked in. I would have missed the very small piece of rolled up paper if it had not had a bright blue string tied around it. I very gently took it out of the Neebing room, closed the door, got up into a half crouch and moved out from under my homewagon. Before I could remove the string, Finn and Meryl walked into the campsite, with Tashi winging in behind and settling on a perch Meryl had rigged on the back of her wagon. They were followed closely by Piper and Jing. I quickly tucked the small paper roll in my pocket.

"I have helped all I can to clear the open space beyond the tangle. Lom and Ealdred stayed behind to study the area some more," Piper stated, as she sat down on a camp chair near my cook fire. "Is that tea in your kettle?"

"Help yourself. I was just taking a break and stretching. Looks like Meryl and Finn are bringing chairs over to join us."

When all were settled with hot cups of tea, Piper began speaking. "I have always been fascinated by the old, old places that can be found scattered about Sommerhjem. There are a number of them in the southern mountains. Yara mentioned an amphitheater she saw when she was in the Tåkete bog."

"Then there is the fountain at the Gatekryss Crossroads," said Meryl. "It has been there as long as anyone can remember. The water flows there even on the coldest days of winter. No one in recent memory has been able to explain how it works."

And then there are the standing stones just off the narrow lane that runs along a ridge near where the Günnary have hidden themselves away. And there is the fountain made of glass or ice, or crystal, not to mention the Huntress herself, I thought.

"I brought up the ancient places for a reason. The longer I studied the archway and the doors we uncovered in the cliff wall beyond the labyrinth, the more and more I get the feeling that they are very, very ancient, like those places we just mentioned," stated Piper. "I have always wondered if our ancestors were responsible for these places, or were others here before us? That has led me to question whether we brought the way of choosing our next ruler by the Gylden Sirklene challenge with us when our folks came to this land, or if that way was already here?"

"Speaking of ancient places, at the request of Lady Esmeralda, Finn and I have been poking around the royal palace and the grounds and have made some interesting discoveries. The royal palace is built over the foundation of a much older structure. Lady Esmeralda let us go down to a lower level and showed us a little-known entrance to an even lower level. It is quite fascinating down there," said Meryl. "There are some carvings you need to see Nissa."

"Very interesting carvings, oh my yes, very interesting," suggested Finn. "Like what we have seen on your homewagon, the firestar rings, bracelet, pendant, and cuff. Like what we have seen, but slightly different. Yes, slightly different."

"You say that Lady Esmeralda requested that you poke around the royal palace and the grounds?" Piper asked.

"Yes," said Meryl. "Seems that while she knew some secret ways and passages within the royal palace, she did not know many. There really had been no one in her growing up years to teach her. When the former regent came to power, he dismissed almost all of the serving folks who had been loyal to Lady Esmeralda's mother, Queen Qctavia, and replaced them with those loyal to him. It is my understanding that Lady Esmeralda has tried to locate many of the older folks who served her mother. It has been only partially successful. So much of the knowledge of the royal palace has been lost. After the former regent was asked to step down, the captain of the royal guard asked Lady Esmeralda if she knew all of the secret ways in and out of the royal palace. It became very clear at that time that she did not. Without that knowledge, and not knowing what the former regent and his followers knew, the royal palace is vulnerable to secret goings and comings."

"And they didn't do any searching before you and Finn arrived?" I asked.

"Oh, sorry, I guess I didn't explain that part. Yes, both Lady Esmeralda and Beezle have spent a great deal of time seeking out the hidden ways within the royal palace, and the head of the royal guard has spent hours looking for hidden ways onto the royal palace grounds," said Meryl.

"Beezle?" I inquired.

"Yes, Beezle. When he was not off somewhere on business for the Crown, he has been helping Lady Esmeralda. Seems he has quite an interest in hidden passages, and such, and is quite good at ferreting them out. He was the one who actually found the place I would like you to see."

"When would be a good time to go?" I asked.

"Let's meet with the others over the noon meal where we can discuss what all of them want to do next," proposed Piper. "If you've a mind to, Nissa, those who want to could go down with you to the space below the royal palace that Meryl and Finn want you to see. I certainly would not mind going along."

While everyone had been talking, I did not realize that Carz had moved in next to me, and was now leaning against me. Warmth flowed from him to me, and the firestar gem on my ring began to warm. The urge to jump up and demand either Meryl or Finn, I did not care which, lead me immediately to the area below the royal palace was very powerful.

Had they found a place that might give us a clue to where the last piece of the oppgave ringe was, or could the ninth piece of the oppgave ringe be hidden in the chamber? I wondered. I did not express this thought aloud, fearing that might somehow make it not so.

"I think going down to see what you have found is a very good idea," I told the others in a very calm voice, a voice was much calmer than I felt. "Just give me a few moments to put away my shutter and tools."

Neither Seeker Eshana, Seeker Chance, Yara, nor Greer returned to the royal palace for the noon meal. Lom, Theora, and Ealdred begged off doing what they referred to as the "dungeon tour," even though Lady Esmeralda assured them that to her knowledge, there had never been a dungeon in the lower levels of the royal palace. That left Piper, Meryl, Finn, and me to take on the task of seeing what we could discover.

At the last minute, Lady Esmeralda decided to join us, which did not surprise me half as much as the fact that Tashi, Meryl's griff falcon, chose to come along also. It was quite amusing seeing the looks on folks' faces as Tashi flew through the halls of the royal palace and glided down the stairs.

After we had wandered along a few corridors in a lower level of the royal palace, Lady Esmeralda led us to a small storeroom at the end of a corridor. It was a rather ordinary room, compared to others in the royal palace. Three walls of the room were lined with shelves holding an odd assortment of bits and bobs, small chests, and a mismatched selection of crockery. Lady Esmeralda went to the wall opposite the door, did something I could not see, and the shelving swung open, revealing a rough stone opening. All of us were going to have to duck to pass through.

"We had best grab several lanterns off the shelves, and light one each before we descend the stairs," Lady Esmeralda said, while lifting lanterns off the shelf on her left. "I had a number of them brought down here after Meryl and Finn told me we would need them to really see what they had found."

Once through the low-arched opening behind the shelving, we walked only about three or four steps before coming upon a narrow stairwell that curved its way down several dozen steps. In the light of the lantern, I could see that the stairs and stairwell we were descending were made by folks rather than being a naturally-occurring cave, or being carved out of the bedrock. At the bottom of the first set of stairs, there was a landing. As I halted to look around, I could see the floor beneath my feet was thick with dust and little disturbed, with the exception of several folks' footprints, which I suspected belonged to Meryl and Finn. I wished they had removed the layers and layers of cobwebs that covered the walls and ceiling and hung down in tatters.

"You know, since you knew you were going to invite us on this grand adventure, could you not have done something about the cobwebs?" I said.

"Picky, picky, picky," Meryl retorted.

"Spiders are our friends, our friends," Finn said. "Just think, they keep the other bugs to a small number, a very small number."

"True," I said, as I brushed yet again another clump of spider web out of my hair and off my face, hoping the spider who built it had not been still on the web. "Any other pests we should be worried about, like rats or mice?"

"I would not worry too much, since you have Carz with you and Piper has Jing. Two very large cats might cause the vermin to think twice before venturing out. Besides, we only have very important, well-mannered vermin in the royal palace's lower levels," said Lady Esmeralda, trying for haughtiness and failing miserably.

After descending a second set of stairs, bringing us two levels below the main floor of the royal palace, we traveled just a little farther forward before arriving at an archway. Stepping through the archway, I could feel we had entered a large area, even though our lantern light did not penetrate very far into the darkness.

"When we were here before, we looked at the walls. Unlike the first set of stairs we came down, where the walls are partly made and partly carved out of bedrock, the walls of this large chamber are totally carved out of bedrock, as are the second set of stairs. It was not until we were heading back up that we noticed the floor. I would like to take a closer look now, for I think I saw a pattern on the floor. I don't want to speculate any further until I have a chance to look more closely," said Meryl. "I also think we need to figure out how this area was once lit up."

"It reminds me of a great room, a great room, from what we have been able to see. Like a small keep, a small keep great room," said Finn.

"Now I am curious. Beezle and I found the entrance to the stairway leading down here a while back. We never had a chance to go any farther than the archway before we had to go back. We ran out of time that day. Since then, other matters have prevented us from coming back. I am grateful that Meryl and Finn have continued to explore," said Lady Esmeralda. "Nissa, Piper, Finn, would you go back up with me, so we can gather more lanterns? Meryl, will you be all right down here by yourself?"

"I'll be fine. I have Tashi, though maybe Nissa or Piper, you could ask one of the cats to stay with me. While I wait, I'll begin to set and light the lanterns we have already brought down."

Both Carz and Jing stayed behind. I think they were too interested in exploring the space, and not at all interested in coming with Piper, Lady Esmeralda, Finn, or me. It did not take us long to find a storeroom filled with useful things, including more lanterns than we could carry. Once we were back with Meryl, we made short work of placing the next set of lanterns and lighting them, which in turn further lit up the large chamber we were in.

Meryl had been right to think the bits of pattern on the floor were significant. Inlaid stone of a clear deep blue formed a labyrinth on the floor. In the center was a symbol I thought I had seen before. When I heard a gasp to my left, I looked over to see Lady Esmeralda staring intently at the mosaic of a quirrelit tree with a patterned border around it.

"Oh, I am sorry. I am going to have to cut my adventure with all of you short. I just remembered, I was supposed to meet with some of the interim ruling council members shortly after the noon meal. I must go. I must be terribly late," said Lady Esmeralda, turning abruptly and heading for the stairs.

Now what was that all about? I wondered. *She is not a very good liar. She had such a look of surprise in her eyes when she looked up from studying the mosaic in the floor. Now where have I seen that border pattern before?*

CHAPTER EIGHTEEN

I was distracted from my thoughts about Lady Esmeralda's reaction to the mosaic on the floor when I glanced up and took a really good look at the walls. Evenly spaced around the chamber were pillars, each one not much taller than me. They did not reach up to the ceiling, so did not function to hold the ceiling up. Upon closer inspection of one of the pillars, I saw that they had never been designed to be any taller than they were. Atop each pillar was a platform wide enough that I could have sat down on it with room to spare. I could not imagine that the pillars had ever been designed as seats for folks, however.

What caught my eyes even more than the height and design of the pillars was what was carved into the pillars themselves. Each one had carvings similar to those I had seen in the Huntress' book and in various other places this past year. Upon closer inspection, I realized what I was seeing. Each pillar had a different design central to it. As I looked at the carved swirls and lines on the pillar in front of me, I began to distinguish within the pattern the shape of an animal. The one I was looking at directly in front of me was carved in the shape of a griff falcon.

"Meryl, would you come here and look at something with me?" I asked.

"What is it you wish me to see?" Meryl asked.

"See here," I said, as I began to trace my finger along the continuous line that formed the griff falcon's image.

"Oh, I see it now," said Meryl.

I withdrew my hand and stepped back. I felt the air over me move. When I looked up, I could see that Tashi had settled herself on top of the pillar and was looking down. Meryl stepped forward and began to trace the line I had been tracing. Piper and Finn had wandered over when I had asked Meryl to come over, so we were all there to see what happened next.

"Oh my, oh my, the line is turning blue, turning blue," exclaimed Finn.

Finn was indeed correct. As Meryl touched the pillar and began to trace the line that formed the image of the griff falcon, the line began to turn blue where she had traced her finger.

"It didn't do that for me," I exclaimed.

"Nissa, over here," Piper called from across the chamber.

I did not realize she had left our group near the pillar with the griff falcon outline glowing blue. As I turned around, I saw that the pillar she was standing next to was also glowing blue. It was not showing the outline of a griff falcon though. It was showing the outline of a mountain cat. Jing was sitting on top of the pillar.

I went looking for a pillar that had a hunting cat outline carved into it. I found it directly across the chamber from where Piper was standing. It did not surprise me to see Carz already sitting on top of it.

"Finn, would you come over here, please?" I asked. "I would like you to try to trace the outline of the hunting cat, if you would."

"All right, happy to, yes, happy to," said Finn.

When Finn traced the outline of the hunting cat, nothing happened. I, in turn, asked both Meryl and Piper to trace the outline of the hunting cat, and again, nothing happened. When I traced the outline of the hunting cat on the pillar, it shone blue, as had the griff falcon and mountain cat outlines.

"Let's look at the other pillars," I suggested.

When we finished walking the circumference of the chamber, we had accounted for all of the companion animals. Besides the ones that now showed fading blue outlines of a griff falcon, a mountain cat, and a hunting cat, there was a pillar each with the outline of a bog fox, a border dog, and a halekrets. Interestingly, the pillar that depicted the night wolf had two night wolves on it. It was the eighth pillar that was most interesting of all, for it did not, as far as we could tell, show the outline of any animal.

While the others went back to looking at other areas of the chamber, I continued to study the eighth pillar. The more I looked at it, the more I thought I saw pictures within the lines. Perhaps a quirrelit tree and what looked like a quirrelit tree seed. Maybe the Huntress' fountain, but then maybe that was just in my imagination. For some reason I could not explain even to myself, I did not call the others over and point out what I thought I was seeing.

"We had best head up," Piper suggested. "Though it is hard to tell how long we have been down here, I think it has been quite a while. We need to get the others to come down here. We can send someone to ask Seeker Chance and Yara to come back from the royal library. Greer is in one of the meeting rooms in the royal palace working with his father, so he should be fairly easy to find."

"I'd be happy to head down to the clearing in the tangle to fetch Lom," I said. "I think you should tell them to invite their companion animals. I agree that the others really need to see this chamber, whatever it is. I'll be right behind you folks. I just want to take a look at the hunting cat pillar again before I come up. I'll take care of turning down the lanterns."

When I got back to the pillar that had the carving of a hunting cat, I found Carz once again sitting on top of it. I asked Carz if he would please jump down. Once he was down, I traced the hunting cat line with my finger. Nothing happened. Then I asked Carz if he would jump back up on the pillar. When I traced my finger on the line that formed the hunting cat in the design, it once again turned blue.

Just on a whim, I walked to the next pillar and tried to trace the outline of the border dog. Nothing happened. I asked Carz if he would please get on top of the pillar with the outline of the border dog, and he refused. He also would not get on any of the other pillars when I asked. He would only get on top of the one with the carving of the hunting cat on it. *How very interesting,* I thought. I would need to tell the others what I had discovered.

It took quite some time to gather everyone back at the royal palace. Lom, Theora, and Ealdred were easy to find and came right away. Greer was also easy to locate. Runners had to be sent to the royal library to fetch Seeker Chance, Seeker Eshana, and Yara. When they finally arrived, they were accompanied by Seeker Odette and the head royal librarian, Eluta. When all were finally gathered on the upper terrace, Lady Esmeralda also joined us.

"Did you make it to your meeting on time?" I inquired.

"Meeting? Oh, ah, yes," Lady Esmeralda answered vaguely.

Something is not right here, I thought. *Lady Esmeralda seems distant and secretive. I hope everything is all right.*

"Sorry, Nissa, I am a bit distracted. Long tedious meeting, you know. Did you discover anything about the chamber below?" asked Lady Esmeralda.

Well, that was quite a quick switch. I wonder what is going on with her? I did not have time to think more about it, for Seeker Chance asked why they had been asked to come back from the royal library. I suggested it would be better if we showed them rather than talked about it.

As we entered the royal palace, one of the interim ruling council members pulled Lady Esmeralda aside. Since I was the last in line, I chanced to overhear their conversation.

"Lady Esmeralda, you missed a very important meeting this afternoon," Lady Furman said, and I could hear the censure in her voice. "It is important for you to be at these meetings. I hope you had a very good reason for not being there."

"Yes, Lady Furman, I had a very important reason for not being there. Now, if you will excuse me."

"What is it all of you are doing now?" Lady Furman asked.

"Another important meeting I am trying not to be late for," Lady Esmeralda said.

"And all those, those animals have to attend?"

"Yes," Lady Esmeralda stated, and excused herself once again.

When Lady Esmeralda turned to follow the rest of us, she noticed I was close by. A look of embarrassment crossed her face. At first, I wondered if it was because I had witnessed her being reprimanded, or because I had witnessed Lady Furman's obvious dislike of the companion animals. What was Lady Furman's problem? Did she think Carz was going to use some over-gilded and stuffed chair to sharpen his claws? I decided neither of those possibilities were what really caused the look of embarrassment on Lady Esmeralda's face, however. I realized it was because she knew that I knew what she had told me earlier was not the truth.

As Lady Esmeralda drew up beside me, she whispered she was sorry for her deception earlier. "I will explain when the time is right. Please trust me for now."

We did not speak after that, for we were in a hurry to catch up with the others. By the time Lady Esmeralda and I entered the chamber, the others had the lanterns turned up. We arrived just as Piper concluded telling the others what had happened when we had been here earlier.

"Did you notice that the labyrinth here is the very same pattern as the one we just finished clearing?" Lom asked.

"Fascinating," said the head royal librarian, Eluta. "We need to consult with Master Clarisse to see if this chamber is mentioned in the Book of Rules. I wonder if this chamber has anything to do with the Gylden Sirklene challenge. So much knowledge has been lost. The long gap of time since the death of King Griswold has certainly added to that loss. The chamber has the feeling of very great age. You say the labyrinth you uncovered at the bottom of the royal palace gardens is identical to the one we see here on the floor?"

"Yes," said Lom.

I had not noticed, but now that Lom mentioned it, I could see it clearly. I stood back while the others, who had not been in this chamber with us earlier, took the time to look around. Once they had a chance to look over the labyrinth on the floor with the symbol of a quirrelit tree in the middle surrounded by a patterned border, and before I was about to tell them what I had discovered, Theora stepped in the chamber.

"I went back to make sure no one had followed us. I also pulled the shelf back into place in case anyone decides to wander down here and becomes curious about where we have all gone," said Theora. "I went back as far as the last set of stairs we took, and heard tentative footsteps heading down. I sent Tala up. I cannot be sure, but I think she might have scared Lady Furman out of a few years of her life. At least, I think it was Lady Furman who tried to follow us. I don't think she is very fond of our companion animals, or us, for that matter."

"I am not at all sure that she is very fond of the Crown or the Gylden Sirklene challenge either," stated Lady Esmeralda.

"My impression also," said Seeker Eshana. "Certainly one to keep our eyes on. Very good thinking to check out the back passage, Theora. Now, Nissa, you looked like you were about to tell us something a moment ago."

"I discovered something after Piper, Meryl, and Finn had gone up to fetch the rest of you. First, ah, Ealdred, would you go and stand next to the pillar that has the depiction of the hunting cat on it? Good. Now, will you trace the outline of the hunting cat?"

"Like this?" Ealdred asked, as he drew his finger along the line carved into the pillar that represented the hunting cat. Nothing happened.

I walked over and stood next to the same pillar. Carz jumped up and settled himself on top. Reaching out, I traced the same line Ealdred had just traced, and the line began to glow blue.

"What I discovered after the others left was the line turns blue when I trace my finger along it while Carz is sitting on top of the pillar. It does not turn blue if he is not sitting on top of the pillar. I also discovered that if I trace my finger on any of the other depictions of our companion animals, the lines do not turn blue. In addition, when I asked Carz to get on top of the pillar that has the carving of the border dog on it, he would not, nor would he get on any pillar other than the one that has the carving of the hunting cat on it. I think we need to see what happens when all of us have our companion animals atop their respective pillars, and we trace the outlines of each of them."

All were in agreement that we should try my suggestion. It was not without a great deal of trepidation that we all stood poised by our particular pillars. Keeper Odette suggested we start with the one closest to the chamber door and work our way clockwise. Those who had not carried a piece of the oppgave ringe, or did not have a companion animal, stepped back toward the doorway. It was quite clear that even though Theora had not brought in one of the rings, she still needed to be present at the pillar that depicted night wolves.

One by one our companion animals climbed, flew, or jumped up to the top of their respective pillars. I was surprised that both Kasa and Toki were able to leap that high. One by one, we traced the outlines of our companion animals. One by one, the outlines lit up. As the last of the outlines was traced, I happened to glance at the empty pillar. Lady Esmeralda was standing right next to it. I saw her reach out to tentatively touch the pillar. I thought I saw a flicker of blue light when she did that, but maybe that was only my imagination.

Chapter Nineteen

After spending quite some time in the chamber two levels below the main floor of the royal palace, we could discover nothing more. There did not seem to be any other way out of the chamber, or at least not one we could find. My feeling was we needed the ninth ring carrier and that folk's companion animal in order to discover anything more about this chamber. For now, the chamber was just another mystery to be added to all the others we could not explain.

Besides the chamber, we did not know who had the ninth piece of the oppgave ringe, or whether anyone did. We did not know the purpose of the oppgave ringe. We did not know just what the Gylden Sirklene challenge entailed. We did not know the purpose of the area we had cleared with the quirrelit tree and the labyrinth. We did not know how to open the doors in the cliff wall, what was behind them, or even if the doors needed to be opened. We did not know where the halekrets were, and what they might want with the rings Lom had found in the royal forest. For that matter, we did not know if the theft of the nine firestar gems from the rover elder Zeroun was connected to any of the other mysteries. I also realized, as I was climbing the stairs, that I had another mystery to solve. With all that had gone on this day, I had forgotten the small roll of paper I had found in the Neebing room earlier. That was at least one mystery I might be able to solve.

I did not have a private time where I could look at the small roll of paper until well after dark when I was back at my homewagon. After we climbed up from the chamber, Seeker Eshana suggested we ask some others to join us for a meeting. I thought he was right in thinking we needed to include others in what we had found over the past several days. Runners were sent to invite Master Rollag, Master Clarisse, Journeyman Evan, Lady Celik, Elek, and several others. We decided to meet at the campsite, for it would be a place where we could talk and not be disturbed or overheard. Lady Esmeralda made arrangements for a meal to be delivered.

When all had arrived, Theora, Lom, Piper, and I asked Tala, Taarig, Jing, and Carz if they would make sure no one came close to the campsite. They swiftly left to settle themselves at various spots around the perimeter. I would think the sight of a night wolf or two, a mountain cat, or a hunting cat would cause anyone to think twice about visiting. Not to be left out, Kasa and Toki settled in at the entrance of the campsite, and Tashi flew off in the direction of where the horses were grazing.

Just as we were all settled in with a meal, I heard the sounds of a wagon approaching. I was not too concerned, for I thought Carz or one of the others would discourage the wagon from coming too close to the campsite, and yet the sounds indicated the wagon was coming ever closer. I looked to the entrance and saw both Kasa and Toki standing at alert, yet neither was giving any warning. Indeed, after a moment, they moved back from the entrance, and Carz walked in, followed by a homewagon.

I do not remember what I did with my plate of food when I leapt up, for it was Da's homewagon that was entering the campsite. I could not imagine what possibly could have brought him to the capital so early, causing him to miss out on several summer fairs, when it occurred to me that I really had lost track of time. It was just a little over a week until the great summer fair. I did not have time to think about that at the moment, since Da had halted the horses, swung down, and was sweeping me up in a strong hug. Soon after, I was greeting Nana. After Da and I took care of getting the homewagon in place and leveled, unhitching the horses and getting them settled, introductions were made all around.

Finally, I was able to ask Da what had brought him and Nana to the capital so soon. I had not expected them until later.

"I had a task to do for Lady Celik. I did not want to deliver the information she asked me to seek out by messenger bird, so I came early. Also, Nana and I had become increasingly aware at the last two fairs that our every move was being watched. Fortunately, between Oscar, Bertram, their families, and the Jalcones, not to mention the time when Shueller and

Tannar were with us, those watching us would have been hard-pressed to get too close," explained Da.

"Are the rest of those you mentioned coming here also?"

"Yes, we came as a group. Oscar and Bertram and their families, along with Shueller, Tannar, and the Jalcones are going to be camping with the rover elders. I thought it best that we camp here with you," said Da.

"I'm so glad you and Nana are here," I told Da.

"As am I," stated Lady Celik. "We have missed you, your knowledge, and your wisdom on the interim ruling council. Now that you and Nissa's nana are settled, please get a plate of dinner. Your daughter and her companions have invited all of us here, for there is much to discuss. Later, if you would, I would meet with you."

Da nodded his head in response to Lady Celik's request for a meeting. He, then, brought two camp chairs over to where we were gathered. It did not take long for Da and Nana to get settled in, each with a plate of food. The animals went back on guard. Lady Esmeralda, and the rest of us, filled in those who had not been to the chamber below the royal palace with what we had discovered. When we ended telling about the labyrinth on the floor, the pillars, and what happened with the pillars, I happened to glance over at Master Clarisse. She had a very thoughtful look on her face.

Before I could ask her what she was thinking, once again Kasa and Toki rose from where they were resting. Carz entered the opening into the campsite, followed by Shueller and Zeroun.

"Glad I am that Carz knows me," said Shueller. "This must be some gathering with guard cats and guard night wolves posted around the perimeter. You are just the group we are seeking."

"Welcome. Here, have my seat, and I will go get a couple more," said Da.

When we were all settled again, Meryl did a quick summary for Shueller and Zeroun of what had transpired in the chamber below the royal palace. Then Lom and Ealdred brought the three newcomers up to date on what we had found in the clearing.

"I was just thinking this afternoon, on my way back from the royal palace to my homewagon, that we keep getting more and more mysteries to solve and fewer and fewer answers," I told the others.

"Perhaps I can provide an answer to one question," suggested Zeroun.

"I have been trying and trying to remember the old tale about night wolves partnering with folks. When you mentioned the door you found in the cliff wall, it tickled something in the back of my mind. There is an old tale about two night wolves, a gardener, and a protector. Now, give me a moment to get my thoughts in order."

We all waited. I could see both Lom and Theora were leaning forward in their seats.

"There is an old tale that speaks of two folks paired with two night wolves. One of the folks is referred to as the gardener, the one who tends the plants. The other is known as the protector, the one who protects the gardener. In times of transition, the four appear and are needed to uncover and monitor the gate. I am not sure what that means exactly. The full tale tells of the trials and tribulations of the two pairs before they do what they are destined to do. Sorry if all this is so vague. So many of the stories which were handed down orally have been lost over time. So few were written down."

"Lom, you and Theora with your night wolves fit the general outline of the tale Zeroun has just told us," said Seeker Chance. "I wonder if the gate the tale speaks of is the set of doors you folks uncovered in the cliff wall beyond the quirrelit tree in the clearing. Without the billhook you found in the royal forest, Lom, getting the vines down would have taken a lot more effort."

"And it is taking continuing effort," Lom said. "Since most of you were not anywhere near the clearing this day, you did not see Ealdred and me cutting away at the vines, which started to grow back to cover the doors."

If the doors in the cliff wall are the "gate" of Zeroun's tale, just what did that mean? If the doors are a "gate," then they are a "gate" to what? Does this tale solve one of the mysteries, or just add to it? I wondered.

"Master Clarisse, does the Book of Rules disclose anything about any of the things we have discovered over the last few weeks? Time is growing desperately short, and we are no closer to knowing what any of these discoveries mean, not to mention where the ninth ring might be found, or just what the Gylden Sirklene challenge is," Master Rollag remarked. "For that matter, just what do we know about the Book of Rules?"

"It certainly was not stored well, for such an important book," suggested Seeker Eshana. "The hermit who had the book kept it in a large wooden crate he used as a table. After much rummaging around, throwing out this thing and that, he pulled out a rectangular object, blew the dust off of it, pounded it on his pants leg a few times, and handed it to me. Asked me if the book with the mouse-chewed pages and torn cover might be what I was seeking. It turned out, as you know, to be the Book of Rules."

"It is indeed a strange and less than pretentious little book," said Eluta, the head royal librarian. "After the confrontation with the former regent in the Well of Speaking, Master Clarisse brought the book to me, for it was certainly not in good repair. After looking at it, I could discern that the cover was fairly new, and that the pages were indeed very, very old. Inside, on what would be the title page, it said 'Book of Rules'. Much of where the writer's name would be on that page had been lunch for a rodent or bugs. All that was left was the word 'Journey'. I am not sure if that was the last name of the writer or more of the title."

"You also need to know that the Book of Rules is never very specific," said Master Clarisse. "Another challenge in trying to read it is trying to accurately translate the old language. It is a very ancient language, for which there are very few texts, and certainly no dictionary. Because my clan, the Høyttaiers, have always been secretive, fearing to write anything down, we have had to rely on folks' memories down through the ages. While I did not have overly much trouble translating the first part of the book when we were at the Well of Speaking and being challenged by Lord Klingflug and his followers, the further I have delved into the book, the harder it has been to translate. As you know, there was mention of the need of a living key, who turned out to be Nissa ...."

My thoughts flashed back to that fateful day in the Well of Speaking when Carz had so spectacularly saved the small key I had found in the Neebing room from being lost in the harbor. It turned out I was the "second key" needed to unlock the vessteboks that day.

"It would seem, upon further reading, that there will be need again for a living key. I do not know if it will again be you, Nissa," said Master Clarisse. "What was that, Yara?"

"Sorry to interrupt," stated Yara apologetically. "I was just thinking about the appearance of the blue, um, what I would call blekbrann, but which you might refer to as will-o'-wisps, who led us to Nissa and Greer. Also, when we were in trouble, the blue blekbrann did not surround all of us to save us from harm. Rather they surrounded Nissa. I think that might be significant. Perhaps she is still a living key. A key to what I am not sure, however."

"You could very well be right," Master Clarisse agreed. "As for the oppgave ringe, the Book of Rules is not very forthcoming. As near as I can translate, there is something about a puzzle or a puzzler, I am not sure which. I have sent for some help with the translating. I do not know if others will come forward, since, as you know, members of the Høyttaiers clan have always been reluctant to reveal themselves, especially during the former regent's rule. And I am sure trust of the interim ruling council has not been established yet."

As Master Clarisse finished speaking, I saw Lom give Ealdred a curious look, but did not know what that was all about. The discussion moved on to whether anyone had heard anything about the ninth ring. Sadly, no one had. The conversation then swung back to the chamber beneath the royal palace, since it directly concerned the ring carriers and their companion animals.

It was good to meet with all of the folks who had gathered this night. Unfortunately, it resolved nothing. We were no closer to answers to the many questions than we had been. For that matter, our level of concern had risen a great deal. At least mine had. Now that I was aware of what day it actually was, and how close we were to the time the ninth ring needed to be found, I could practically hear the clock ticking louder and louder with each passing minute. It was also disconcerting to think of myself as a living key and that I might still have a role to play in the unfolding future.

I certainly was not going to solve any of these mysteries this night, so, after everyone had left and I had said goodnight to Da and Nana, I pulled the covers up and settled into bed when I suddenly remembered the small roll of paper I had found in the Neebing room.

CHAPTER TWENTY

I sat up in my bed with Carz stretched out beside me, and turned the flame up on the lamp hanging next to me. Very carefully, I unrolled the small piece of paper that had been left in the Neebing room. On the paper was a drawing of a symbol made of lines that intertwined. The drawing was similar to the type of patterns in the book the Huntress had given me. Shueller had called them Neebing patterns.

These patterns seemed to be showing up in all sorts of unexpected places, or perhaps I was more aware of them since I had been given the book by the Huntress. In talking with others over the past week or so, I had noticed Neebing patterns on boxes, rings, bracelets, wrist cuffs, walking sticks, doors, and pillars, to mention a few. Both Shueller and Zeroun had told me the patterns had once been carved on shutters and houses. They told me that they used to be found throughout Sommerhjem. That had been the practice long ago at any rate. For some reason, that practice had faded over time.

Thinking about traditions and knowledge lost in the past was not, however, going to help me figure out what the symbol on the small piece of paper I was holding meant. I wished I knew why it had been left for me. Just as I thought that, I realized it was not the first strange thing that had been left for me in the Neebing room. There had been the firestar gem. Also, I had been left a quirrelit seed. Of course, at the time, I did not know what it was. I also did not know how very rare it was, or how important it was, until the night I met the Huntress. Then there was the small key that had been left in the Neebing room, which had turned out to be one of the two keys needed to open the vessteboks set in the sea wall of the Well of Speaking.

Sitting and staring at the symbol on the paper was getting me nowhere, other than raising more questions, so I turned down the light, pulled the covers up, and tried to sleep. Sleep was a long time coming, for I had difficulty turning off all the thoughts swirling around in my head. I was certainly not well rested the next morning.

Lady Henrietta Green was shown into the formal parlor upon arriving at Lady Farcroft's capital town home. She was surprised to find several others sitting there, calmly partaking in an afternoon tea. The urgency of the note she had received asking her to come to Lady Farcroft's town home had made her think something monumental had happened, or was going to happen. These folks sitting calmly drinking tea belied that belief, until Lady Green took a good look at Lady Farcroft, who was pacing in front of the fireplace.

Noticing that Lady Green had entered the parlor, Lady Farcroft walked swiftly to the door, gave instructions to the man who had escorted Lady Green, and closed the doors.

"We should be very secure here," Lady Farcroft stated. "Time grows very, very short, so I have gathered you folks here to discuss any new information any of you have discovered. Also, we need to review our plans to cover all of the contingencies for what could possibly happen on the third day of the capital fair."

"We finally got through to those ineffectual idiots on the interim ruling council," Lord Mostander stated. "We were finally allowed to see what those folks who carried pieces of the oppgave ringe into the capital have been working on at the bottom of the royal palace gardens."

"And that they should have any say in what we of noble birth are allowed, or not allowed, to do is just not right," complained Lady Padde. "Why those who carried the rings in are just peasants, laborers, minor merchants, and a librarian, of all things. One might be a noble now, but was raised on the streets of Høyhauger. The lass, Piper, comes from a family of some standing. However, she is the only one. And then, there is that rover, Nissa," Lady Padde said disgustedly.

"Yes, well, we all know how you feel, Lady Padde. More to the point is just what is at the bottom of the tangle," Lady Farcroft asked.

"Strangely enough, there is very little," stated Lord Mostander. "Just a path to a labyrinth with a single quirrelit tree in the center. Just before the labyrinth, the path divides, and then reconnects beyond the labyrinth and leads to the cliff wall. Set into the cliff wall is an opening holding a large, elaborately carved set of doors. There seems to be no way of opening the doors, other than taking a battering log to them."

"Have any of you heard what might be the purpose of this area?" Lady Farcroft asked. No one gathered had any explanation.

"There is something else. Lady Esmeralda missed an important meeting the other day. When I confronted her, she was with all of those folks connected with carrying the pieces of the oppgave ringe into the capital. She was there in the royal palace with them and their disgusting, flea-ridden, dirty animals," Lady Furman said, revulsion evident in her voice. "They headed into the lower levels of the royal palace and were gone for quite some time. When I tried to find out what they had been doing down there, I was blocked from going any farther down the stairs to the level under the main floor by one of those awful black wolves. Very politely mind you, but nevertheless, he did not allow me to go where those folks had gone. There was no way to follow them. First these common folks are becoming uppity, and now their flea bitten animals are."

"While I realize Lady Esmeralda has lived in the royal palace all of her life, and the interim ruling council has made it clear it is her home until the next ruler of Sommerhjem is chosen, you should not have been prevented from going where you wish to go in the royal palace, and those wild animals should not be given the free roam of the palace or the grounds," Lord Hindre said emphatically. "That young woman has assumed too much about who gets to make decisions now!"

"Be that as it may, there is not much we can do at this moment about Lady Esmeralda. Her time will come, when one of us becomes the next ruler of Sommerhjem. Now, any more news or information?" inquired Lady Farcroft.

Time was moving much too quickly, and yet, not moving fast enough. The time of the great summer fair in the capital was way too close at hand for a number of reasons, not the least of which was there still was no word about anyone finding the ninth piece of the oppgave ringe. I noticed Ealdred, Master Clarisse, Seeker Chance, and a journeywoman from the Glassmakers Guild were spending time together. My suspicion was they were trying to translate more of the Book of Rules. Seeker Eshana, the head royal librarian, Eluta, and Yara set off every day for the royal library to meet up with Seeker Odette. They continued to try to find out what they could about the Gylden Sirklene challenge, and any other information that might pertain to the oppgave ringe, or to the chamber we had found below the royal palace.

Lom spent most of his time studying the doors in the cliff wall. He said it was hard to be away from them, for the pull from whatever was beyond them was very strong. One day at a meal, he laughingly suggested he would climb up the vines like the halekrets had, if he thought he had a real chance of making it to the top and not falling to his death.

The interim ruling council had gotten wind of the clearing and had insisted they be allowed to see what was going on. Piper and Theora had taken on the task of making sure any who entered the clearing stayed on the path. A few folks had tried to disregard their instructions and had been warned back by Jing and Tala. Taarig was also there with Lom. He, however, stayed very close to Lom and let the others do the patrolling.

Meryl and Finn kept busy each day, poking into places in the royal palace and grounds that may not have been poked into for a very long time. Beezle and Lady Esmeralda joined them when they could, and they had discovered a number of hidden passageways within the royal palace that had not been used in years. Beezle told me that the dust they had walked through in some of those passageways was inches deep. Other passageways and hidden places in the royal palace had been used more recently, and frequently, which was worrisome.

That left Greer and me at loose ends. I certainly could occupy my time with my wood projects, and Greer could meet with his father and work on business. However, Greer had told me, there was just so much business that could be done in the capital, and he and his father had taken care of most of it. I was certainly grateful for his company while I worked on my carving. I had given him a knife and some instructions about whittling. It turned out he had a talent for it. It helped him pass the hours.

During one morning while the others were away, we sat in

companionable silence, each working on our respective projects. I had reached a point where I really needed to stand up, stretch my legs, and do something different for a while. I asked Greer if he wanted to take a break.

"I would be happy to," remarked Greer, standing and brushing wood chips off his clothing. "The waiting to see what is going to happen next is weighing on me. Not being able to help find the answers is difficult."

"I know what you mean. All too soon the meeting in the Well of Speaking is going to happen. It is frightening to think of what will transpire if the ninth ring doesn't show up," I suggested.

"Even if the ninth ring does appear in time, we don't know what will happen. And then, there is the matter of the challenge. What exactly is the Gylden Sirklene challenge anyway? No one seems to know," said Greer.

"I can appreciate what you are saying, and you are not the only one saying it. Da told me the questions you are mulling over are what most of the folks of Sommerhjem are also thinking about. I don't even want to imagine the reactions if the ninth ring is found, if the challenge takes place, and if a new ruler is chosen because of the challenge. Not everyone is going to be happy with the final choice. Oh, muddle fuddle. Nothing is going to happen this day, and I am tired of working. Walk with Carz and me?"

"With pleasure. I am sure Kasa would not mind stretching his legs. Any particular place in mind?"

"Yes, I want to go back to the chamber below the royal palace. I want to take a really good look at it. Are you up for a little underground exploring?" I asked Greer.

"By all means. Lead on."

Lady Esmeralda had posted a pair of guards at the entrance to the room that led to the way down to the underground chamber. She had left instructions that if any of us who had been there before wanted to reenter, we should be allowed to do so. When Greer and I reached the chamber, I was pleased to discover that a number of lamps and lanterns had been left by the entrance. I suggested we light only two at first.

"Why only two?" Greer asked.

I decided it was time to take at least one person into my confidence concerning the small roll of paper I had found in the Neebing room.

"You may not be aware that over the last year, I have come into possession of a number of items that have been significant."

"I know you carried two pieces of the oppgave ringe," Greer said, "and the key needed to open the vessteboks."

I decided I did not need to mention the quirrelit seed, for then I would have to explain the Huntress, and I was reluctant to do that. "Yes, well, I seem to have been given something else recently. A small piece of rolled up paper was left in my homewagon. I'm not sure why, or if it is even significant or related to what is happening now, but I have a strong suspicion it could be. It appeared in my homewagon right about the time we discovered this chamber. I have nothing that justifies my thinking that what is on the small piece of paper has something to do with this chamber, and yet, I think it does. Does that make any sense?"

"About as much sense as anything else that has happened to either of us this past year," Greer stated ruefully. "May I see the small piece of paper?"

I held the paper out to Greer and lifted my lantern, hoping it would shed enough light on the paper so he could see what was drawn there.

"It looks very much in the style that you have carved on your homewagon and on the shutters you are working on. It also looks very much in the style of the carvings on the pillars here," said Greer.

"It certainly appears to be in the old style that we have seen on a number of things which have only recently been found …."

"Like Theora's bow …."

"And Lom's billhook. I want to look closely in this chamber and see if we can find a symbol matching the one on the paper. Here, I made a copy, thinking the looking would go faster if there was someone else looking with me. Again, I don't know why I think we might find something, but I do."

Greer and I had been in the chamber below the royal palace for about an hour. He had taken one wall of the chamber and I had taken another. Neither of us had found anything that resembled the symbol on the small piece of paper left in the Neebing room. Just as I was about to turn the corner and start on the next wall, I spotted the symbol at about eye level.

"Greer, come over here. I think I found it."

Chapter Twenty-One

When Greer came over to my side of the chamber, I pointed out the symbol I had found. He concurred that the symbol on the wall matched the symbol on the small piece of paper I had shown him.

"What do you think it means?" asked Greer.

"I have no idea. I suggest we see if there is something we can push, or pull, or turn, or twist, which might do something, such as open up some section of the wall. Maybe the last piece of the oppgave ringe is hidden here. We can only wish it is that straightforward and simple."

Greer and I worked for over an hour, covering every inch of the wall where I had found the symbol. We found nothing. We then went back to looking at the rest of the chamber's walls. We did not find another symbol like the one on the small piece of paper, nor did we find any way out of the chamber other than the door where we had entered. Finally, we decided to call it a day and head back up to fresh air and, hopefully, sunshine.

When we reached a door heading out of the royal palace, the air was indeed fresh, due to the torrential rain that was pouring from a very dark and ominous sky. Not wanting to become soaked to the skin trying to get to my homewagon, I agreed with Greer that waiting out the rain in the small side parlor assigned to us in the royal palace was the best idea, so we headed there.

I was not surprised to see others of our group also in the parlor. I was thankful that someone had had the foresight to light a fire and set out a late afternoon tea. Even before we discussed with the others gathered there what we had discovered, and had not discovered, in the chamber below, the atmosphere in the small parlor was about as gloomy as the day outside. Lom had no luck finding a way to open the doors in the cliff wall. The seekers, along with Yara and the head royal librarian, Eluta, had found nothing more concerning either the whereabouts of the ninth ring or the Gylden Sirklene challenge. Journeyman Evan, who had stopped by and been delayed going back to the Glassmakers Guildhall, told us Master Clarisse had gathered others to help translate more of the Book of Rules, but it was slow going.

The mood in the room took a further nosedive when Lady Esmeralda joined us and reported that the amount of tension and unrest throughout the country of Sommerhjem was on the rise. It was very clear to all of us that the closer we came to the third day of the great summer fair in the capital, the more anxious everyone was becoming. So much was still unknown.

I had a question that needed to be asked, and since almost all of us were assembled here, I thought now was as good a time as any.

"I know my next statement will seem a bit selfish, compared to what we have just been discussing. However, no matter the outcome of the challenge, which I somehow think will happen, I still need to earn a living. Sooner than any of us want, the fair here in the capital is going to begin. Da, Nana, and I all will need to set up our booths."

The first reaction from the others was that it would be too dangerous for me to leave the royal palace grounds.

"I really appreciate all of your concern. The fact remains, however, as I said, I need to be able to sell my wares, and hopefully gain some commissions. I also want to submit my shutter project for judging. I know, on the one hand, this seems irrational and foolish on my part. On the other hand, if I work my booth, a part of me will feel better."

"How can you feel better when you are putting yourself at risk?" asked Theora.

"I'm sure that you and the head of the royal guard will make sure I get to and from the fairgrounds safely each day. Master Rollag has made arrangements for me to have my booth on the Glassmakers Guild grounds, next to the booth Journeyman Evans is going to be running. Nana and Shyla will both be in the booth with me. Trust me, Nana is someone you do not want to cross, especially if she thinks I am in any type of danger.

Da is going to set his booth up with the other metalsmiths, and I'm sure he will be well looked after by them."

"I think you have the right of it, being at the fair," stated Lady Esmeralda quietly. "The decision to bring you folks here to keep you safe was a good one. However, sequestering you on the royal palace grounds may have been a double-edged sword, so to speak. While we have kept you safe, we have also kept you out of the public's view. Some folks see that as keeping you safe. Others see you as hiding, thinking you know something they do not. Rumors are going around that you may have even left the capital, because you know that some type of disaster is about to happen. Those who oppose the Crown are pushing this view. They think they might be able to use this idea to their advantage, should the ninth ring not be placed in the vessteboks when it is supposed to be."

"So, you think Nissa has the right of it, and should set up and tend her booth at the fair?" Theora asked.

"I think she should, yes," said Lady Esmeralda. "I also think the rest of you, with great caution and under well-planned circumstances, should attend the fair with your animal companions. Folks need to know that you are confident that everything will work out all right on the third day of the fair. I know you are all discouraged that the ninth ring has not appeared yet. I have confidence that somehow, some way, all will be well when we once again meet in the Well of Speaking."

I wished I was feeling as confident as Lady Esmeralda. I did not even want to think about what might happen if the ninth ring was not found and placed in the vessteboks by the third day of the fair. I was sure Lord Klingflug and his followers would have plans in place, should the ninth ring not be found in time. I knew the interim ruling council and others had been meeting and would also have plans in place. That was all very well and good. However, it seemed to me that, if the challenge could not happen, we might become a land divided.

An additional worry for me came from a conversation I overheard between Theora, Piper, and Piper's mother. All had served as border guards, so they were very aware of the lands to the south and east. In addition, Piper's family guarded the southern pass. They had talked about being worried that, if we did not have a strong leader, if Sommerhjem looked divided, the rulers of Bortfjell to the north, and Rullegress to the south, might think Sommerhjem was ripe for the plucking. The land to the east held too many unknowns for anyone to even speculate what might happen there.

Fortunately, I had little time to worry about what other countries might do in the future, since there were too many very immediate things to worry about. For one, with the great summer fair at the capital just days away, I needed to spend some time finishing up my entry to the Woodworkers Guild contest. I had won a medallion of excellence last year, which had gone a long way toward building my reputation as a woodworker. I had no such expectations for this year, but having my shutters on display would at least let folks see my work and, hopefully, bring some commissions my way.

With the rain's passing, and the sun's reappearance, we all walked out into the cool summer afternoon and went our different ways. Greer and Kasa decided to take a bit of a walk to stretch their legs, and I walked back to the campgrounds with Carz, deep in thought.

I had to think positively, for the alternative was too scary to contemplate. I hoped Lady Esmeralda's comment that all would be well would turn out to be true. For now though, I needed to get to work. Besides the shutters to finish, I needed to make handles for a number of Da's knives and carve a few more whimsies. Once I sat down to work, I tucked my worries into the back of my mind and fell into the rhythm of carving and sanding. When I heard Da calling my name, I was surprised by how much time had passed.

"Nissa, ahem, Nissa. 'Tis suppertime. Time to put your tools away and join the rest of us on the terrace," said Da.

When I stood, I let out a muffled groan, for I was stiff and sore from being hunched over, carving the shutters.

"Are you almost done with those shutters? They are very beautiful. I think I need to put in an order for my cottage," Da suggested.

"A commission for shutters is it now? We will have to discuss price."

"You would charge your dear ol' Da?"

"Of course," I said laughingly, as I brushed wood shavings off my clothes and generally tried to straighten up. "I was taught how to drive a hard bargain by the best, you know."

I was grateful for that lighthearted moment with Da, for the discussion at the evening meal was less than encouraging. Still no word on the ninth ring. Too much word about how anxious folks were becoming, both in the capital and in the rest of the land of Sommerhjem. No information on what the chamber below the royal palace was all about. No progress on just what the doors in the cliff wall opened up to, or how to open them. No new information on why there was a labyrinth in the middle of the clearing. No sightings of the halekrets. No word on the missing firestar gems. No new information on what the Gylden Sirklene challenge was. No new plans on what was going to happen on the third day of the great summer fair if the ninth ring were not placed in the vessteboks.

So very much was up in the air, and the clock was ticking. Sometimes when I was lying in my bed at night, I thought I could hear the clock in the clock tower of the royal palace ticking away. As I listened hard in the dark, I thought I could hear those ticks coming faster and faster. I know that was just my imagination.

Or maybe not, for two nights before the first day of the fair found me rearranging my cart, so I would be ready to move it to my spot in front of the Glassmakers Guildhall. I had taken my shutters over to the Woodworkers Guildhall without incident earlier in the afternoon. It had felt good to be off the royal palace grounds, even if it was with an escort of royal guards. My rover heart longed to be free to walk the streets with just Carz and myself. For that matter, I really wished I could skip the fair all together and head my homewagon anywhere away from here. I needed to be back on the road almost as much as I needed air to breathe and water to drink.

On the morrow, I would go and set up my booth and, in just four short days, we would gather in the Well of Speaking to see what would happen.

Chapter Twenty-Two

The first day of the great summer fair in the capital started on a bright, beautiful summer morning. The sky was cloudless and a brilliant blue. There was enough breeze to keep the smells of burning fires, sweet and savory cooked food, animal droppings, and the other assorted smells of a fairgrounds at bay. It was good to be back in my booth.

Last year was the first time I had been to the great summer fair in the capital for a number of years. I had forgotten how huge it was and how many attended. Of course, I had just a bit on my mind last year at this time, what with having smuggled the then royal heir, Lady Esmeralda, into the fairgrounds. If we had been discovered, I probably would not be sitting behind my booth this day, trying to stay calm.

This year I was more prepared for the size of the fair and the large number of folks. That did not make me any less anxious, as I sat trying to carve a whimsy, this one a combination of a bunny and a fox. That would make it a funny or a box. Not good names, I supposed. Perhaps a fobbit or a rabbox would be better.

I sometimes wonder if I will ever have the chance to set up a booth at the great summer fair without having six to a dozen things to worry about. I envied those folks who were less aware of what was going on concerning what was to happen in several more days. The one thing I did notice right away, when folks began wandering the lanes that made up the fair, was there seemed to be more folks this year. More folks being here, however, was not putting more coin in my pocket. With the fair being as big as it is, most folks take to wandering about looking at as much as they can before they part with any coin. While that is pretty typical of the first day of the fair, I noticed, while there were more folks this year, I had fewer sales this day than on the first day last year. If anything, folks seemed more reluctant to part with their coin this year than last year. Sales were few and far between, to say the least.

What also struck me was the difference in the various groups that wandered by. Some seemed to be overly enthusiastic about being at the fair, their reactions to what they saw, or the foods they sampled, seemed overly exaggerated. It was as if they were trying too hard to pretend everything was normal. Then, there were what I thought of as the doom and gloom bunch. These folks wandered about the fair looking morose, picking things up to look at, and then putting them back, muttering about how it was not worth spending good coin on anything when they did not know what the morrow would bring. The tension among those folks was so thick it could be cut with a very dull knife.

During the day, a number of the other ring carriers wandered by my booth. It was interesting to see the reactions of the fair goers when one of the ring carriers would stop to chat. I am not sure what attracted the folks most, but I suspect it was the companion animals.

I tried to put myself in others' shoes and imagine what it was like for them to see two night wolves calmly walking down the fair lanes. I remembered what it was like for me when I first saw them, and I am fairly used to folks with uncommon animals. Those two night wolves made a striking pair, all midnight black with silver tips to their fur, like starlight had been sprinkled on their backs. Just their size alone would give one pause. Lom and Theora were striking in their own right: he with a vine growing out of his pocket and up into his beard, billhook strapped to his belt, and she with her bow and quiver slung over her shoulder, wearing the special royal guard uniform.

I was glad that Seeker Eshana, and sometimes Seeker Odette, accompanied Seeker Chance, for the little halekrets, Ashu, attracted a lot of attention, especially from the wee lads and lasses. Of course, wandering around the fair with a mountain cat and a bog fox drew Piper and Yara their own curious glances. Meryl, with Tashi, the griff falcon, perched on her shoulder, was also turning heads. Only Greer seemed to be able to wander the fair without attracting too much attention, except for those who knew border dogs. His father accompanied him with his own border dog at his side, and the four of them were a striking sight.

I came to the conclusion that Lady Esmeralda was correct. We who had carried rings into the capital needed to be seen. Maybe by being seen calmly going about our business, we would give some reassurance to the folks in the capital that all was well, or would be well on the third day of the fair. I had noticed that the time of the gathering on the third day of the fair in the Well of Speaking had been posted for the first hour past noon. I imagine those who sided with the former regent had been quite insistent on that time, for it would be exactly one year from the day the Gylden Sirklene challenge had been called. In truth, the challenge had been called a bit later than the first hour past noon. I did not think that was going to matter much, however.

I know the interim ruling council, and other groups that supported the Crown, had been burning the late night lamps, trying to have plans in place to cover as many possible outcomes for that gathering as they could think of. I am sure those who opposed the Crown were meeting late into the night, making their own plans. We needed to know what we should do if the ninth ring was not found in time. We needed to know what we should do if it was.

I knew that the captain of the royal guard, the captain of the royal palace guard, the captain of the special guards, and representatives of the various border patrols had been meeting in preparation for the potential outcomes. Lady Celik and her son had tapped into all of their many informants to try to gather information concerning the plans of those who would oppose the Crown. Master Clarisse had been meeting behind closed doors with others, whose identities were hidden under hooded cloaks, trying to read and decipher the Book of Rules. More and more members of the Order of Seekers were arriving daily in the capital and were meeting with the royal librarians, the royal historians, and the rover elders.

Lom spent so much time at the cliff wall trying to decipher the carvings and trying to figure out how to open the doors, we had finally moved a bench back there, so he could sit down occasionally. Theora made him take breaks for meals and to sleep. Greer and I had had no luck finding out anything more when we had gone back to the chamber in one of the lower levels of the royal palace. Meryl and Finn continued to explore the royal palace grounds and the royal palace, looking for other hidden places to no avail. Lady Esmeralda and Beezle also used what little time they had to spare looking for hidden areas or passageways within the royal palace.

I certainly wished I could help more, or do more. I just did not know what I could do. I knew sitting, thinking heavy thoughts, and not whittling, was fairly unproductive. I had just picked up my carving knife when Shyla, who was helping me at my booth, called my name to get my attention.

"Your pardon, Nissa. There is a Lady here who wishes to talk with you."

While I did not recognize the very well-dressed middle-aged woman who stood at the booth counter, I recognized her voice the moment she spoke. I had crossed paths with her in Glendalen and learned she had been responsible for my being kidnapped in Tverdal. All of the information gathered by the Crown also suggested she had strong ties with Lady Farcroft, who was clearly on the side of the former regent. Some even thought that Lady Farcroft had her own plans, which did not include the former regent or the Crown. I needed to school my face, so as to look like a rover woodworker eager to get a fine commission from Lady Green and not look like someone who had a grievance with her.

"M'lady, how may I be of assistance?" I asked politely.

"Ah, yes, well, I, um, saw the chest you carved and entered in last year's Woodworkers Guild contest. I admired your designs and wish to, um, hire, yes, hire you to do some carvings for me," said Lady Green.

"How kind of you," I told her. I did not continue talking, for I wanted to see what Lady Green would say next. I certainly had no reason to trust what she was saying. I did not think she sincerely liked my carving designs or really wanted to hire me.

"Ah, well, yes. Now then, I wish for you to make me a chest. Yes, a large chest for the foot of my town home bed, to hold blankets and such. You will need to come by my town home to take measurements, of course. How about after the fair this night? I would, well, make it worth your while to get this started right away."

I was saved from having to answer when Master Rollag stepped up to the booth. "How nice to see you, Lady Green. I see you admire Nissa's work as much as I do." Directing his comments to me, he went on. "Now, I could not help overhearing that Lady Green wants to commission you to make a chest for her. What a grand offer. I almost hate to remind you that you promised to finish that project for me in the next day or so. I do want to be able to present my niece with the chest as a gift at her wedding, which takes place in less than a week."

Of course, I had no idea what Master Rollag was talking about, since he had never commissioned a chest from me. Then I realized he was trying to give me an excuse not to go to Lady Green's town home that evening.

"It would take less than thirty minutes for you to come by the town home, measure the area, and figure out what size chest would fit," suggested Lady Green. "I could send a carriage."

The last time I had taken a carriage ride in the capital had not turned out well. Before I could think of a way to use the excuse Master Rollag had given me in order to refuse Lady Green without offending her, Master Rollag stepped in again.

"Ah, Lady Green, I think I have a way to solve both our problems and save Nissa some time. The head of the Woodworkers Guild owes me a favor and would certainly send one of his journeymen over to take measurements."

"Well, ah, that just will not do. No, it will not do," stated Lady Green emphatically, trying very unsuccessfully to look appalled. "A strange man in my bedchamber. Oh, my, no!"

"I can see how that might be a concern. I will make sure that the head of the Woodworkers Guild sends a journeywoman or a woman Master. Would that be suitable, Lady Green? Nissa?"

"It would be a great relief. This night, once I have the measurements, I will sketch out several possible designs for your approval. Would that be acceptable to you, Lady Green?" I asked politely.

Lady Green accepted our solution. I think she was wise enough to know that, if she had continued to argue, she would have appeared too insistent, or too eager, and less than gracious. In these unsettled times, it was not wise to attract too much attention to oneself.

Once she left the booth, I asked Shyla to cover the counter and walked behind the booth to have a quiet conversation with Master Rollag. Before I could even get the first word out, he began to speak.

"My apologies for butting in. I know you could have handled that situation very well on your own. I was just unsure if you were aware of the strong connection that Lady Green has with Lady Farcroft. I do not trust her motives for wanting to hire you. Mind you, I think she would be very wise to give you a commission, for your work is outstanding. You know I greatly admire it."

"Thank you for liking my work. And more importantly, thank you for butting in. I must admit, I was hard-pressed to quickly come up with an excuse for not going to her town home after the fair closes this night. It would have been very bad form not to try for a commission from a woman of Lady Green's standing. I'm all too aware of Lady Green's connection to Lady Farcroft and those who follow the former regent."

I took a few moments to fill Master Rollag in on my adventures in Tverdal and Glendalen before I got back to the subject of commissions.

"So, I'm making a chest for your niece, am I? We can hope that Lady Green does not come back and want to see it."

"Why would she do that?" Master Rollag asked, genuinely puzzled.

"It would be a perfect example of what I might carve on her blanket chest. She might say that my drawings just do not give her a true sense of what her chest might look like, so would ask to see the one I am carving for you."

"Oh dear, I never thought of that."

"It is good, then, that I have a chest already three-quarters completed in my cart which might suit. I will get it out now and work on it. If she wanders back, or sends others to check on what I'm doing, it will give credence to your story. I have one question."

"Yes?"

"Do you actually have a niece who is getting married at the end of this week?"

"As a matter of fact, I do. Mind you, I have a beautiful stained glass made for her as a gift."

"In that case, I will not hold you to the commission for the chest you have lied to Lady Green about," I told Master Rollag.

"Actually, I am going to have you hold me to my request, for I have other relatives who may need a gift down the line, or perhaps I might just want a piece of your work for myself. I will not hold you to the end of the week deadline, however. Now, let's see how much I can talk you down on the price."

I was glad when the fair closed at the end of the day. I was equally glad when my escort arrived to make sure I got back to the royal palace safely. Our late supper on the terrace was not a cheerful or a noisy one. All of us were lost in our own thoughts and worries, since there were just one and a half days before the meeting in the Well of Speaking was to take place, and nothing new had been discovered.

Chapter Twenty-Three

I was glad that the first day at the fair had gone mostly without incident, as did the second day. No word had come from any of the many sources concerning the ninth ring. Not knowing what was going to happen on the morrow was nerve-racking, to say the least. At the end of the second day, I had hoped to return to the royal palace grounds and go to my homewagon. I just wanted to spend the evening quietly around the campfire with Da, Nana, and any of the others who wished to join us. Unfortunately, I did not get my wish and was not even able to be alone with my family and friends until quite a few hours after the evening meal.

A week before the opening of the great capital fair, Lady Esmeralda had gathered together those of us who traveled with companion animals, along with a number of royal tailors and royal dressmakers. We had apparently become important folks for whatever was to come in the next weeks and needed to dress the part. In addition, Da was included in this gathering, along with Ealdred, Finn, and the seekers. When the rather pompous head royal tailor and an equally pompous head royal dressmaker started in on what magnificent dresses, robes, or suits they saw us in, I was not the only one who had a look of concern on my face. The dressmaker and the tailor both waxed on and on about how they could color coordinate the men's outfits with the women's dresses. Or else, one of them suggested, they could match our clothing to the colors of the animals who accompanied us. Then one of them suggested that jeweled collars could be made for each of the animals that would match accompanying jewelry we would wear. I wished I had a way of preserving the looks of horror on the others' faces. Before I could say anything, Lady Esmeralda stepped in.

"I am sorry if I gave you the impression that you were about to design new outfits for each of these kind folks. Much as I think all of your ideas are really quite splendid, what we need is for you to make sure each of these folks has appropriate clothing that fits well and is what they wish to wear. Take Nissa, for example. She is a rover, and I am sure she has formal rover wear, but it may need cleaning or mending. Perhaps you could work with her to produce a fine cloak. Nissa, do you have material in your clan plaid that they might incorporate in a cloak?

"Yes, I have some in my homewagon. My mother was a very fine weaver, and I have some of the cloth she wove. Da, do you still have some of Mother's cloth also?"

"Yes. I would be happy to get some of it out." Turning to the tailor, he asked, "Are you aware of the cut and make of formal rover wear?"

The head royal tailor answered in the affirmative. He looked insulted that he would even be asked such a question. I must admit that, once the head royal tailor and the head royal dressmaker understood what was being asked of them, they were very efficient and asked what was needed from each of us.

Now, it was the night before the third day of the fair and all of us were gathered in the small parlor set aside for us. We once again met with the head royal tailor and the head royal dressmaker, who presented us with the clothing we were to wear the next day. I, personally, thought getting all dressed up was a bunch of fuss and bother. Lady Esmeralda, however, suggested that appearances were going to matter the next day. She assured me that Lord Klingflug and his followers would most probably be dressed in their finest and would present a united front. We needed to do the same. It would not do, she had suggested, if we appeared as a raggle-taggle group. I had to take her word for it.

Once we all had our finery for the following day, we met briefly. There was really no reason to sit around and go over all the plans that had been put in place, so, after a short briefing, all of us headed out. Since there was nothing to be done but hope the ninth ring showed up on the morrow, the other ring carriers decided to join those of us who were camping on the royal palace grounds.

To my surprise, when we arrived at the campsite, other folks were already there, sitting around the campfire. It was Bertram and Oscar and their families, Shueller and Tannar, the Jalcones, and Journeyman Evan. I could smell some type of berry tart bubbling away in a cast iron pot set in the coals. Oscar was just tuning up his fiddle. Piper excused herself to go get her mountain flute.

"After the fair closed, we got to thinking," stated Oscar. "It seemed a shame for those of us who have been together since the beginning of this adventure, not to be together on the night before the big meeting at the Well of Speaking. I don't know about you, but I am not sure how soon sleep is going to come this night. Since we don't know what might happen on the morrow, we thought we might have a little lively music and some of Mistress Jalcone's fine cooking to while away the hours."

"Master Rollag and Master Clarisse said to save spots for them, along with Beezle, for they will be along in a while," said Journeyman Evan.

I was feeling better than I had when we were gathered in the royal palace parlor. One bright thing that had come out of the past year was the friendship of folks I had met along the way since I first left home on that rainy night over a year ago. I was certainly glad to be surrounded by most of them this night. I grabbed my camp chair and pulled it into the circle around the campfire. No matter what happened at an hour after noon the next day, I had this night filled with the smell of wood smoke mixed with the smell of sweet berries, the glow of the embers in the fire pit, and the sounds of music, sometimes the wild music of the high hills, sometimes the long forgotten melodies of childhood.

As time passed, other folks joined us, straggling in one by one, or in small groups. It was shortly after Beezle had arrived to add his flute to the music being made that Lady Esmeralda arrived, dressed in rover clothing.

"Can an honorary rover join this group?" she asked. It seemed fitting that she was part of the gathering, since she had traveled with me last summer disguised as a rover. That disguise had saved her from Lord Klingflug and his followers, who had determined she was expendable.

Long hours later, the musicians finally put their instruments away, and Oscar and Bertram sent their protesting younger children off to bed. We sat around the fire talking quietly, until it burned down to coals, and the group split up. Finally, all of us headed to bed. All that could be done had been done. All that folks could think of to plan for what could possibly happen had been thought out and planned. We had spent most of the night gathered together. For just a little while, we had put our worries aside. Dawn would come soon enough.

"Come on, Carz, let's check the horses and then head to bed. Morning is going to come very early."

On the morning of the third day of the fair, all of us were up very early. I spent a brief moment wondering if I might have been better off staying up for the rest of the night, rather than catching a few hours of sleep. I certainly did not feel very rested. I rather envied Carz, for I knew, while I worked at my booth, he would be under it, napping.

I felt rather funny walking to the fairgrounds dressed in my formal rover clothing. I had thought of just taking my formal clothes there and changing in my cart. I knew I would not normally be carving, whittling, or sanding wood in my good clothes. Dwelling on clothes at a time like this, on a day like this, seemed foolish. Not really knowing what the day would bring, I decided that changing clothes was just one more thing to worry about. The folks of Sommerhjem had far more important things to worry about this day than whether I had sawdust or wood shavings on my formal clothes.

The atmosphere at the fair was subdued. It did not help that the morning fog took a very long time to burn off. There was enough gloom among those folks with whom I had walked to the fair, and the late receding fog certainly was not helping. The fact that there was still no word about the whereabouts of the ninth ring had been the topic of conversation at breakfast. It had been an odd gathering on the royal palace terrace. There we were, all of us dressed in our finery, sitting about, pretending we were very interested in what was set before us for breakfast, yet with few of us eating much.

I was glad of Shyla's company, and of having Journeyman Evan in the booth next to mine. I wished the trade were brisker, so my mind would not keep going over and over all of the talk and plans from the night before. My fervent hope for the day was that the ninth ring would show up, and I would not be called upon to do anything other than watch what was to unfold in the Well of Speaking. I had little care for what happened after that. My greatest wish was to be able to pack up my homewagon at the end of this fair and move on to the next fair down the road. I certainly had neither the inclination nor the wish to attempt the Gylden Sirklene challenge and become the next ruler of Sommerhjem, not that I had any illusions that I could possibly be chosen.

The morning dragged on and on. There was a lot of milling around among the folks at the fair. As near as I could tell from what I observed, very few were purchasing anything in our lane of booths, nor were folks carrying any bundles or bags suggesting they had purchased things from booths in other lanes. I did not even see very many folks walking by eating a sweet pastry, or anything else for that matter. It was also unusually quiet for that many folks in one place. Lads and lasses did not race down the lane. There was little to no laughter among the folks who wandered by.

When the royal guard came by to escort me to the Well of Speaking, it was almost a relief. The waiting would at least be over. Carz fell into step with me, as if being surrounded by royal guards was an everyday occurrence. I wished I felt as calm as Carz looked. When I looked closer at Carz, I realized he was not as calm as he outwardly might appear to others. Since he had been with me since he was a kit, I had become very adept at reading his body language. He might look calm, but he was also on alert.

When we arrived at the Well of Speaking, I could see the other ring carriers and their companion animals. Lady Esmeralda may have had the right of it about all of us dressing up for the occasion. Even the animals looked mighty fine, for they had allowed us to brush them until their coats shone. Not without disgusted looks as we did so, mind you. I do not know what Meryl did, but Tashi's gold and red feathers were almost brighter than the sun.

All of us were gathered in an area to the side at the top of the Well of Speaking. Though I had been here before, I was still a bit in awe of the place, a huge amphitheater that sloped down to the sea with seats that held hundreds. The most amazing feature was how sound carried from the lowest level all the way to the top. Someone could stand at the sea wall and whisper and a folk sitting in the topmost row would be able to clearly hear what was said. The seawall itself was also very interesting, for it was elaborately carved, except for one very plain stone. I now knew, as did most folks gathered, that the plain stone was the very stone into which the vessteboks was set.

More and more of the general seats were filling up and, while there was a lot of noise from the conversations going on, the mood in the Well of Speaking was somber. Like the first time I had come to the Well of Speaking, what was going to happen over the next hour or so was going to affect not just the folks here, but all of Sommerhjem. Like the last time, there were still folks outside the walls of the Well of Speaking going about their day, attending the fair as if nothing were more important than what type of berry tart they wanted to try, or seeing whether their entry had won a prize. I felt some irony about that last thought, since the woodcrafts were to be judged this afternoon and, depending on the outcome of the next hour or so, I might never know or care whether my carved shutters were considered worthy by the judges.

Suddenly, a quiet came over the gathered crowd and, looking over at another entrance, I saw the interim ruling council begin to descend the stairs. Upon reaching the bottom of the stairs, the group headed to the Speakers Platform and seated themselves. After the interim ruling council was seated, a patrol of royal guard formed a line in front of the platform. Other patrols of royal guards took positions along the outside edges of the Well of Speaking. I know the interim ruling council had requested the presence of the royal guard as a precaution. I just hoped we would have no occasion to call on them this day.

Once the interim ruling council was seated, those who had reserved seats closer to the sea wall began to make their way down. Elders were always given seats close to the Speakers Platform. I saw a group of elder rovers begin the downward descent. I was glad to see Zeroun and Shueller among them. After the elders were seated, others I recognized began to take their seats, including the head royal librarian, Eluta, accompanied by the head royal historian. Master Rollag, Journeyman Evan, Seeker Eshana, and Seeker Odette came down the stairs, accompanied by Beezle, his mother Lady Hadrack, Lady Celik, and her son Elek. As I scanned the crowd, I found Bertram, Oscar, the Jalcones, and Finn all seated together. It was strange to see Da seated among them. Last year on this day, I did not know where Da was, or if he was safe. Even as the events unfolded that day, I was not sure if he would end the day a free man, no longer pursued by Lord Klingflug's followers, or if both of us would be locked away in some deep, dark dungeon, never again to see the light of day. I could not find either Master Clarisse, or Lom's mentor, Ealdred, which had me a bit worried.

I was distracted from searching the crowd when a group of well-dressed folks began to descend the stairs. Leading the group was the former regent, Lord Cedric Klingflug. Others I recognized were Lady Farcroft and Lady Green. As they moved down the stairs, the noise in the Well of Speaking quieted down to a very soft murmur. Time had just run out. Whatever was going to happen this day was about to happen, for it was now a year from the day that the Gylden Sirklene challenge had been called by Lady Esmeralda.

CHAPTER TWENTY-FOUR

As a heavy silence fell over the crowd, an official-looking gentleman stood up from his seat on the Speakers Platform. With grave dignity, he invited those of us who were still standing at the top of the Well of Speaking with our companion animals to please descend the stairs. I felt really self-conscious, since the entire crowd assembled was looking at us.

Before we were even seated, Lord Cedric Klingflug stood up and demanded attention. I was surprised once again at what a very ordinary-looking man of middle years the former regent was, dressed conservatively in black. This man, who had caused so much heartache and trauma for so many in Sommerhjem, should look imposing and downright evil, not like someone you would pass on the street and not even give a second glance. Even his voice, when he started speaking, did not ring out with power or command.

"I demand that this farce of an interim ruling council be disbanded. We have gone along with your foolishness long enough concerning an oppgave ringe and a challenge. Well, even your precious Book of Rules said that there needed to be nine rings in the vessteboks by this day. Are there nine? You, rover, yes you, the one with the mangy hunting cat, go count the rings in the box, since you are the so-called key."

Well, the former regent certainly has not improved his manners or his like for rovers over the last year, I thought. *His eyesight also has not improved, since Carz' coat is shining in the bright sunlight. Mangy indeed!*

As reluctant as I was to do as the former regent had so ungraciously asked, I stood up and, with as much dignity as I possessed, walked to the seawall where the vessteboks was housed. Slowly, I opened the small gold box, hoping beyond hope that the ninth ring would be there. Unfortunately, there was still an empty post where the ninth ring should rest. I turned to face the crowd and quietly said that there were only eight rings present.

"What did you say, rover?" Lord Klingflug asked, with a sneer in his voice. "No ninth ring, did you say? Well then, I demand that the Gylden Sirklene challenge be termed null and void. Done. In addition, I demand I be placed back as regent. After all, I have the most experience."

"There is actually one who has a better claim to the rule of this country than you," stated Lord Hadrack from the Speakers Platform.

"I suppose you think it should be Lady Esmeralda. Well, she had her chance a year ago to stand up and take her place as the next queen of Sommerhjem. She was an untried lass, then, who was not very popular with the folks she was supposed to rule. She stepped down and called this ridiculous challenge instead. She does not get to just change her mind a year later. 'Oh well, now that the challenge is not happening, I guess I will be queen after all'," Lord Klingflug said, in a high-pitched voice, mimicking Lady Esmeralda.

"I think you might be surprised as to Lady Esmeralda's popularity among the folks of Sommerhjem," Lord Hadrack interrupted. "She may have been young and untried a year ago. She may have been less than popular with those she was to rule, as you intended by keeping her isolated. This past year, she has grown into an outstanding young woman and leader. The trouble with you, Lord Klingflug, is you rarely check what the common folk are thinking and feeling. If you did, you would have noted that Lady Esmeralda has become very well-liked and respected, not only here in the capital, but in the surrounding countryside. I think we would be well-led by Lady Esmeralda, if it comes to that."

All of us in the Well of Speaking were now leaning forward in our seats. There was not a sound to be heard, other than the voices of the two men speaking. The tension was thick. I am not sure anyone was even breathing.

"Gentlemen, I think I can resolve this dilemma we find ourselves in," said Lady Esmeralda quite calmly, as she rose from her seat.

"I will not agree to you standing there and declaring yourself queen, nor will many others," said Lord Klingflug, his face red with anger.

"I have no intention of going back on my word, given when I stepped down as heir to the throne and called the Gylden Sirklene challenge. I truly believe that we need to go back to the old ways of choosing the next ruler of Sommerhjem. Do I think I have just as much of a right to go through the challenge as you or anyone else in Sommerhjem? Yes, I do."

"Fat lot of good those lofty words are going to do you. The challenge is never going to happen, since the ninth ring is not in the vessteboks right now," stated Lord Klingflug.

"If I may interrupt this debate for a moment," said Master Clarisse, who had been joined near the sea wall by Ealdred and a master from the Glassmakers Guild.

I wondered what others in the amphitheater thought of the trio standing there. Master Clarisse had a presence about her that commanded attention, as did Ealdred, a very tall thin man with vines growing out of his boot tops and twining up his body into his beard. The master from the Glassmakers Guild was a slender woman who would be distinctive wherever she went, for, like the glass she made, her skin was translucent in appearance, and her hair was the color of frosted glass.

I had not seen any of them come into the Well of Speaking, since, like all of the others, I had been watching the exchange between Lord Klingflug, Lord Hadrack, and Lady Esmeralda.

"What, you want to add more sketchy information from the so-called Book of Rules?" Lord Klingflug asked impatiently. "Once again, you could be telling us anything, since most of us cannot read the old language."

"That argument is old and tiresome," suggested Seeker Eshana, rising from his seat. "As you well know, the rover Shueller is here, and I am sure he has brought his truth stone with him. Would you like to test the truth stone yourself this time?"

Lord Klingflug quickly stated that would not be necessary. I guess I could understand why the former regent was nervous about handling a truth stone, considering what he probably had to hide. I am sure many in the amphitheater would have liked to get a truth stone in Lord Klingflug's hands and ask him questions. Alas, this was not the time or the place for that to happen.

"I, for one, would welcome a truth stone. Shueller, would you be so kind as to bring yours forward?" asked Master Clarisse. "Any volunteers to make sure that the stone Shueller is bringing to me is actually a truth stone?"

There was complete silence in the amphitheater. Finally, a well-respected grain merchant stood up.

"Merchant Ryman, if you would step forward, please. Thank you for volunteering for something which is most likely going to be painful," said Seeker Eshana. "Is Merchant Ryman acceptable to you to test the truth stone, Lord Klingflug?"

It was interesting to see what was happening within the group that had come with Lord Klingflug. Lady Furman, Lord Hindre, Lady Padde, and Lady Green, all folks who had been pointed out to me as folks aligned with Lady Farcroft, had moved slightly away from Lord Klingflug and were talking among themselves. Lady Farcroft moved closer to Lord Klingflug and whispered something in his ear. Despite the amazing acoustics in the Well of Speaking, I could not hear what she said. Whatever it was certainly did not please Lord Klingflug. Turning to Seeker Eshana, Lord Klingflug reluctantly accepted Merchant Ryman as a tester of the truth stone.

"You and others sitting with you still have a chance to be the tester, if you would like," Seeker Eshana said to Lord Klingflug. "No takers, then? All right, Merchant Ryman, I thank you for volunteering. In advance, I would like to apologize for any harm that may come to you."

"No need to apologize. I was here a year ago and know what to expect."

"Shueller, if you would be so kind as to place the truth stone in Merchant Ryman's hand and ask him a question."

Shueller stepped forward and handed the truth stone to Merchant Ryman. "Now then, is your last name Ryman?" Shueller asked.

"Yes."

All in the amphitheater could see the merchant standing tall, holding the truth stone. Nothing had changed when he was asked his name. Nothing changed when Shueller asked him if he was a grain merchant, and if he was particularly knowledgeable about the grain rye. It was when he asked the merchant if he lived in Farlig Brygge, and Merchant Ryman answered "yes" that things changed. It was obvious that he was lying, since his family had lived in the capital for as long as anyone could remember. Merchant Ryman grimaced and almost dropped the truth stone. Anyone with eyes could tell that he was hurting.

"Do you wish for us to continue to ask Merchant Ryman questions that he needs to lie to, or are you convinced that the stone is indeed a truth stone?" Seeker Eshana asked.

Lord Klingflug was wise enough to state he and others were satisfied that the stone that Merchant Ryman was holding was indeed a truth stone. Merchant Ryman, with heartfelt relief, quickly handed the truth stone back to Shueller, who in turn, placed it Master Clarisse's hand.

"What the Book of Rules clearly states is that all of the pieces of the oppgave ringe need to be here one year from the day the Gylden Sirklene challenge was called," said Master Clarisse.

"Well, it is a year from the day that the challenge was called. We have checked the vessteboks and there are only eight pieces of the oppgave ringe there. I would suggest that the conditions of the challenge have not been met, so we need to adjourn this assembly and meet to figure out what to do next. I, for one, am qualified to return and rule Sommerhjem," said Lord Klingflug smugly.

All at once the Well of Speaking was filled with any number of folks, all talking at the same time. Finally, the same official-looking gentleman who had invited those of us accompanied by companion animals to come down into the amphitheater stood and pounded his staff on the Speakers Platform and called for silence.

"If I may continue," said Master Clarisse. She waited until there was relative silence once again. "The Book of Rules states that all of the pieces of the oppgave ringe need to be here a year from the day the challenge is called."

"Yes, yes, we all know that. So, as I just stated, time is up," said Lord Klingflug, quite emphatically. Those gathered around him were nodding their heads in agreement.

"Actually, time is not up," said Master Clarisse. "The Book of Rules does not state that the pieces of the oppgave ringe need to be in the vessteboks at the exact hour and minute that the challenge was called. It says the pieces need to be here a year from the day, and the day has not ended yet. Before you and others go declaring that you should be made ruler of Sommerhjem, perhaps you need to wait until the clock strikes midnight."

Mutters and murmurs, multiple conversations, and arguments began swirling around the Well of Speaking. Once again, the official-looking gentleman pounded his staff and called for order.

"You are just stalling for time," Lord Klingflug retorted. "You and I both know there has been no word, no trace of the ninth piece of the oppgave ringe. All of the folks you have had looking for it have failed."

"As far as I can tell, all of the folks you have had scouring the countryside and waylaying innocent folks have also failed," countered Lady Celik. She held up her hand to prevent Lord Klingflug from speaking. "I, for one, am willing to wait until the midnight hour before conceding that the ninth piece of the oppgave ringe is not going to arrive. You can leave the amphitheater if you wish. Anyone else willing to wait, please stand up."

The noise of hundreds of folks rising to their feet should have been deafening, and yet it was eerily quiet. Well over two-thirds of the folks in the Well of Speaking stood up.

"I think you have your answer as to whether folks here wish to have this assembly dismissed," suggested Lord Hadrack. "If the ninth piece of the oppgave ringe has not appeared by the stroke of midnight, we will dismiss this assembly and convene in the morning here to discuss what should happen next. Each group, including yours, Lord Klingflug, can bring your ideas before the interim ruling council."

"Why do you get to decide what to do next?" Lord Klingflug asked petulantly.

"You really did not think that if the challenge failed to materialize, that you could just step back into being the regent, did you?" questioned Lord Hadrack.

Before Lord Klingflug could answer that question, Tashi, the griff falcon took flight, her golden wing feathers and red tail feathers flashing like fire in the sun. I looked down and saw that all of the other companion animals had also begun to move.

Chapter Twenty-Five

Carz gave an impatient glance over his shoulder, which I interpreted to mean he wanted me to go with him. I noticed the others also began to walk with their companion animals. Carz and I led the way, followed by the rest of the group in pairs, with Meryl taking up the rear. We headed straight to the Speakers Platform where the interim ruling council was sitting.

"Now, just what foolishness is this? What is going on here?" Lord Klingflug asked, almost shouting. His face was turning an alarming shade of purple.

Other voices joined Lord Klingflug's, and the noise level in the Well of Speaking again began to rise. All talk abruptly ceased when Seeker Eshana drew himself up to his impressive height, flung his formal blue seeker's robe over his shoulder, and pounded his walking stick on the stone pavers. The sound of his walking stick hitting stone rang out like claps of thunder.

"I would suggest that we remain seated and silent."

That was all he said, and I will tell you, if I had been one of the folks standing or talking at that moment, I would have sat down and been as quiet as a mouse. As it was, I was trying to stay next to Carz, and look like I knew what was going on, which was difficult, since I did not know what was happening.

When we reached the Speakers Platform, the animals split apart, forming two lines. Each of us stood next to our companion animal. Carz and I stood next to the steps. Those sitting on the Speakers Platform were looking at us and each other, not sure if we were there for them, not sure if they should get up, descend the stairs, and walk out along the pathway we had formed. Tashi took that decision out of their hands when she glided down and headed straight toward Lady Esmeralda.

Lady Esmeralda instinctively held out her arm. Tashi landed on it and climbed up to her shoulder. I heard a collective sigh rise from the gathered crowd. Those members of the interim ruling council who were seated between Lady Esmeralda and the stairs stood and stepped behind their chairs in order to let Lady Esmeralda and Tashi pass.

I felt someone come up to stand opposite me. Glancing over, I saw it was Meryl. When I gave her a questioning look, she just slightly shrugged her shoulders. She seemed to have no more idea as to what was happening than I did.

Lady Esmeralda walked to and descended the stairs. When she reached the bottom of the stairs, Tashi left her shoulder and settled on Meryl's. Very quietly, Lady Esmeralda said, "It is all right. I did not expect an escort, however."

I could hear soft murmurs running through the crowd, for they had heard what Lady Esmeralda said. As she began to pass down the corridor we had formed, I heard Lord Klingflug speak out.

"I demand to know what is going on here. What trickery is this? Does anyone else not realize this is just a delaying tactic? They have trained that bird to perform this trick so we do not get to the real issue here, and that is the fact that the so-called challenge is a farce. I should never have been forced to step down. I am still the regent. Royal guard, stop those folks."

I took a quick glance in Lord Klingflug's direction, and he was so mad he looked to be frothing at the mouth. Once again, Seeker Eshana struck his walking stick on the stones beneath his feet. Silence again fell over the gathering.

"I think we should all settle down and see what is about to happen," stated Lord Hadrack. "Lord Klingflug, I would respectfully suggest you take your seat. The royal guard is not going to stop what is going on. For that matter, I am not sure they could. If you personally would like to tangle with two night wolves, a bog fox, a well-trained border dog, a hunting cat, and a mountain cat, not to mention a halekrets and a griff falcon, please be our guest." Lord Hadrack paused to look at Lord Klingflug and those seated with him. "No? Then we need to all take a collective breath and see what is about to unfold here."

By the time Lord Hadrack had finished speaking, Lady Esmeralda had walked to the head of the column we made and was leading us back to the seawall where the vessteboks was. When she reached the vessteboks, she turned and faced the assembled crowd.

"It has long been the tradition to break the royal seal when a ruler dies and to make a new one for the next ruler. When my mother, Queen Octavia, died, her royal seal was broken and replaced by one made for me, since it was assumed I would be the next queen."

"Yes, yes, we all know that. So what?" Lord Klingflug said under his breath, forgetting he was in the Well of Speaking and all could hear him.

"Kindly allow me to continue, Lord Klingflug," Lady Esmeralda stated graciously.

Lord Klingflug ducked his head and looked for all the world as if he were concentrating on a spot on his pants.

"As I was saying, when a ruler dies, the royal seal of that ruler is broken, and a new seal is struck for the new ruler. In breaking the seal, the stem that holds the seal remains intact and is used again. When I abdicated the Crown, no one thought to break my seal. Just recently, I discovered there is more than one reason to break the seal. The first would be obvious. Once a ruler has died, the ruler's seal is no longer valid. The second reason is that inside the holder of the seal is a small compartment, which I was not aware of until about a week ago."

Lady Esmeralda drew out a chain and held it up. At the end of the chain was a golden pine spider silk pouch. She opened the pouch, and very carefully tipped the royal seal holder out onto her hand. She then tipped the royal seal holder upside down. I was not close enough to see what fell into her hand, but whatever it was flashed brightly in the sun.

"Interestingly enough, the ninth piece of the oppgave ringe has been in the capital all along, as I suspect it always is, for inside the small compartment of the royal seal I found a piece of the oppgave ringe. I also suspect it is not usually the ninth piece placed in the vessteboks, but the first."

"This is a trick. Can you folks not see that? This is just a trick," stated Lord Klingflug emphatically.

"If this is a trick, then nothing is going to happen when I place the ring in the vessteboks," stated Lady Esmeralda calmly.

Lights had risen out of the vessteboks each previous time a piece of the oppgave ringe had been placed, and I could only hope that that was what would hold true when Lady Esmeralda placed the ninth ring. If not, who knew what would happen next? I think all of us held our breaths when she placed the ring in the vessteboks. Nothing happened.

I was sure that Lord Klingflug and others would not be very patient at this point. I was expecting another outburst to come any moment. I turned to see what was happening behind me. Lord Klingflug was just opening his mouth to speak when he abruptly closed it. I turned back to see what had silenced him. I certainly was not prepared for what happened next. Flowing up over the seawall came dozens and dozens of blue will-o'-wisps. At the very same time, a golden light began to rise out of the vessteboks, rising higher and higher, until it arched out in all directions. I cannot tell you how long the light lasted. When it finally faded, it sounded like everyone in the Well of Speaking took a collective breath.

The majority of the blue will-o'-wisps continued to hover over the vessteboks. The remaining blue will-o'-wisps broke away from the others and headed toward those of us standing next to our companion animals. As I watched the blue specks of light drift toward us, Carz leaned against me. I found great comfort in him being so close. In the next few moments, I needed that comfort and reassurance, for the blue will-o'-wisps came straight toward me, forming a line from me to the vessteboks. Carz gently grabbed my hand in his mouth and pulled me forward. As I moved forward, the blue will-o'-wisps retreated.

Once I was standing by the vessteboks, Master Clarisse stepped forward. Giving me a reassuring look, she turned and faced the folks assembled in the amphitheater.

"According to the Book of Rules, when the last piece of the oppgave ringe is placed in the vessteboks, once again two keys will be needed to remove the box from where it rests in the plain stone in the seawall. A year ago, the metal key that Nissa brought to open the vessteboks was placed in safekeeping. Master Rollag, do you still have the key?" asked Master Clarisse.

I had, over the last year, never even wondered what had happened to the key I had used to open the vessteboks. So much had happened that day that the key had completely slipped my mind. It is a good thing that others had thought to rescue it.

It took a few moments for Master Rollag to make his way down to where we were standing. He reached in his shirt and pulled out a pouch made of golden pine spider silk. Opening the pouch, he tipped its contents out onto his hand. The little key looked very tiny in his large hand. He turned to hand the key to Master Clarisse. She shook her head and indicated that she thought he needed to give the key to me.

So much for getting all dressed up and going with the others to the Well of Speaking just to see what was going to happen, I thought. *My wish to not have anything more to do with the Gylden Sirklene challenge or the oppgave ringe, to just be able to go back to my booth and settle in to being a rover woodworker, is not about to happen this day.*

It was with some reluctance I stepped forward and accepted the key from Master Rollag. I reached down to touch Carz, just for reassurance, and I felt something swiftly run up my arm. I remember that happening the last time I had been about to place the key in the very small key hole. As I had a year ago, I did not jump when I felt something run up my arm, nor did I try to brush it off. I felt a very slight weight settle between my shoulders beneath the thick single braid that fell down my back. A feeling of extreme peace settled over me.

As I took a deep breath, it seemed like I was being transported back to the first time I had been asked to be the living key. Like then, no one stopped me. No one said a word. There was an unnatural stillness to the air, and I once again felt as if time had stopped. I was no longer aware of the sound of the sea crashing on the rocks below me, or the blue of the sky above me. I no longer could hear the rustle of the clothing of hundreds of folks behind me. I was only aware of the key in my hand, which grew warmer with each step I took toward the plain stone set in the sea wall, and of the slight weight on my back, which also grew warmer with each step I took. The only difference this time was I was surrounded by blue will-o'-wisps.

Even though the keyhole was very small, it was once again easy to see, for it was emanating a slight bluish glow. Holding my hand steady, I inserted the key into the keyhole and turned it once to the right. I heard a click. As I had done the last time, I then turned the key to the left and heard a second click and a grinding noise.

I wondered what was going to happen when I turned the key that last turn back to the right. When I had reached this point a year ago, I had turned the key one more time to the right, the vessteboks had sunk farther into the recess in the plain stone, and a light had shone forth of such intensity that all of us had stepped back and shielded our eyes. When I turned the key to the right again this time, that did not happen. Rather than sinking farther down into the stone or sending up another shaft of light, the vessteboks rose up out of the plain seawall stone, its lid closing slowly. I did not even think about what I should do next, but instinctively stepped forward and lifted up the vessteboks. The blue will-o'-wisps continued to surround me.

Master Clarisse's voice rang out. "The nine pieces of the oppgave ringe have been placed in the vessteboks in the proper time, fulfilling the first step in completing the Gylden Sirklene challenge. Does anyone here contest this?"

I stood holding the vessteboks surrounded by blue will-o'-wisps, all the while holding my breath. I wondered what those who opposed the Crown and did not wish the Gylden Sirklene challenge to happen would do. There was only silence.

"I ask again, does anyone dispute that the nine pieces of the oppgave ringe have been placed in the proper time in the vessteboks?" Master Clarisse asked.

Once again, there was only silence in the Well of Speaking. Finally, Lady Farcroft spoke up. I am sure she surprised those gathered here, for most of them probably only saw her as a somewhat ineffectual, dithering woman. Very few knew her as a shrewd, cunning adversary of the Crown. It would seem she had had enough of hiding as a very silent partner behind Lord Klingflug.

Lady Farcroft stood and, looking down her nose, asked in a haughty tone, "What does your precious Book of Rules suggest we do next, now that the ninth ring is here?"

CHAPTER TWENTY-SIX

"Thank you for asking," said Master Clarisse in reply to Lady Farcroft's question. "According to the Book of Rules, the oppgave ringe needs to be put together ...."

Before Master Clarisse could finish speaking, Lord Klingflug not so gently pushed Lady Farcroft back. "I suppose the interim ruling council is going to take over the vessteboks now. I demand that others of us be present when the oppgave ringe is being assembled."

"Well now, that is an interesting suggestion," Master Clarisse said mildly. "I think the one who is supposed to put the oppgave ringe together should have the choice of whether she wants an audience or not."

"She, what do you mean, she? Who is she?" asked Lady Farcroft, stepping forward again, casting a shadow on Lord Klingflug, since she was half a head taller than he was.

"Why, I think it would be obvious. Nissa, of course. I do not know about you folks, but I do not think I would want to, or even could, take the vessteboks out of Nissa's hands. Besides, who better to try to figure out the puzzle of putting the oppgave ringe together than one who makes beautiful, very difficult, and complex puzzle boxes?" Master Clarisse suggested.

As I stood there surrounded by blue will-o'-wisps holding the golden vessteboks, I could not believe what Master Clarisse was suggesting. *Oh, this cannot be happening. Making puzzle boxes does not make me a puzzle expert. Maybe I can just hand the vessteboks over to someone else,* I thought.

Even as I was thinking of turning and handing the vessteboks over to Seeker Eshana or Master Rollag or Master Clarisse, anyone but me, the blue will-o'-wisps drew in even closer. In addition, something shifted slightly on my back under my braid, and a reassuring warmth spread through my body, calming me. I brought my attention back to what was going on around me. Lady Farcroft was still speaking.

"Once the oppgave ringe is assembled, then what? For that matter, is there a timeline for when this needs to be done?"

"I cannot answer your second question, for the putting together of the oppgave ringe will take as long as it takes," replied Master Clarisse.

"What is to prevent that rover lass from stalling?" asked Lord Klingflug, pushing his way forward again. When he said the word "rover," no one could fail to hear the loathing in his voice.

"To be honest, there is nothing to prevent the rover Nissa from taking her own sweet time. Knowing Nissa, however, I cannot see her doing anything other than working day and night to solve the puzzle of the oppgave ringe. Now," said Master Clarisse, turning to Lady Farcroft, "in answer to your first question as to what happens after the oppgave ringe is put together, the Book of Rules, as usual, is not specific. What I can tell you is the oppgave ringe is the key to the next step. What the Book of Rules suggests, is that the oppgave ringe will unlock a way to the Gylden Sirklene challenge. It suggests that there is a gate that needs to be found."

Before either Lady Farcroft or Lord Klingflug could ask any more questions or raise any more objections, Lord Hadrack began to speak.

"The interim ruling council has asked me to announce that the first condition of the Gylden Sirklene challenge has been fulfilled. As you all know, when Lady Esmeralda called the challenge last year, the nine pieces of the oppgave ringe needed to be in the vessteboks a year from the day. That has now happened. This assembly is now dismissed. I suggest we all go and enjoy the rest of the fair."

Over the objections coming from those who opposed the Crown, the interim ruling council stood, stepped down from the Speakers Platform, and began the long climb up the stairs of the Well of Speaking, followed by the elders. In an amazingly short time, the only ones left in the amphitheater were the seekers, Da, Master Rollag, Master Clarisse, Beezle, Journeyman Evan, Finn, Lady Esmeralda, and the eight of us who stood with our companion animals. Also remaining were several patrols of royal guards, who waited discreetly at the top of the stairs. Other royal guard patrols had escorted Lord Klingflug and Lady Farcroft's contingent and all other stragglers out of the amphitheater. I would be remiss in my counting of who was there if I forgot to also mention the several dozen blue will-o'-wisps who still surrounded me.

Lady Esmeralda turned to me and asked if I was all right.

"A bit bewildered. I also must admit that while the vessteboks is not all that heavy, I am getting a bit uncomfortable holding it."

"Of course you are," suggested Master Clarisse. "I propose we move from here and head back to the royal palace."

"I do have a request," I told the assembled group. "I left Shyla and Nana alone at my booth. Da, would you be so kind as to go and tell them what is going on. Give them the choice to either keep the booth open or close it."

"Knowing your Nana, she will insist on keeping it open. I think a discussion needs to be had the next time the interim ruling council meets about some compensation for you, since you are losing valuable sales and chances for commissions while carrying out tasks for the Crown," said Da.

I was not sure how I felt about Da's suggestion. Now was not the time to discuss it, for I really wanted to move from here and find some place to set the vessteboks down. Da assured me he would talk to Shyla and Nana, and told me I was not to worry. When he told me not to worry, he could not keep his own worry out of his eyes.

Another reason I wished to leave the Well of Speaking was I wanted to ask Lady Esmeralda a few questions, as I am sure others in our group did. I just thought it prudent not to ask her here, for anyone remaining, even those at the top of the stairs, would be able to hear our questions and her answers.

By the time we reached the small parlor we usually met in, I was very tired. Not so much from carrying the vessteboks, but from the added burden that I was supposed to assemble the oppgave ringe. Wooden puzzle boxes I understand. I had never worked with any type of puzzle that had to do with metal rings. As I sat down, Master Clarisse came over to me.

"I think it would be all right if you want to set the vessteboks down for a moment and have something to eat and drink," Master Clarisse said gently. "Even the blue will-o'-wisps seem to have backed off."

I realized I had not noticed. They were still there, but were scattered about the room, mostly near the ceiling, and their light had faded to a soft blue. Gratefully, I sank back into a comfortable chair and accepted a cool fruit drink from Seeker Chance.

Before any of us could ask the main question that was on all of our minds, Lady Esmeralda spoke up. "I imagine all of you have questions about the ninth piece of the oppgave ringe. Theora, will you please check to make sure no one is lingering outside, and then close the door? Beezle, will you please check the secret panel by the fireplace and make sure no one is lurking nearby?"

Beezle and Theora did as Lady Esmeralda asked.

"First, I must apologize for not telling any of you that I had found the ninth piece of the oppgave ringe. I am not sure I can explain why I did not. It is not that I do not trust every one of you in this room with my life. I have already done that with a number of you. Something just held me back."

"I personally think that was a very wise idea," stated Piper. "We all know that there have been and are folks here in the royal palace who are not as loyal to the Crown as those gathered here in this parlor. Had it leaked out that you had found the ninth ring, who knows what might have happened."

"Now, the real question is, how did you discover it?" asked Seeker Chance.

"There is some irony that you are the one to ask that question," said Lady Esmeralda.

When Seeker Chance raised an inquiring eyebrow, Lady Esmeralda explained.

"It was actually Ashu's doing."

"Ashu?"

"Yes. About a week ago, when we were all concentrating on some text or map, I cannot remember exactly what, the chain that holds the royal seal was bothering my neck. One of the links has a kink in it, and it was scratching me. I lifted the chain over my head and laid it down on a table, which incidentally held some of Ashu's favorite nuts."

"You do spoil him, you know," admonished Seeker Chance. "I have even seen him sit on your lap while you patiently crack open the nuts for him."

"Ah, well, yes, you are correct. I have been known, upon occasion, to crack open a nut shell or two for Ashu. That day, however, I was busy with some of you, and Ashu took it upon himself to crack open the nuts. Since the table top was made of polished rock, all he needed was something to pound the nut with."

"I am beginning to get a glimmer of where this story is going," said Seeker Eshana.

"It would seem that although the royal seal is very sturdy for using with sealing wax, it is not really built to be used to crack nuts. In the process of trying to crack the nut, Ashu knocked the royal seal out of its holder. I looked up just in time to see him scamper off the table and pick up the royal seal, which oddly enough had not broken in the process. When I reached him, he handed the royal seal to me, and then looked at me expectantly."

"What a little rascal," laughed Seeker Chance. "I bet he was hoping you would crack a few nuts. I really should not be laughing, since he should not have been using the royal seal to pound nuts ...."

"There is some humor in the whole scene," said Lady Esmeralda. "At any rate, I quickly put the royal seal and its holder in my pocket, cracked a few nuts for Ashu and, then, got back to whatever we were studying. I did not get back to looking at the royal seal until later that night when I was getting ready for bed. I had examined it before and noticed that the border around the quirrelit tree symbol we found in the middle of the floor in the chamber here matches the border around the royal seal holder. I had found nothing else at that time. This time as I looked at the seal and the holder and tried to figure out whether I could put them back together, I noticed something was loose inside the holder. It was then that I discovered the ninth piece of the oppgave ringe. Ashu really is the hero of the day."

I was glad for the humor and distraction of Lady Esmeralda's tale. It took my mind off the task it would seem I had been chosen for. When it was quiet again and I had a chance to think more, I realized I had questions for Master Clarisse.

"Master Clarisse, does the Book of Rules specifically state a very reluctant rover lass is supposed to be the one chosen to put the oppgave ringe together?" I asked.

"Were that the Book of Rules was that specific. It would certainly make this whole Gylden Sirklene challenge easier to figure out. No, the book only says a living key needs to put the oppgave ringe together. You have proven to be a living key. It is also good that you have a puzzle-solving type of mind," said Master Clarisse.

"So there might be another living key?" I asked hopefully.

"There might," replied Master Clarisse. "You seem reluctant to take on the task. That, you should know, is completely understandable. All of you gathered in this room have been asked to take on a great many tasks and risks for the Crown during the last year. As anxious as you all may be to return to your former lives, or to get on with the new paths you are now journeying along, I think we all need to see through to its end what Lady Esmeralda started when she called the challenge."

"We could each of us approach the vessteboks and see what might happen. Maybe it will be different this time." Greer explained that they had gone to the Well of Speaking one day and thought to try to touch the rings. None of them had been able to do so.

"So, you, Nissa, are the only one who has handled more than one of the rings," said Master Rollag, who had been quiet up to this point.

"I have held at least three of them so far," I answered.

"I'll go first," said Lom.

I was surprised that he had volunteered to go first, for he was more apt to stand back and observe what was going on before acting. When I thought more about it, I realized he might be the logical one, since he was highly sensitive to objects of power.

Lom stepped forward. He did not get within a foot of the vessteboks before the blue will-o'-wisps swarmed forward, blocking his way.

"Well, that went well, didn't it?" Lom said, stepping quickly back.

Once he stepped away, the blue will-o'-wisps retreated back up to the ceiling. Each of the others, in turn, stepped forward to open the vessteboks. Each time they got within a foot of the table it rested on, the blue will-o'-wisps swarmed forward.

I had to conclude, very reluctantly, that I was the one chosen to put the oppgave ringe together, since it seemed no one else could even get near the vessteboks.

"I guess I had better get started, then," I said.

Chapter Twenty-Seven

Before I could even think about getting up from my chair, much less figuring out where I wanted to work on the oppgave ringe, I heard a discreet knock on the door, followed by the royal steward entering the parlor. He addressed Lady Esmeralda.

"Begging your pardon for the interruption, Lady Esmeralda. Several delegations of nobles headed by either Lord Klingflug or Lady Farcroft are in the entry hall demanding an audience," said the royal steward.

"I had an inkling they would arrive sooner or later. Seems they have arrived sooner," said Lady Esmeralda. "Since I do not want to keep all the fun of meeting with them to myself, Master Rollag, Master Clarisse, Thorval, seekers, would you be so kind as to accompany me?"

"Your pardon once again," said the royal steward. "Several members of the group in the entry hall slipped away before the royal guard contained the group. The head of the royal guard patrol has sent guards off to find them. I just thought I should let you know."

"Thank you, Reave. Please invite those gathered in the entry hall to make themselves comfortable in the Rose parlor. Provide tea and a cart of small cakes and biscuits, please. Let them know we will be there shortly. And please ask the captain of the royal guard to make her presence known," said Lady Esmeralda.

"The Rose parlor? You really do not like those two groups, do you?" said Beezle, chuckling.

"Why would you say that? Just because I had them sent to the most garish, most ugly, and most uncomfortable room in the royal palace does not necessarily mean I do not hold them in high regard. After all, I did request tea and cakes for them," stated Lady Esmeralda.

"Right. What would you like us to do?" asked Beezle.

Lady Esmeralda, all serious now, turned to the rest of us. "Beezle, Meryl, and Finn, would you take Piper, Jing, Theora, and Tala with you and check the passageways within the royal palace? Check first those which the servants and others would most likely know. See if you can find our stray wanderers and escort them out."

"Do you think it is wise for both Piper and me to be away from guarding Nissa?" inquired Theora.

"Oh, I think the vessteboks and I are sufficiently well-guarded," I told the others. "After all, with Carz, Lom, Taarig, Yara, Toki, Greer, Kasa, and Ealdred, plus the blue will-o'-wisps, I should be quite safe."

"Hey, you forgot me," said Journeyman Evan, trying to look quite hurt, which was less than successful, since he was holding a berry tart in one hand and a small drizzle-covered pastry in the other.

"Ah, yes," I said. "My hero, who would fend off a hoard of angry nobles by pelting them with berry tarts and pastries."

"What, and waste good berry tarts? Not to mention pastries," Journeyman Evan quipped, pulling the sweets closer to his body in a mock protective stance.

After all that had happened building up to this day, and the tension of what had gone on in the Well of Speaking a short while ago, it was good to laugh at Journeyman Evan's silliness. After the others departed, those left behind sat back down. For a while, all of us were silent, sipping our tea, and catching our breaths. Finally, Yara broke the silence.

"What do you wish to do next, Nissa?" Yara asked.

"My most fervent wish would be to pack up my homewagon, attach my cart, hitch up my horses, and take to the open road."

"And I would join you," Yara said, with great sympathy in her voice.

"Yet I know that is not a choice I will or would make. So, to answer your question, I would like to get out of this stuffy parlor and go sit on Lom's bench by the doors we uncovered in the cliff wall. I think much better when I am out in the sunlight and fresh air. I should be safe enough, if Lom and Ealdred could ask the tangle to close up behind me. Would that be possible?"

"I think it would be more than possible," Lom answered. "I also am more than grateful for the idea. The pull to the back of the garden has been growing stronger since you brought the vessteboks here. It has been all I could do to sit inside this long."

Most of us could not stand up fast enough to move out of the parlor and out of the royal palace, with the exception of Journeyman Evan, whom I saw take the time to swipe a few more pastries. I raised an eyebrow in his direction. He just grinned back at me and told me he was still a growing lad.

Though the royal guard set outside the parlor objected, they stepped back when I exited the parlor surrounded by blue will-o'-wisps and my companions. I was so glad when we stepped out of the royal palace and onto the grounds. When I glanced up at the blue sky, I thought I could detect a slight golden haze still in the air, but that may have been my imagination.

Once we got to the tangle, the foliage drew back so we could walk down the path. The others stepped back from where they had stationed themselves to surround me. Greer suggested I go first.

Tucking the vessteboks more comfortably under my arm, I stepped forward onto the path that led through the tangle to the clearing. When I looked over my shoulder past those who were following me, I could see the tangle closing up behind us. As I entered the clearing, blue light shot up from the blue half-globes set into the path edge. The blue will-o'-wisps spread out away from me and began to perform a beautiful dance around and through the blue lights. I stopped for a moment just to watch. Carz, not quite as entranced as I was, nudged me from behind, suggesting I get a move on.

I decided to walk the labyrinth. I am not sure why. I could have just walked to the cliff wall without going through the labyrinth. It simply seemed like the respectful and proper action to take. Just before I stepped onto the labyrinth path, I thought about what Seeker Eshana and Seeker Chance had said about what they knew about labyrinths. The herbalist whose labyrinth they walked had suggested that it could be helpful in calming the mind and finding pathways to answers. I certainly needed a calm mind and answers.

I stopped, took a deep calming breath, and tried to empty my mind of all thoughts other than putting the oppgave ringe together. I, then, stepped forward. Sound and time began to fade away. I felt as if I was wrapped within a warm cocoon of calm and peace. As I moved farther and farther through the labyrinth, I was aware of only the path and Carz. Even my awareness of them faded. Soon I was moving without thought and was surprised when I stepped back out of the labyrinth. Taking the left hand path toward the cliff wall, I knew, without knowing how I knew, that I needed to study the carvings on the cliff doors before I opened the vessteboks.

"I want to thank the rest of you for going with me to meet with Lord Klingflug, Lady Farcroft, and the others. I was certainly not looking forward to the meeting in the Well of Speaking, even though I knew I had the ninth piece of the oppgave ringe. I think if the royal guard had not been there to escort them out of the amphitheater, we might still be there. They certainly do not give up easily," said Lady Esmeralda.

"They always think they have more rights and privileges than anyone else," said Master Rollag. "Wealth and power does not always bring out the best in folks. Some folks are spoiled by privilege, and they are the first to complain about the success of those like Lord Hadrack. He is a fair and kind overseer of the land he holds."

"Or Chance's father, Lord Avital, a man who works right alongside those who live on his land. His success in the wool and weaving trade is strong proof of what really works," suggested Seeker Eshana.

"Master Clarisse, I would like you to be my partner in taking the lead for this meeting we both do not want to be at," said Lady Esmeralda ruefully. "If things begin to get out of hand, I hope I can count on you, Seeker Eshana, Seeker Odette, and Seeker Chance, to take your imposing and commanding seeker stances. Feel free to pound your walking sticks, or whack folks with them, or whatever gets their attention quickest."

"I think we will refrain from hitting any of the gathered nobles. Bad form," said Seeker Odette with a slight grin.

"Your choice," said Lady Esmeralda, adjusting her skirt as if adjusting her armor in preparation for battle. "Let us see if we can send this group packing with as little fuss and bother as possible." Putting a welcoming smile on her face, which clearly did not reach her eyes, Lady Esmeralda nodded to the royal steward to open the Rose parlor door.

"Ladies, gentlemen, I hope you have been comfortable while you have waited. Please excuse our delay," said Lady Esmeralda graciously.

"We demand to have someone present to watch what this rover lass is doing. Do you not understand that rovers are thieves and worse? You must know they are not to be trusted. Why that Nissa ..." Lord Klingflug sputtered, practically frothing at the mouth, "... right this minute she, she ...."

"Are you suggesting that my daughter and I, along with all other rovers, are not to be trusted? Are you suggesting Nissa cannot be trusted to do what is right for Sommerhjem?" asked Thorval. His voice was as hard and as hot as the metal he worked fresh out of the forge.

Lady Farcroft stepped forward, realizing that Lord Klingflug's attitude and approach would get them nowhere. "What we really wish for is to have a representative or two here at the royal palace monitoring what is going on."

"You already do," suggested Master Rollag. "Like the guilds, the merchants, the fishers, the farmers, the foresters, and others, including the rovers, we all have representatives on the interim ruling council. To add more nobles to the mix would violate the instructions in the Book of Rules. Just like the rest of us, you need to talk to your representatives. Would that not be correct, Master Clarisse?"

"I believe so," answered Master Clarisse.

"Anyone else? No? Then, please, feel free to finish your tea. I think this meeting is concluded," said Lady Esmeralda, turning and leading her group back out of the Rose parlor. She could hear Lord Klingflug sputtering behind her. "That was thoroughly unpleasant. Makes me want to go take a long hot soak, like you want after traveling in a hard cold rain on muddy roads. Let us get back to the small parlor and friendly folks."

I sat down on the bench we had moved near the cliff wall and the doors. The others arranged themselves either under the quirrelit tree or a bit away from me, giving me space to try to puzzle out what I should do next. While I suspected all of them had a great many questions, I was extremely thankful they held back from asking them, for I did not have any answers. The only thing I knew for sure was coming here to this bench was the right choice. I set the vessteboks down and began studying the arch over the doors, and the doors themselves. I had a very strong feeling there were clues here, if only I could decipher them.

After quite some time, being no closer to an answer than when I had sat down, I picked up the vessteboks and opened it, surprised in a way that it was not locked, even though I had pocketed the small key I had used at the seawall this time. I knew I would be able to touch the first two rings lined up in the box, since I had placed them there. I also knew I could touch the fourth ring, the one Meryl had placed in the vessteboks, for I had held it before. The real test would be if I could pick up any of the other rings.

I slowly reached into the vessteboks, hesitated just a short moment, and then picked up the two rings I had placed in the vessteboks and lifted them off their carved quirrelit wood posts. Other than the rings feeling slightly warm, nothing happened. Next I picked up the fourth ring. Again nothing happened, except the fourth ring was also slightly warm.

Others, who had tried to hold one of the pieces of the oppgave ringe and were not supposed to, have come away with very injured hands. As a woodworker, I could not afford to have a hand injured. I needed both of them. It was with some trepidation I reached into the vessteboks for the third ring.

CHAPTER TWENTY-EIGHT

When I reached into the vessteboks for the third ring, the blue will-o'-wisps did not swarm me. I had to look around to see if they were still here. It took me a moment to find them, since they were scattered about in the vines that covered the cliff wall. Although they had protected me on both of the occasions I had encountered them, I was not sure what they would do if I was not the one who should pick up any of the other pieces of the oppgave ringe.

Encouraged, I reached farther into the vessteboks. When I picked up the third piece of the oppgave ringe, the one Greer had carried to the capital, again, nothing happened. Lights did not flash, the wind did not howl, my hand did not feel searing pain. All I felt, as I held the third ring in my hand, was that it, like the others, was slightly warm.

Since nothing untoward had happened to me so far, I took out the next four rings and set them beside me on the bench next to the first four. All that was left in the vessteboks was the ninth ring. *In for a copper, in for a silver,* I thought, as I reached my hand into the vessteboks one last time. Again, nothing happened. It was almost anticlimactic.

Next, I took the time to take a look at each ring individually. They were all misshapen gold rings, but mighty odd-looking ones. While it was true they were gold rings, they were not a band the likes of which some married folks wear, nor did they have any stones set in them. Each very narrow band looked as if it had been bent out of shape. The more closely I inspected them, the more it looked like the rings had been made that way. Each ring had deep scratches along the band which did not look like a regular pattern. The scratches looked like they had been carved into the band, rather than put there by hard wear. While each ring was similar, the twists in each of them were slightly different, and the grooves just slightly off. None of them matched.

I was a little bit leery of trying to put the rings together, since I remembered something that had been said about the oppgave ringe. A warning had been given that only those who felt that they truly had the right to rule should even attempt the Gylden Sirklene challenge. There, of course, would be those who foolishly thought the Crown should rightfully be theirs, as well as those who would also attempt the challenge but should not. Individuals who fell into both groups attempted the challenge at their own risk. I remembered having heard that the next ruler would be chosen by being able to handle the oppgave ringe without coming to harm.

Did that mean that if I put the oppgave ring together and could hold it unharmed, I was rightfully the next ruler? I wondered. That was certainly enough to give me pause. I knew I did not want to rule Sommerhjem. I just wanted to get back on the road. Being confined to the royal palace grounds these last few weeks had been difficult. I could not imagine having to stay in the capital most of the year, year after year.

Before I did something like putting the vessteboks on a table in the small royal palace parlor, excusing myself, and fleeing, I thought I had best talk to Master Clarisse. I carefully put the rings back into the vessteboks in the order I had taken them out. I was not sure I needed to do this, but I was not taking any chances. Carefully closing up the golden box, I stood up, tucked it once again under my arm, and began to walk the path back toward the tangle. The blue will-o'-wisps left their resting spots on the vines and drifted toward me. The other folks who had accompanied me here fell silently into step behind me.

Once we were out of the tangle, I told the others that I wanted to go to my homewagon, and asked if one of them would ask Master Clarisse to please join me there. Yara volunteered. The rest of us headed back to the campsite. Once we arrived there, I told the others that I had decided to take a break, that I had some questions for Master Clarisse before I continued.

"I can't imagine what is going through your head right now, nor the pressure you are putting on yourself, not to mention the pressure you must feel from the situation you have been put in. I think I would be torn between my duty to Sommerhjem and my want to run to the farthest and highest hill in the land," said Greer.

"And how did you get to be so wise?" I asked.

"Guess it comes from living on the streets for most of my life and now having a home and family in Sommerhjem. The question of what you do and what is needed to survive changes when you have folks who care about you and whom you care about," answered Greer.

"This adventure for you, Greer, reunited you with your family," said Meryl. "My bringing the piece of the oppgave ringe into the capital gave me an excuse, I guess you could say, to leave an unwelcoming family situation and create my own family. In a way, Finn is more of a father to me than my stepfather ever was, and he has unselfishly taught me a trade."

I looked over at Finn and noticed his cheeks were just a bit pink. It was such a contrast to his normally gray appearance. He was saved from having to respond, for at that moment Toki entered the campsite, followed by Yara and Master Clarisse.

"Yara said you needed to speak with me, Nissa," said Master Clarisse.

"Yes, if you please. I hope the rest of you are not offended, but I would like to speak with Master Clarisse alone. We'll just step into my homewagon."

Not one of those gathered objected, so I got up and climbed into my homewagon, followed by Master Clarisse and Carz. I set the vessteboks on the table and sat down, inviting Master Clarisse to join me.

"I'm not sure how to start," I said.

"However you feel comfortable," Master Clarisse replied.

"As I was sitting on what we call Lom's bench in the clearing looking at the doors in the cliff wall, it occurred to me that part of the challenge indicated that whoever would be chosen as the next to rule needed to be able to handle the oppgave ringe."

"According to what we have been able to translate from the Book of Rules, that is correct."

"That is where my dilemma lies. I'm called upon by that same book to assemble the oppgave ringe because I am the living key. Is that correct?"

"Yes."

"That means I will be able to handle the oppgave ringe in pieces and when put together. Does that then mean I'm supposed to be the next ruler of Sommerhjem?"

"Do you wish to be the next ruler of Sommerhjem?" Master Clarisse asked gently.

"Absolutely not."

"Why not?

That question caught me by surprise. I had to take a moment to think about it.

"Besides the fact that the open road calls so strongly to me, that I am a woodworker by trade, that I have no idea how to rule a country?"

"Yes, besides those things."

"I also do not think at this time that a rover being chosen as the next ruler would be in the best interest of Sommerhjem. That is not to say that there are not wise and capable folks among the rovers. Elder Zeroun comes to mind, or my Da. It is just that Lord Klingflug and many of his followers think rovers are the scourge of the earth. I think they could muster an opposition that would tear this country apart, if a rover, especially a young rover, were to become the next ruler."

"Elder Zeroun is not the only wise rover in the capital at this moment. You are also wise, and quite possibly correct in your assumptions," said Master Clarisse gravely.

I glanced questioningly at the vessteboks that sat on the table between us.

"From all we can glean from the Book of Rules, which I have repeatedly stated does not give direct clear instructions, the living key who is to assemble the oppgave ringe should not come to any harm. The living key's tasks are to put the oppgave ringe together and find the gate to the challenge. Apparently, the writer of the Book of Rules was aware that there would be questions concerning the living key's safety. It implies that the living key will not be harmed doing those tasks. That does not answer your main question, however, which is does being able to handle the oppgave ringe automatically make you the next ruler of Sommerhjem? The answer to that question would be 'no'."

I am sure Master Clarisse could see the look of relief on my face.

"Remember, the Book of Rules suggests that anyone who truly feels they have the right to rule can try the challenge. I think that sentence should have been read differently. All of us have the right to rule, if we fulfill the Gylden Sirklene challenge. Willingness to rule also would not be accurate either, for we all know Lord Klingflug, and others who do not side with the Crown, are more than willing to rule. When I read the Book of Rules when the challenge was called a year ago, I was skimming it. Now that I have had time to study the book, it would be more accurate to suggest it was not the right to rule, but the heart to rule. The challenge is supposed to bring forth someone who has the land of Sommerhjem's best interests at heart. It is important to note that the Book of Rules does not say the country of Sommerhjem, but the land of Sommerhjem. I am not sure what to make of that. I do, however, think it is important. Well, that was a pretty longwinded answer to your question," stated Master Clarisse.

"Thank you for sharing the information. I'm relieved that I do not have to unwillingly become the next queen. What you have told me brings up another question. Suppose that someone like another rover, or a gardener like Lom, is supposed to be the next ruler? Won't they be reluctant to come forward to try the challenge, thinking they are not worthy or not qualified?"

"I have thought about that, and I think those who are of the right heart, so to speak, will be somehow called to try the challenge. There is nothing in the Book of Rules that suggests that, mind you. It is just a very strong feeling I have."

"So you think that some folks who have never thought of themselves as a folk who could rule Sommerhjem might be called to go through the challenge?"

"Yes, I truly believe that. Otherwise, how else would you get the true and rightful ruler, if everyone thought that only a wealthy merchant or a higher noble should be the one to rule? It would not be good if someone thought they were just common folk and should not even try, even if they are just what the land needs. Now mind you, a wealthy merchant or a higher noble might be the one chosen. So too, could a weaver, a shepherd, a farmer, a forester, or a rover be the next rightful ruler of Sommerhjem."

"I'm truly glad to know it will not be this rover."

"All I can really say for sure is that, even though you assemble the oppgave ringe and can handle the parts and the whole, you do not automatically become the next queen. I cannot speak for the land," said Master Clarisse.

I was not as relieved as I had hoped I would be by the outcome of my conversation with Master Clarisse. At least I was fairly reassured that, if I could get the pieces of the oppgave ringe together, I would not instantly become the next queen of Sommerhjem. On that note, I accompanied Master Clarisse out of my homewagon and thanked her for her information. She wished me luck in solving the puzzle of the oppgave ringe. Yet I wondered if there was something she was not telling me.

Just as Master Clarisse was leaving, Piper, Jing, Theora, Taarig, and Beezle came through the entrance to the campsite, followed by several royal palace servants carrying trays and baskets.

"As a reward for finding the misplaced members of Lord Klingflug's and Lady Farcroft's entourage, we have provided ourselves with a high tea. Journeyman Evan will be along shortly, along with a few others. He was last seen heading toward the royal bakery, trying to convince Journeywoman Clare to send us some of her pastries. I still have not figured out if Journeyman Evan lingers about the royal palace bakery because he is fonder of Journeywoman Clare or her pastries," said Beezle. "So how is the puzzle of the oppgave ringe coming?"

"The rings are still in the vesteboks." I went on to explain the worries I had expressed to Master Clarisse and her reassurance that being the living key and putting the oppgave ringe together would not instantly make me the next queen of Sommerhjem.

"You would make a good queen," said Lady Esmeralda, who had entered the campsite shortly after those who had accompanied Beezle. "You are brave, courageous, intelligent, and clever. You have faced adversity well and will likely continue to do so. You have been willing to risk your life for others and your country. You have traveled about Sommerhjem and are aware of her many and diverse folks. Do not sell yourself short as a possible candidate."

"Thank you for those kind words. I fervently hope that my becoming the next ruler of Sommerhjem does not come to pass. I feel certain that my destiny lies in being a rover. With that settled, let's see what these kind folks holding those heavy trays and baskets have brought. I suddenly find myself very hungry."

After eating too much, I felt ready to tackle the oppgave ringe. Something I had seen while I was sitting in the clearing was niggling at the back of my mind. I told the others I needed to go back to look at the doors in the cliff wall one more time before the daylight was gone.

Chapter Twenty-Nine

As I moved across the royal palace grounds, more and more blue will-o'-wisps gathered around Carz and me. It was a good thing I was not trying to sneak anywhere unnoticed. Once again, the entrance to the path leading through the tangle opened. The blue half-globes flared and sent up columns of blue light as I passed by. When I reached the doors built into the cliff wall, I realized I was not going to be able to find what I came for, since the sun had already begun to set, and the royal palace prevented the light from reaching this lower back part of the garden. I would need to return on the morrow. Once the sun was up, I would have a little better light than I had now. I also intended to bring a few lanterns. Somewhat discouraged, I headed back to the campsite.

Over the evening meal we had talked about what to do with the vessteboks overnight. It had been finally decided that leaving it in my possession was as good a plan as any.

Yara had remarked at that time, "Who knows what will happen after you get the oppgave ringe put together? I, for one, want to be around to see this through, so I think I will stay close to you and that vessteboks, after what I went through to bring in the sixth ring. I know the others feel the same way. It will be a beautiful night with almost a full moon, and the stars will light up the sky overhead."

Piper, too, had decided she was going to camp out with us for the night, as did Lom, Yara, and Greer. I do not know of anyone who would be so desperate to get the vessteboks that they would be willing to face a hunting cat, griff falcon, two night wolves, plus a mountain cat, a bog fox, and a border dog. Ashu was an unknown, but, after hearing some of the

188

things he had done while traveling with Seeker Chance, I was not going to count him out either.

Later, as I lay in my bed that night listening to the night sounds, I felt more than safe with all of those who were camping with me, two-legged, four-legged, and winged.

Surprisingly, I woke early the next morning, refreshed. It was just after dawn, and yet, I felt no need to wiggle down under the covers and sleep any longer. I got up, dressed, and grabbed the vessteboks off the table where I had left it the night before. It had not occurred to me before I went to bed that I should hide the vessteboks away somewhere in my homewagon. As I headed down the steps of the homewagon, I noticed that Finn had already started a fire and had the kettle on.

"You're up early," I said.

"Always good to greet a new day at dawn, always good. Like the quiet, I do, like the quiet. You'll have tea, yes, you'll have tea?" asked Finn.

"I think I will take a pass on the tea. I want to go back and look at the doors in the cliff wall."

"You should wait for the others, wait for the others."

"Somehow, I don't think anyone will approach us. I heard Lady Esmeralda say that the number of royal guards patrolling the grounds has been doubled. I think Carz and I will be all right. Also, if you will notice, the blue will-o'-wisps are gathering, even as we speak."

"I will go with you, then, go with you," Finn said, and began to rise.

"Please stay here. Know I welcome your offer. I think, however, this is something I need to do alone."

Finn sat back down. I knew he did so reluctantly. I asked him to inform the others where I had gone and ask them to give me a little time before they came looking for me. Now, my only concern was whether the tangle would open the path for Carz and me. I grabbed a few lanterns and set off.

I guess I should not have worried, for, when I arrived at the spot to enter the tangle, it pulled back, allowing me to walk down the path. Once I was on the path, I looked back to see the tangle closing up behind me. Once again, I walked through the labyrinth, letting my mind go blank. When I reached Lom's bench, I was not surprised to see Lom there with Taarig lying beside him.

"Do you sleep here now?" I asked.

"No, but I understand why you might ask that," Lom said, and then yawned a huge yawn. "Theora makes me leave each night. I can stand the pull for just so long though, and then, I need to come back here. There is something on the other side of those doors that continues to pull at me. What brings you here so early and with only Carz and the blue ... what is it that Yara calls them?"

"Blekbrann."

"Ah, yes, blekbrann."

"I wanted to take a look at the doors and the arch over them. Something about them is niggling at the back of my mind, and I thought if I took another look, I might be able to bring it forth."

"Do you mind if I stay?" Lom asked.

"Somehow I don't think either of us could be anywhere else right now."

I went up to the doors and hung the lanterns on hooks I found conveniently built into the door frame. After that, I went back to the bench.

"Scoot over and share the bench, if you would, please," I requested of Lom.

We sat for a long time in companionable silence, each in our own thoughts. Finally, I opened the vessteboks and took out the rings, placing them on the bench in the order they had arrived. I took my time picking up each one, looking at it carefully, and then putting it back on the bench. Again, I picked up the first ring. I realized that one set of grooves on the first ring had a particular mark, and I had seen that mark before. I studied the doors and the arch, looking closely. It was then that what had been hiding in the back of my mind finally floated forth and connected with what I was seeing. There was an identical mark carved into the arch.

I realized I had made an error in my thinking. I had been so careful to keep the rings in the order they arrived in the capital, since that is how they had been placed in the vessteboks. I had been so worried that I would somehow mix them up and never be able to solve the puzzle of how to put the oppgave ringe together. Looking at where I now found the matching mark on the arch made me suspect that, just because I had carried the first ring in and placed it on the first post in the vessteboks, it did not mean it was the first ring.

I quickly picked up the second ring, looking for a distinctive mark. Now that I thought I knew what I was looking for, I quickly found it on both the ring and the arch over the doors. On a hunch, I picked up the ninth ring. I found the mark and then the matching mark on the far left of the arch. I placed it in the vessteboks on the first post, hoping against hope that I was guessing right about how to determine their order. I had placed all but the last ring in the vessteboks when Lom spoke up.

"Ah, Nissa?"

"Yes," I answered, as I picked up the last ring.

"You might want to look up for just a moment," suggested Lom.

"Oh …." I did not get the question why I should look up out of my mouth, for I could already see why. The blue will-o'-wisps had left their resting spots on the vine leaves and were drifting closer and closer. "Now that could be worrisome."

"Why?"

"Either they are drifting closer because I'm doing something right, or they are drifting closer because I'm doing something wrong."

"Ah. Which do you suspect it is?"

"I think I'm doing something right."

I went on to explain to Lom about the marks on each of the rings matching up with the marks on the arch, and that I was arranging the rings in the vessteboks from left to right in the same order as the marks on the arch. I showed him the mark I was referring to on the last of the rings, which I still held in my hand.

"I would fully understand if you wanted to leave and distance yourself from me, since while I'm fairly sure I'm making the right choices, I could be wrong," I told Lom.

"Thank you for the offer. I trust your instincts, so I think I will stay put."

Since sitting there for the rest of the morning holding a misshapen golden ring in my hand arguing with myself as to whether I was right in my assumptions was not going to get me anywhere, I placed the last ring in the vessteboks. The blue will-o'-wisps swirled around us both, moving faster and faster until they became a blur of light, and then suddenly winked out.

"I'm still not sure if I chose right," I said.

I really did not want to admit to Lom how shaken I was by the blue will-o'-wisps' display. *Had that light show been because they were disapproving or approving? Had I done the right thing, or had I really made a mess of things by mixing up the pieces of the oppgave ringe?*

"I think it might be all right," said Lom. "Look at the arch over the doors."

When I looked up and saw what Lom was referring to, I began to feel much better. Many of the blue will-o'-wisps had settled themselves in the marks carved into the arch over the doors that matched the marks on the rings. Others had gone back to resting in the leaves of the vines.

"I guess they approve," I said. *Might have been nice if they had settled in the marks carved into the arch over the doors earlier. It would have saved so much time and rumination,* I thought wistfully.

"Would have been nice if they had done that earlier," Lom said, echoing my thoughts. "Nothing about finding the pieces of the oppgave ringe came easily for any of us, so I don't know why I would expect the rest of the Gylden Sirklene challenge to be easy."

I did not know what had surprised me more, the blue will-o'-wisps settling themselves in the marks carved into the arch above the doors, or the length of Lom's sentence.

"Now that I have the rings in what I think is the right order, I guess I should get on with the task of putting them together. I'm going to go sit in the shade of the quirrelit tree, for it is getting rather hot out here in the sun. If you will excuse me."

"I think I'll stay here. Thank you for closing the vessteboks."

When I gave Lom a questioning look, he explained that the rings all together pulled very hard at him, stronger than what drew him day after day to the bottom of the garden. He hoped distance would help.

"Either that, or you will feel pulled in two directions, which I imagine might get really uncomfortable."

"If it becomes too much, I will move back up to the royal palace," Lom assured me.

"Have you ever considered having a cloak made that is lined with golden pine spider silk? I wonder if it would do for you what the golden pine spider silk pouches have done to mask the power of the rings?"

Lom chuckled and explained he had just gotten a vision of himself in a cloak that had drawstrings at the hood and the hem. If he was becoming overwhelmed by the pull of an object of power, he could turn the cloak into a pouch.

"Of course, that is if a cloak of golden pine spider silk could work in reverse of the pouches that have concealed the rings. Maybe golden pine spider silk only works one way," I said, now that I had a chance to really think my idea through. I have to admit I did walk off chuckling at the image of Lom all wrapped up in his folk-sized pouch. The humor of the whole idea helped relieve much of the tension I was not aware I had been feeling. I felt the muscles in my neck and shoulders begin to relax.

I became even calmer as I entered the labyrinth and walked its path to the quirrelit tree. Carz padded alongside me, and I was glad of his company. I sat down with my back to the quirrelit tree. Carz lay down beside me. I took a moment to give him a good scratch between his ears. The soft rumble of his purr was soothing, and I think I might have just stayed there in the shade, drifting, if a small quirrelit branch had not dropped directly on my head.

Reluctantly, I drew myself together. I picked up the vessteboks from where I had set it on the ground and placed it on my lap. Opening it carefully, I picked up the ring that was now on the first post on the left side of the box, and the ring directly to its right. I, then, closed the vessteboks and set it aside. I took my time looking at one ring and then the other. I was beginning to see a pattern in their shape. While each ring appeared misshapen, they really were not that different. I began to try to match up their edges. I put two edges together and began to rotate them. The edges did not line up. Then I flipped the one in my left hand over, and still they did not line up. Almost, but not quite. The scratches for the most part lined up but not the edges. I then flipped the ring in my right hand over and still no success. Flipping the ring in my left hand once again, I was hopeful, so I began to rotate the rings. Finally, all of the edges and scratches lined up. I was astonished as to what happened next. The two pieces of the oppgave ringe drew together, and no matter what I did, I could not get them apart. I could only hope I had put the right ones together, for there was no turning back now.

Assuming I was right, assembling the rest of the oppgave ringe would not be as difficult, since I only had two sides to worry about rather than four. The work went swiftly, and in no time at all, all of the pieces of the oppgave ringe were fitted together, and nothing I could do, short of pounding them with a hammer, was going to break them apart. Actually, I had a strong suspicion that even a hammer would not break the oppgave ringe apart.

I leaned back, resting my back once again against the quirrelit tree. I do not know how long I had been sitting hunched over working on the oppgave ringe, but it felt good to rest against the tree. I took a long moment to look at the assembled rings. *Now what?*

Chapter Thirty

Now that I had the oppgave ringe together, I took a really good look at what I had assembled. The more I turned it over in my hand, looking at it from all angles, the more I became convinced its function was not as a ring to be worn on the hand. While each of the pieces looked like rings you might wear on a finger, the assembled oppgave ringe would be a mighty funny ring, for it was now far too long for the average finger, and would probably limit movement of the knuckle of even a larger than average hand. So what I had was not a ring, but a cylinder.

I took a long hard second look at the cylinder I held in my hand. Now that the oppgave ringe was put together, what had looked like scratches all lined up and formed a pattern. I could see how the marks on each individual ring, which corresponded to the marks I had found above the doors on the cliff wall, now became just a part of the whole design on the cylinder.

My mind began to drift, thinking about the pattern on the cylinder, and the woodworker in me began to imagine the same design, or a design like it, carved on a walking stick. With that thought, I sat up abruptly and realized I had seen a similar design on a number of walking sticks. Four walking sticks to be exact. At least four walking sticks that I could recall. Head royal librarian Eluta, Seeker Eshana, Seeker Odette, and Seeker Chance. *As if I needed any more unsolved mysteries or unanswered questions, now I am wondering about designs on walking sticks and just what that means.*

I got up, stretched, and looked around. Lom was still on the bench by the doors. Other than the sun rising just a bit higher in the sky, nothing had really changed while I put the oppgave ringe together. I do not know why I thought anything would.

After stretching out the kinks in my shoulders, I nudged Carz and told him I was going to go over and talk to Lom. I asked if he wanted to come along. He just looked up, yawned a huge yawn, dropped his head, and put one paw over his muzzle. I took that to be a rather large "no" as to accompanying me, so I left him napping, walked out of the labyrinth, went to where Lom was, and sat down next to him. Taarig lifted his head, saw that it was me, and went back to his nap.

"Ah, to be a hunting cat, or a night wolf, and have nothing better to do than nap during the day," I said to Lom. "Do you mind if I sit down next to you again?"

"I would welcome the company. Did you figure out how to put the oppgave ringe together?" Lom asked.

"Yes," I said, as I held my hand out and opened it.

Lom made no move to reach for the oppgave ringe. He did take quite some time studying it, motioning with his hand when he wanted me to rotate it so he could see another side.

"I really don't know why I even asked if you had the pieces of the oppgave ringe together. I could feel the pull of it even as you sat under the quirrelit tree. It is more powerful than anything I have ever felt. Any idea as to what it is, or what it is supposed to do?" asked Lom.

"None whatsoever. I was struck when I was looking at it that the pattern that is now formed on the cylinder is very similar to some designs I have seen on a number of walking sticks."

"You are right."

"Not that I know what significance that has, by any means. I guess I should do something with the oppgave ringe now that I have assembled it. Putting it back in the vessteboks would probably be a good start. I left the vessteboks by the quirrelit tree. It's next to Carz. I don't think anyone will try to take it while he is next to it. I'll pick it up when I head out."

"It would be difficult for anyone to take it even without Carz next to it, since the tangle is still closed," Lom pointed out.

I looked back and saw that he was correct. The tangle was still closed, and there were no other folks in the clearing.

"I would like to spend a little longer looking at the doors. Ever had something just hovering on the edge of your mind, and yet be unable to bring it into the light?" I asked.

"You would ask this of someone who has been staring at the doors for days?" Lom questioned.

"You might have a point."

I settled back on the bench and began to really take a good look at the doors. I realized that the design carved into the doors was not really as random as it might first appear. As I continued to stare at the doors, one small section of the design suddenly came into sharp focus. I stood up and motioned that Lom should accompany me.

Pointing at the small section in the design that had drawn my attention, I asked Lom, "Doesn't that remind you of a griff falcon?"

Lom looked where I was pointing. I traced my fingers along the lines to indicate what I was talking about.

"I think you are right. I'm going to stand back and see if I can see any of the other companion animals."

Thinking that was a really good suggestion, I stepped back with Lom and began searching for a hunting cat. I suspected he might be looking for a night wolf or two.

"Nissa, look here," Lom said, pointing to a place on a door. "I think these lines form two night wolves intertwined. What do you think?"

"You are right. Look here. While I was looking for a hunting cat, I think I found a mountain cat instead."

Lom agreed with me that what I had pointed out to him did indeed look more like a mountain cat. While I had been looking for the lines that might form a hunting cat, I had noticed something else.

"Lom, see where the griff falcon, the two night wolves, and the mountain cat are placed on the doors?"

"Yes."

"Picture them as being laid out in a circle. Start at the griff falcon and follow where you think the circle might go to the left. I will follow it to the right. I suspect that we will find the other companion animals evenly spaced in a circular pattern."

"Ah, I think I just found a halekrets," said Lom.

"And I just found a bog fox."

It took us only moments to locate a hunting cat, and a border dog.

There was a gap between the bog fox and the night wolves. The lines there were blurred. That is the only way I could describe it. They were not worn away or weathered. It did not look as if the carver of the doors had just not finished those lines.

"Look here, Lom. Can you make out what is carved in this area?" I asked.

"No. Now, that's odd. The more I look at that area, the less distinct the lines become."

We both stared at the area we could not make out for quite some time before moving back to the bench.

"How did you think of looking for the rest of the companion animals along the arc of a circle?" Lom inquired.

"I remembered the pillars we found in the chamber in the lower levels of the royal palace. Once we had found the griff falcon, the mountain cat, and the night wolves, it struck me that they were placed in similar positions in the chamber with the pillars. I just made a guess that perhaps the animal carvings on the doors would follow the same order in a circle. I'm thinking that we need to go back to that chamber."

"I think you are right."

I went back into the labyrinth to collect the vessteboks and Carz. When I got there, though Carz was still napping, the vessteboks was gone. My first action was to wake Carz up and get him to move, thinking somehow he had shifted on top of the vessteboks while I had been on the bench with Lom. Though he gave me one of those "why did you wake me?" looks, he did stand up and stretch. The vessteboks was not underneath him. I called over to Lom to please come join me. He must have heard the slight panic in my voice, for he came rather quickly.

"Is something wrong?" Lom asked.

"The vessteboks is gone. I left it here where I was sitting, and now, it's gone. I didn't see anyone in the clearing, and the tangle didn't open, as far as I can tell. I can't understand how the vessteboks has gone missing. I certainly didn't hear anything while we were at the doors."

"I don't think anyone came in from outside of the tangle. I think I would have sensed the plants moving. I did when you entered the tangle earlier this morning," stated Lom.

"Can you give me a boost up? I need to climb up in the quirrelit tree and see if I can spot anyone or anything."

Lom gave me a boost up. Once I was in the quirrelit tree, it was an easy climb up almost to the top. The branches were thick and sturdy. I closely examined each branch and found nothing. I looked carefully at the trunk to see if there were any holes where the vessteboks could be hidden. Again, nothing. Finally, after looking over and under every branch and leaf, I climbed back down.

"Did you find anything?" Lom asked.

"No, nothing. No folks hiding in the branches, no animals that I could see, no holes of any kind, nothing hanging from the underside of any branch. It is just a very lovely quirrelit tree. I don't understand how this could happen. This is not going to be easy to explain to the others. I'm having a great deal of trouble explaining it to myself. I guess I had best head up to the royal palace. If nothing else, I need to find some golden pine spider silk to wrap the oppgave ringe in."

"You will not need to go to the royal palace for that. I have some with me."

When I raised an inquiring eyebrow, Lom explained that he carried it as a precaution. Ever since his experience in the royal forest south of the capital, when he was looking for a piece of the oppgave ringe, he had become more sensitive to things that held some power. He wanted to be prepared to be able to shield himself or an object, whichever might be more prudent, should he find something that held power.

The piece of golden pine spider silk was more than adequate to wrap the oppgave ringe in. I carefully wrapped it up and tucked it into an inside pocket. While I had been in the campsite surrounded by folks and animals, I had not worried about having the vessteboks with the pieces of the oppgave ringe inside. I had not worried this morning when I carried everything to the clearing, for I was sure nothing would get past the tangle. It seems I was wrong not to be worried, since the vessteboks was now missing.

I felt very vulnerable as I stepped out of the tangle with the assembled oppgave ringe in my inner pocket. I know Carz would certainly not let anyone harm me. I was sure that Lom and Taarig would also deter anyone trying to get close. I was glad the blue will-o'-wisps were still with me. Yet, that did not make me any less anxious about getting to a point where I was no longer responsible for the oppgave ringe. Who knew when or how that would come about?

Lom and I headed up toward the royal palace. No one came near us, much to my relief. I knew that the next folk I needed to talk to was Master Clarisse. After all, she was the one who could read the Book of Rules. Though it did not seem to give very clear instructions, maybe it would tell us what to do next, which would be nice. I was also beginning to get a glimmer of an idea as to something I wanted to try. I would need all those who had carried the rings into the capital or were accompanied by a companion animal.

When we arrived at the royal palace, I ran into Yara and Toki heading toward the small parlor where we often assembled.

"Have you seen Master Clarisse this morning?" I asked.

"Yes, we have been working in the royal palace archives this morning. She and the seekers were going to come to the parlor for a break and a bit of refreshment shortly. I was just on my way to see if I could get that set up. I'll meet you there in a bit."

Good to her word, Yara came into the parlor saying that the refreshments were on their way. Shortly thereafter, Master Clarisse entered the parlor, followed closely by the three seekers.

"Did you spend time this morning working on the oppgave ringe?" Master Clarisse asked.

"Yes, and I was successful in putting it together." I did not explain I had not been so successful in keeping the vessteboks in my possession. I wanted to talk to Da first about that. However, that was not my main concern at the moment, for I could not talk to Da until after the fair closed this day. Now, I wanted to ask a few questions.

"Master Clarisse, does the Book of Rules tell us what needs to happen once the oppgave ringe is put together?" I asked.

"Not clearly. It does suggest that a gate needs to be found or opened."

"I have an idea about that," I said.

CHAPTER THIRTY-ONE

I asked the others who had gathered for tea to pass the word along that I would like all of those who had carried rings to the capital to meet with me after the evening meal. In a way, I wished I were still working on putting the oppgave ringe together, for that would give me something to do while I waited. Instead, I walked back to the campsite.

I settled inside my homewagon with Carz and got out the book of designs the Huntress had given me all those many months ago. If I did not have the book and the ring with the firestar gem that she had made me, I might have begun to think that my meeting with the Huntress had been just a dream. I passed the time looking at each page, each design, and thinking about the designs I had seen that were similar to those in the book. Most recently there had been the cuff Beezle wore, the ring Lom wore, the bracelet Piper wore, and the pendant Jing wore. Then, there was Lom's billhook and Theora's bow. Now that I had seen the oppgave ringe put together, I had realized that the design on the oppgave ringe was similar to that on a number of walking sticks. In addition, similar designs were on the doors and archway set into the back wall of the royal garden, and on the pillars in the chamber several levels below the main floor of the royal palace. What all that meant, whether that was at all significant, I did not know. Certainly something to think about. My musing was interrupted when I heard a soft knock on my homewagon door.

"Nissa, may I come in?" asked Da.

"Please do," I wondered what had brought him back from the fair so early.

"It's not past fair closing time already, is it?" I asked.

"No, I decided to leave early. Too many folks milling about asking whether my daughter had put the oppgave ringe together yet."

"Oh, Da, I'm sorry. Must not have been good for sales."

"Actually sales were good. Especially by folks who wanted a knife that had one of the handles you carved. Problem is, I could not tell if they wanted them because they are beautiful and have a fine blade, if I do say so myself, or …."

"Or if they were just getting one so they could have bragging rights," I said, suggesting what I thought would be the ending of his sentence.

"You have the right of it, I think. At any rate, even after I raised the price for the knives, they still sold. I actually came here to see if you have any more handles made."

"Before we get to that, I need to tell you something. Or maybe several somethings," I said, stalling for time.

"Go on," said Da patiently.

"I have managed to put the oppgave ringe together, for one."

"I had no doubt that you would be able to do so."

"I also seem to have managed to lose the vessteboks."

"Did you now?"

I was surprised that Da did not seem either perturbed or surprised that the vessteboks was missing. I went on to explain that I had left the vessteboks under the quirrelit tree next to Carz, that Lom and I did not think anyone could have gotten into the clearing, and that we had not seen anyone.

"Nissa, I think you have more important things to worry about than the vessteboks," suggested Da.

I realized at that moment that I had never asked Da how he came to be in possession of the vessteboks a year ago, just when it was needed. It had never occurred to me to ask him, and it should have. Before I could say anything about that, he began speaking.

"Someday, after the challenge is completed, we need to talk more about the vessteboks. Right now, all I can tell you is, I think you need not worry about it. My suspicion is it is right where it needs to be at this time. Now, back to more important matters. Do you have any more knife handles ready?"

I laughed, gave Da a hug, and gave him instructions on where to find more knife handles in my cart at the fair.

"I have been carving them over the last few weeks, along with whimsies, to replenish my supply. I guess I had great hopes that once my part in this whole challenge was done, I might be able to move on to the southern fairs, and you and Nana would do so also. If I could, I would be on the road this day."

"I certainly understand your need to take to the open road. Your Nana and I have been talking it over and, once this challenge is over and Sommerhjem has a new ruler, we hope to head back to the cottage in Mumblesey." When Da saw the look of disappointment on my face, he went on. "This traveling from fair to fair has been good this summer, especially those few fairs we did together. Next summer, maybe we will do this again. Right now, while you have a hankering to get back on the road, I've a hankering for the peacefulness and simple village living at my cottage by the sea."

I was disappointed, though I really could not be upset with Da for wanting to return back to his cottage. I knew that being on the road had been hard for Da since the death of my mother. I could only hope that next summer we could at least share the summer fair circuit for a little while.

After he left, I spent time doing some of the chores I had neglected over the last few days. I was glad when it was time to head up to the evening meal. Once the meal was over, I invited those who had carried pieces of the oppgave ringe to the capital to accompany me to the chamber. I asked Master Clarisse, Da, Finn, Ealdred, and the seekers to come also. I wanted those who had not carried rings to the Well of Speaking to stand guard outside the chamber. I was not sure if what I suspected about the chamber was going to be right. I was sure that I did not want anyone to disturb us while we were down there.

Once we were through the storeroom, and all of us were heading down the stairs, I asked the last folk in line to please close the opening to the stairs. Fortunately, at the bottom of the stairs, there was room for some of us to gather. The rest of the group stood on the lower steps. The animals did not stop, but headed right into the chamber behind me. Since we had not yet lit the lanterns in the chamber, I could not see where they had gone.

"Thank you all for trusting me enough to come with me here. When we were here last, we noticed that each of the pillars represents one of the companion animals we traveled here with, with the exception of one of the pillars. We, as most of you know, found that when our companion animal was atop a pillar, and we traced the outline of the lines that represented that animal, the outline turned blue. Actually, to be clearer, when Carz was sitting atop the pillar that had the lines carved into it representing a hunting cat and I traced those lines, the outline turned blue. When others tried to trace the hunting cat lines, nothing happened. That was true of the other pillars. They only turned blue when the right animal was on the right pillar, and the line was traced by their companion. Is everyone following me so far?"

All of those huddled in the small landing and on the stairs nodded or murmured agreement.

"When Lom and I were in the clearing looking at the doors, we found line drawings of all of the companion animals carved into the doors in a circle in the same order as they are on the pillars in the chamber behind me. As I stand in the doorway moving clockwise, equally spaced is the pillar of the night wolves, followed by the pillars of the hunting cat, border dog, halekrets, griff falcon, mountain cat, and bog fox."

"That is all eight of the animals on only seven pillars," commented Seeker Eshana.

"And I know there are eight pillars, for I stood next to the eighth, the one just to the right of the entrance to the chamber," said Lady Esmeralda.

"You are both correct," I said. "Lady Esmeralda, you stood next to the eighth pillar before you put the piece of the oppgave ringe in the vessteboks. I am not sure I really saw what I thought I did, but when you traced something on the pillar, I thought I saw it turn blue, for just the briefest of time."

Lady Esmeralda looked surprised. "I had thought so too, and then I thought I was just imagining it, or perhaps the blue from one of your pillars was reflecting off the one I was standing next to. I really could find none of the companion animals on the pillar I was standing next to."

"I suspect you will not find one of them. I'm not sure you will find any animal. When Lom and I were looking at the doors and began to look at the spot in the circle where the eighth pillar's line drawing of an animal should appear, the more we looked, the less we could distinguish in that spot. It was most strange."

"Lom, was that what you observed, too?" Ealdred asked.

"Yes, the more I looked, the more the place on the door became less distinct. It was very strange."

"So, are you here hoping that now that Lady Esmeralda has put the ninth ring in the vessteboks, that lines on the eighth pillar will turn blue?" asked Seeker Eshana.

"That is one possibility."

"Not the one you called us down here for though," said Seeker Eshana.

"No, not the one I called you down here for. I suspect that, now that all of the pieces of the oppgave ringe are in, and the oppgave ringe is assembled, this chamber has something to do with the next step. Master Clarisse, any thoughts?"

"Yes. There is a paragraph in the Book of Rules which suggests that one needs to walk the path and follow the light to the door. I had thought that perhaps that meant the clearing you all have been so diligently working on. If I understand what you have been telling me, I am not sure how this chamber matches that instruction, since you say the pillars show some blue light when you trace the outline of your animal. I do not know how you might follow them."

"There is something else."

I was not sure how I was going to explain this, but I needed to try. I really did not want to discuss the Neebing room in my homewagon with all these folks, but I also did not want to lie to them.

"I found a small piece of paper that had been left in my homewagon. It was rolled up and tied with a small piece of blue string. It had a symbol drawn on it. Lom and I searched this room to see if we could find that symbol anywhere here. Please do not ask me why I thought we might find it here, but we did. Finding the symbol did not lead anywhere, for nothing happened when we pushed and prodded that section of the wall. I do not know if it is significant. I just have a very strong feeling about all of this."

"Do you have that small piece of paper with you?" asked Master Clarisse.

"Yes."

"May I see it?"

Master Clarisse walked down the steps as the others let her by. I handed her the small piece of paper, which she carefully rolled out. Then she pulled the Book of Rules out of an inner pocket and began to leaf through the pages until she found what she was looking for.

"You remember I said there was a paragraph suggesting that one needs to walk the path and follow the light to the door? Well, on that same page there is a drawing. Interestingly, it is identical to the drawing on the paper you just handed to me. I think you may be on to something. Please proceed with your idea," suggested Master Clarisse. "What do you wish to do next?"

"I think those of us who carried the pieces of the oppgave ringe should enter the chamber, starting with Lady Esmeralda. I think we need to walk the labyrinth on the floor, and then walk clockwise to our pillar. Theora, I think you need to go last."

"Let me get the order straight," said Yara. "First Lady Esmeralda, then myself, followed by Piper, Meryl, Seeker Chance, Greer, Nissa, Lom, and then Theora. Is that correct, Nissa?"

"I think so."

"What do you wish us to do then," asked Seeker Chance, "once we are all in place?"

"I think we need to trace the outline of the animal on our pillar. Lady Esmeralda, I suspect you will know what to do when it is your turn. At least, I think so. You all do understand that I really don't know what I'm doing here. All of this is just guesswork."

"You need to do what you feel is right," said Master Clarisse.

I motioned for Lady Esmeralda to enter the chamber. Carrying a lantern to light her way, she walked the labyrinth clockwise to the pillar just to the right of the opening to the chamber. One by one the rest of us followed.

Once each of us was situated at the correct pillar, it was easy to see the chamber clearly, as each had brought a lantern. Atop the pillars were our respective companion animals, with two exceptions. The two night wolves were atop the pillar Lom and Theora stood next to, and there was nothing atop the pillar Lady Esmeralda stood next to. At least, I did not think so.

"What next, Nissa?" Lady Esmeralda said. "Should I start, or should all of us trace the lines on the pillars at once?"

I do not know where the idea came from, but I felt both of those two suggestions were not right. "I think that Lom and Theora should start. I don't know why."

"As good a guess as any," said Greer.

When Lom and Theora traced the lines representing the two night wolves, several things happened at once. The outlines of the night wolves turned blue, a grinding noise could be heard, and out of both sides of the opening of the chamber, stone doors swiftly slid out, and closed off the chamber. Carved into the doors was a bow the same shape as the one Theora carried.

CHAPTER THIRTY-TWO

"Well, that was certainly unexpected," I said, as I stared at the sliding doors that had closed off the chamber. Once I got over my shock, I noticed that Tala had jumped off the pillar she shared with Taarig, and stood in front of the doors. "I don't think we need to panic yet. Theora, would you move over next to Tala?"

Theora did as I asked. "You have an idea, do you not?" Theora inquired.

"I think so. Try tracing the outline of the bow carved into the doors."

Theora reached up and traced the outline of the bow. It turned blue just like the outlines of the night wolves had turned blue. A slight grinding noise was heard, and the doors opened. Many voices spoke up at once, asking what had happened, and if all of us in the chamber were all right. Theora held up her hand, asking for silence, and explained.

"I think I now have a better understanding of what Zeroun has been trying to explain about my role in all of this," Theora stated. "He has suggested that the old tales call for a protector. It would seem that my role here, at the very least, is to guard this door so no one goes in or out, until such time as whatever we are called to do here is completed. Now that we have all caught our breaths, I suggest that we, once again, close this chamber up and get on with what we are supposed to do next."

I noticed that the minute Theora had begun to trace the outline of the bow on the doors, the blue outlines of the night wolves on the pillar immediately ceased to glow blue.

Theora stepped back to the pillar next to Lom. Tala again jumped up to sit next to Taarig. Lom and Theora traced the outlines of the night wolves carved into the pillar. The doors slid out and sealed off the chamber.

Tala again jumped down and went to stand next to the doors, followed by Theora. The outline of the two night wolves continued to glow blue.

Once the doors were again shut, I addressed the group. "It would seem that whatever is going to happen here is definitely sealed off from anyone getting in and trying to stop us. I think we need to continue what we started."

I traced the outline of the hunting cat, followed by Greer tracing the outline of the border dog, and so it went in order around the circle until it came to the pillar Lady Esmeralda stood next to. She hesitated for a moment and then reached up and traced something on her pillar. Unlike what had happened on our pillars, where the outline of a companion animal began to glow blue, the entire pillar Lady Esmeralda was standing in front of began to glow blue.

In addition, a thin line of blue flowed out from the bottom of that pillar, past Lady Esmeralda, past Theora and Tala, and flowed onto the labyrinth pathway, following each turn, until the blue line exited the labyrinth. It continued to flow around the edge of the chamber past Lom and Taarig. I expected it to continue to circle around the chamber, on past all of us until it reached Lady Esmeralda. That was not to be the case. Just as the blue line reached my feet, Carz jumped down from the top of the pillar behind me, settling at my feet. I really did not know what to make of that. How long I would have stood there was anyone's guess, if it had not been for Greer.

"Ah, Nissa, you might want to take a look at that symbol we found on the chamber wall," Greer suggested.

I looked up toward the spot where Greer and I had found the symbol that matched the symbol drawn on the small piece of paper that had been left in the Neebing room. It was glowing in a light green color. I was not sure what surprised me more, that the symbol was glowing, or that the symbol was glowing in a light green color, and not blue.

Seeker Chance took a step away from his pillar to take a closer look at the symbol, and immediately stepped back when Meryl told him to stop.

"Almost instantly, when you stepped away from your pillar, the blue outlines and the blue line on the floor began to fade. I think we all need to stay put, with the exception of Nissa," stated Meryl.

When Seeker Chance stepped back next to the pillar Ashu was sitting on, the blue outlines and the blue line on the floor of the chamber began to glow brighter.

"Why do you think it will be all right for me to move?" I asked.

"There was no change in the brightness of the blue lines when Carz jumped down. None of the other animals seem inclined to move. Ashu did not jump down when Seeker Chance moved. When Seeker Chance moved, the blue lines began to dim," said Meryl.

"In addition, the blue line on the floor stopped at you," added Yara. "It bypassed Lady Esmeralda, Theora, and Lom, and then stopped when it got to you. Try stepping toward Greer and see what happens."

I took a tentative step toward Greer. The blue lines held steady in their brightness. Carz padded ahead of me, heading straight toward the light green symbol glowing in the wall. The blue outlines on the pillars and the blue line on the floor did not dim once Carz had moved away from me. He reached the section of the chamber wall where the light green symbol continued to glow steadily. I took another tentative step forward. The blue line on the floor shot forward straight to the wall that held the light green glowing symbol.

Once again, Seeker Chance stepped away from his pillar to follow the blue line on the floor, and when he stepped away from his pillar, the blue lines on the floor and on the pillars began to dim. Not only did the line on the floor begin to dim, but it also moved back to my feet.

"Well, it would seem that I'm supposed to stay put," Seeker Chance said.

I stepped forward one step, and once again the blue line on the floor moved swiftly to where Carz was standing. When the blue lines continued to stay at the same level of brightness, I took another step. Carz looked back at me impatiently.

"All right, Carz, I'm coming."

I did not know what difference it was going to make if I walked slowly or rushed, since neither Greer nor I had been able to find any break in that section of the chamber wall, nor discern why the symbol might be important. Of course, it had not been glowing light green when we looked at it before. When I got to the wall where the light green symbol was glowing, I reached my hand up, but did not touch it. When I reached my hand up, an arc of light pulsed out from the firestar gem on my finger to be met by an arc of light from the light green symbol. Several things happened at once.

The section of wall I was standing in front of silently swung inward, creating a door-sized opening in the chamber wall. A few, and then more and more, blue will-o'-wisps came out of the opening and surrounded Carz and me. Carz took my hand gently in his mouth and pulled me forward. We took ten or so steps before Carz released my hand, the blue will-o'-wisps faded back, and the door to the chamber swung closed.

"What just happened here?" Yara asked, as she watched Toki and the other companion animals jump down off the pillars and head toward Theora and Tala.

"I have no idea," said Seeker Chance. "Nissa stepped up to the wall of the chamber, held her hand up toward the light green light, the symbol she and Greer had found earlier, then an arc of light came out of the symbol, to be met by an arc of light from the firestar gem in her ring. After that, a portion of the wall swung inward, creating a doorway."

"That is what I saw also," confirmed Meryl, who had seen what had happened from the side opposite Seeker Chance, since the door had opened up between their two pillars. "Once the wall opened up, blue will-o'-wisps came out through the opening, a few at first, and then in greater numbers. They, as you saw, surrounded Nissa and Carz. I did see Carz take Nissa's hand in his mouth and pull her through the opening. Then, the door swung shut."

"Did all of you notice at the very moment that Nissa stepped through the doorway, the animals began to jump or fly down off the pillars?" inquired Greer.

"Yes," stated Piper. "At the same time the animals were getting down, the blue outlines on the pillars and on the floor began to fade."

"I suspect we are done here," said Lom. "What we are done with remains the question."

"And what happened to Nissa and where did she go are also questions," suggested Theora.

"I cannot imagine that she has come to any harm, since the blue will-o'-wisps are with her. Do any of you know if she had the oppgave ringe with her?" Lady Esmeralda asked.

"I believe so," said Theora. "My question is, do we try to open the opening she went through? If that does not work, do we remain in this chamber until she returns, or do we leave here?"

"I have a suspicion that we are to leave here, since Jing is pawing at the door," said Piper.

"You may be right," stated Greer. "I have been trying to get the wall with the symbol on it to move to no avail. The symbol is not glowing light green, or any color for that matter. I can see no seam or break in the wall where the doorway was, and that makes absolutely no sense. I think there is nothing we can do here now."

"Much as I hate to agree with Greer, I think he has the right of it," stated Lom. "Theora, do you think you can open the door to the stairs again?"

Theora reached out and traced the line carving of the bow in the doors. It flared briefly blue in color, and then the doors slid open. The others were still waiting on the stairs.

"Is everything all right?" questioned Master Clarisse.

"We are not entirely sure," answered Lady Esmeralda. "Before we speak of what just happened in the chamber, would one of you go to the top of the stairs and make sure we are still alone down here?"

"Where is Nis …?" Nissa's father, Thorval, began only to have Lady Esmeralda caution him to wait.

Once Ealdred returned to the bottom of the stairs, Lady Esmeralda began to speak.

"My sincere apology to you, Thorval. I can understand your concern, for we are all concerned as to what has happened to your daughter, and where she might be now. Let me explain."

Lady Esmeralda described what had happened in the chamber, with the others adding information or confirming what Lady Esmeralda was saying.

"It is some comfort that the blue blekbrann are with her, I think," said Yara. "So far they have proven to be protectors of Nissa, and I, for one, can't see why that would suddenly change."

"I sincerely hope you are correct," said Master Clarisse, whose face took on a thoughtful look.

"What are you thinking?" asked Seeker Eshana.

"Earlier when we discussed the Book of Rules, a paragraph suggested that one needed to walk the path and follow the lights to the door. I had thought perhaps that meant the path in the clearing you all have been so diligently working on, and yet …."

"And yet, Nissa just followed a blue line and walked through a door," suggested Seeker Odette, speaking up for the first time. "Did she have the oppgave ringe with her?"

"Yes," answered Thorval. "Since she took possession of the vessteboks, and was charged with putting the oppgave ringe together, it has not been out of her possession."

"So, we do not know if it is good or bad, that Nissa and the oppgave ringe are now out of our reach," stated Lady Esmeralda.

"So it would seem, so it would seem," said Finn.

I hoped the blue will-o'-wisps would continue to stay with me, for I found myself in a tunnel without a lantern. My only light was that which the blue will-o'-wisps gave off. As we moved through the tunnel, I became aware we were not walking in a straight line. We would come to other tunnels leading off from the one we were walking down. Sometimes we would continue straight ahead. Sometimes we would turn down another tunnel. I was hopelessly lost after a number of turns and growing quite anxious. Once, when I stopped, Carz came and leaned against me. It helped to have him close.

I do not know how much time we spent in the tunnels, or how far we walked. When we turned yet another corner, I became aware that the tunnel no longer smelled of damp and dust. Rather, I could smell fresh air filled with the scents of flowers and green growing things. I also noticed that the tunnel began to lighten up. Ahead of me I could see a bright haze of fog. I felt more than saw that I had stepped out of the tunnel, only to have the fog close in around me. Suddenly, I felt frozen in place. I had felt this way once before. From out of the haze, I heard the cries of hunting cats, answered by one from Carz.

CHAPTER THIRTY-THREE

As I stood surrounded by fog, I could see nothing, and I think quite some time passed, but maybe not. I am not really sure. What I do know was that I could not move, even after the fog began to lift. I found myself standing with my back to a cliff wall, unable to move anything but my head, surrounded by four hunting cats. Striding toward me was one of the tallest women I have ever seen, and this time she actually looked happy to see me. Dressed all in forest green, tunic, leggings, boots, and gloves, she held a spear as one who knew how to use it.

"I am not surprised it is you who is the one who has been sent to open the gate," the Huntress stated. "Come, Neebing blessed, follow me."

I was about to comment that it would be difficult to follow her, since I was mostly frozen, and mostly unable to move, when I realized that was no longer the case. Like the last time I had met the Huntress, Carz had placed himself protectively next to me, and the feeling of being immobile had worn off. I took a tentative step forward and found I was not stiff at all. As I looked forward to follow the Huntress, I really began to take in my surroundings.

"Come along, Nissa. Don't gawk. We have much to discuss and little time to do so."

It was hard not to stop and take in what I was seeing. I was standing inside a small valley surrounded on all sides by sheer cliff walls. Waterfalls fell from great heights. Rainbows arced through the mist created by the falling water. Ahead of me a stone path wound through waving grasses and a profusion of wild flowers in a multitude of colors. Beyond that was a huge grove of ancient quirrelit trees. I thought I saw something running along one of the branches, maybe one of the halekrets. Butterflies rose up in clouds of color when we walked past them. Song birds lent their musical notes to the air. Other birds rode the thermals, soaring above us. As I looked ahead, I could see sunbeams dancing on small ponds and pools of water scattered over the landscape. I was so taken by the beauty of the place that I did not realize I had stopped walking.

"Must I send the hunting cats back to push you along?" the Huntress asked.

"What? Sorry. It's so beautiful and peaceful here. I got distracted."

"Move along now. As I said, we have much to discuss. I would rather do so sitting down, over some tea."

The Huntress led me along the path heading toward the quirrelit grove. Before we reached the grove, she turned off on a side path and headed toward a smaller quirrelit grove that grew next to a cliff wall. She walked up to an ancient tree trunk that looked like it had grown out of the wall. There she did something, and a section of the trunk of the huge old quirrelit tree swung open. Her four hunting cats slipped through the doorway. The Huntress then stepped through, motioning for Carz and me to follow.

"I think we will be more comfortable here while we talk."

I looked around, half expecting to have somehow found myself in the Huntress' home where I had been before. I guess at this point I would not have been surprised if we were in her home in the woods outside of Crestbury. As I looked around the interior of the quirrelit tree, I discovered this was not the case. The carvings within the tree, and the general layout, were similar to the Huntress' home, but not quite the same.

"As you have observed, this tree home is similar to mine, but not mine. Actually, this will be the temporary home for the gardener and the protector during the time of the challenge. Since you are here, I know they must be also. There is still much to be done to make the main quirrelit grove ready, for it has been far too long since the ruler of this land has been chosen as he or she is supposed to be chosen. The land of Sommerhjem has suffered for it, as has this valley, for here dwells the heart of this land. Now then, let us each get a mug of tea, and discuss what your next tasks need to be."

I did as the Huntress requested and filled a mug with hot tea, adding a bit of honey to sweeten the flavor. Carz and the other hunting cats all settled in for a nap. I envied Carz and suspected I would be much happier settling in for a doze in front of a warm fire than I was sitting here sipping tea and waiting to hear about what I had been chosen to do next.

"You have three tasks to do this day. You need to open the gate, you need to instruct the gardener and the protector, and you need to place the oppgave ringe where it needs to be during the Gylden Sirklene challenge."

I would have liked it better if the Huntress said I had only three tasks left to do period, and then my part in all of this would be over. Stating that I had three tasks left to do this day suggested that I might have other tasks to do in the future. I had no desire to be the new queen of Sommerhjem and hoped that would not be one of my future tasks.

Since the Huntress remained seated, sipping her tea, I thought this might be an opportune time to ask a few questions of my own. "I tried to find your home in the forest outside of Crestbury."

"Did you now?"

"Yes. I could see the top of the young quirrelit tree we planted last year. It seems to be growing well. When I headed in its direction, I found it, but could not find the grove your home is in."

"I was probably away. Now then, we had best get to the gate, so you can open it. I imagine those who were in the chamber with you are beginning to get quite anxious."

The Huntress' answer to my question did not make it any clearer why I could not find her home. It also occurred to me as we left the quirrelit tree that there were more important questions I should have asked. I should have asked just where we were now, or how she knew about the chamber. The Huntress was striding so quickly away from me that I had to rush to catch up. When I finally did so, I thought I had an answer to where we were now. I found myself looking at a carved archway built into the side of the cliff wall. Set into the archway were two carved wooden doors, very similar to those we had discovered under the vines in the clearing at the bottom of the royal palace garden. I noticed that the doors had a much different design on them. I could find no circle of animals on the doors. Rather, woven in among the very intricate intertwined lines was the outline of what I thought of as Theora's bow and what I now recognized as a billhook, like the one Lom carried.

"Before you open these doors, there are a few things you need to know. Within the quirrelit grove straight behind us, there is a circle of standing stones and a stone within the circle of those stones. At the moment, the bases of the standing stones and the stone within the circle are covered with vines and other greenery. That all needs to be cleared away by the gardener. The halekrets will help. Once the center stone is cleared, you will need to place the oppgave ringe where it belongs, along with the key to the vessteboks."

"Ah, there may be a wee bit of a problem. I no longer have the vessteboks," I said.

"Yes, I am aware of that. It is where it needs to be. You need worry no longer about it. You also need not worry about knowing what to do with the oppgave ringe. You will know. Now listen, I have much to tell you and little time."

The Huntress then proceeded to give me the instructions that I would need to pass on to the gardener and the protector, whom I suspected would be Lom and Theora. When she had finished, she said, "Now then, I would suggest you open the gate."

I turned to look at the doors and then turned back toward her to ask what she meant, what gate was she referring to, only to find she was no longer standing behind me. I looked all around and could see neither her nor any of the four hunting cats who had accompanied her. I did not know how they could all just vanish like that. It was some distance to the quirrelit groves, and between Carz and me and the quirrelit trees, there really was nowhere to hide.

Since I did not think it would be either appropriate or appreciated if I wandered this valley trying to find the Huntress, I turned back to study the doors. I could see no keyhole in the doors, which was probably good, since I was all out of keys. Well, that was not quite accurate, for I did have the small key to the vessteboks. In addition, there were no door handles, and no bar across the door that needed to be lifted.

How long I would have continued to stand studying the doors is anyone's guess. Finally, Carz moved up to one of the doors and put both front paws against it. *Could it be that simple?* I wondered. *All I need to do is just walk up to the doors and push?* I walked up, placed both hands on one door, and pushed. Carz pushed on his door at the same time. Both silently and easily swung open. I was not surprised to find Lom sitting on his bench on the other side. He certainly was surprised to see me.

"We have got to stop meeting here. Folks are going to begin to talk," I quipped. I really could not resist. Injecting some humor into the situation was needed on my part, considering the day had started in the chamber, had led through a maze of tunnels following the blue will-o'-wisps, continued with meeting the Huntress again, and now with the opening of the doors. I am not sure Lom appreciated my sense of humor. Before either of us could say anything, Taarig raced down the path toward the opening of the tangle and disappeared.

"I think Taarig is off to find Theora," suggested Lom. "Are you all right?"

"I'm fine. I followed the blue will-o'-wisps through tunnels to ...." I had to stop and think what to call this place where the Huntress said the heart of this land dwells. I guess valley was as close as I could come. "The blue will-o'-wisps led me to the small valley you see through the doors. I was met there by ...."

I found I could not get the next words out. I knew I wanted to say I had been met by the Huntress and four hunting cats. I tried again, and again I could not get the words out.

"Ah, there are things we, you, Theora, and I, need to do, so I do hope Taarig has gone after Tala and Theora."

"I'm not sure I can wait. The pull to go through those doors is almost overwhelming."

"Hold on for just a little longer. I know both of you are going to be needed in there. I'm afraid if you go through those doors without Theora, they might close behind you and trap you. Just a wild guess on my part, which I don't think we should test out. Besides, here comes Theora, running our way, following the two night wolves."

"Nissa, you are here. How ...." Theora trailed off when she noticed the doors in the cliff wall were open. "I was about to ask how you got here. I would guess you came through the doors in the cliff wall. That brings up a great number of other questions."

"I think we might have to wait on the questions, for there seem to be a number of folks heading out of the tangle. We need to get through the doors and close them."

Both Theora and Lom were in agreement, having assessed who those folks were who were making rapid progress toward us. We swiftly followed Carz and the two night wolves through the doors.

"Are you sure if we close these doors we will be able to get out again?" Theora asked.

"The only thing I'm relatively sure of at this moment is I don't think letting those young nobles into this valley at this time would be good for them. I don't have any explanation for why I think that. As to whether we will be able to get out …." I paused as I helped Lom and Theora push the doors shut. "I can't guarantee I will be able to open the doors again. I suspect you two might. Take a look at them."

It did not take either Lom or Theora long to recognize the carvings of Lom's billhook and Theora's bow. We could hear very muffled pounding on the doors from the other side. Then, abruptly, the pounding stopped.

"I hope you will trust me that what I'm about to tell you is the truth. I wish I could explain how I know this. Let me show you something."

I wished I had pen and paper at that moment, so I could have drawn sketches of both Lom's and Theora's faces when they finally turned around and got a good look at the valley. It really was a beautiful place. I led them down the path the Huntress and I had walked earlier, leading them to the quirrelit tree next to the cliff wall. I need not have worried that I would not be able to get the door open, for it was open when we got there.

"It is my understanding that this beautiful home within this tree is to be your temporary home for the duration of the challenge. It is my guess that you two are now the gatekeepers of this valley. Let's go inside and I will tell you what I can."

CHAPTER THIRTY-FOUR

I could only hope that Lom and Theora would trust me, since I was not able to tell them where I had gotten my information. I guess I would not blame them if they thought I was making the whole thing up.

When they stepped through the door into the tree home, I could see by their faces that they were having the same reaction to the interior as I had had when I first stepped inside the Huntress' tree home. Lom and Theora took some time to explore before we finally sat down to talk.

"This is an amazing place," stated Theora. "It's much bigger inside than you might expect. Nissa, the woodworker in you must be itching to copy all of the designs carved into every wall, every cupboard, and every chair. The upstairs is equally beautiful. Both of the bedrooms look like they were designed for us. Each room has a bed for a folk and one for an animal. All very cozy, and mysterious."

"Mysterious?" I questioned.

"Why yes," said Theora. "Who might dwell within this valley, and who dusted the rooms and put clean linens on the beds? Towels are laid out and the pitcher next to the wash basin is full of clear water. It certainly seems that someone either lives here, or …."

"Or you and Lom have been expected," I suggested.

While Theora had been speaking, Lom had been opening cupboard doors. "There are plenty of general supplies in the cupboards, and the handle of the small pump next to the sink works smoothly. The water that flows out of it is clear and tastes refreshingly clean," Lom stated, as he brought another handful of water to his mouth.

I noticed that Carz was pawing at a braided rug near the cupboards. "Carz, stop that. This is not our home."

Carz did not stop. Rather he moved the rug over several feet revealing a metal ring set in the floorboards. Then he sat back looking smug and began to wash his left shoulder. Lom moved the rug some more, declaring that Carz had uncovered a trapdoor. He reached down and opened it.

"What do you see?" I asked.

"It is not so much what I can see; rather it is what I smell. It smells like a root cellar. Let me grab the lantern that is hanging from the first rung of the ladder and light it. I'll go down and check to see if I'm right."

"Maybe I should go ahead of you," said Theora.

"I thank you for taking your role as protector seriously. However, neither the night wolves nor Carz has so much as twitched a whisker since I opened the trapdoor, so I think it might be safe for me to go down."

Theora nodded her head in reluctant agreement. Lom lit the lantern and began to climb down the ladder. A few moments later, he reappeared at the opening.

"It is indeed a root cellar, and filled with enough supplies to last through a cold season. We could live quite comfortably here for some months and never have to leave. Not that I would want to, mind you."

"Who could have done all of this? Does someone live in this valley?" questioned Theora.

I knew I could not give Theora an answer to her first question, and I really did not know the answer to her second one. Since I could not answer either question, I thought this might be a good time to let Lom and Theora know what I could of what the Huntress had told me.

"As I said earlier, this tree home is to be your home until the Gylden Sirklene challenge is completed. You are the gatekeepers. The gate that Master Clarisse has been suggesting needed to be found and opened is not the opening I walked through in the chamber with the pillars. The gate mentioned in the Book of Rules is the pair of doors built into the cliff wall at the bottom of the royal palace garden. Did you take a good look at the doors when you closed them?" I asked.

"Yes, they had line drawings of both a billhook like mine and a bow like Theora's."

"Also, line drawings of two night wolves," added Theora. "Much as I might be reluctant to agree with your statement that Lom and I are supposed to be the gatekeepers, I think your information is correct."

"I suspect," I said, "if I were to go out through those doors into the clearing surrounded by the tangle and the doors closed behind me, I would not be able to get back in. I think my opening the doors was a one-time-only action on my part. I was the key to the doors, and I believe my job is now done concerning finding and opening a gate. I have not had a chance to look and see if I can return through the tunnels to the chamber below the palace. I would need the blue will-o'-wisps to guide me, for if I tried it on my own I would become hopelessly lost. For that matter, I have not seen any of the blue will-o'-wisps since I arrived in this valley."

"Do you want to go look?" Lom asked.

"No, I think I'm finished opening gates for a while. However, I have been left with a few more tasks this day, as have you. I, at least, need to do my task this day, since I'm not sure I can return here once I leave. Unfortunately, I cannot do what I am charged with doing until you, Lom, do something for me. If you both have explored this tree home enough for now, I think you should follow me to the larger quirrelit grove."

"Before I forget and you leave here, just in case neither Lom nor I can go past the doors, could we put together a list of what we might need from my wagon and Lom's tent?" requested Theora.

I had really not thought through what it might mean for Theora or Lom if they were not able to leave this small valley. The thought of them here for weeks and weeks without a change of clothing brought an interesting picture to my mind of them opening the doors each successive day in dirtier and more ragged clothing. I did not think I should share this picture with them. Rather I suggested they find something to write a list on before we left the tree home. Once that was done, we set off toward the quirrelit grove.

From a distance, it looked as though the quirrelit grove was circular in shape. The grove itself was a number of rows deep. The closer we got to the quirrelit grove, the more I could discern the trees were both huge and very old. In addition, the path into the grove was not straight. Rather it wound around the huge trunks. Once I passed the last row of trees, I stepped into a glen.

The Huntress had told me that there was a circle of standing stones within the quirrelit grove. I do not know what I was expecting. Perhaps standing stones similar to those where I had met the Günnary for the first time. Those had been ancient stones, weathered gray with time, mottled with lichen, still as tall and proud as the day they were raised. The standing stones I was looking at now could have been carved yesterday. Though they showed no signs of age, I had a very strong feeling that they were even older than the standing stones I had seen before. Unfortunately, the standing stones were covered about halfway up by vines.

Another thing that was different from the standing stones I had seen before was there was a mound of vines in the middle of the circle. From what the Huntress had told me, there was a stone under all of the vines and other greenery.

"I think under all of that green growing mass in the middle of the standing stones is a stone that needs to be uncovered, along with uncovering the base of each standing stone. I think this is where you come in, Lom," I said.

"Good thing there are three of us, for it is going to take all of us to clear this away. I have tried to ask the vines to move. Unfortunately, they are as uncooperative as the vines that hang down over the archway and the doors in the cliff wall. I have had to cut them back each day, for they grow very fast and do not withdraw upon request," said Lom.

"As for clearing away what you cut, I think we will have help," I suggested. "You might want to cut the vines in short sections."

Before Lom could even ask why I had suggested he cut the vines in short sections, the reasons began climbing down out of the quirrelit trees.

"I think our helpers have arrived," said Theora, followed by a chuckle. "Those little halekrets really are quite endearing, aren't they? I'd check your pockets to make sure you are not carrying any valuables, Lom."

"Traveling with Theora is like traveling with a teasing big sister," groused Lom. "Remember, one should never tease a folk who carries a really, really, sharp billhook," said Lom with mock fierceness.

"If you two are through, the sun stops its passage across the sky for no one," I gently suggested.

Both Lom and Theora just grinned at me. Then Lom began to cut the vines away from the mound in the center of the standing stones. He cut them in short lengths, as I had suggested. Theora and I pulled away the cut vines and put them behind us. The halekrets then grabbed some of the vines and either dragged or carried them out of the quirrelit grove. In practically no time at all, we had cleared away all of the foliage that had covered the stone in the center of the standing stones.

Then we started on the vines and other greenery that covered the bases of the standing stones. As we cut away the foliage, I noticed that the base of each standing stone was really made up of two stones. The stone closest to the center rose only about four feet high, whereas the stone behind the first stone rose far above my head. I did not have much time to think about this, for I was too busy tugging and pulling vines away.

I had not noticed that Theora had left the glen, until I saw her re-enter carrying both long-handled brooms and a short-handled broom. It did not take long for her to brush the remaining debris and dust off the top of the stone we had uncovered. While she did that, I began to sweep up the little bits of branches and leaves that were scattered around the stone. The halekrets grabbed up any piles I swept together.

Once Theora had cleared away the top of the stone in the middle of the clearing, Lom and I walked over to see what she had uncovered. The top of the stone was flat for the most part, rectangular in shape, and very smooth and polished. I noticed a rectangular indentation on the front left side of the top of the stone, what looked like a carving of a circle in the center of the stone, and a small knob right in front of that carved circle.

Since I really did not know what we were supposed to do, more specifically what I was supposed to do, I took up my broom once again to clear off what remained on the ground around the middle stone and the standing stones. After a while, I stopped sweeping for a moment to stretch the muscles in my back, and for the first time really took a good look at the standing stones. I do not know why I was surprised when I saw line carvings on the standing stones like the ones we had seen in the chamber below the royal palace, and also on the doors built into the cliff wall. I began to count the standing stones and, as in the chamber, there were eight of them. I immediately looked toward the pillar that I thought would correspond to the pillar from the chamber that had the line drawing of a hunting cat on it. Sure enough, I found the line drawing of a hunting cat on the standing stone I had suspected it might be on. I pointed that out to Lom and Theora. They, in turn, walked to the standing stone just to the left of the path we had entered the glen by and traced the outline of two night wolves.

It did not take us long to find the line drawings of the other companion animals on the other standing stones, which were in the same order around the circle as they had been in the chamber below the royal palace. It made me wonder about the two places. Had they always been connected? Was one built before the other? If so, which one was older, the chamber or what we were looking at now? I was summoned away from my questioning by Lom, who called to me to look up from my examination of the standing stone with the line carving of the hunting cat.

"Nissa, look what that halekrets is carrying," said Lom.

One of the halekrets was walking toward the stone in the middle of the standing stones, carrying what looked to me to be the vessteboks. She walked up to the stone and stood beside it. When I reached the halekrets, she held the vessteboks out and handed it to me.

"Thank you, I think," I said, as the halekrets climbed up on the stone and reached out her tiny hands. I placed the vessteboks back into them, and she walked to the left side of the top of the stone and placed the vessteboks in the rectangular indentation I had noted earlier. Then she reached out her hand to me again. I did not know what she wanted.

"I don't know what you want," I said.

The halekrets pointed to a small hole in the top of the stone right in front of the vessteboks. It looked similar to the key hole in the plain stone on the sea wall in the Well of Speaking.

"Is it the vessteboks key you want?" I asked.

CHAPTER THIRTY-FIVE

I did not know what to do. The halekrets seemed to be in the habit of running off with items. First, they had taken the nine rings that Lom had found in the royal forest south of the capital. Just now one of them showed up with the vessteboks, which I had last seen sitting next to Carz under the quirrelit tree in the clearing at the bottom of the royal palace garden. It could be argued that the halekrets did not actually take the vessteboks, but had been given it. That idea did not make me any less nervous about handing over the small key to the halekrets, who was holding out her hand to me at this moment.

Giving the halekrets the benefit of the doubt, I slid a golden pine spider silk pouch out from under my shirt and opened it, took the small key out, and gave it to the halekrets. She took the key and, much to my relief, did not run off with it. Rather, she stuck it in the small keyhole in the stone in front of the vessteboks. When she inserted the key into the keyhole, like I had in the Well of Speaking, she turned it once to the right, and I heard a click, but nothing happened. She then turned the key to the left, and I heard a second click and a grinding noise. The vessteboks sank down into the stone, so that only the very top of it was now visible. The halekrets then turned the key one more time to the right, and the lid opened. What I saw next caught me by surprise.

No light shone out of the vessteboks as it had the time I had opened the vessteboks in the Well of Speaking. Then, a light had shone forth of such intensity that all of us had stepped back, shielding our eyes. It had been a column of light that rose up out of the box in a steady stream. Rose up was an understatement at best, for the light from the box, which carried all of the colors of a rainbow, rose and rose until it almost touched the clouds. Then it had arched out in all directions until it formed a canopy in the sky and shone as far away as the very borders of Sommerhjem.

The light shining forth then had been a big surprise. What I saw now was no less of a surprise, just not as spectacular in form. Inside the vessteboks were nine rings, one on each of the nine posts, each set with a firestar gem.

"Lom, Theora, would you come take a look at this?"

As Lom and Theora walked over to stand beside me, the halekrets climbed back down. I said a quiet "thank you" to her as she walked away. When I looked around, I realized that all of the halekrets were gone out of the glen. Turning back, I asked Lom and Theora to look in the vessteboks.

"Lom, you will note that there are nine rings. I think they are made of a material similar to your billhook and Theora's bow. From what I can see, the design on each ring is just a little bit different. What do you think? Are these the rings you found in the royal forest south of the capital?"

Lom did not pick up any of the rings to examine them. His first reaction was to tell me that the rings that he had found did not have firestar gems set in them. Upon closer inspection, he got a thoughtful look on his face.

"What?" Theora asked.

"I'm a bit embarrassed to admit to you that I often would take each ring out of its pouch and spend time studying it. I did this late at night by lamplight or early in the morning, before anyone was up. I got to be quite familiar with them."

"Why would you be embarrassed?" I asked.

"I really don't know. For some reason I was fascinated by them."

I ventured a guess. "Even though each of these rings has a firestar gem set in them, you think they are the same rings you found in the quirrelit tree in the royal forest, and that the halekrets somehow acquired."

"That is certainly a much kinder way of saying one of the halekrets was a pickpocket," suggested Theora chuckling.

"However the rings came to be here now, however they came to have firestar gems set in them, I'm almost positive those rings are the ones I found in the quirrelit tree along with the piece of the oppgave ringe," said Lom.

"And now, we have nine rings set with nine firestar gems. Incidentally, nine firestar gems recently went missing from the elder rover, Zeroun. I'm not a real big believer in coincidence. I suspect the firestar gems set in these rings are the ones missing from Zeroun," said Theora.

"I would tend to agree."

I had once witnessed a ring being made out of what I suspected was quirrelit wood. I had watched the Huntress take a firestar gem that had been left for me in the Neebing room and mount it in a ring made of quirrelit wood. I saw her toss the ring, mounted now with the firestar gem, into the fire. I remember wanting to rush to the fire to rescue it. The Huntress had calmly informed me I need not worry, for the fire would not harm either the wood or the firestar gem. The fire would join them together and make both stronger. It would seem she knew what she was talking about, for a short while later, she used tongs to draw the ring out and drop it into a bucket of cold water to temper it. It was the ring I still wear to this day. I wondered if the Huntress had been the one who had set the firestar gems into the rings that now rested in the vesseboks.

"I note that none of us are reaching our hands in to take any one of the rings out," I said.

"I can find no reason to do so," said Lom.

"Neither can I," said Theora. "What about you, Nissa?"

"Interestingly enough, I'm feeling more pushed away than drawn toward the vesseboks. None of these rings should be mine," I stated simply. "These new rings in the vesseboks are just another mystery that, hopefully, in time, will be solved. I think that I have one more task to perform."

While we had been looking at the rings in the vesseboks, I had been feeling the oppgave ringe begin to warm in my pocket, even though it was wrapped in golden pine spider silk. Golden pine spider silk could mask an object of power, and it could also contain some heat. The growing warmth I was feeling in my pocket suggested to me that the oppgave ringe was getting quite hot.

I reached into my pocket and drew out the wrapped oppgave ringe. Once it was out of my pocket, the small bundle began to cool slightly. I am not sure if it became cooler because it was no longer closed in my pocket or because it was now out in the cooler afternoon air. I slowly unwrapped the oppgave ringe from the golden pine spider silk and rolled it into my hand. *Now what?*

Unfortunately, a convenient halekrets did not come walking into the glen to show me what to do next. No blue, green, or any other color will-o'-wisps floated in to form an arrow pointing the way. I was on my own. As I glanced at the top of the stone where the vessteboks now resided, I saw once again what looked like a carving of a circle in the center of the stone and a small knob right in front of that carved circle.

No matter where I looked, trying to figure out what I should do next, my eyes kept being drawn back to that knob. Finally, I leaned across the stone to take a closer look. From the small amount of debris caught around the part of the knob that met the top of the stone, I suspected it either pulled out or unscrewed. I tried pulling the knob up. It did not move. Next, I tried to unscrew it. To my great surprise, it turned smoothly. And turned, and turned, until I had unscrewed a cylinder very similar in shape and markings as the oppgave ringe. It, however, was only a third as long. I took a good hard look at the knob, and then held it next to the oppgave ringe. The markings on the knob were identical to the markings on one end of the oppgave ringe.

I turned to the others and held out my hands. "I think the oppgave ringe is a key. As you can see, the markings on the part of the knob that was screwed into the rock match the markings on the bottom third of the oppgave ringe. I think the oppgave ringe screws into the hole in the top of the rock."

Both Lom and Theora took a good look at what I was holding out. Neither one of them made any move to touch either the knob or the oppgave ringe. Both agreed with me that my assumption was probably correct. I suggested that they might want to distance themselves from me and the stone in the middle of the standing stones. Neither Lom, Theora, the two night wolves, nor Carz chose to do so. As a matter of fact, Carz moved closer to lean against me. Lom and Theora with their night wolves chose to flank me, one on each side.

Taking a deep breath, trying to relax, I reached over and set one end of the oppgave ringe into the hole. Very slowly and carefully, I began to turn the oppgave ringe to the right. It began to slide into the hole easily, until it was one third of the way in, then it stopped. At the same moment it stopped, the carved circle sank into the stone and slid sideways until I was looking at an opening. Very, very slowly, a glass dome began to rise out of the circle. At least it looked like glass, but then the Huntress' fountain had looked like it was made of glass or ice, but I do not think it had been made of either. Perhaps it and this dome were made of carved crystal. I suspected it could be broken by hitting it with a hard object, but perhaps not. When the dome stopped rising, I saw it rested on a stone base. In the side of the stone base was another hole about the same size around as the knob and the oppgave ringe.

It was what was inside the clear dome that caught all of our attention. I heard a quick intake of breath from Theora and felt Lom shift. Inside the dome were two slim circlets made of an intertwined combination of gold, silver, and what looked to be quirrelit wood. Each portion of the circlets had what the rover elder, Zeroun, had called Neebing patterns carved into them. They were strikingly beautiful in their simplicity.

Theora was staring at the circlets in the dome. "They are so simple in design, and yet, so very beautiful. I suspect one of these is the crown for our next king or queen."

"I have seen paintings in the royal palace of King Griswold and his daughter who was the next queen. The circlet you see on the left looks like the circlet he is wearing in the painting," said Lom.

"Is the circlet on the right a match for what his daughter wore when she was queen?" I asked.

"No. She is always depicted as wearing a gold crown with several jewels scattered about it," said Lom. "However, I have also seen the circlet on the right, or something like it, in portraits of earlier queens of Sommerhjem."

"So, we might assume that the circlets here would belong to the rightful king or queen of Sommerhjem," suggested Theora.

"I think you may have the right of it, which suggests that the Gylden Sirklene challenge takes place here," I said.

Before anyone could say anything more, I found myself reaching forward to unscrew the oppgave ringe, and replace it with the knob. The dome did not begin to descend back down into the opening. I then took the oppgave ringe and placed it in the hole at the base of the clear dome. I turned it several times and it stopped. I do not know why I knew to do what I did. It felt right, however.

We all took a very quick step or two back when the circlets began to glow, and then, a very narrow golden light shot straight up out of the dome. It rose higher and higher, broadening until the base of it spilled over and down the rock in the center of the standing stones, encompassing the entire rock. We kept stepping farther back, until we were outside of the standing stones. As the golden light continued to rise upward, we looked up and watched it form the shape of the trunk of a quirrelit tree, growing taller and taller until it topped the rim of the cliff walls surrounding the small valley. Once it was at least twice as high as the valley, the golden light began to form branches.

I could only guess it was forming a complete quirrelit tree made of golden light that was branching out over all of the capital and beyond. Folks far out in the countryside would be able to see it from very far away. Was this then the signal that the Gylden Sirklene challenge had begun? As I stood there, I waited for the light to fade, as had the lights that had risen from the vessteboks each time a piece of the oppgave ringe had been placed. The golden light did not fade.

"Ah, are you about done with your task, now?" asked Theora.

"I certainly hope so. I'm not sure how much more my heart can take this day. I think I need to find a place to sit down," I told Theora and Lom.

"A very excellent idea," said Lom. "I must admit, I find my knees are just a little bit wobbly."

The six of us moved farther back along the path toward the doors built into the cliff wall. Finding a small knoll covered with grass about halfway between the quirrelit grove and the doors, we climbed up and sat down facing the quirrelit grove.

"How did you know to do what you did with the oppgave ringe?" Theora asked.

"I have no idea, absolutely no idea. It just seemed right at the time."

"What do you think happens next?" Lom asked.

"My best guess is whoever is to be the next king or queen needs to be able to handle the oppgave ringe and gain one of the circlets." I suggested.

CHAPTER THIRTY-SIX

"There is no stopping it now," said Lady Farcroft, addressing the others in the room. "Any fool with eyes can see the golden light in the shape of a quirrelit tree rising up out of the cliff behind the royal palace. It is obvious that dreadful rover lass, Nissa, has put the oppgave ringe together, and done whatever she was supposed to do."

"Now, we do not know that for sure," said Lady Green.

"Do we not?" Lady Farcroft snapped. "Once the ninth ring was placed in the vessteboks, it was only a matter of time before Nissa, or someone, figured out how to put the oppgave ringe together. We have had reports from our folks in the royal palace that the whole group of ring carriers and their animals have been going off somewhere in the bowels of the royal palace where others have been barred from going."

"My son reported to me earlier that he and his friends saw three folks, accompanied by the two night wolves and a hunting cat, go through the doors built into the cliff wall at the bottom of the royal garden. My son and his friends tried to get to the doors before they closed, but were unable to," said Lord Mostander.

"It is now that I wish I had been able to stop Lord Klingflug from trying to keep Lady Esmeralda from becoming the next queen. He was in the ideal position to be the rule behind the throne. She was so naïve and unaware of so much about Sommerhjem," said Lord Hindre. "With the right handling, she could have been influenced to do our bidding. It was never enough for him though. He wanted the Crown for himself, and look where that got us."

"Did you see him at the Well of Speaking, all puffed up, still demanding that he should be ruling Sommerhjem? At this point, any one of us could be the next king or queen," suggested Lady Padde.

"That is more or less correct," said Lady Farcroft. "Anyone who feels they are called to be the next queen or king, anyone who thinks they have the right to be the next king or queen, can take the Gylden Sirklene challenge, whatever that might entail. My suggestion is we make sure we are in line first to try. Others might be too late to try, since one of us may have beaten them to it."

"Unfortunately, the Crown may have anticipated much more than we suspected," said Lord Mostander. "Whether they knew that Lady Esmeralda had the ninth ring ..."

"I think they did not," said Lady Farcroft. "Too many folks would then have known, and a secret is hard to keep with that many folks knowing."

"... or they just hoped it would arrive on time. They sent messages out to the far corners of Sommerhjem inviting any and all who felt called to be the next king or queen to arrive at the capital this week. The point ...."

"Certainly a clever way to get more folks to attend the great summer fair," suggested Lord Hindre snidely.

"Be that as it may." Lord Mostander, having now been interrupted twice, gave Lord Hindre a quelling look. "The point, here, is most anyone who thinks they should be the next ruler of Sommerhjem is probably already here in the capital, or fairly close. With that golden light like a lighthouse beacon in the sky, it is going to be very clear that something important is happening. I am sadly afraid we will have to take our place in line."

"How can this be? We of the noble houses should demand that we be allowed to take the challenge first. It is our right, is it not?" questioned Lady Furman. "I hate to admit that I am hoping that Lord Klingflug does not win, or pass, or whatever one has to do for the Gylden Sirklene challenge. If he becomes the next king, I am not sure he will be as helpful to those of us who backed him when he was regent. Then he needed us. If he is to become the next king, well ...."

Before Lady Furman could continue, Lady Farcroft held up her hand for silence. She had heard a discreet knock on the door. Walking to the door, she opened it a crack and listened to the folk on the other side. Closing the door, Lady Farcroft turned back to those gathered.

"It would seem that Lord Klingflug is here. It is probably not wise to prevent him from entering my house. I suggest we all get comfortable and take up our tea cups. No sense in letting him know we were doing anything other than having a late afternoon tea together," said Lady Farcroft calmly.

Moments later, Lord Klingflug entered the room, glanced around, and looked like he was about to say something, when Lady Farcroft spoke up.

"I see you got my message to come to tea."

"Message? What message?" Lord Klingflug sputtered.

"I sent a message over earlier this day inviting you to a late tea. Of course, that was before that golden light was shining in the sky. I just assumed you had been held up. So glad you could make it," Lady Farcroft said smoothly, creating an excuse as to why all the others were gathered. "We were just speculating that the column of golden light rising up out of the cliff behind the royal palace suggests that Nissa, or someone, has managed to put the oppgave ringe together."

"Ah, well, yes, then, that is the very reason I am late. I have been trying to find out from my sources just what is going on," stated Lord Klingflug, straightening his jacket, accepting a cup of tea from a smiling Lady Farcroft.

Lady Farcroft heard him muttering very quietly under his breath, "Why did my steward not give me Lady Farcroft's invitation to this tea? I will be having words with him later."

"And were you successful?" asked Lady Green, who had been unusually silent during the previous discussion.

"Yes. I have it on good authority that that rover Nissa has assembled the oppgave ringe," said Lord Klingflug, unable to keep the sneer out of his voice. "I should have done more to get rid of those rovers when I had a chance. I was way too soft. When I become king, you can be sure I will not make that mistake a second time."

"What else have you learned?" asked Lady Farcroft, trying to get Lord Klingflug off his rant about rovers and back to the subject at hand.

"My sources at the royal palace have informed me that Master Clarisse made a general announcement this afternoon that the gate mentioned in the Book of Rules has been found. It is the pair of doors built into the cliff wall at the bottom of the royal palace garden. She also stated that the oppgave ringe is now in place, and the gatekeepers are that garden laborer,

Lom, and that border guard, Theora, along with the two night wolves. They will be in charge of opening and closing the gate each day."

"That is just outrageous," stated Lady Furman. "That Lom lad is a nothing who comes from nothing. How can this be? We need to march ourselves right up to the royal palace and demand that one of our choosing be the gatekeeper."

"There is more," said Lord Klingflug.

"Go on," suggested Lady Farcroft.

"It seems anyone from street thief to noble will be allowed, one at a time, to walk the labyrinth to get through the clearing and enter through the gate to what has been described as a small valley. There the Gylden Sirklene challenge will take place. The gate will open at dawn and be closed at dusk. I went up to the royal palace before I came here to confront Master Clarisse and demand that I be the first to take the challenge. I was told I needed to be there at dawn and get in line. I, the former regent, was told I had to get in line!" Lord Klingflug said in disgust.

"This just cannot be right. I shall demand a meeting of the interim ruling council this very night to rule that we nobles, large land owners, or very successful merchants be allowed to go first to try the challenge," said Lord Hindre. "After all, I cannot imagine that one of us would not fulfill the challenge and be the next king or queen. We certainly are the most qualified. Why waste any more time letting common folk try the challenge when it should all be decided by choosing one of us."

"A splendid idea," said Lady Padde.

Before anyone else could respond to Lord Hindre's suggestion, once again, a knock came at the door. Lady Farcroft moved swiftly across the room to answer the knock, opened the door, stepped out of the room, and left the door open a sliver behind her. She could hear a heated conversation was being carried on by the various folks in the room. When Lady Farcroft reentered the room, Lord Klingflug was insisting quite loudly that he be the one to take the challenge first.

Gradually the room became silent when the folks noticed that Lady Farcroft had returned and was not looking pleased. She was holding a crumpled poster in her hands. Smoothing it out, she held it up for all in the room to see.

"You can clearly see from this poster, which one of my servants has brought me, demanding a meeting of the interim ruling council is not an option. Posters like this one have been put up all over the capital. Swift riders have been dispatched to the far reaches of Sommerhjem. As you can see by the seal on the bottom, this is an official announcement by the Crown concerning the Gylden Sirklene challenge. It commences on the morrow at dawn and will continue from dawn until dusk until the next ruler of Sommerhjem is chosen. All who feel called to try the challenge are welcome. No one will be refused. No one group, rank, guild, occupation, and so forth, will have preference," said Lady Farcroft.

"We have once again underestimated those representing the Crown," said Lord Mostander. "They could not have gotten all of those posters made up in the last few hours. They must have had them ready in anticipation of the ninth ring arriving on time, the oppgave ringe being assembled, and the gate that was mentioned in the Book of Rules being found."

"Those supporting the Crown have had entirely too much luck as of late," Lady Furman groused.

"More than as of late," muttered Lord Klingflug under his breath.

"What did you say?" asked Lady Farcroft.

"I said 'more than as of late'. When Queen Octavia died and I was appointed regent, I anticipated that one day we would have to give the rule of Sommerhjem over to a young, untried princess. It was then that many of us who are gathered here in this room began to plan for that day, and how we could prevent it. I had scholars looking through dusty tomes, scrolls, ancient text, and books in both the royal library and the royal palace archives to find out how we might prevent her from taking the throne."

"And what you found, instead, was the fact that, since the time of King Griswold's death, we had broken from tradition as to how we choose our next ruler," said Lady Farcroft.

"It was then I put several plans in place. The first was to isolate the princess, so she would not know what was happening in Sommerhjem, while we gained more control over the land and increased our holdings. In addition, by isolating the princess, her subjects became less and less enchanted with her," said Lord Klingflug.

"It was a plan that certainly worked well," stated Lady Padde. "Having watched her this last year gain respect and popularity, I am not sure how long we would have been able to control her after she came of age."

Ignoring Lady Padde, Lord Klingflug went on. "Once I was aware of the Gylden Sirklene challenge and the oppgave ringe, I put in motion all that I could to prevent the challenge from being called. I sent folks out to comb the royal library, the royal palace archives, and any place else I could think of to find the Book of Rules. I tried to find and remove all of the Høyttaier clan, so there would be no one who could read the Book of Rules, if someone besides us found it. I had folks scouring the countryside for most of a year to find Thorval Pedersen, because rumor had it that he knew something about the vessteboks."

"Unfortunately, none of those plans worked," said Lord Mostander. "The crowning blow, pardon the pun, was when Lady Esmeralda called the Gylden Sirklene challenge a year ago. Then our only option was to find the pieces of the oppgave ringe before the supporters of the Crown did. Unfortunately, at every turn, those who had acquired or found one of the rings, always managed to slip through our fingers, no matter how well we had them located or contained. Sometimes, I feel like there are unseen forces at work here."

"I held out such hope that, if we could not locate the ninth ring, those loyal to the Crown would also not be able to find it," said Lady Green. "There is some irony in the fact that it was already here in the capital during most of the year while we were looking for it. To think that we once even had it in our possession and did not realize it!"

Lady Farcroft gave Lady Green a quelling look, for she had been the one who had temporarily had the princess' royal seal in her possession, but then had lost it. "That is all water under the bridge at this point. Might I suggest that there is one last thing we can try before dawn?"

CHAPTER THIRTY-SEVEN

All of us who had carried pieces of the oppgave ringe into the capital were gathered on the terrace of the royal palace, along with others who had been key to bringing the Gylden Sirklene challenge to the point it was now. Besides the ring carriers, Da, Lady Esmeralda, Lady Celik, Elek, Master Rollag, Master Clarisse, Journeyman Evan, Eluta, Zeroun, Finn, Seeker Eshana, and others were gathered to discuss what needed to happen next.

"Now that the Crown has posted that the Gylden Sirklene challenge is to commence on the morrow at dawn, in anticipation of folks showing up at any time, probably even before the sun sets this night, I have asked the captain of the royal guard to work with the captain of the royal palace guard, and post more patrols at the royal palace," said Lady Esmeralda. "Since it has been known throughout Sommerhjem for months that we anticipated the challenge was to take place this week, everyone who has ever aspired to rule Sommerhjem will be here to line up at the royal palace gates, from the lowest of the night wagon haulers to the highest of dignitaries, including those from other countries."

"It is a good thing everything fell into place so quickly from the time the ninth piece of the oppgave ringe was placed in the vessteboks, or we might have had riots on our hands," said Master Rollag. "The reports of folks drifting in over the last week or so certainly have led us to suspect that not all who have arrived here from the far ends of Sommerhjem and beyond are here for the capital summer fair. I suspect there is not a spare room left to rent in town, and all of the campsites are very overcrowded."

"I am glad so many have come," said Lady Esmeralda, "though it has caused a great strain on the city's resources, and the royal guards and peacekeepers have certainly had their hands full. For every one folk who genuinely feels they are called to try the challenge, there are at least four or five who just think they should be the next ruler."

"Theora and I have been talking to the head of the royal guard, who says that, besides the normal challenges of keeping the peace during the capital fair, there are additional challenges of added folks who are here for the Gylden Sirklene challenge and those who would take advantage of those folks," Piper said. "She has told us of an increase in the number of pickpockets and swindlers. It is her sincere hope that a new ruler will be chosen soon, and the Gylden Sirklene challenge will not drag on for days and weeks. Master Clarisse, does the Book of Rules give any indication of what the timeline might be for the challenge?"

"What the Book of Rules suggests is that those who are seeking to be the next ruler of Sommerhjem must go through the gate. It has been determined that the gate that is being referred to is the pair of doors in the cliff wall at the bottom of the royal palace garden. The book, for once, is clear that only one person is allowed to enter through the doors at a time. Since that is the case, it will take as long as it takes for all those who think they should be the next ruler to enter the small valley beyond the doors."

"If that is the case, choosing the next ruler of Sommerhjem could go on for months," said Seeker Chance.

"That is certainly possible," replied Master Clarisse.

"You do not think that is going to be the case, though," stated Seeker Chance.

"No, I do not. I think that many who enter the clearing and walk the labyrinth will change their minds about going farther," said Master Clarisse. "Some may, by force of will or conviction, go through the gate, overriding the urge to turn back."

"I think others will go through the gate because they are called to do so, and yet, will not be chosen to be the next queen or king," I told the others.

"Why do you think so?" Da asked.

"Because of the nine rings with the firestar gems that rest at this moment in the vessteboks inside the quirrelit grove. I don't think they are there for no reason. I don't know who they may be for. I do think they are important," I replied.

I had told those gathered here about the vessteboks being in the valley and what it held. I had not told them about the standing stones, or about the stone within the standing stones. I felt as incapable of telling others about the standing stones as I was of saying anything about the Huntress.

Before the discussion could go any further, the royal palace steward made a discreet coughing noise to get Lady Esmeralda's attention. "I beg your pardon, Lady Esmeralda. Lord Klingflug, Lady Farcroft, and a number of others are here and wish to speak with you. I put them, once again, in the Rose parlor."

"Thank you, Reave. Nissa, Piper, perhaps you and your cats would accompany me. Being flanked by a hunting cat and a mountain cat might intimidate some of Lord Klingflug's followers. Being accompanied by a rover will probably put his undergarments in a twist," Lady Esmeralda said, leading the way off the terrace.

"You really don't like the former regent, do you?" I asked Lady Esmeralda.

"Not in the slightest. Knowing that he, Lady Farcroft, and others seriously discussed ending my life prematurely does not make me fond of them."

"I can certainly see how that might sour a relationship," said Piper. "I wonder what they might want now. Wasn't Lord Klingflug already here demanding to be the first to take the Gylden Sirklene challenge? Didn't he already get turned down on that request?"

"Yes, and yes. I do not know what brings him and his followers back. Ah, here we are. We shall soon find out," said Lady Esmeralda.

Carz, Piper, Jing, and I followed Lady Esmeralda through the door into the Rose parlor. I was not surprised to see Lord Klingflug, Lady Farcroft, Lady Green, and Lady Furman among those gathered there.

"There is no need for you to be accompanied by these, these others, and their animals," stated Lady Furman. "We merely wish to have a calm and sensible conversation with you, Lady Esmeralda."

The look on Lady Furman's face when she saw the cats made it very clear that she did not think much of being in the same room as Carz and Jing. I could not understand her objection, since they were often better groomed than many of the folks who visited the royal palace. They were certainly better mannered.

Ignoring Lady Furman's objection to the presence of Piper, the cats, and me, Lady Esmeralda said, "The hour grows late. What is it that you wish to discuss?"

Lord Klingflug stood up, cleared his throat, and said, "We have a number of things we wish to discuss. First, we wish to make it clear that we think it was presumptuous of the interim ruling council to put the Gylden Sirklene challenge on a first-come, first-served basis. That needs to be changed. You have influence with the interim ruling council. You are of noble birth, and surely you can see the logic of having those of our kind go first."

"First, all of the folks of Sommerhjem are my kind. Second, the Book of Rules states that anyone who feels called to try the challenge should be allowed to do so. The emphasis here is on the word 'anyone', so the interim ruling council concluded that no one should be excluded and no one should be given preference. They will not be inclined to change their minds, and I would not be inclined to ask them to do so," stated Lady Esmeralda firmly. "What else do you feel the need to discuss?"

"It concerns the gatekeepers," suggested Lady Padde. "We feel that a royal palace day laborer and a minor eastern mountain border guard are really not suitable choices for such an important role."

"I would suggest that the choosing of who is to be the gatekeeper, or in this case gatekeepers, is not and has never been in the hands of the interim ruling council. They, Lom and Theora, are the only ones who are able to open the doors in the cliff wall. A great many of us have been studying those doors for a number of days and have not found a way to enter. Nissa, along with the assembled oppgave ringe, was the living key to open the doors," said Lady Esmeralda.

"Why, then, is Nissa not the gatekeeper, and why can she not give that duty over to one of our choosing?" asked Lord Mostander.

"Because my only task was to unlock the doors. Once that was done, it became very clear to me my task was done. I concluded that once I stepped outside of the small valley inside the cliff, I would not be able to open the doors again. They can now only be opened by what the elder rover, Zeroun, refers to as the gardener and the protector, Lom and Theora. Also, I don't think I want to challenge not one but two night wolves any time soon," I told the gathered nobles.

"When Lady Esmeralda called the Gylden Sirklene challenge over a year ago, she set in motion something that, I have come to the conclusion, none of us has any control over," suggested Piper.

"I agree. So many generations have passed since King Griswold's death," said Lady Esmeralda. "So much knowledge has been lost concerning the Gylden Sirklene challenge, and yet, somehow, despite great difficulty, all of the parts have fallen into place. The Book of Rules, which had been lost, was found, and there was someone available to read it. The vessteboks arrived when it was needed, as did the keys needed to open it. All nine pieces of the oppgave ringe were found, carried to the capital on time, and assembled. It is now placed where it is needed for the challenge. I and the interim ruling council feel that what has happened was meant to happen. Folks chosen for each of the tasks were meant to be the ones chosen."

There was silence in the Rose parlor for a moment. I could see one, and then another, of the gathered nobles looking like they were about to say something, and then thinking better of it. Finally, Lady Farcroft spoke up.

"We have heard that you and Lord Hadrack's nephew, Aaron Beecroft, have been disappearing at times. It has been suggested that you and he have been trying to locate the hidden passageways that are rumored to riddle the royal palace. How do we know that you did not find a way into that valley that any one of us could use to set ourselves up as the gatekeepers?"

"I can assure you that neither Aaron nor I have discovered a secret passageway leading to the small valley surrounded by the cliff at the bottom of the garden of the royal palace."

"We know you discovered a chamber below the royal palace and have not allowed anyone down there," stated Lord Hindre.

"You are very well informed, and also correct," said Lady Esmeralda.

"We demand to see this chamber," shouted Lord Klingflug. "You cannot keep us from there."

"Actually, I can, since the interim ruling council has declared this my home until such time as a new ruler is chosen." Before Lord Klingflug could speak, Lady Esmeralda went on, "But I have no objection to taking you down there. You are welcome to spend as much time in the chamber as you wish."

I am not sure who was more surprised that Lady Esmeralda was allowing the assembled nobles to go to the chamber below the royal palace, the nobles or Piper or me. The more I thought about it, the more I came to the conclusion it was a wise decision on her part.

"If you will follow Nissa, Carz, Piper, and Jing, they will lead the way. If I remember, Piper, we left all of the lanterns there, did we not?" Lady Esmeralda asked.

"Yes. I was the last one to leave, the last time we were there, and I blew out all of the flames," Piper answered. "I suspect there is still enough oil to last for a while once the lanterns are re-lit."

I remember talking to Seeker Chance after I had left the small valley about what had happened in the chamber after I had gone through the opening following the blue light. He had told me that the wall had closed up after I had gone through, and they had tried to get it to open again to no avail. They had waited for quite some time for me to return. When that did not happen, Theora had reopened the door to the stairway. Those waiting, after explanations had been given, had come into the chamber, and also could not find a way to follow me. After much discussion, Piper had volunteered to wait in the chamber for a while longer, before turning out the lanterns and leaving.

When we arrived at the storeroom, Lady Esmeralda asked the nobles to wait in the corridor while she went into the storeroom. I noticed she shut the door behind her when she went in. Time passed, and I could feel the folks behind me getting fidgety. Finally, Lady Esmeralda opened the door, holding a lantern aloft. I could see she had lit a number of other lanterns while she had been in the storeroom. I felt movement next to me as Carz and Jing slipped by me and headed through the storeroom, disappearing through the opening to the stairs to the chamber below.

"Please take a lantern to light your way and follow Nissa and Piper. I will take up the rear," said Lady Esmeralda. "The second set of steps are old and worn, so be careful. We think the chamber you are about to go down to was built before the present royal palace and is very old. It may have been part of a keep built on this site long ago, but that is just a guess."

While the nobles were gathering just inside the doorway to the chamber, Piper and I went and lit the lanterns that had been left inside. With everything lit up, I could see nothing had changed from the first time I had explored here.

"The reason a number of us came down to explore this chamber was we were thinking that perhaps the ninth piece of the oppgave ringe might have been hidden here. As you know, it was not. While the royal historians or the seekers might find this chamber of interest, as you can see, it is just a large chamber with beautiful pillars. Little is known about its origin or use," said Lady Esmeralda. "Feel free to explore it."

I marveled at how deftly Lady Esmeralda had actually told the truth about the chamber without telling its function or what had happened here earlier. Piper and I took positions on either side of the entrance to the chamber. Carz and Jing joined us. It did not take long for the assembled nobles to grow bored with wandering around the chamber. Finally, Lord Klingflug announced he had seen enough, and it was growing late. The others agreed and began to move out of the chamber and up the stairs. Once we reached the main floor, Lady Esmeralda asked if they had any more questions. None of them did.

Just as they were leaving, I heard Lord Klingflug say to Lady Farcroft, "It would seem I am not the only one whose plans do not work."

Chapter Thirty-Eight

Lady Esmeralda, Piper, and I escorted Lord Klingflug, Lady Farcroft, and the others to the main royal palace doors and wished them a goodnight. Both Carz and Jing followed them partway down the steps before the two cats stopped, sat, and began grooming. It was all I could do not to laugh. Here were all of these nobles puffed up with their own importance basically being snubbed by a hunting cat and a mountain cat.

Once the nobles were out of sight and hearing, Lady Esmeralda turned to Piper and me. "If I were able to swivel my head around to lick my backside with disdain, you would see me right now sitting between Carz and Jing and joining them in grooming. Why is it that so many folks who have wealth think they should have more privileges and power than hardworking folks? Listening to them this night made me somewhat nauseated. They think they should be first in line, and that they should be able to choose the gatekeeper, and they are convinced one of them is going to be the next king or queen. Lord Klingflug and his cronies have spent a great deal of time and effort to prevent the Gylden Sirklene challenge from ever happening. Now that it is inevitable, they want to control it and its outcome. I wonder when they are going to realize the Gylden Sirklene challenge has never been even the slightest bit under anyone's control."

"Even when they get what they want, they're not happy," said Piper. "They wanted to be able to go down and find out what we had discovered beneath the royal palace. You could see that they were all ready to argue with you."

"You certainly took the wind out of their sails on that one," I chimed in, chuckling as I remembered the astonished looks on the nobles' faces when Lady Esmeralda told them she would take them down to the chamber.

"And yet, they really did not spend very much time there looking or asking questions," suggested Piper. "Mostly, they just complained."

"Do those disgusting cats have to go with us? Oh, eww, cobwebs!" said Lady Esmeralda, in a fair imitation of Lady Furman's voice.

"And then there was Lady Green, all of a dither about getting the bottom of her gown dusty. What did she expect?" Piper asked.

"Lord Klingflug did only a cursory inspection of the chamber. I noticed that Lady Farcroft and Lord Mostander spent more time taking everything in. I don't know why I'm concerned more about Lady Farcroft than the others," I said.

"Probably because there are two very different sides to her," said Lady Esmeralda. "She presents an image of being as much a ninny as Lady Green. All of the reports that Lady Celik and others have made about Lady Farcroft paint an entirely different picture of her. She has been behind a number of plans that have almost succeeded in stopping pieces of the oppgave ringe from reaching the capital. You are right to be more concerned about her than Lord Klingflug, whom we also cannot discount. We had best get back to the others. There is still much to discuss and last-minute plans to go over before dawn on the morrow. I do not think any of us will be getting much sleep this night."

Lady Esmeralda was correct about none of us getting much sleep. On our way back from seeing Lord Klingflug, Lady Farcroft, and the others out of the royal palace, we were met by the royal steward, who directed us to one of the larger meeting chambers where members of the interim ruling council and others had gathered.

"I am sorry if you folks have been waiting long for Nissa, Piper, and me to join you. We were detained by Lord Klingflug and others, listening to their demands. As Lady Furman put it, they merely wanted to have a calm and sensible conversation with me. What they were hoping for was that I would side with them concerning just who should be eligible to be first in line to attempt the Gylden Sirklene challenge. I think they were also hoping I would side with them concerning the need for someone of noble birth to be the gatekeeper. They are pretty put out that 'a mere lowly day laborer and a very minor eastern mountain guard' are the gatekeepers and not one of their rank and choosing."

"Oh, is that all?" questioned Master Rollag.

"Not by any means. They are fairly upset with the interim ruling council for opening the Gylden Sirklene challenge to all on a first-come, first-served basis. They think the rabble, anyone who is not them and noble, should be put to the end of the line, and they should go first. Lord Klingflug went so far as to suggest that, since I supposedly have influence over the interim ruling council and am, of course, of noble birth, I surely would see the logic of having 'our kind', his term not mine, go first. I told him I would not bring it up to the council, and I did not see you changing your minds."

"You are correct in that," said a member of the interim ruling council.

"They even wanted to know why I could not be the gatekeeper," I told those gathered. "Of course, if I could be the gatekeeper, then they assumed I would just turn the task over to one of them."

"So, was that the end of their demands?" asked Lady Celik.

"No. They wanted to see the chamber with the pillars," said Lady Esmeralda. "All of you have been informed that Aaron Beecroft and I found a chamber below the royal palace that we suspect was here before the present royal palace was built. Since the ninth ring was not there, as all of us now know, I could see no reason to not allow them to look around the chamber."

I could hear an increase of murmuring in the room. The interim ruling council had been informed of the discovery of the chamber, and that we had searched it, hoping it might contain the ninth piece of the oppgave ringe. Only those who had been present on the day we had gathered in the chamber and opened the door that had led me to the small valley with the standing stones were aware of what happened that day. We had concluded that was information that needed to remain among the few of us.

"I think your allowing them to take a look around the chamber was a wise choice," said Lord Hadrack. "It is now one less thing they can complain about or throw in our faces, if one of them is not chosen as the next king or queen of Sommerhjem."

"It was also very wise of you to take Nissa, Piper, Carz, and Jing with you. I bet Lady Furman was just delighted to spend time in the Rose parlor with Carz and Jing," said Seeker Chance.

"She could hardly contain her enthusiasm," said Piper dryly.

"I can't imagine Lord Klingflug was all that happy that Nissa came with you. He does not care very much for rovers," commented Da.

"Back to the business at hand," suggested Master Clarisse. "The Book of Rules does not explain just what the challenge is. It does tell us that one must follow the path to have a clear mind before entering through the gate. I suspect that means that one needs to walk the labyrinth before going through the doors in the cliff wall. What happens after that is anyone's guess."

When I opened my mouth to talk about the two circlets that were on the stone in the middle of the standing stones, nothing came out. My suspicion, of course, was that only the rightful king or queen would be able to use the oppgave ringe to obtain one of the slim circlets. I had also come to the conclusion that so little being written down about how to put the oppgave ringe together, how to find and open the gate, what to do with the oppgave ringe, and about other parts of the Gylden Sirklene challenge had a lot to do with not being able to even say anything about it if you actually knew something. Just as I had not been able to tell Lom and Theora about the Huntress, I could not tell those gathered here about the two circlets.

The meeting went on into the wee hours of the night. Finally, it broke up when Lord Hadrack suggested we were as prepared as we could be for all the possible outcomes and what might happen on the morrow. As I walked out of the meeting room, Da stopped me.

"What do you think you will do this day?" he asked.

"I have not thought that far. I know that curling up under the covers and sleeping the day away is most likely not an option. I think, however, my tasks are complete concerning the oppgave ringe and the Gylden Sirklene challenge."

I can only hope I misunderstood the Huntress when she suggested my tasks were done for the day, and she was not implying there were other tasks to be done on other days. That was not a comforting thought, all things considered.

"You are not thinking of getting in line for the challenge so you can become the next queen of Sommerhjem?" Da asked.

"Not even on a good day. You?"

"Not on any day. I feel no call to be the next king of Sommerhjem. I may not want to be a fulltime rover again, but I know I would much prefer my nice quiet cottage in Mumblesey to living in the royal palace. I have decided not to leave here until the challenge is fulfilled, providing it does not drag on for weeks. I know many of the crafters are going to pull up stakes and move on to the next fair in another day or so. The royal metalsmith has invited me to work in his forge until I take to the road again. I think he is hoping to learn the secrets to my knife making."

"I know I need to head into the fair this day," I told Da. "It is time I get back to being a rover, and I can see no need to stay here and watch the parade of folks who wish to be the next queen or king wait in line. Even though I am quite tired, it is way too late to go to bed now. I think I will go get cleaned up, grab something to eat, and head to the fairgrounds at first light."

Da and I walked back to the campsite in companionable silence and parted ways at our homewagons. Carz followed me up the steps and headed straight toward the bed. I rummaged around, finding clean clothes and some of the sweetly-scented soap made by Nana, and gathered them together to take with me to the bath house.

"Heading up for a bath, Carz. Want to come along?" He lifted his head up briefly, and then laid it back down, and put a paw over his eyes. "I'll take that as a 'no' then."

Dawn had broken when I walked back into the campsite after a long hot soak. I had not expected to find any of the others up, but there was a small group gathered around the cook fire. When I really took a good look, I noticed Seeker Chance had a look of distress on his face, and Meryl looked upset. Piper came toward me, and I could see the look of great concern on her face. I was also surprised to see Greer and Yara standing with the group.

"Has something happened?" I asked, as I tried to move past them toward my homewagon. I was suddenly very afraid that something had happened to Carz.

"Wait," Piper said quietly. "They are gone. All of the animals are gone. They left just a short while ago."

"Carz?"

"Carz, Jing, Ashu, and Tashi have all left," replied Piper.

"Where …."

"They have gone through the gates to the small valley," said Seeker Chance. "I was awake when I felt Ashu move off the bed and head out of the tent. Was still dressed, for I had thought to just lay down for a little while when we got back from the meeting early this morning. I could not figure out why he had left the tent, so I got up. When I looked out the tent flap, I saw that Carz and Jing were with him, and they were heading out of the campsite. When I caught a glimpse of Tashi winging overhead, I left the tent and followed."

"What happened next?"

"As they headed across the royal palace grounds, they were joined by Kasa and Toki," said Seeker Chance, "followed shortly by Greer and Yara."

"I could not understand why Kasa wanted to go out, since it had not been that long since we had been outside. He was quite insistent, so I opened a door for him, and he rushed off," said Greer.

"The same happened with Toki, so I followed," said Yara.

"All of the animals headed straight toward the tangle," said Seeker Chance, taking up the conversation once again. "When we got through the tangle, we saw them walk the labyrinth and then take the path to the gates. Just as they arrived at the doors, the doors opened, and all of the animals walked through. We followed their steps and were met at the doors by Lom and Theora. We knew better than to ask to enter and so turned around and left. There was nothing we could do."

I felt a great need to find something to sit on, for I was not sure my knees would hold me up any longer. I had always feared that one day Carz might leave me. I just thought I would be able to say goodbye.

Chapter Thirty-Nine

Once I caught my breath, I wanted to rush right out of the campsite, go to the doors in the cliff wall, and demand to be let through. I knew in my head that I would not do that. My heart did not agree and was still arguing with my head when Da came, sat beside me, and took my hands in his.

"It is not like you to expect the worst, daughter. All of us gathered here now have had some task or tasks to fulfill to bring us to this day and the commencing of the Gylden Sirklene challenge. Eight of you have been accompanied on that journey, each by a very special animal. Is it possible that they have not left you, but rather are just carrying out one of their tasks this day?" questioned Da.

I grabbed onto that thought the way an unwary swimmer, being swept out with the tide, grabs on to a piece of flotsam. "Do you think that might be so?"

"I think it is entirely possible," said Da. "I just can't imagine the possibility that each and every one of the companion animals would abruptly disappear from each and every one of your lives. You all have too close a bond with them."

I gathered that idea close as I got up to go to my homewagon and pack up various tools I had lying around. Since all of what I had been called to do concerning the oppgave ringe and the Gylden Sirklene challenge was done, I could see no reason to linger in the campsite this day. After all, the capital fair was still going on, and I still had a living to make.

Though the fair would not open for several more hours, I decided I was going to go in early, since I had not been at my booth for a while. I wanted to check what inventory had sold, what I needed to restock, and to just straighten up in general. I knew Shyla would have done a fine job keeping the booth open and things straightened up. I just needed the familiar routine after the goings on of the last few days.

Da decided he would accompany me, as did Nana. It felt very strange not to have Carz walking beside me. Oh, I know that I had walked to my booth at other fairs without him when he had chosen to stay behind at the campsite. I guess I somehow always knew he would be there when I returned after the closing bell rang each night. I had no such assurance this day.

I arrived at my booth well ahead of most of the folks who had booths along the Glassmakers Guild's lane. It was quiet, and the morning was cool, with a slight breeze bringing the smell of salt water up from the harbor. I have always liked that quiet time early in the morning before the hustle and bustle of the fair begins. It felt good to be back.

After I had had a chance to straighten up the cart that formed my booth, swept up errant wood chips and done other tidying chores, I realized that I was very hungry. Knowing I still had a bit of time before the fair opened, I set off to find my favorite baker's booth and get something to eat. I remembered a shortcut I had found last year that took me on a more direct route to the baker's booth, so I cut down that way. It took me along the backside of some of the booths. I had just rounded a tree when I was grabbed from the side and pulled through the back flaps of a tent of a rug merchant, thrust into a chair, and bound. I felt a knife press against my neck.

A voice spoke out of the shadows. "I would strongly suggest you remain very still and very quiet. It was very foolish of you to wander the fair all alone, without your cat or your guards. Here is what is going to happen now. I have some questions for you. If you answer them promptly, you will be released. If you refuse to answer my questions, it will be rather painful for you. Is that clear?"

"Very." *How could I be so stupid as to think that now that my tasks are done, I would be free to return to being just Nissa, the rover woodworker? Carz leaving and lack of sleep is no excuse for my lapse of judgment.*

"Good. Now then, I wish for you to describe what lies beyond the two doors set into the cliff wall in the lower part of the royal garden."

I could see no reason not to give a general description of the small valley. It was going to get difficult, and possibly painful, should she, and I think it was a she questioning me, ask for specifics. There were some things I would not be able to tell her, no matter how much I might want to. I could feel sweat begin to trickle down my back. I did not think Carz and Master Clarisse would rush into the rug merchant's tent any time soon to rescue me, as they had when I had been snatched off the streets of Tverdal.

"It is a small, very beautiful valley. Waterfalls cascade from atop the cliff. There is a profusion of grasses and flowers, and a path winds through them. It is a very peaceful and quiet place, with the exception of birds singing and insects buzzing. Sunlight glints off several ponds and pools. There is a large quirrelit grove a ways down the path."

"What else?" the woman in the shadows demanded.

"There is a small grassy knoll on the left side of the path to the quirrelit grove."

"A grassy knoll, birds singing, a large quirrelit grove. Enough! Tell me how the challenge takes place."

I decided to try another approach, for I was fairly sure I was not going to be able to tell this inquisitor about what was within the quirrelit grove. "I know as little as anyone else about what the Gylden Sirklene challenge is, or how it takes place, and I really don't want to know. I have always been a reluctant participant in all that has gone on over the last year concerning the oppgave ringe and the challenge. Believe me, I have no desire to take the challenge and become the next queen of Sommerhjem. My tasks were finished when I assembled the oppgave ringe."

"How did you get into the valley in the first place?"

This was going to be trickier to answer. "I put the oppgave ringe together, and then once it was together, I tried the doors and they opened." That was the truth as far as it went. I was glad I was not being made to hold a truth stone, for I am not sure how my answer would stand up. I just hoped she would not ask me about what I did with the oppgave ringe.

"What did you do with the oppgave ringe?"

"It was the key I used to open the doors." Again, I was really not lying to this woman who had a henchman holding a knife to my throat. Once the oppgave ringe had been assembled and all of us were in the chamber below the royal palace, we had been able to put in motion what had been needed to open the wall of the chamber and allow me to get to the valley to open the doors from the inside. Of course, I was really going to try not to tell this woman that, if I could. Actually, I was not sure it was possible for me to tell her that.

I began to wonder how much longer they would be able to keep me tied up here. I could hear sounds of folks opening their booths. I could hear the normal noises of merchants and crafters yelling to one another across the lanes. Would not someone notice that the rug merchant had not opened his tent? The opening hour of the fair had to be soon. It then occurred to me that these folks who were holding me probably had not picked this tent at random.

It also occurred to me I could concentrate on the firestar gem set in the ring the Huntress had given me. She had made me a clan friend of the forester clans and said if I was ever in trouble all I needed to do was call for help. I did not want to do that just yet. And maybe I would not need to do it, for I caught a slight movement near the roof of the tent behind the woman who stood in the shadows.

"Let us try this again," said the woman. "This time I want details. No more waxing poetic about the beauty of the valley. Just how big do you think the valley is? How far from the gate to the quirrelit grove? How many paths wander through the valley, and in what direction? What do you see directly in front of you when …?"

I had ceased to listen to her questions for I could tell that the interior of the tent was getting slightly lighter. Blue will-o'-wisps were gathering in large numbers behind the inquisitor. They were glowing very, very dimly. I suspected that the folk who was holding a knife to my throat was bent over and not looking up. If he did, he would not fail to see the blue will-o'-wisps.

I found the fact that they were hovering near the roof of the tent a comfort, and yet worrisome. A comfort because I hoped they might intervene should the two who were holding me move to harm me. Worrisome, because, since I had fulfilled my tasks both concerning the oppgave ringe and being the key to opening the gate, I thought I was done, and the blue will-o'-wisps would therefore no longer be concerned with me. That they were here now was giving me pause.

I was brought out of my reverie abruptly when I felt the knife at my throat nick my skin and heard the woman suggest I needed to pay attention and answer her questions. Suddenly, the blue will-o'-wisps flared to brightness and flew straight at the knife-wielding man. I could see nothing, but I heard the knife drop and the sound of the man stumbling back. Then I heard rapid footsteps as the man ran out the back of the tent.

Just as the man was running out of the back flap chased by the will-o'-wisps, the front flap of the rug merchant's tent was flung open. A forester entered. Before he could do more than ask what was going on, the inquisitor rushed out of the shadows, pushed the forester aside, and ran out of the front of the tent. The forester was torn between following her or coming to my aid. He chose to come to my aid.

"We really need to stop meeting like this. The last time you asked for my help you were all tied up too. What is it with you and folks tying you up? Where is your hunting cat? Carz, wasn't it? They don't have Kiaya somewhere too, do they?" asked Frayne, as he was untying me.

Frayne must have seen something in my face, for he asked if I was all right, if I was hurt in any way.

"I am fine. Feeling rather foolish at the moment. I did not call for help. How did you know to come?"

"I, uh, let me think on that while I finish untying you. There you go. Can you stand?"

"I have not been tied up all that long, so I am fine to stand and to get out of this tent. Let's move quickly before the rug merchant who owns this tent finds us and calls the peacekeepers to arrest us for rug stealing. We can answer each other's questions when we are safely back at my booth. Will you go with me there?"

"Of course, clan friend."

When we arrived at my booth, I asked Shyla if she would check with the Glassmakers Guild's cook and see if she had anything to spare, for I was famished. That left the booth empty so I could have a discreet conversation with Frayne.

"I will try to answer your questions. First, I don't know who it was who snatched me off the path behind the booths. I have my suspicions. I'd rather not say, however, for I have no proof. I do know they wanted information about the challenge and the oppgave ringe. In all honesty, I could not give her any information, any more than I could give any to you now. Something prevents me. I foolishly thought my role was over, since I had put the oppgave ringe together and unlocked the gate for the challenge. I just didn't think this morning when I went off to find breakfast that I might still need to be careful."

I invited Frayne to sit down on one of the chairs behind the counter so we could continue to talk.

"As to Carz, well, he has tasks of his own this day, and so is not with me. And Kiaya is just fine and safe."

I felt odd answering Frayne's question about Kiaya. Few folks knew that was the rover name we had given Lady Esmeralda when she had traveled with me disguised as a rover to keep her safe until her coming-of-age day last summer. Frayne had been one of the foresters who had rescued us at one point on our journey to the capital from Snoddleton, but that is a story for another time. Right now, I needed to find out how he knew to find me in the rug merchant's tent, since I had not called him.

"How did you know I needed rescuing again?"

"You called."

"No, I don't think I did. I thought about calling and dismissed that idea when the roof of the tent began to fill up with blue will-o'-wisps."

"Blue will-o'-wisps? You did say blue will-o'-wisps, did you not?"

"Are you asking about their color or their existence?" I asked. It was all I could do not to laugh out loud at the look on Frayne's face. It was good to want to laugh, after what had already happened this morning.

"The color. I have heard of the green will-o'-wisps that are supposed to be in the marshes and swamps near Farlig Brygge, except I think they call them blekbrann there. Never heard of blue ones, though."

"As far as I am aware, no one else that I know has either. As I was saying, I had thought to call for help from a forester if one was close at hand. I thought I had not called, since the blue will-o'-wisps have come to my aid in the past. I hoped that was why they were gathering on the underside of the roof of the rug merchant's tent."

"Now that I have had a chance to think about it, I don't think you called either. I remember what your call felt like, and this call was different."

Chapter Forty

I would have liked to ask Frayne more. Unfortunately, just before I could get my questions out, Shyla returned with bread, cheese, and a few tarts.

"The guild cook apologized for the meagerness of the fare. Seems he was swamped by visitors to the guild this morning and said they ate like scavengers. I asked him who had come to breakfast besides Journeyman Evan, which gave him a good laugh," said Shyla.

Journeyman Evan, who was minding the booth next to mine, overheard Shyla's remark and, of course, had to respond. How long that teasing exchange would have gone on is hard to tell, had not folks wandered up to both of our booths. As Frayne began to slip out of my booth, I thanked him once again for coming to my rescue. I also asked if he would mind doing me a favor by taking a note up to the royal palace and placing it in the hands of the royal palace steward and none other. He agreed.

It took me a few moments to write the note, addressing it to the royal palace steward. I wanted the others who had carried pieces of the oppgave ringe into the capital to know that we were not yet safe outside the royal palace. We were now, more than ever, vulnerable without our companion animals, as I well had found out just a short while ago.

It was midafternoon when the traffic slowed down just a bit in front of my booth. Sales had gone well, for which I was very thankful. I was certainly glad the day had continued to be uneventful after its rather scary start. Piper and Greer, accompanied by a small contingent of royal guards, had stopped by briefly to let me know they had gotten the warning, and to thank me for sending it. I really did not have a chance to talk to them at the time because a number of fairgoers, wanting to look at the whimsies, had gathered at the booth. I told Greer and Piper I would catch up with them later.

It was interesting to listen to the talk that swirled around the booth as fairgoers wandered by, or gathered in groups near the booth. Much of the talk was of the golden light that was still shining out of the small valley behind the royal palace. I heard one of the passing fairgoers telling another that she found it odd that the golden light in the shape of a quirrelit tree had very few leaves.

"Do you not think it is odd," she had said, "that the golden tree has so few leaves?"

"Well, it certainly had few yesterday when it first came pouring out from that cliff behind the royal palace. I noticed that there are more leaves this day."

"Are you sure?"

"Oh, yes. My young son is very into counting these days, ever since he learned to count beyond one hundred. It was he who pointed out that there were more leaves this day."

"I wonder what that means."

"I wonder what it all means," said the first speaker.

I could not hear much more of their conversation, since they had walked farther down the lane. It got me to wondering. I had noticed the golden light formed a quirrelit tree trunk and branches when it rose right in front of me. I guess I did not think about whether those branches were bare or had leaves. Thinking back, I realized that there had been very few leaves on the tree. Like the folks I overheard, I too was curious as to whether there were more leaves this day as compared to yesterday. And, if so, I wondered what that meant, if anything.

I also heard from time to time about this folk or that folk who was thinking about trying the Gylden Sirklene challenge, for they thought they would make a good king or queen. I do not think many of them were really serious about actually going to try the challenge, however. As at most fairs, there were always groups of folks my age wandering through the fairgrounds with a few coppers or silver coins burning holes in their pockets. I could hear the teasing and the bravado among them, daring each other to try the challenge, or bragging about what they were going to do when they became the next queen or king. I suspected this kind of foolish talk was likely to go on until the rightful ruler for the land of Sommerhjem was chosen. I could only hope that the true next ruler would be chosen soon.

As I worked at my booth through the afternoon, I wondered what was happening back at the royal palace. Had Lord Klingflug pushed his way to the front of the line and demanded he go first? Had folks been respectful while standing in line waiting their turns, or had there been problems? Had the nobles made more demands? I also wondered how Lom and Theora were doing. I did not envy them their job as the gatekeepers. Mostly, when I could no longer keep it out of my mind, I wondered where Carz was, and if he would come back.

Just as Shyla and I were packing away our wares, a small patrol of royal guards approached the booth.

"We are here to escort you back to the royal palace grounds," said one of the guards. "The other half of our patrol has gone to escort your father and grandmother back."

While I did not like the fact that I might need an escort, I was not going to be foolish and refuse it. I knew most of this small patrol, which helped. It was a relief to know that Da and Nana would also have an escort back. I have to admit, while I was happy to have an escort, I was looking forward to the day I no longer needed one.

Much as the royal palace campground was a beautiful place to camp, and certainly came with good food and good company, I missed camping at the fair. I missed Mistress Jalcones' cooking. I missed the nightly gatherings of old and new friends around the cook fires. I missed the talk, the laughter, and the music that happened at night after the fairgoers had all gone home. Tucking those thoughts away as Shyla and I tucked the last of our wares into the cart, I bid her farewell until the morrow. It was with great reluctance I headed back to the royal palace and then to an empty homewagon.

The first topic of discussion among those of us gathered on the terrace for the evening meal was unfortunately about my being snatched that morning. I was glad that the focus of the talk concerning my being grabbed in broad daylight was more on how to protect all of us while the challenge was going on than how foolish I had been to head off on my own.

Dinner on the terrace was saved from being a quiet and solemn meal by the stories being told by various folks about what had gone on at the royal palace this day concerning the Gylden Sirklene challenge. I think they purposely kept up an ongoing patter, for they knew those of us who had traveled with uncommon animals were hurting with them being gone.

"While I was not surprised by how many folks had lined up at the royal palace gate well before dawn, I was surprised by how little trouble there was with all those folks standing in line for hours," said Seeker Eshana.

"Especially considering what a varied group it was, with a baker standing next to a very wealthy merchant, a fisher standing next to a small land owner, a noble standing next to a forester," commented Master Clarisse. "What I found most curious were the few folks who had a look of confusion on their faces as if they could not quite figure out how they found themselves in the line. They did not have that look of determination that some had, nor did they have that look of self-righteous smugness that others had."

Seeker Eshana nodded. "I remember seeing a few of those. I had the feeling that no one was more surprised than they were to be standing in the line. I saw one of them begin to step out of line and then step back in, as though someone had pulled her by the back of her shirt. I thought it rather odd at the time."

"Did anyone try to push their way to the head of the line?" I asked, for I was curious as to whether Lord Klingflug had continued to insist that he be first.

"Actually, that was one of the big surprises of the day," said Master Rollag. "Lord Klingflug did not show up at all, nor did Lady Farcroft, nor any of the others of their group. I find that rather worrisome, considering their demands of the night before."

"I cannot imagine that Lord Klingflug has changed his mind that he is destined to be the next king of Sommerhjem," said Lady Esmeralda. "I also found his absence here this day troubling. I wonder if he has decided to let what he would consider 'the rabble' try first and thinks he will then succeed at the challenge and can be magnanimous in saying 'I let those inferior folks try the challenge and they failed. I must be the rightful king as I have said all along. After all, I am a noble and most suited for the task of ruling Sommerhjem.' Can you not just hear him?"

"What I found interesting," said Seeker Chance, "is there was not a single rover waiting in line. Not a single one."

"Rovers have always had wanderlust," said Thorval. "We are folks who for the most part are not content to stay in any one place for long. There is always something waiting over the next hill, across the next bridge, around the next bend. I actually am an odd rover, since I have a cottage in Mumblesey. I had thought I was content there. What this summer has shown me is I am, for the most part. Yet the allure of the open road will always be a part of me. Nissa and I have talked of doing some fairs together next summer, and I think it will not take much persuasion on her part for me to agree."

"I'm glad of that, Da. On another subject, I heard talk at the fair this day that the golden light in the shape of a quirrelit tree that continues to rise up out of the valley had mostly bare branches yesterday. I really did not notice that then. I can see that they were right as I look at the golden tree now," I said.

"You are correct, there are more leaves on the golden quirrelit tree now than there were at dawn," stated Master Clarisse. "I have spent most of this day here on the terrace, which gave me a good view of the end of the garden. I watched as each folk entered the tangle. Most were not gone all that long, coming out shortly after they entered. My suspicion is they either turned around at the entrance to the clearing, or after walking the labyrinth. I cannot imagine they got as far as the doors in the short amount of time they were there."

"You would be correct," said Theora, as she and Tala stepped up onto the terrace.

Chaos ensued for the next few minutes, not because Theora was standing on the terrace and had left the gates, but because those of us who had carried pieces of the oppgave ringe to the capital were too busy hugging and ruffling the fur, or in the case of Tashi, the feathers, of our companion animals.

I finally let go of Carz when he began to squirm. He gave me a slight look of disgust, I think because I had been holding him too tight. It could have been because he knew I had thought he would not come back. I was very glad he chose to lie down right next to me. If he had moved away, I probably would have gone to sit next to him. I could not imagine the others not feeling the same way. I almost burst out laughing at the image of all of us moving from spot to spot following our companion animals all over the terrace as they moved. Once I had my mirth under control, I realized that not only Theora and Tala were on the terrace with us, but also Lom and Taarig.

"You have left the valley. Has a king or queen been chosen?" I asked.

"No," answered Lom. "When dusk came, the other animals who have been with us this day began to head out of the valley. Taarig and Tala literally pushed us out the doors. The doors swung shut behind us."

I am sure Lom and Theora now faced a group of folks who had various looks of concern on their faces. If the gatekeepers were outside of the valley, would they be able to open the doors from the outside?

"The minute the doors closed behind us, we immediately turned around and tried to open them. They opened easily," stated Lom. "We do not think anyone can get into the valley, for when Theora tried to open the doors by herself, they would not open. Once we were through the tangle, it closed up behind us. I again turned around and tried to go back to the clearing. The tangle opened up right away."

"We do not think it will be wise for us to leave the valley each night. We are most vulnerable from the tangle to here. We felt it was all right this night, since we were surrounded by all of the companion animals," said Theora. "We just felt you might like to know what happened this day."

"Let us move this conversation to a more secure place within the royal palace," suggested Lady Esmeralda.

Once we were all settled inside, Theora told us what their day had been like, with Lom adding bits and pieces to her tale.

"It has certainly been an interesting day. There has been, as you know, a steady stream of folks, one at a time, at least getting as far as the clearing. Many who made it that far, turned around and headed back. Then there were the folks who made it to the quirrelit tree in the center of the open space and walked the labyrinth."

"Most of them, after walking the labyrinth, very quietly just continued back on the path, through the tangle, and were gone," said Lom.

"Of the great number of folks who came forth this day to try the Gylden Sirklene challenge, only a handful or two actually walked through the doors," continued Theora. "Some turned back before they entered the quirrelit grove. Others entered the grove, but were back out quite quickly. A very few of the folks who entered the valley were gone for some time in the quirrelit grove."

"Some of the folks who left the quirrelit grove, who had spent some time there, could not seem to leave the valley fast enough. They ran as if a pack of night wolves were pursuing them. Their faces held a look of terror," said Lom. "Some left more slowly. Some even smiled at us on their way out of the doors."

"Those folks seemed content with whatever had happened to them in the quirrelit grove. There were a couple of folks who were different. They had a look of, I guess you could call it awe, as they passed us."

"When each of the folks who entered the doors passed us by, I did not feel any pull that any of them had an object of power on them. That was not the case when those who had what Theora described as a look of awe on their faces passed us on their way out of the valley."

"You think they carried something that held power out of the valley?" said Master Clarisse.

"I do," answered Lom.

"Do you have any idea what it might have been?" asked Master Clarisse.

Lom paused a moment and looked as if he was going to speak. Another moment passed before he answered Master Clarisse. "I truthfully really cannot tell you."

I wonder if they were carrying one of the nine rings we had seen in the vessteboks?

CHAPTER FORTY-ONE

Lom and Theora stayed for a little while longer, and then said they were going to head back. I volunteered to walk them back as far as the opening to the tangle. The others gathered on the terrace were also beginning to head to their respective living quarters, or back to the campsite. Da suggested he would walk with me, but Nana asked him to walk back with her. I was just as glad, for I wanted to talk to Lom and Theora alone.

Once we were far enough away from the royal palace and the others, I asked Lom if he thought those few he had felt something about might have been carrying one of the rings from the vesseboks.

"I think that is what they were carrying. The firestar gem on my ring warmed when each of them passed. If one of them had been wearing one of the rings from the vesseboks openly, my firestar gem might have arced."

"Do you know who any of these folks were?" I asked.

"No. I think by his dress and manner, one was a farmer. Not young, yet not old either," said Lom.

"One was a woman. She was well-dressed and had a set of keys attached to her belt. I would guess she was a small merchant of some kind. She was probably older than me by five to seven years. I really can't explain why I think so, but I think those two folks were not drawn to the quirrelit grove because they thought they should be the next ruler of Sommerhjem."

"You both think they were drawn there to choose one of the rings out of the vesseboks," I stated.

"Yes," answered Lom with conviction.

"And yet, when Master Clarisse asked you if you had any idea about what they might have been carrying out of the valley you said you could not say."

"I told her the truth. I really could not say. I can talk to you about it. I can talk to Theora about it. When I tried to answer Master Clarisse, I could not get the words out. Maybe it was so I would not describe the folks who might have been carrying the rings from the vessteboks to anyone other than you."

"I completely understand. This morning when I was being held in the rug merchant's tent, I was glad rescue came so quickly, because I could not have answered the woman's questions even if my life might have depended on it. Ah, here we are at the tangle. It will be another long day for you two on the morrow, so I will leave you here to head to your quarters in the valley."

I bade the two goodnight and watched them enter the tangle with the two night wolves. What I really wanted to do then was head back to my homewagon and just sit on the steps with Carz at my side. I wanted to tell him how scared I had been to find him gone, and how very glad I was that he was back. It was all I could do not to reach down and touch him every few steps, just to reassure myself that he was still walking beside me.

I was about halfway to the campsite, when I noticed someone sitting near one of the fountains. As I drew closer, I could see in the dim lamplight that it was Master Clarisse. When I came closer still, she stood up and waved me over. It would seem that my step-sitting was going to have to wait.

"I was hoping to catch you before you reached your homewagon," Master Clarisse said.

"Is something wrong?" I asked.

"No. No, I just wanted a quiet time to have a chance to ask you some questions, without being surrounded by so many folks," Master Clarisse replied. "After hearing about your ordeal this morning, it occurred to me that we never thought to ask you about what happened after you left the chamber below the royal palace, or anything about your time in the small valley. Those who would oppose us certainly thought of those questions, and yet, we did not. A puzzle for sure."

"I would like to think that you did not think to ask those questions for you felt it was none of your business, that it would give you an unfair advantage concerning the challenge, which is what I think my inquisitor was trying for this morning. What I can tell you about what happened after I left the chamber below the royal palace, and before I opened the doors in the cliff wall, is nothing, other than a brief description of the valley. Please understand that I would trust you with more information. It is not a matter of me holding back. Rather, it is a matter of me being unable to tell you. Something prevents me from saying anything, and believe me, it's not me."

"I thank you for explaining. Something the seekers, Yara, and I have been discussing has been about the vagueness of the Book of Rules. As we have noted, it gives some specifics, but very few. It has gotten us to wondering if so little is in the Book of Rules to prevent folks from knowing too much, and thereby having an advantage, or from being able to find a way around the challenge ..."

"I hear another 'or' here."

"... or, if some parts leading up to the challenge are kept vague because it is not the same each time. All that has led up to this day has certainly been complicated by the amount of time that has passed since the challenge was last called. So much knowledge has been lost over time."

"I've wondered about something ever since Lady Esmeralda found the ninth ring in the royal seal holder. It had to have been there since the time of King Griswold. I know that King Griswold became king when he was quite young and lived an extremely long life. Surely, a great many folks at that time were still knowledgeable about how he had been chosen to rule Sommerhjem. How then did his daughter become the next queen without going through the Gylden Sirklene challenge?"

"This is a question the seekers, the royal head librarian, the royal head historian, Yara, and I have also been asking of late. It could be that the folks of Sommerhjem just got used to her taking over more and more of the rule as her father grew older. It could be somewhat more complex and sinister. Eluta, the head royal librarian, told me when we were discussing that time period that she often wondered why there were so few books and other sources about the time when King Griswold's daughter became queen. Eluta has made it a priority to get someone in the royal library to do a deep search. Seeker Eshana and Seeker Chance, when they have time, are looking in the royal palace library and archives. Once the challenge is over, Yara has added looking for those references to her list of what to look for in the out-country."

When I stifled a yawn for the second time, Master Clarisse took pity on me and thanked me for talking with her. Carz and I walked back to the campsite. By the time I got there, a fine mist was falling. I was glad for the dampness, for it meant no one would fault me for going directly to my homewagon. I needed the time alone with Carz and my thoughts.

The next morning when I awoke, Carz was once again gone, as were the other companion animals. I did not leave my homewagon with as empty a heart as I had the day before. I felt optimistic that Carz would return at full dusk and held on to that thought as I was escorted to the fair. Since the capital fair was the largest fair of the summer, it ran several more days than the outlying fairs. Most folks stayed the whole time, although some left early to catch a few of the smaller village market days on their way to the next fair south. I had originally planned to leave at the end of the capital fair. I was not sure now when I would leave, for I was not going to leave without Carz. It would appear that Carz was not going to leave before a new ruler was chosen.

Each day was the same, I would get up to find Carz gone, I would be escorted to the fair, spend the day in my booth, and then be escorted back to the royal palace. Each evening, we would gather on the terrace for a meal and discuss what had happened during the day. When dusk fell, our companion animals would find us. Lom and Taarig, and Theora and Tala, however, did not come up to the terrace after the first day.

As the days passed, the number of folks lining up to attempt the Gylden Sirklene challenge grew smaller. Lord Klingflug and his supporters had not come to stand in line, and that was causing more and more concern. It was also curious that, with each passing day, more and more leaves appeared on the golden quirrelit tree rising up out of the small valley.

Listening to the folks who stopped at or passed by my booth, I found it interesting to hear what they were saying about what was and was not happening concerning the Gylden Sirklene challenge. It was certainly apparent to me that something needed to happen soon, for many folks' feelings had gone from being mostly excited and positive when the ninth piece of the oppgave ringe had been found and the quirrelit tree of golden light first lit up the sky to becoming anxious and disillusioned.

On the last day of the fair, I made arrangements with the head of the royal guard for Carz and me to have an escort, once dusk had arrived, to the area on the fairgrounds where the rovers and others were camped. Since I knew I was not going to be able to travel on with my friends the next morning, I wanted to be able to spend their last night in the capital with them. Just as I was going to leave the royal palace grounds with Da, Nana, and Carz, I was hailed.

I turned around to see Lady Esmeralda striding toward me. I knew it was Lady Esmeralda. Few others would recognize her, since she was dressed as a rover and had changed her appearance to look older, just as she had when she had traveled with me.

"I have been saddened that I have not been able to spend any time with the rovers, especially Oscar and Bertram's children," said Lady Esmeralda. "Like you, I would like a night among friends, filled with laughter and music."

When Lady Esmeralda had traveled with me last summer disguised as the rover Kiaya, it had turned out she was a great storyteller and quite popular with the children. While I could certainly relate to her wanting to get away from the royal palace and all of her responsibilities, I was worried about her being away from the great number of royal guards who had been keeping us safe.

"I'm sure there are quite a few of the children, and a number of adults for that matter, who would welcome a story or two from the rover Kiaya, but … ah, Kiaya, do you think …."

"… it's wise that I leave the royal palace grounds? Now, do not you start, too. I have already had a heated discussion with the head of the royal guard about this night. While she is not pleased, she is providing a highly trained and loyal patrol to get us there and back. It is my hope whoever is watching the royal palace will just notice you and Carz accompanied by several other rovers. I took great caution to leave the royal palace by a little-known way. Anyone keeping track of my movements in the royal palace will have seen me go to my chambers and lock myself in for a long night of studying interim ruling council business. I cannot imagine anyone being able to get near my door to disturb me, since I have left clear orders that unless the royal palace was falling down, I was not to be interrupted."

Having gotten to know Lady Esmeralda while she traveled with me and then, again, during these last few weeks, I knew nothing was going to dissuade her from coming with me. She was correct that none of the escorting guards gave her a second glance as we walked to the fairground's campground. The walk was peaceful. When we arrived there, I was not surprised to find Beezle and Journeyman Evan already settled in comfortably around the campfire.

The rest of the evening was all I had hoped it would be, filled with music and laughter. It was hard to say goodbye to my friends. I hoped I would be able to catch up with them a few weeks down the road. I was especially going to miss Shyla, who would travel on with her family. I found some comfort that Zeroun, Shueller, and a few others of the rover elders were going to stay on at the capital until the challenge was completed.

The walk back to the royal palace was a quiet one, and we arrived without incident. Once we were on the royal palace grounds, our escort left us. While Da walked Nana back to their homewagon, Carz and I escorted Lady Esmeralda to a place where she could enter the royal palace undetected.

"I want to keep this rover disguise as much of a secret as possible. You never know when it might be needed again. I have been seriously considering that, once the new ruler is selected, and I move out of the royal palace, I might like to travel as a rover once again. I was making a fairly good living with my knitting, traveling with you last summer. Perhaps I could travel with you again."

I did not know what to say, for I was not sure if Lady Esmeralda was serious or not. I knew that, when the new ruler of Sommerhjem was chosen, Lady Esmeralda would need to leave the royal palace. Her family had retained several estates, and she would most likely move to one of them.

"You would always be welcome to travel with Carz and me. If you decide that the rover life is for you long term, I am sure Da and I could help you build your own homewagon, for a generous fee, of course. Would be a great project during the cold months."

Lady Esmeralda just laughed and said we would haggle about the generous fee another day. She then slipped in between some hedges and was gone. I walked quickly back to my homewagon with Carz, for I knew morning was again going to come too soon.

Early the next morning, just at the break of dawn, I bridled one of my horses and was leading it out of the campsite, hoping to go to the fairgrounds to retrieve my cart, which I had packed and closed up the day before. I stepped out of the trees surrounding the campsite and glanced over toward the pathway leading to the tangle. I could not believe what I was seeing.

Chapter Forty-Two

Strutting, and that is the only word that could really describe it, strutting down the path leading to the tangle was Lord Klingflug, all dressed up as if he were on his way to a royal ball. His manner of walking and his dress would have captured my attention in and of itself. What really surprised me was he was walking down the path toward the tangle dragging a muzzled hunting cat on a leash. It was a small young one, but a hunting cat nonetheless.

He either had been the first in line this morning, or had pushed his way to the front. It was obvious to me that he was expecting to walk into the valley, take the challenge, and be chosen the new ruler of Sommerhjem. *Did he think that being accompanied by an uncommon animal would improve his chances?*

It was very hard to stand by and do nothing. Where had Lord Klingflug gotten a hunting cat? I suspected that he had not found him the way I had found Carz, all tangled up in a very crude canvas and twine bag that someone had carelessly discarded. Carz had gotten his head caught in an open slit in the bag, and then, while trying to get out, had tangled not just one but three of his legs in the twine. He had looked exhausted and bedraggled when I found him, so I can only guess he had been there quite some time. It had taken time and patience on both of our parts to get him loose and, in the end, we seemed to have formed a bond. That was a number of years ago, and he has been with me ever since.

I cannot imagine Lord Klingflug wandering the forest in the eastern mountains and just happening across a hunting cat. It was clear from the way the hunting cat was being pulled along, and the fact that he was muzzled, that the former regent did not have any sort of bond with him. It was all I could do not to drop the reins of my horse, rush right over to Lord Klingflug, and grab the leash out of his hand. I refrained, but just barely. I knew I could not interfere with Lord Klingflug, since he was obviously heading to take the challenge. If I did that, those who opposed the Crown would most likely use that to their advantage.

I stood rooted to the spot for a moment, and then began to move up toward the royal palace to where Master Clarisse was sitting. I tied up my horse and went to sit with her.

"You just showed remarkable restraint," said Master Clarisse. "It must have been very hard to watch that pompous self-important man drag that reluctant hunting cat down the path."

"It's a young one, too, barely of age to leave its mother. That worries me."

"Worries you?"

"Yes. I worry that Lord Klingflug sent hunters off to capture an uncommon animal, in this case a hunting cat, and the hunters may have harmed the mother in capturing the offspring. I wonder if this is part of the reason he and others who support him have not shown up to try the challenge until this day. I hope we will not see others marching in with various other uncommon animals."

"That is entirely possible. His walking in with a hunting cat on a leash certainly proves that, while he may have had scholars researching all things pertaining to the oppgave ringe and the Gylden Sirklene challenge, he really does not understand what he has been told about those of you who carried pieces of the oppgave ringe to the capital," stated Master Clarisse.

"Why would you say that?" I asked.

"If he had, he would have known that none of you chose the companion animal you now travel with. They chose you."

"But I found Carz, and Yara found Toki. Greer rescued Kasa, so they don't fit your idea that they chose us."

"Do they not? Especially in the case of Carz and Toki. You once told me how you found him. Once he was free of that bag, he could just as well have run off. Same with Toki. Once he was well and away from the capital, especially once he was back in the bog, he could have left Yara at any time. Neither animal chose to leave you folks. As for Kasa, he was a young, untrained pup, and yet he stuck with Greer through some fairly hair-raising adventures."

I took a moment to think about what Master Clarisse had just suggested. There was a ring of truth in what she said. I almost missed what she said next.

"He certainly is dressed as if he were on his way to a royal ball. I am surprised he did not have a sash made to drape across his chest with the words 'KING' in capital letters embroidered on it," Master Clarisse said sarcastically. "It will be interesting to see what happens in the next little while. Will Lord Klingflug be one of those who turns around at the edge of the clearing, do you think?"

"No. He is much too determined to be the next king. I think he will even walk the labyrinth, though I don't hold out much hope that he will empty his mind and feel the peacefulness of being near the quirrelit tree," I remarked.

I felt movement behind me and looked back to see Lady Esmeralda approaching.

"I asked the head of the royal guard to make sure that I was informed when Lord Klingflug, or any of his major supporters, arrived to take the challenge," said Lady Esmeralda. "I could not imagine, even though they had not shown up before now, that they would not eventually show up. Once I had word, I sent servants to inform those of you who were staying here in the royal palace. I waited until Lord Klingflug had entered the tangle before sending someone to alert those in the campsite."

I glanced in the direction of the campsite and saw one of the royal guards moving swiftly that way. I could certainly applaud Lady Esmeralda's foresight to make sure we were warned when one of those folks who opposed the Crown decided to take the challenge. We were very unsure and uneasy about what would happen to us if one of them became the next king or queen of Sommerhjem.

"He should have entered the small valley by now, don't ...." The rest of my words were snatched away by a fierce wind that blew up from the bottom of the garden. Brushing the grit and hair out of my eyes, I looked up. A large dark cloud had formed over the cliff, shrouding the golden quirrelit tree. The branches of the quirrelit tree made of golden light were thrashing about, as if caught in a violent storm.

"What is happening?" asked Yara, as she stepped out onto the terrace. "I came as soon as I could."

"We are not sure," said Master Clarisse, very calmly. "Moments ago, Lord Klingflug entered the tangle, dressed as if he were heading off to a royal ball, dragging a young hunting cat on a leash. I cannot imagine that dark, angry-looking gray cloud and the thrashing of the golden quirrelit tree are signs that Lord Klingflug has been picked as the next king of Sommerhjem. At least, I sincerely hope not."

Yara was followed closely by the others who were staying in the royal palace. I could also see those who were camped with me beginning to run toward the terrace. They arrived at the terrace at about the same moment that Lord Klingflug came stumbling out of the tangle. He certainly did not look as grand as he had when he had entered. His cloak was in shreds. His fine clothes were torn and covered in dirt and leafy debris. The smudges of dirt on his face covered up neither the scratches nor the look of terror on his face. Dangling from his hand was what was left of the leash that had held the young hunting cat.

Lord Klingflug kept looking over his shoulder, and I imagine what he saw following him caused him to attempt to move even faster. Shortly after he emerged from the tangle, I saw that he had been followed by both of the night wolves and the rest of the companion animals. Lom and Theora were the last to emerge from the tangle.

Lady Esmeralda called to a royal guard standing nearby and asked him to run and fetch the royal physician. She, followed closely by Master Clarisse and Seeker Eshana, moved swiftly down the terrace to intercept Lord Klingflug in his erratic, stumbling flight across the royal palace grounds. The rest of us followed, trying to meet with our companion animals. By the time we reached Lord Klingflug, he was in a heap on the ground, curled in on himself, surrounded by the companion animals.

Lady Esmeralda stepped through the circle. None of the animals stopped her. She crouched down and laid a gentle hand on Lord Klingflug's shoulder. I was at once struck by her bravery and her compassion. Here she had boldly stepped through the ring of companion animals, who could have very painfully prevented her, and she had reached down to help the man who had plotted against her throughout her whole young life, to the point of being ready to order her death.

"Would you kindly ask the animals to move back?" asked Lady Esmeralda. "I do not think Lord Klingflug will be trying the challenge again any time soon."

"At least not this day," said Lom. "The challenge is closed for the day. The valley needs time to recover. The challenge will commence again at dawn on the morrow. Nissa, if you would accompany us. Your assistance is needed."

With that said, Lom and Theora turned and began to walk back toward the tangle, accompanied by Taarig, Tala, and Carz. I followed. It was a quiet walk. I did not feel it was the time to ask questions, and Lom and Theora did not offer any conversation. The quiet walk gave me time to reflect, not so much on what Lom had said, but on how he had said it. There was such maturity and authority in his delivery of the news that the challenge was finished for the day. No one who heard him make that pronouncement would have dared question him or his right to make that decision. At that moment, he was every inch the gatekeeper of the Gylden Sirklene challenge.

When we reached the doors in the cliff wall, Lom and Theora opened them, we stepped through, and they closed the doors behind us.

"If you will follow us to our quarters, please," Theora requested. I could hear fatigue in her voice. The responsibility of being one of the gatekeepers for such an important undertaking had to be wearing.

When we got to the door of the quirrelit tree home that was Lom and Theora's temporary quarters, they and their night wolves stopped.

"We think it is best that just you and Carz go inside. We will wait out here," said Lom.

I did not know what to expect. The lighting was dim inside the tree home, due to the fact that the dark cloud that had formed over the valley had not moved out yet. Carz padded quickly across the room toward a shadowed corner. I followed quietly. Lying in the shadows in a very tight ball was the young hunting cat. I could see he was shaking all over. The muzzle was still in place, and the broken leash trailed from his collar.

Carz leaned down and licked the young hunting cat between the ears several times. The young hunting cat looked up at me with such a look of fright on his face, it almost broke my heart. I knelt down, and slowly, ever so slowly, I reached my hand out to let him smell me. I hoped the smell of

Carz on my hand along with my scent would reassure the young hunting cat that I meant him no harm. I then stroked his head all the while talking quietly to him.

"His name is Üba, Carz." Just as I do not know how I knew Carz' name when I first came upon him, I would not be able to tell anyone how I knew this hunting cat's name was Üba. I sat down next to Üba, continuing to talk soothingly to him. Moving very slowly, I unfastened the muzzle first. I had no fear that Üba would bite me. After removing the muzzle, I took the collar off and flung both away from me in disgust.

I continued to talk quietly to Üba while I ran my hands gently over his body to make sure he had not been injured or harmed in any way. I had just finished with my examination of Üba when he stood up, stretched, crawled into my lap, turned around several times, and plopped down with a sigh. He was asleep in seconds, snoring softly.

"Carz, can you go see if you can get the door open and invite Lom, Theora, and the night wolves in? As you can see, I'm not going to be going anywhere anytime soon."

Upon entering the tree home, Theora said, "I can see we made the right choice, asking you to come back with us. He was so frightened."

"His name is Üba," I said. "Please don't ask me how I know. I just know."

"We understand," said Lom. "When Üba ran out of the quirrelit grove, the night wolves helped us get him back here. We quickly closed the door, and then, went back and located Lord Klingflug, who was huddled on the ground outside of the quirrelit grove, surrounded by the rest of the companion animals."

"We got him on his feet and moving. He was not in good shape. When he became aware that the animals were essentially herding him out of the valley, he moved out fairly quickly," said Theora.

"What happened in here? From our view from the terrace, first there was a fierce wind, and then, the dark cloud formed over the valley. The golden quirrelit tree's branches shook wildly."

"Lord Klingflug was the first challenger to walk out of the tangle this morning. He was strutting along the path to the quirrelit tree in the center of the clearing as if he were in a parade. We were both appalled when we spotted the young hunting cat being dragged along. It was all we could do not to interfere," said Lom.

"I know the feeling," I said.

"He walked very briskly through the labyrinth, as if he knew that was part of the routine, but I don't think he really used the time to clear his mind and be open to what would then fill it," said Theora.

"In other words, he was just going through the motions," I commented.

"We think so. He just walked up to us, dismissed us as if we were nothing, marched through the doors, and headed straight toward the quirrelit grove. As he passed us, I thought I detected he was not as confident as he wanted us to believe," said Lom.

"Then what happened?"

"We cannot tell you what happened within the quirrelit grove. We felt the great wind come up and saw the dark clouds move in. We huddled in the archway for protection as the dark cloud descended and encompassed the quirrelit grove. There were cracklings of lightning and howls from within the grove. We feared for the companion animals, for it is within the standing stones they spend the day," stated Theora.

"It must have been a feeling of great relief when you saw the night wolves come out of the grove. For the sake of Üba, I thank you for closing down the challenge for the rest of the day. I don't think this valley will be a very welcoming place until that dark cloud has lifted. One thing is for sure. I don't think Lord Klingflug is likely to be our next king."

"I think you are right," said Theora. "Will you take Üba with you and Carz? Maybe when this is all over, you can return him to the wild."

I stayed on the floor, holding the sleeping young hunting cat for a while longer. Finally, I needed to move, so I gently set him on the floor, stood up, and stretched. Üba stood up and stretched too. That brought the first smile of the day to my face.

Addressing the two hunting cats, I asked if they were ready to go. Carz led the way out of the quirrelit tree home, and Üba followed. Our little procession of three moved without incident through the valley, out the doors, across the clearing, out of the tangle, and back to the campsite and my homewagon. Now that I knew what had happened within the small valley, I was anxious to find out what had happened outside after I left.

CHAPTER FORTY-THREE

When I walked into the campsite, I was not surprised to find many of the others sitting around a cook fire. I had hoped the campsite would be relatively empty, for I was concerned about how Üba would react to others besides Carz and me. I was afraid he might get frightened and run away. Having a young hunting cat loose and scared on the royal palace grounds would be a disaster waiting to happen. When those sitting around the campfire noticed Carz, Üba, and me, they became very quiet.

"Ah, good," said Piper. "I'm glad Lom and Theora had the presence of mind to think to call you and Carz to look after the young hunting cat. A bit shy, is he?"

I could not imagine why Piper thought Üba was shy, until I glanced over my shoulder. I almost panicked for a moment, since I could not see Üba until I half turned and looked down. He was hiding behind me, peeking around my legs.

"The young one you see behind me is named Üba. He is underfed, but otherwise in fairly good shape, other than having been mistreated. If you will all remain still and talk quietly, I will try to get him to join the group."

I had just finished speaking when Jing rose and walked toward me. I had not worried about Üba with Carz. I was not sure how mountain cats and hunting cats got along in general, Carz and Jing possibly being an exception. Jing and Üba stared at each other for a short moment, while the rest of us held our breaths. I think something passed between the two cats. Üba slowly came out from behind my legs, touched noses with Jing, and followed him and Carz to a spot near the campfire. All three settled in. I let out a huge sigh of relief.

I walked over and took a seat near the cats on a vacant camp chair. I looked around for Da, but could not find him among the group.

"Your Da asked us to tell you, if you should arrive back here before he did, that he and your nana have gone to fetch your cart and his," said Meryl. "Is everything all right in the valley? Are Lom, Theora, and the night wolves all right?"

"Other than some downed branches and leaves, the valley is fine. As I was leaving, I caught sight of the halekrets beginning to clean up the path. By dawn on the morrow, the valley will probably look as if this day's excitement never happened. What happened after I left? How is Lord Klingflug?"

"Once we asked the animals to back off a ways, Lord Klingflug pulled himself together. Physically, he really was none the worse for wear," said Greer. "However, whatever happened to him in the valley left him a broken man. All the swagger and bravado is gone. He asked us to call for his carriage to be brought onto the grounds. He did not want anyone to see him."

"He also asked for us to send a runner with a message to his steward, asking him to begin packing. Lord Klingflug informed Lady Esmeralda he would be leaving the capital and heading back to his estate. He certainly looked shaken and very, very frightened," suggested Seeker Chance. "When Master Clarisse asked him what had happened to him in the small valley, a great shudder went through his body, and he said he could not speak of it."

"Whatever happened to him has left him a shell of who he was," said Yara. "I have no doubt that he will not return to try the challenge a second time, nor will he be the next ruler of Sommerhjem. We can only hope that his experiences in the small valley will be a warning or a lesson for others who have followed his path in opposing the Crown and harmed others for their own gain."

The group broke up a short while later. When Da and Nana arrived, I helped them settle the horses and level the cart. Toward midday, a steady rain began, so the two hunting cats and I moved into my homewagon. I actually welcomed the rain. I needed time to myself. While the two cats napped, I took time to straighten up the homewagon.

Finally, I curled up on the bed, turned the lamp up, and began to sketch a design for the lid of the chest Master Rollag had commissioned. In the morning, I intended to take the lid for the box, tools, and the pattern I was drawing now with me to the terrace. I wanted to see what happened on the morrow when the doors to the small valley opened at dawn.

The next morning, Üba and I settled ourselves on the terrace with Master Clarisse. I found myself surprised, though maybe I should not have been, that the first one to attempt the Gylden Sirklene challenge was Lady Green. As I watched her walk toward the tangle, Lady Esmeralda came out onto the terrace to join us.

"After the experience Lord Klingflug had yesterday, I had hoped the others of his crowd would see that as a warning sign, decide to go home to their estates, and forget the Gylden Sirklene challenge. Instead, they must have taken that as a sign that they could now take his place in the order of things. I just took a look out an upper window of the royal palace at the line of folks who want to try the challenge. The line is full of major and minor nobles, all in their finery, thankfully not accompanied by any sort of animals," said Lady Esmeralda. "I sincerely hope we do not have a repeat of yesterday with wind, dark clouds, and the doors into the small valley closing."

At the speed at which the folks passed down the path to the tangle and back, I do not think very many actually made it to the doors into the small valley. Lord Mostander certainly moved more quickly back off the royal palace grounds than he had when he entered. Lady Green did not even make it into the tangle and, as for Lady Furman, I was surprised at how fast she could move. She shot up the path from the tangle as if she were being chased by night wolves.

Lord Hindre was very red of face when he marched back up the path. Lady Padde started down the path, turned around, and went off and back onto the royal palace grounds at least four times. We did not see her after that.

It was very late afternoon when Lady Farcroft walked onto the royal palace grounds. She had a look of great determination on her face and fairly marched into the tangle. As I sat there waiting, my tools stilled, I wondered how far she would go. Would she turn around at the end of the tangle? If she kept going, I thought she was smart enough to do more than lip service to the labyrinth. I suspected her determination and self-righteousness would carry her all the way through the doors and into the small valley.

Lord Hadrack had once remarked that he thought Lady Farcroft, while a supporter of Lord Klingflug, had always had her own plans and had carried them out. Now that Lord Klingflug had failed the challenge, I am sure she felt that opened a door for her to be the next queen. More accurately, now that Lord Klingflug had failed the challenge, it probably reinforced her thinking that she really was the rightful next queen of Sommerhjem.

When I felt the wind pick up and noticed a dark cloud beginning to form once again over the cliff, I began to worry we were about to have a repeat of yesterday. The branches on the golden quirrelit tree of light began to thrash about, although not as violently as they had the day before, nor for as long. When Lady Farcroft emerged from the tangle, she was not followed by all of the companion animals. Rather she was escorted out of the tangle only by Taarig and Tala. Once she was again on the path heading up toward the royal palace, they turned around and went back.

Lady Farcroft's clothing was not torn. She was not covered in dirt and debris. She was not stumbling and shambling up the path. She was slightly hunched over, holding her stomach. Even from a distance, she looked decidedly ill. I had a strong feeling her attempt at the Gylden Sirklene challenge had not gone the way she had expected.

After Lady Farcroft, the number of folks entering the royal palace grounds to attempt the challenge slowed down to a trickle. I got up, stretched, and called to Üba, asking if he wanted to stretch his legs and walk back to the campsite with me. I had finished the lid for Master Rollag's chest and needed to get something else to work on. As long as I was basically stuck in the capital, I might as well use the time wisely and build up my stock.

I climbed inside my cart to look for a particular carving tool. Üba climbed in with me. He was less than helpful, sticking his head in every drawer I pulled out and in every box I opened. I turned away from him for just a second, and when I turned back, he was gone. I quickly jumped out of my cart and glanced around the campsite, just in time to see the tip of his tail as it vanished out of the entrance of the campsite. I rushed after him.

Once I was beyond the trees that surrounded the campsite, I could clearly see Üba. He was sprinting across the royal palace grounds, heading straight for the terrace where we had been sitting with Master Clarisse and others. I ran after him. I did not know Üba like I know Carz. I did not know why he had run from me, or what would happen next. I was very out of breath when I finally reached the terrace. I can only imagine the surprised look on my face matched the surprised look on the face of the forester upon whose lap Üba was now curled.

"Well, Üba, it would seem you have made a friend," I said, once I had caught my breath. Üba looked up when he heard me speak, gave a slow yawn, and put his head back down. "Are you all right?" I asked the forester, who looked to be about my age.

"Yes. Fine. Surprised to say the least. He's a young one, isn't he? I think he likes me."

I had to admire the young man's poise, for there were not many folk, I suspect, who would be sitting quite so calmly, after having had a hunting cat jump into one's lap.

"Nissa, this is Nowles," said Yara. "He is from the forester village where I was before being summoned back to the capital. One of their elders named Nelda had once shown Seeker Chance a very old book that contained drawings and descriptions of animals, including a drawing and description of halekrets. I had been attempting, with the help of Nowles here, to copy the book. He is quite a fine artist."

I saw the color begin to bloom on Nowles' cheeks. He looked embarrassed by Yara's compliment.

"Nowles arrived here just a few short minutes before Üba, and then you, arrived. He has completed the drawings and the rest of the descriptions from the book we were working on. When he arrived in the capital, he went to the royal library to find me to give me what he had done, only to be directed here. Nowles had no more sat down and taken the bundle he was carrying out of his day pack, when Üba rushed up and made himself at home."

"I'll see if I can get Üba to come back to the campsite with me," I told Nowles.

"He really isn't a bother," said Nowles, and I could hear a wistfulness in his voice.

"It will certainly make a great tale to tell the children back in your home village," said Yara chuckling. "Yup, had me a little journey to the capital and found myself sitting on a terrace of the royal palace, sipping tea, with a hunting cat on my lap."

Nowles gave Yara an amused grin and reached a tentative hand down to stroke Üba's back. We sat on the terrace for quite some time, having a late afternoon tea. It had been close to half an hour since the last folk had entered the royal palace grounds and headed for the tangle. I wondered if word of what had happened to Lord Klingflug and other nobles had gotten out, discouraging folks from trying the challenge.

Just as I thought that, Üba jumped off Nowles' lap. I was about to stand up and invite Üba to head back to the campsite with me when he took Nowles' hand between his jaws and pulled him out of his chair. Üba dropped Nowles' hand and paced away about ten feet. When Nowles did not follow, Üba repeated taking Nowles' hand and tugging on it. Again, Üba dropped Nowles' hand and paced off.

"I think he wants you to follow him," I told Nowles. He gave me a questioning look. "Go ahead, try, and see what happens."

Nowles reached down, grabbed his day pack, and stepped off toward Üba, who in turn began to walk slowly off the terrace, heading along a path that bisected the path that led to the tangle. I watched as Nowles, all of a sudden, stood up taller and began to move more quickly, catching up with Üba. We all sat on the terrace and watched in amazement as Nowles followed Üba into the tangle.

"Oh my," said Journeyman Evan, who had just walked out onto the terrace followed by Master Rollag. "Was that a forester accompanied by a hunting cat who just entered the tangle?"

CHAPTER FORTY-FOUR

We waited on the terrace for Nowles and Üba to return. An hour passed, and then two. Others arrived from their various tasks and settled in. Servants brought out our evening meal, and still no sign of the forester and the young hunting cat. At one point, someone remarked that at least the wind was just a slight breeze, and there was not a cloud in the sky. The shadows began to lengthen across the royal palace grounds as the day headed toward dusk, and still no sign.

"He has been gone a very long time. None of the others who have attempted the challenge have been gone this long. He surely would have made it through the labyrinth by now, even if he was moving just an inch at a time. I know those who seek to take the challenge should not be interfered with. Yet, I cannot imagine that Lom or Theora would allow him to linger in the clearing. They certainly would have asked him to move on after this long a time. They would have suggested he enter the small valley before the doors closed," said Master Clarisse.

Seeker Chance then asked the question that was on all of our minds. "Is it possible that Nowles is Sommerhjem's next king?"

Moments before the sun was surely going to set, I looked up and saw movement at the opening of the tangle. Soon I could make out Nowles and Üba slowly turn and take the path heading not toward the royal palace, but toward the campsite. He was followed out of the tangle by our companion animals. All except Carz headed toward us. Carz stood looking our way, and then turned, and followed Nowles and Üba. I found myself standing quickly and heading toward the campsite.

Half way to the campsite I turned back to see if the others were following. They were not. The rest of the companion animals had formed a line blocking the exit from the terrace. It looked as if I was on my own. When I arrived at the campsite, I found Nowles looking dazed, standing in the middle of the area flanked by both of the hunting cats. Before I could say anything, a light arced from Nowles' hand to mine. I could see that startled him. I saw him stumble over to a camp chair and abruptly sit down.

"I have tried to tell myself it was all a dream, and I somehow found myself here in this campsite. I thought one of you must have put something in my tea, so that I was knocked out, and while knocked out, I had amazing dreams. You folks didn't put anything in my tea, did you?"

"No, we did not. We were sitting on the terrace with you when Üba got you to stand up and follow him. You followed for a short distance, and then something happened, for you caught up with him. The two of you walked side by side into the tangle. You have been gone for hours. We suspected that you went through the doors of the cliff wall into the small valley and took the Gylden Sirklene challenge. What do you remember? Can you talk to me about it?"

"I, I …. Was it a dream? Is she real?"

"Is who real?" I asked, though I thought I knew the answer.

"The Huntress," Nowles said in a whisper.

"Yes. I take it you met her."

"I thought it was all a dream, that maybe I had fallen and hit my head or something. It wasn't a dream, was it?"

"No, it wasn't."

"We talked for quite a long time. Oh, before I forget, she gave me something to give to you. She said you would know who to give it to, so it can be returned."

I watched as Nowles opened his daypack and, to my great surprise, pulled out a bundle wrapped in golden pine spider silk. He handed it to me. I strongly suspected that the bundle I held was the vessteboks itself.

"Thank you. If you would wait right here for a moment, I think I should put this right away. I will be right back. A question, though, before I go. Is it empty?"

"Yes."

Instead of going to my homewagon, I headed straight for Da's. Since he was the one who had brought the vessteboks to the capital a year ago, I knew he was the one who needed to take care of it now that it was no longer needed. Every rover homewagon has a hidden compartment that even another rover would be hard-pressed to find. I, of course, knew where to find the one in Da's wagon. It did not take me long to open the compartment, hide the vessteboks, and return to the fire pit. When I sat back down, Nowles asked a question.

"That arc of light from the firestar gem in the ring I now wear, it arced to you. Do you also wear a firestar gem?"

"Yes." I wondered if I could tell him about the fact that my ring had been made by the Huntress. Since he had met her, I thought I would take a chance on it. I had never been able to speak of the night I had spent with the Huntress to anyone until now, so I was surprised at the words that came out of my mouth. "The Huntress made my ring out of quirrelit wood and a firestar gem that had been a gift to me from the Neebings. I suspect that the ring you now wear was on the farthest post to the right in the vessteboks." Nowles gave me a 'how did you know?' look. "Tell me about how you acquired yours."

"The closer and closer I got to the quirrelit grove in the valley, the more and more urgent it seemed to me that I should go there," said Nowles. "I was surprised to find a ring of standing stones inside. I was drawn to the stone in the middle. Just as I reached there, a fog rose up and blocked out the quirrelit grove. I can tell you I was very afraid, and became even more afraid when I could not move."

How well I remember that feeling of being very afraid and unable to move.

"I became even more afraid when this tall woman carrying a spear strode out of the fog, accompanied by four hunting cats."

"Did she happen to hold you at spear point and threaten your life, by any chance?"

"No. Üba very bravely stepped in front of me, looking for all the world like he was going to take on all four grown hunting cats and the woman holding a spear. He was much braver than I was at that moment, I am ashamed to say."

"What happened next?"

"She said, 'Good, you have bonded with Üba. Now go take the last ring out of the vessteboks.' I did as she asked. She is not someone you would want to argue with."

"You certainly speak the truth there."

"We talked for a while. She told me about the properties of the ring I had taken from the vessteboks. While you were putting the vessteboks away, I was trying to recall what else we talked about. It is all quite hazy now."

"I think there are some things that you just cannot or should not tell anyone else about your experience with the Huntress. I suspect that when the others come back to the campsite, you will not be able to tell them much about what happened to you in the valley, including about what is within the quirrelit grove."

"The last thing I remember her saying was I am Neebing blessed, and it is time for the Neebing blessed to walk the land. She said it had been far too long. Do you know what that means?"

"You have no idea how very much I would like to be able to tell you. Every time I think I'm about to get an answer to just what it means to be Neebing blessed, something interrupts."

"One other thing. The Huntress suggested that I needed to stay here until the challenge is completed. She also said I needed to leave the capital afterward very, um … I think her words were … I 'should slip out of town unnoticed'."

"I think it might be best if you and Üba stay with us for now. Where did you leave your gear?"

"The foresters once again have a small headquarters in the capital. Lady Esmeralda made the former regent's tenants give it back to us. At the moment, a forester named Frayne is in charge. I left my gear there."

"I know Frayne. I will get a message to him to come to the royal palace and bring your gear. If you are all right now, I think we should let the others who camp here know they can join us. When I left the terrace as you were walking to the campsite, all of the other companion animals were basically blocking the way for the others to follow me."

Just then I heard the sound of wings overhead and looked up to catch Tashi gliding in. She was followed by Meryl walking into the campsite, carrying a loaded basket.

"The others will be here soon. I brought some bread and cheese, for I thought Nowles might be hungry."

For a little while it got to be quite comical, for, as each person who was wearing something with a firestar gem set in it entered the campsite, an arc would flash from their firestar gem to Nowles'. Things had just settled down when Master Rollag arrived accompanied by Lady Esmeralda, Master Clarisse, Beezle, and Journeyman Evan.

"I certainly hope that is the last of the light display," commented Meryl. "After each arc of light, it takes a while to get my vision back."

When everyone was finally settled around the fire, Master Rollag asked Nowles what he could tell us.

"I'm afraid I can tell you very little. I remember feeling pulled to go into the tangle, to walk the labyrinth, to go through the doors in the cliff wall and, after that I have very little recall. I really do not know how much time passed. Then I found myself walking out of the tangle, Üba at my side, and this ring with the firestar gem on my hand. At that time I felt compelled, I guess you might say, to come to this campsite and find Nissa. I can't really explain why."

"Nowles also told me he has a strong feeling that he should stay here for now," I told the others. "I would agree. He is now one of us who walks with a companion animal. We don't really know how safe any of us are outside the royal palace walls at this time. From all the reactions of our various firestar gems to his, I would suggest that he is someone who is loyal to the Crown and has the best interest of Sommerhjem at heart."

I drew Master Rollag aside and asked him if he might get a message to the forester Frayne and ask for Nowles' gear to be brought here. Journeyman Evan overheard, and said he would go take care of the task right away. I knew we could count on his discretion. He had me laughing, as I watched him tiptoe to the seekers' tent, frequently glancing over his shoulder, and then slip into the shadows, pretending he was a sneak thief.

After he left, the talk turned to a discussion of what had happened this day, with one noble after another attempting the Gylden Sirklene challenge and being unsuccessful.

"Has your aunt or uncle, Lord or Lady Hadrack ever indicated that they felt drawn to try the challenge?" I asked Beezle. "From what I have observed, either one of them would be a good and fair ruler of Sommerhjem."

"I think so too, so you can imagine my disappointment when both of them told me that they felt they were not called to be the next ruler. I have urged them to try anyway. Since this whole challenge process is taking days and, so far, no one has emerged as the next ruler of Sommerhjem, some folks are becoming very anxious," said Beezle.

"How about your father, Greer?" Beezle asked. "He too would be a fine ruler."

"My father and I are both of the opinion that being in the clear air of the high hills of Dugghus is where we want to be, not in the capital. To be honest, we can hardly wait to get back."

"You actually want to get back to those pesky sisters of yours?" teased Journeyman Evan.

I had not noticed that he had returned.

"Yes, even back to my pesky sisters."

"Nowles, I dropped your gear off at the royal palace. I did not know where you might wish to stay here. Forester Frayne had heard about your afternoon adventures. News travels fast, for he already knew of your connecting with Üba and trying the challenge. It is hard to keep anything quiet around this place."

"You are welcome to share my tent, my tent," said Finn. "Plenty of room, yes, plenty of room."

"I accept. I think Üba and I would enjoy camping here more than staying in the royal palace. No offense," said Nowles.

"None taken," responded Lady Esmeralda.

"So, getting back to the former subject," I said. "Finn, how about it? Don't you think you should be the next king of Sommerhjem?"

The look of panic on Finn's face was comical. The discussion then turned back to putting out ideas as to who else might possibly be a likely candidate to be called to rule Sommerhjem. Finally, the group broke up, and all planned to meet on the terrace for breakfast at the latest. Some planned to join those of us who were making a habit of being there at dawn.

As I lay in bed, I reflected on the conversations that had swirled about the campfire this night. While there had been teasing and laughter along with serious talk, underlying it all was the feeling that time was running out. That concerned me a great deal.

CHAPTER FORTY-FIVE

Lady Green was ushered into Lady Farcroft's parlor where Lady Farcroft was pacing back and forth in front of the bay window, scowling. Lady Green turned back toward the parlor door, apparently not wanting to become the brunt of Lady Farcroft's agitated mood. Before Lady Green could take a step, Lady Farcroft whirled and began to speak in a very controlled voice.

"The news of the spectacular folly and failure of Lord Klingflug has spread across the capital. I am sure that the news, in every humiliating detail, is now just as swiftly making it to the out country. His supporters are leaving the capital in droves, heading back to their own estates and lands, the cowards. Countless folks are now trying to distance themselves from Lord Klingflug. It also does not help that every single one of us who has supported Lord Klingflug and the disposition of Lady Esmeralda has tried the Gylden Sirklene challenge and failed, or has not even tried," said Lady Farcroft disdainfully, looking straight at Lady Green.

"I know you think I am a coward like the rest of them. I did try. I really did," said Lady Green, almost whining. "No matter how much I tried, I just could not make myself go into that tangle of greenery. I was too afraid that what happened to Lord Klingflug would happen to me."

"You should have tried harder."

"Like you did? No thank you. What happened to you?" Lady Green snapped back, tired of always being criticized by Lady Farcroft. "I heard the reports about your try at the Gylden Sirklene challenge. I heard that the wind picked up, and that the dark clouds started moving in like they had for Lord Klingflug. I heard you got escorted out by the night wolves and looked ill when you left the royal palace grounds."

Lady Farcroft turned her back on Lady Green to look out the window. She would never be able to tell anyone what had happened to her in the standing stones inside of the quirrelit grove. She had been judged, and made to face all that she had done, all the choices she had made, and the immediate and far-reaching consequences of those choices. In addition, she had been shown what Sommerhjem would be like if she were to become the next queen. Even thinking about it now made her feel ill. Though she would never admit it to anyone, she did understand why those of her group who had tried the challenge had packed up and left the capital.

However horrible her experience had been in the standing stones, there was a small part of her that wondered if it had all been an elaborate trick by the Crown to ensure that none of Lord Klingflug's followers were chosen as the next ruler. She wondered if there was something growing in that quirrelit grove that made her think she was being judged, and made her think she was not worthy to be the next ruler of Sommerhjem. *That had to be it. All is not lost. We just need to regroup.*

The next few days were uneventful as far as the Gylden Sirklene challenge was concerned. The number of folks who were lined up at dawn had slowed to a trickle. While I had to admit I was getting a great deal of work done sitting all day on the terrace, my longing to be on the road was growing stronger and stronger with the passing of time.

I was not the only one who was having trouble with the waiting. I noticed as the days passed that Lady Esmeralda did not seem like herself. She looked anxious to me. I also found it odd that she was spending more and more time on the terrace with us or wandering the royal palace grounds. When she had discovered and carried the ninth ring of the oppgave ringe, she had shown no nervousness. Anyone would have been hard-pressed to know she carried such an important secret and burden around. Now that her task was over, I suspected she might be a bit anxious about having to leave the royal palace once the new ruler was chosen. After all, it had been her home all of her life. Heading off into the unknown would make anyone a little nervous. The worry that a new ruler had not been chosen yet was causing all of us concern. Maybe that was what was causing her restlessness. Whatever the cause, I was particularly concerned for her.

I had just stood up to stretch my back and shoulder muscles when Beezle stepped onto the terrace and came over to stand beside me. I was glad of the company. I had been alone on the terrace since Master Clarisse had gone off to the Glassmakers Guildhall shortly after the noon meal, and it was now midafternoon.

"I am worried about Lady Esmeralda," Beezle said, echoing the thoughts I had just been having. "She does not seem to be able to stay at one task for very long. She seems really distracted. The other day I found her pacing around a fountain, talking to herself. I really could not hear what she was saying. I felt like she was arguing with someone, and yet no one was there."

"Perhaps she was having a quarrel with herself. When I'm trying to make a hard decision, I sometimes argue with myself. I do have the advantage of talking it over with Carz. He, however, never agrees with either side of my arguments."

"I think I will go and catch up with Lady Esmeralda," said Beezle. "Maybe she just needs someone to talk to. It has been a long year for her, filled with such uncertainty. Not knowing the outcome of the challenge has certainly been weighing on all of us. I can only imagine how much more it must weigh on her."

I was struck once again by how kind and thoughtful Beezle was. He was so unlike some of the young nobles we had seen wandering the royal palace grounds. Beezle had his feet solidly on the ground. He once remarked it was often mucky ground, since his family's main endeavor was producing prize-winning and very prized cheeses, and his family's estate had a lot of cows.

I watched Beezle lead Lady Esmeralda over to a bench sheltered by an arbor and begin to talk with her. After that, I did not pay much attention. I do not know how long I had been working on a carving when I heard Master Clarisse call my name. I had not even been aware she had returned.

"Nissa, look …."

"Huh, what? Look where? Look at what?"

"Look toward the tangle. Both Lady Esmeralda and Beezle are headed that way," said Master Clarisse.

"Oh, Beezle is probably just going for a walk with Lady Esmeralda. She has seemed a bit agitated lately. I have noticed her walking the grounds quite a bit. Beezle went to talk to her a little while ago," I said, and then looked back down at my carving.

"I do not think Lady Esmeralda is just out for a stroll," Master Clarisse remarked. "She just entered the tangle."

"What?"

"She just entered the tangle, and now Beezle is pacing back and forth in front of the entrance. No, wait, he is now heading up here."

Beezle had no more than stepped foot on the terrace when we both asked him at the same time whether Lady Esmeralda was about to attempt the Gylden Sirklene challenge.

"Yes. She told me she has been wrestling with whether or not to take the challenge ever since the doors in the cliff wall were opened. When confronted in the Well of Speaking by Lord Klingflug, she had stated she had just as much right to take the challenge as anyone else, even though she stepped down as heir to the throne a year ago. Since then she has struggled with doubts. I suggested to her that, since she was never really rightfully the heir to the throne in the first place, she never had a throne to abdicate. I reminded her that according to the Book of Rules she had just as much right to take the challenge as anybody."

"Your words must have had quite an effect," said Master Clarisse.

"I do not think you should give me very much credit. I think my words may have been just a last wee push to send her on a path she had already chosen, but had not admitted to herself. Lady Esmeralda also told me that the pull to go to the small valley within the cliff has been building each day to such a point that she could no longer suppress it. I hope ...."

Beezle broke off what he was about to say, for the wind had begun to pick up. I looked toward the top of the cliff to see if dark clouds were moving in. They were not. Something, however, was happening to the quirrelit tree made of golden light. It looked like the light was pulsing.

"Something is wrong," said Beezle.

I could hear the concern in his voice. I did not understand why he would think that. Yes, the reaction of the golden light quirrelit tree was a little different, but that did not necessarily make it a problem. It was not until I stopped looking at the top of the cliff that I saw what might be causing Beezle's concern. Lom and Theora were walking out of the tangle, trailed by tendrils of fog.

Before Lom and Theora were halfway up the royal palace grounds from the tangle, Beezle had leapt off the terrace and was rushing toward them. The three stopped, had a brief discussion, and then Beezle set off at a fast run toward the tangle. Lom and Theora continued up toward us.

I watched as Beezle raced toward the opening to the tangle that was now completely shrouded in fog. Just as he reached the entrance, I thought I saw a fox emerge from the fog, beckon to Beezle, then turn back into the tangle. I shook myself, and then scolded myself for having such a wild imagination, thinking a fox the color of fog had really been there. *Just a fanciful thought, like the ones that come to you when you lie on your back on a summer's day trying to see pictures in the clouds overhead.* I was brought back when I heard Master Clarisse ask Lom and Theora what was happening, why they were not at the doors.

"We are not sure what is happening. We saw Lady Esmeralda enter the clearing," said Lom.

"And it was about time, in my opinion," stated Theora. "So many have entered the clearing these long last days who had neither the skills and, more importantly, the heart to rule Sommerhjem."

"All right, she entered the clearing. That does not answer why you are not at the doors," I said impatiently.

"We stood at the doors and watched Lady Esmeralda walk the labyrinth. She took her time, walking it slowly," said Lom.

"She stopped for a time, with her hand resting on the trunk of the quirrelit tree, before she completed the labyrinth and headed toward us at the doors," stated Theora.

"She smiled at us as she passed by," said Lom.

"And there was such a look of peace on her face," added Theora. "We have seen looks of resolve, determination, and fear on folks' faces, but never before that look of peace. Once she passed through the doors, several things began to happen. The wind started up. I am sure you felt that."

We nodded that we had indeed felt the wind. Lom then picked up the tale.

"A ground fog began to send tendrils out from the quirrelit grove, growing thicker and thicker, rising higher and higher. Lady Esmeralda disappeared into the fog."

"We knew we could not go after her. It was hard not to, for we feared what might happen to her," said Theora. "Just after she disappeared into the fog, Taarig and Tala emerged out of it and headed toward us. Never before had they left the grove any time from dawn to dusk when someone was in the grove, except the times they escorted Lord Klingflug and Lady Farcroft out. And yet, here they were heading straight toward us."

"And maybe Toki, too. I thought I saw the shape of a fox in the fog following them. I can't be sure," said Lom. "Anyway, when the two night wolves reached us, they, well, they basically herded us out the doors, which then swung shut behind us."

"They swung shut behind you? Where are Taarig and Tala now? Did they stay in the clearing?" I asked.

"Sorry, I wasn't quite clear," said Lom. "Once the night wolves had successfully gotten us out of the small valley through the doors, the doors began to swing shut. Taarig and Tala swiftly turned around and slipped back through the doors before they were completely closed."

"Of course, we turned around and tried to open the doors to get back into the valley. As you well know, we have never had any trouble gaining entrance to the valley since the doors were first opened," said Theora.

"I take it the doors did not open for you this time," said Master Clarisse.

"No, they did not," disclosed Lom.

"And now, Beezle has rushed off and entered the tangle. What was he thinking? If the fog is as thick inside the clearing, even with the blue half globes lighting up, he is going to find getting to the doors very slow going and difficult. Then once he gets there, what is he going to do with the doors closed?" I asked.

"Look, something is happening to the golden quirrelit tree of light," exclaimed Master Clarisse.

Chapter Forty-Six

I looked toward the top of the cliff at the golden light in the shape of a quirrelit tree. Master Clarisse was correct in her observation that something was indeed happening. The light was continuing to pulse in a slow and steady rhythm. That was not what had drawn Master Clarisse's attention. Leaf buds were forming on all of the branches and, even as we watched, some of the buds were very slowly beginning to unfurl into leaves.

From the time the doors into the small valley had been opened to allow folks who wanted to try the Gylden Sirklene challenge until now, the golden quirrelit tree made of light had gone from being almost bare to having a few leaves. When it had first appeared, it had reminded me of a tree late in the cold season, with branches mostly bare, having only a few leaves that had held on with great tenacity through the cold months. As the days had gone by since the doors were opened, some more leaves had appeared on the branches. What was happening now was very different.

Lom called my attention away from the golden quirrelit tree.

"Look, the tangle has closed up. The fog that followed us out of the tangle has withdrawn since Beezle entered, and the tangle has closed up. I don't think it would open for me, or even for Ealdred and me together, at this point."

"I think you are probably correct. All we can do now is wait," said Master Clarisse.

And wait we did. Soon others began to arrive from wherever their tasks had taken them this day, to wait on the terrace as the hours very slowly slipped by. It was quite a gathering. All of us who had carried pieces of the oppgave ringe were there, along with Da, Nana, Master Rollag,

Journeyman Evan, Ealdred, Finn, Seeker Eshana, Seeker Odette, Lady Celik, Elek, Lord Avital, and Eluta, the royal librarian.

It did not take long for Lord Hadrack and the rest of the interim ruling council to join us on the terrace, along with a number of elder rovers, including Shueller and Zeroun, who had been meeting with Eluta and the seekers. There was a small commotion when Lady Farcroft, Lady Furman, and a number of others pushed their way onto the terrace, demanding to know what was going on. Lord Hadrack took charge and drew them aside. Once he had finished talking, he escorted them to a set of chairs that had been brought out by the royal palace servants to accommodate the growing crowd.

I also noticed that the captain of the royal guard had called in several patrols and had them scattered about the terrace. They looked extremely alert. I watched the captain confer with Master Clarisse and Lord Hadrack. After the conference, she swiftly left the terrace. When Master Clarisse again sat down beside me, she explained what she and the captain of the royal guard had talked about.

"The captain is putting in place one of the plans that has been discussed for use when there was a significant change happening concerning the challenge. That quirrelit tree of light can be seen for miles, and you would have to be blind not to notice it is pulsing, much less that it is filling out with leaves at a very rapid rate. That certainly has already attracted attention and will continue to do so. The captain of the royal guard is posting patrols of guards to prevent folks from rushing the royal palace and the royal palace grounds."

"It would seem they were not in place fast enough to prevent Lady Farcroft and her ilk from entering," suggested Piper.

"It is actually good that they are here," said Master Clarisse.

"Why in the world would you suggest that?" questioned Piper.

"While I appreciate that all of you who have carried pieces of the oppgave ringe here, and those who helped you bring those pieces here, have faced untold dangers and hardships, often created by Lord Klingflug, Lady Farcroft, and others, if something significant is now happening, it is good that they are here to witness it. If only those loyal to the Crown were here right now, those who oppose the Crown could always claim afterward that we just made up whatever happens now."

I could see Master Clarisse's point. Enough of those who had supported Lord Klingflug had tried and failed the Gylden Sirklene challenge. If something significant was happening now, they needed to witness it. At least I was trying to see her point when Lady Farcroft stood up abruptly and marched over to Master Clarisse.

"Whatever is happening now is wrong. I demand you call this off!"

"Lady Farcroft, it is not in my power to call the Gylden Sirklene challenge off any more than it is in your power," stated Master Clarisse.

"You said we had to enter the challenge one by one. That is not what is happening here. It is my understanding that Lady Esmeralda entered the tangle, the gatekeepers were kicked out of the valley, and then Aaron Beecroft entered the tangle."

"That is correct, other than the fact that the gatekeepers were escorted out, rather than kicked out," said Master Clarisse.

"That is not the point. Aaron Beecroft did not wait his turn, so whatever is now happening is null and void, for the rules have been broken."

"Actually, they have not," stated Master Clarisse with authority and conviction.

I could not imagine how anyone would not believe Master Clarisse. Somehow, and I cannot explain how, Master Clarisse became something more than a master of the Glassmakers Guild at moments like this. I had seen this happen several times over the past year. She rose up to her full height. In a voice that brooked no argument, Master Clarisse stated that no rules had been broken.

"The Book of Rules states that each candidate needs to enter the gate to the Gylden Sirklene challenge alone. Those of us who can read the ancient language interpreted that to mean that folks should go one at a time. There was no one in line when Lady Esmeralda entered the tangle. She did not step in front of anyone to take the challenge. As a matter of fact, there was no one in line when I left the royal palace at noon. Nissa, were you on the terrace all afternoon?"

"I was. Several folks headed for the entrance to the tangle prior to Lady Esmeralda after you left. One made it to the entrance to the tangle and then turned around and left. The other entered the tangle and returned quite quickly. For an hour or so before Lady Esmeralda entered the tangle, there had not been anyone else in the area."

"That does not explain enough. Aaron Beecroft entering the tangle after Lady Esmeralda makes what is happening now unacceptable," said Lady Farcroft.

"The Book of Rules states that only one folk at a time may enter the gate to take the challenge. It does not state that one or more other folks cannot be in the valley at the same time or experience the challenge at the same time. More to the point, as I stated before, I think the first thing that you are not taking into consideration is the fact that none of us here on this terrace, including you, has, or has ever had, any control over the Gylden Sirklene challenge," said Master Clarisse calmly.

Lady Farcroft looked taken aback by Master Clarisse's last statement. Before she could say anything, Master Clarisse went on.

"None of us know what is happening now. We know that Lady Esmeralda walked through the doors in the cliff wall, the gate, and walked into the small valley. Lom and Theora were then escorted out of the valley by the two night wolves, who then returned to it, slipping back through the closing doors. We know when Lom and Theora tried to reopen the doors, they were unsuccessful. They were followed out of the clearing and through the tangle by tendrils of fog that became so thick we could not see down the path."

"Yes, yes, I know all of that. My question ...," started Lady Farcroft.

"I am not finished yet. I think all here should have the information you are requesting. When Lom and Theora were about halfway from the entrance of the tangle to here, Aaron Beecroft left the terrace and met them for a brief conversation."

"He asked why we were no longer at the doors," said Theora. "He was very concerned that Lady Esmeralda was in danger. We advised him that we did not think that was so. He did not wait to listen to why we thought that. Instead, he rushed to the opening of the tangle and entered. Once he had entered the tangle, it closed up behind him. There is no way of knowing if he even made it to the labyrinth. There is no way of knowing if he made it to the doors in the cliff wall. There is no way of knowing if the doors opened for him. In other words, there is no way of knowing just what is happening right now."

"Lady Farcroft," said Master Clarisse, "all any of us know is that something different is happening now. What that means is anyone's guess.

299

When Lord Klingflug took the challenge, the wind practically howled across the royal palace grounds, dark clouds with lightning within moved in over the valley. When the challenge was over, he was escorted out of the tangle by all of the companion animals. He looked very much the worse for wear. When you took the challenge, the wind picked up, some dark clouds moved in, and when you left the tangle, you were escorted out of the tangle by the two night wolves and looked ill."

"There have been a few folks who, when they left the small valley after having been there a while, had a look of awe about them. We do not know what happened to them while they were in the valley. We suspect it was something quite, I don't know, quite, well, like something had really changed for them. I don't know how to explain it otherwise," said Lom.

"As you can plainly see," said Master Clarisse, picking up the narrative once again, "something completely different is happening now that Lady Esmeralda and Aaron Beecroft have entered the tangle. The quirrelit tree made of golden light began to pulse and has settled into a steady rhythm. Buds have appeared on all of the bare branches, and those buds are growing into leaves. I will not be surprised if the quirrelit tree of golden light is soon in full leaf."

Lord Hadrack stepped forward and suggested to Lady Farcroft that he would be glad to escort her back to a comfortable chair and have someone bring her a soothing cup of tea. I heard her remark as she walked away that she still did not feel it was right that Beezle had followed Lady Esmeralda into the tangle. He remarked that it was hard to tell what was right, since it had been a great number of years since the last Gylden Sirklene challenge. He told her we had to trust that what had worked for the land of Sommerhjem for time out of mind would hold true, and a ruler would be picked who would be good for the land.

It worried me that, even after Lord Klingflug's and her own experiences of the Gylden Sirklene challenge, Lady Farcroft was still questioning its validity. I guess there are always going to be folks who would think they should be the rightful rulers of Sommerhjem, or that the rule should be inherited. Once the new ruler of Sommerhjem is chosen, I cannot imagine that everything will just fall in place without some serious issues needing to be resolved. Not everyone was going to quietly and gracefully welcome the new ruler and the new rule.

Time passed slowly as the shadows grew longer and longer on the royal palace grounds. The royal palace cooks and bakers had outdone themselves providing tea, tarts, pastries, and cakes in the late afternoon. As the hours slipped toward dusk, a dinner buffet was set out on the terrace.

No one left. Conversation was now very quiet. The golden quirrelit tree was now covered in the full leaves of summer, pulsing in a slow and steady rhythm. I began to wonder how long all of us would remain on the terrace. When day turned into night, would all of the folks still be here waiting? I continued to wonder if Beezle had gotten into the small valley, and just what was happening in there.

I hoped Lady Esmeralda and Beezle were all right. I realized that over the last year both of them had become my friends. I am sure that others sitting on the terrace were thinking the same thing. Piper would be particularly worried about Beezle, as would Lom, for they had both traveled for a time with him. Lord Hadrack would be especially concerned, since Beezle was his nephew.

And then, there was Lady Esmeralda, who over the last year had become a beloved figure to so many who had been harmed under Lord Klingflug's regency. She had worked tirelessly to make sure the foresters were returned to their home forests. She had been an advocate with the interim ruling council to set up courts throughout the land and appoint good and fair men and women as judges to hear the cases of the multitude of folks who had lost lands and livelihoods because of edicts and taxes under the rule of the former regent.

Just as dusk was about to slip into full dark, something began to change. A murmur began to travel through those gathered on the terrace. Spears of blue light could now be seen above the top of the tangle.

Chapter Forty-Seven

As we watched, the now fully-leafed quirrelit tree made of golden light rose higher into the air and its branches spread even farther out of the small valley. The tree grew brighter and continued to pulse in a steady rhythm. The light from the golden quirrelit tree lit up the royal palace grounds, pushing back the darkness and shadows. We could see clearly all the way to the tangle, which had reopened.

I think all of us on the terrace stopped breathing. At least I know I did. It was so quiet I thought I could hear the waves crashing on the shore far down in the harbor. There was such a stillness, a waiting, not knowing what was about to happen, only knowing something was. I heard someone whisper, "Look, there, there at the tangle."

I looked up to see Tashi glide out of the tangle, the light from the golden quirrelit tree causing her gold and red feathers to blaze. I heard gasps and sighs from those standing near me. Tashi was followed out of the tangle by the two night wolves, Taarig and Tala, walking side by side. The silver tips of their midnight black coats sparkled in the light. The night wolves were followed out of the tangle by the border dog, Kasa, and the bog fox, Toki, also walking side by side. Their coats, too, gleamed in the blazing light from the golden quirrelit tree.

I let go of the breath I had been holding when I saw Carz walk out of the tangle next to Jing, the mountain cat. The two cats looked aloof and fierce, their coats blazing in the light. There was a feeling of great dignity and solemnity about the procession heading out of the tangle. I cannot imagine that any of the folks on the terrace, grounds, or looking out of the royal palace windows did not, at that moment, have their eyes trained on the opening to the tangle.

Lady Esmeralda and Beezle stepped out of the opening to the tangle, side by side. I heard Seeker Chance, who was standing next to me, release a breath when he saw that Ashu, the halekrets, was riding on Beezle's shoulder. I then heard a collective intake of breath when those gathered saw what I had begun to expect might have happened as we waited all those hours. Lady Esmeralda and Beezle were each wearing one of the slim circlets made of an intertwined combination of gold, silver, and what had looked to me to be quirrelit wood with the Neebing patterns carved into them. Under the dome on the stone in the middle of the standing stones, the circlets had looked strikingly beautiful in their simplicity. On the heads of Lady Esmeralda and Beezle, they shone radiantly.

I had wondered why there had been two circlets under the dome on the stone in the circle of standing stones. I had thought that maybe one was for a future king and the other for a future queen, depending who was successful at the Gylden Sirklene challenge. I never considered that there were two circlets because there would be both a king and a queen at the same time. That was certainly going to cause talk.

As the procession of companion animals, Lady Esmeralda, and Beezle made its way slowly up the path from the tangle, I began to listen to the conversations that had started around me. I could hear the surprise in many of the voices, the joy in others. I could hear some folks saying that this combination of Lady Esmeralda and Aaron Beecroft was brilliant.

I could hear members of the interim ruling council talking among themselves, and then consulting with Master Clarisse. Then the same official-looking gentleman who had pounded his staff and called for order at the Well of Speaking when the ninth ring was placed in the vessteboks, once again pounded his staff to get our attention.

"Your attention, please. Master Clarisse, you have the floor."

"The fact that Lady Esmeralda and Aaron Beecroft are approaching us wearing circlets that match those paintings and sketches housed in the royal palace and the royal library should be enough to draw the conclusion that both have completed the Gylden Sirklene challenge and have been chosen as the new rulers of Sommerhjem. The Book of Rules mentions a circle as a symbol."

"They could have taken those circlets into the clearing and never taken the challenge at all," said Lord Hindre.

I could see Lord Klingflug's followers standing with Lord Hindre and nodding their heads in agreement.

"The second mark of the chosen ruler of Sommerhjem is the ability to touch and remove the oppgave ringe from where Nissa left it in the small valley. Those of you who have taken the challenge will know what I state is truth. Lady Farcroft, you entered the small valley and took the challenge. Do I speak the truth?" Master Clarisse asked.

I could see Lady Farcroft trying not to answer Master Clarisse's question. Try as she might, and as much as she was reluctant to answer Master Clarisse's question, she finally spat out, "Yes."

"So then, if Lady Esmeralda and Aaron Beecroft have the oppgave ringe in their possession and are able to handle it without harm, that should answer any misgivings any of you have about one or both of them being the next and rightful ruler or rulers of Sommerhjem."

As I moved closer to the stairs where Carz and the procession would climb up onto the terrace, I came closer to where Lady Farcroft and the others were. Lady Furman's voice was so loud and strident it was not difficult to hear what she had to say.

"This cannot be. Lady Esmeralda gave up the throne," said Lady Furman.

I heard Lord Hadrack repeat what Beezle had said to Lady Esmeralda earlier in the day, suggesting that Lady Esmeralda could not abdicate a throne that had never rightfully been hers. In addition, he told Lady Furman, according to the Book of Rules, Lady Esmeralda had just as much right to take the challenge as she or any of us standing on the terrace.

"So you are saying I must accept her as our new queen?" questioned Lady Furman irately.

"By all indications, that would be so. Do you not see what she is wearing on her head?" inquired Lord Hadrack. "As near as I can tell from this distance, as Master Clarisse stated, it is the same as past queens have worn. Just look at the paintings in the royal palace. The same goes for the circlet that my nephew is wearing. It can be seen in portraits of past kings of Sommerhjem."

"So you are saying that our next queen is an untried lass, and in addition, the challenge has also chosen a king? That our new king is a minor dairy farmer? This cannot be right." Lady Furman said disgustedly, as if she suspected Beezle of smelling of cow pies, of being someone who might drag something unpleasant into the royal palace on his boot.

"Yes. Now if you will excuse me, I would like to go and greet our new rulers and pledge my heartfelt allegiance. You are welcome to stay or go. What I will tell you is the Gylden Sirklene challenge is over. In a very surprising and unexpected way to be sure, but the new rulers have been chosen."

"Not so fast, Lord Hadrack," said Lady Farcroft. "They may be wearing circlets that look like the ones past kings and queens have worn, but we have not yet confirmed the second requirement that Master Clarisse spoke of."

"Nissa, would you come forward, please?" requested Lord Hadrack. "Ah, Shueller, would you also come forward?"

Both of us moved to stand next to Lord Hadrack.

"Shueller, do you have the truth stone with you?"

"Yes, sire."

"Would you place it in Nissa's hand? Lady Farcroft, you or any of your acquaintances are welcome to test the veracity of the truth stone. No? Then will you abide as truth what Nissa tells us while holding the stone?"

They reluctantly agreed.

"Good. Nissa, please describe the oppgave ringe. I know others here on the terrace have seen it, so we can question them also."

"I would be most happy to hold the truth stone and answer your questions. I would suggest we hurry, since I, for one, would like to greet Lady Esmeralda and Bee ... Aaron when they arrive here."

I was a little worried, not so much about holding the truth stone, but that I would not be able to answer the questions the way I had not been able to speak of the Huntress and other things.

"Nissa, please describe the oppgave ringe, once you had it put together."

"While each of the individual pieces looked like rings you might wear on a finger, the assembled oppgave ringe would be a mighty funny ring, for it is far too long for the average finger, and would probably limit movement of the knuckle of even a larger than average hand. So what I assembled was not a ring, but a cylinder. When it was assembled, the scratches on the rings created a pattern similar to those patterns you will find on the seekers' walking sticks."

"What did you do with the oppgave ringe?" Lord Hadrack asked.

I was concerned that I would not be able to tell them, since I had not been able to talk about the standing stones or the rock within, much less the circlets, or my suspicion that the oppgave ringe was the key to opening the clear dome the circlets resided in.

"I left it in the small valley …."

I was glad that Master Clarisse spoke up at that point, for I was not sure I could have said any more.

"Is there anyone here who will dispute the truth of what Nissa is saying? No? Then, let us proceed. Remember, other than the one charged with assembling it, only the rightful king or queen of Sommerhjem can handle the oppgave ringe. We know that those who were not the rightful ring carriers were harmed trying to handle even one piece of the oppgave ringe. Think of how much more harm would come from trying to handle all nine pieces fused together."

At this point, the procession of the companion animals followed by Lady Esmeralda and Beezle had reached the stairs leading up to the terrace. Royal guards had lined up, one to a step on each side of the stairs. The gathered crowd had moved aside to create a space for the companion animals, Lady Esmeralda, and Beezle. Once they were on the terrace, the companion animals formed a protective ring around them. Tashi circled in. Lady Esmeralda instinctively held out her arm. The griff falcon landed on Lady Esmeralda's arm, walked up onto her shoulder, settled herself, and then began preening her feathers. Ashu remained on Beezle's shoulder.

Master Clarisse stepped forward and addressed the two standing inside the circle formed by the companion animals. I noticed that neither of them looked uncomfortable or dazed. There was an air of command about them which I had not seen before. They stood before us straight and strong, and yet supremely at ease.

"Lady Esmeralda, Aaron Beecroft, do you have the oppgave ringe with you?" asked Master Clarisse, her voice ringing out so clearly and loudly I was sure anyone within a block or two of the royal palace would surely be able to hear her.

"We do," said Beezle, opening his hand and holding it out, making it visible for all those close enough to see.

"Lady Esmeralda, would you please take the oppgave ringe from Aaron

Beecroft's hand? You all can clearly see that no harm has come to either of them from handling the oppgave ringe. Nissa, would you please step forward?"

I did as Master Clarisse asked.

"As all of you well know, Nissa has, up to this point, been the only one who has had the ability to handle the oppgave ringe. Nissa, before I ask you to handle it again, do any of the rest of you wish to step forward and try to hold the oppgave ringe? Know you do so at your own risk," stated Master Clarisse.

Lord Mostander shoved his way forward through the crowd. "I will handle the so-called oppgave ringe to prove to you that this is just a trick by the Crown. All of this business with the circlets and the trained animals is just a sham to make us believe that those two are the next rulers of Sommerhjem."

He has obviously never lived and traveled with a hunting cat, I thought, *for there is nothing remotely trained about Carz.*

Lady Esmeralda walked to stand behind Carz and reached across his back to hand the oppgave ringe to Lord Mostander. The oppgave ringe had no more than touched his outstretched hand when he screamed, flung it into the air, and dropped to his knees, clutching his injured hand. Several folks rushed forward to aid him up and to a chair. The royal physician was called to attend to him.

Meanwhile, I watched the oppgave ringe's path of flight as it arced back inside the circle of companion animals to be caught handily by Beezle. He then walked to the edge of the circle, reached across Jing's back, and held out his hand to offer the oppgave ringe to me. I heard a crescendo of voices telling me to take, or not to take, the oppgave ringe from Beezle's hand.

CHAPTER FORTY-EIGHT

I did not hesitate. I had never been harmed by handling the pieces of the oppgave ringe when they were apart, and I had not been harmed when assembling the oppgave ringe. I reached across Jing's back and took the oppgave ringe from Beezle's hand. It felt warm to the touch, but that was all.

"As you can plainly see, Nissa, who has always been able to handle both the individual pieces of the oppgave ringe and the assembled oppgave ringe, can do so now. Does anyone else wish to dispute the fact that Nissa now holds the assembled oppgave ringe?" asked Master Clarisse.

"I do," said Lady Furman, pushing her way through the crowd. "I just know you and that, that dairy farmer who is trying to claim he is the next king of Sommerhjem, are doing some sort of sleight of hand trick. You, rover, keep your hand straight out in front of you so I can see it and the so-called oppgave ringe. I know that one of you has switched the one that Lord Mostander held.

"Lady Furman, I caution you to reconsider what you are asking to do. Nissa is holding a truth stone. Nissa, I ask you again, is the object in your hand the oppgave ringe that you assembled from the nine rings from the vessteboks and left in the small valley at the bottom of the garden?"

"Yes, it is."

"Nissa has indicated that the object she is holding is, in truth, the oppgave ringe. Let me remind you that only Nissa and the one, or in this case the ones, who have taken the Gylden Sirklene challenge and have been chosen as the next rulers of Sommerhjem can handle the oppgave ringe. Lady Furman, are you sure you wish to take the oppgave ringe from her hand?"

"I know there is a trick here, so I am going to prove to all of you that these two standing in the circle of disgusting dirty animals are not the next rulers of this land."

I felt sorry for Lady Furman, for I knew what was going to happen when she took the oppgave ringe from my hand, and it was going to be very painful. I watched as she reached for the oppgave ringe. Her fingers barely touched the cylinder before she screamed, snatched her hand back, and fainted. Fortunately, Master Rollag, who was standing behind her, caught her before she hit the terrace flagstones.

"Is there anyone else who wishes to try holding the oppgave ringe?" asked Master Clarisse. No one stirred. No one pushed through the crowd. "It is my opinion, based on the writings in the Book of Rules, that the Gylden Sirklene challenge has been met. Lady Esmeralda and Aaron Beecroft have successfully completed the challenge and have been chosen to be the new rulers of Sommerhjem."

"As the present chairman of the interim ruling council," said Lord Hadrack, "I speak for the council. We too declare Lady Esmeralda and Aaron Beecroft to be queen and king of Sommerhjem. I suggest we now adjourn this gathering. We will assemble in the Well of Speaking at noon on the morrow for the formal presentation of our new rulers and their installation as king and queen of Sommerhjem."

It took some time to clear the terrace and the royal palace of both well-wishers and disgruntled folks. During all that time, the companion animals never moved from their protective circle. Once the terrace was cleared of stragglers, Lord Hadrack addressed those of us remaining.

"Perhaps now that most everyone has left, might those of you who are partnered with a companion animal request they open their most appreciated circle of protection and allow our new queen and king a chance to move and sit down?"

Before any of us could say anything, the companion animals began to move. Tashi flew to Meryl for a brief moment before she flew up to her favorite perch on a tree next to the railing of the terrace. Each of the other animals greeted their individual companions before settling in for a nap. Ashu swiftly scrambled up Seeker Chance to perch on his shoulder. I had to chuckle, for Ashu checked out each of Seeker Chance's coat and shirt pockets on the way up.

It was not until I heard Master Clarisse address Lady Esmeralda and Beezle as "Your Majesties" that it really hit home for me that Lady Esmeralda was now Queen Esmeralda and Beezle was now King Aaron. It was going to take me a while to get used to addressing Beezle as "Your Majesty." Even calling him "King Aaron" would take some getting used to. To my mind, he would always be Beezle.

"I do not know about the rest of you," said Lady Esmeralda, "but it has been a long and rather surprising day. I, for one, would welcome a soft chair along with some warm tea and a nibble of something. I am finding myself surprisingly hungry. If you would join me, please."

Just as we stepped inside the royal palace, the royal steward, the royal tailor, and the royal dressmaker all rushed forward, requesting the attention of the new king and queen. They exclaimed that there was so much to be done before the morrow and the formal presentation in the Well of Speaking.

Lady Esmeralda addressed the three standing before her. "Both Aaron and I appreciate your concerns. As for what needs to happen to prepare for the presentation in the Well of Speaking, I think we can find something suitable in each of our wardrobes that will be more than adequate for the occasion. If I recall, in my wardrobe, I still have the coming of age gown that I did not get to wear last year, which should suit."

"I too have formal wear at my uncle's town home. I am sure it can be brought here and dusted off before the presentation on the morrow," suggested Beezle.

"I will see to it, Your Majesty," said Lord Hadrack.

I saw Beezle, and I think I will always think of him as Beezle, look startled. That was probably the moment for him that it really sank in that he had been chosen to rule Sommerhjem.

"On a more immediate concern," said Lady Esmeralda to the royal steward, "Reaves, would you see if Cook could put some simple fare together for this group? Have it sent to the Sea Green parlor. It should be big enough to hold all of us. Also, would you ask Cook if she could send something up for the companion animals? Now, if the rest of you would please accompany me to the Sea Green parlor, we have much to discuss."

When we entered the parlor, Beezle flopped himself down in a comfortable chair next to the fire, took the circlet from his head, and spent a moment staring at it. "Well, this is going to take some getting used to."

"Yes, indeed," agreed Lady Esmeralda.

"Lady Esmeralda, we now know that you have been feeling a very strong pull to try the Gylden Sirklene challenge for days," stated Master Clarisse. "We are also aware that you felt you did not have any right to try the challenge. I, for one, am glad you finally gave in to the pull."

"Thank you, I think. I have to admit I am more than a bit surprised and overwhelmed at the moment," said Lady Esmeralda.

"And as for you, Beezle, how long have you felt the pull to try the Gylden Sirklene challenge?" asked Master Clarisse.

"For quite some time," Beezle admitted. "I just kept trying to ignore the pull. I kept hoping Lady Esmeralda would finally realize she should try the challenge. I always thought she should be the next ruler of Sommerhjem. This day, however, after she went through the tangle opening, try as I might, I could not stop myself from following her. At first, I told myself she might be in danger or harmed, so I would just go and try to make sure she was safe. Once I entered the tangle, I knew I could no longer lie to myself."

"Lie about what?" I asked.

"Well, number one, Lady Esmeralda is perfectly capable of taking care of herself. She did not need me to rush in and hold her hand during the challenge. Anyone the challenge would choose to be the next ruler of Sommerhjem would certainly not be some fair damsel in distress. Since I had never thought of Lady Esmeralda as anything other than a highly capable woman, I do not know why I was trying to fool myself that she was not."

"Is there a number two?" I questioned.

"Yes. As I rushed headlong toward the opening of the tangle, I could no longer deny the overwhelming pull to go and attempt the challenge myself."

"Can you tell us what happened next?" Master Clarisse inquired.

"Once I was a few feet within the tangle, the fog thinned considerably. When I got to the clearing, the blue half-globes flared, giving off enough light for me to find my way to the labyrinth. Oddly enough, all the urgency I had felt to reach the tangle fell away when I entered the labyrinth. I took my time walking the labyrinth, trying to empty my mind, as you, Seeker

Eshana, had suggested. Once I was through, I felt a tremendous sense of peace."

"We saw a look of calm and peace on your face, Lady Esmeralda, when you passed us going through the doors to the small valley. Is that how you felt also after walking the labyrinth?" asked Theora.

"After all of the self-arguing about whether I had a right to take the challenge, and whether I would, once I walked the labyrinth, I knew I had made the right choice, and so, yes, I was at peace," said Lady Esmeralda.

"As was I," said Beezle. "When I arrived at the doors built into the cliff wall, I found them standing wide open, which surprised me, since after I ran from the terrace and before I headed to the opening of the tangle, Lom and Theora had told me the doors had closed behind them, and they had not been able to reopen them."

"It sounds like you were expected," commented Lom.

"There was still quite a heavy fog in the small valley when I stepped through the doors. I thought I saw the shape of a fox in the fog, and thinking it was Toki, I followed him to the quirrelit grove. Now, I am not so sure it was Toki. Something to think on another time. At any rate, I am afraid I cannot tell you any more about what happened after I got to the quirrelit grove. Perhaps Lady Esmeralda can."

"I cannot. Not that I do not want to. I do know we must have been in the grove for quite some time. I do know there is much we learned there, and much that needs to be done for the land of Sommerhjem. I also know that, much to my surprise, I have been chosen to be one of the two rulers of Sommerhjem, and Aaron Beecroft here is to be the other. I do not find it odd that the Gylden Sirklene challenge has chosen two rulers. It feels right for this time."

I thought about what Lady Esmeralda had just said about having two rulers of Sommerhjem feeling right for the land at this time. I had to agree. Lady Esmeralda understood the inner workings and intrigues of the capital, and Beezle knew the out county, not only as a minor noble, but also as a traveling musician, and from other roles he had played for the Crown. The two of them created a balance, something Sommerhjem sorely needed.

After several hours passed, many of those gathered in the Sea Green parlor began to take their leave. Much needed to be done before gathering in the Well of Speaking the next day. It had been decided there would be no grand reception, for the new rulers had determined one of the first acts in their rule would be to eliminate foolish and excessive spending on the privileged trappings of rule, which was the total opposite of what the former regent had done.

"The royal treasury, besides being rather low at the moment, needs to be spent wisely on the priority needs of this land. Holding lavish parties to celebrate us does not fit with who each of us is, much less help repair the damage Lord Klingflug's rule has done to Sommerhjem. We think we need to set a precedent as to how we intend to rule, right from the beginning," said Lady Esmeralda.

"Uncle," Beezle said, directing his comment to Lord Hadrack, "would you be so kind as to get a message out to the interim ruling council to attend a meeting day after next? Let us make it early afternoon."

"Now that Sommerhjem has both a king and a queen, you wish to thank them for their service and dismiss them?"

"On the contrary. While yes, the interim ruling council will no longer be needed, an advisory council will be. Lady Esmeralda and I have talked prior to this day about how we hoped the new ruler of Sommerhjem would keep a council made up of folks across clan and class lines. We have always felt that all groups need to be represented and heard. Now that we are the new rulers of Sommerhjem, we want that to happen."

"I would be honored to send out your very wise request, Your Majesty," stated Lord Hadrack.

"Thank you. I have to say, this being addressed as 'Your Majesty' is going to take a bit of getting used to. We will talk more about that later, Uncle."

"One more request," asked Lady Esmeralda. "Those of you who carried pieces of the oppgave ringe to the capital, along with Theora, Seeker Eshana, Ealdred, and Finn, would you folks stay with us in the Sea Green parlor for a little while?"

CHAPTER FORTY-NINE

Once the rest of the group had left, Beezle got up and closed the doors to the Sea Green parlor, locking them tight. He then went over to the fireplace, did something at the mantle, and a wall panel opened. Beezle slipped inside and was gone for a brief time. When he returned, he closed the panel and threw himself back into the chair by the fire, stating all was clear.

"Thank you all for staying," said Lady Esmeralda graciously, "and please do not give me any of that 'we are yours to command' garbage that those fawning nobles are apt to do. I count all of you as my friends ...."

"As do I," said Beezle.

"Over the next few weeks especially, and in the coming years, we are going to need folks who are our friends first and subjects second."

"Being addressed as King Aaron, or Your Majesty, is going to feel mighty strange to me for a long, long time. I am going to need folks who know me, and in private still call me Beezle."

I found myself rather inappropriately chuckling. "King Beezle does have quite a ring to it, though it might lack some panache."

"Just plain Beezle will be just fine," said Beezle, sending me a mock scowl. "In all seriousness, I think it would be all too easy to get caught up in being the ruler and forget who we are ruling. Sommerhjem does not need another Lord Klingflug. I do not want to lose the man who slogged along in the rain with you, Nissa, who played the mountain flute in manors large and small, at harvest festivals, and in smoky pubs with you, Piper, or who escaped the Raven's tower with you, Lom."

"And I do not want to be the isolated princess I was before I spent those weeks traveling with you, Nissa, learning about the country I now find myself surprisingly picked to rule. Both Beezle and I need all of you to remain our friends. We also have a number of tasks left to do together, now and in the future, which we will talk to you about in several days. For now though, it is enough to just be able to be ourselves with you, if you all agree."

I, for one, was honored that the new king and queen of Sommerhjem counted me as a friend. It was good after the events of the last few weeks, and especially this day, to sit back with Carz draped across my feet and carry on quiet conversations among folks I had come to respect and care about over the last year. It was late when our group finally broke up, and Carz and I walked back to the campsite.

The next morning was a flurry of activity. All of us who had carried pieces of the oppgave ringe to the capital were asked to be part of the honor guard escorting the newly-chosen king and queen of Sommerhjem to the Well of Speaking. We all gathered on the front steps of the royal palace buffed, shined, polished, combed, and brushed to within an inch of our lives. Our new queen and king, against the very strongly worded advice of the head of the royal guard, were determined to walk to the capital fairgrounds and the Well of Speaking, rather than to ride in the royal carriage.

"We want everyone to know right off that we are of the folks, not above the folks, of Sommerhjem. You never get to have a chance for another first impression, so we are determined to make this one count," said Lady Esmeralda.

Once we left the royal palace grounds, I could see the wisdom in what Lady Esmeralda had said. The lanes leading to the fairgrounds were lined with folks, all wanting to catch a glimpse of their new king and queen. It did not surprise me that every inch along the way was crowded with folks, not to mention folks hanging off balconies and out of windows, and folks looking down from rooftops.

The two new rulers looked, I think, more regal in their plain formal wear and simple circlets surrounded by us and our companion animals than they would have dressed in splendid expensive finery, riding along in a gilded carriage, wearing crowns weighed down with jewels.

We reached the Well of Speaking without incident. The interim ruling council had gone before us and was already seated on the Speakers Platform. The elders had been seated. General seating was jammed. Meryl launched Tashi, who soared above the crowds, circled the amphitheater several times, and came back to rest on her outstretched arm. That certainly got the assembled crowd's attention, and conversations quickly shifted from a quiet murmur to silence.

Meryl, Tashi, Seeker Chance, and Ashu led the procession down the steps to the bottom of the Well of Speaking. The rest of us, with our companion animals, followed. I heard a collective gasp from the gathered crowd when the newly-chosen king and queen of Sommerhjem stepped through the archway.

The journey down the stairs went quickly for all of us. When we reached the bottom, we lined up along the sea wall facing the crowd. I tried to spot folks I knew. I found Seeker Eshana sitting with other seekers. I located Da and Nana sitting with Master Rollag, Journeyman Evan, Ealdred, and Finn. I also found the group of nobles who had supported Lord Klingflug seated together. Lord Klingflug was conspicuously missing from the group. I could only hope they would not cause a disruption of the proceedings here this day.

The same official-looking gentleman, who had called the assembled folks to attention in the past, pounded his staff, though it was quite unnecessary, since all eyes were on us at the bottom of the Well of Speaking. Lord Hadrack stood, stepped down from the Speakers Platform, and addressed us.

"As chairman, I speak for the interim ruling council. Would Master Clarisse step forward, please?" Master Clarisse stood up from where she was seated in the front row and went to stand next to Lord Hadrack. Both moved to stand with Lady Esmeralda and Beezle. "I cannot imagine that anyone assembled here, and for miles and miles around the capital, did not yesterday see the changes in the quirrelit tree made of golden light. Unlike when Lord Klingflug and others attempted the Gylden Sirklene challenge and the golden tree thrashed amid dark clouds, yesterday the branches budded and then fully leafed out. It also rose higher and spread its branches wider, lighting up the royal palace grounds. While that was happening, Lady Esmeralda and Aaron Beecroft were inside the small valley taking the challenge. When they emerged, they were wearing the circlets you see them wearing now, circlets identical to those seen in paintings of past kings and queens of Sommerhjem. More importantly, they carried with them the oppgave ringe."

Master Clarisse took over the narrative. Standing tall and commanding, holding the Book of Rules in front of her, she looked at the assembled crowd.

"The Book of Rules states that the folk who would be the next ruler of Sommerhjem after the passing of the previous ruler must take and complete the Gylden Sirklene challenge. The Book of Rules indicates there will be a clear sign given when that folk has been chosen. It would be hard for anyone to deny a quirrelit tree made of golden light unfurling into full leaf while Lady Esmeralda and Aaron Beecroft were taking the challenge is a clear sign. In addition, the chosen ruler must be able to hold the oppgave ringe without harm. Both Lady Esmeralda and Aaron Beecroft are able to do so."

"Yesterday," said Lord Hadrack, "both Lord Mostander and Lady Furman tried to prove that the oppgave ringe was false, though it had been declared by the rover Nissa while holding a truth stone to be the actual oppgave ringe. The resulting pain each of them endured trying to hold the oppgave ringe went a long way to convince them that the object was what it had been declared to be. It is the opinion of the interim ruling council, and other folks who were on the terrace of the royal palace yesterday and witnessed what happened, that Lady Esmeralda and Aaron Beecroft have fulfilled the Gylden Sirklene challenge and are the new rulers of Sommerhjem. Let word be sent throughout the land that Sommerhjem has chosen its new rulers the way rulers have been chosen here since time out of mind."

A great cheer rose up from most of the crowd. I noticed Lady Farcroft and those nobles sitting with her were not very enthusiastic in their cheering. As word of the announcement rose up and out of the Well of Speaking, I could hear a roar also rise up from the huge crowds of folks gathered on the capital fairgrounds outside of the amphitheater.

The crowd was brought back to silence by the official-looking gentleman on the Speakers Platform once again pounding his staff to get their attention. Once he had their attention, he announced that the new rulers needed to accept their positions and swear an oath to protect the land of Sommerhjem. He turned our attention back to Lord Hadrack.

"Lady Esmeralda, do you step forward to claim the position of Queen of Sommerhjem, having been chosen by right of having completed the Gylden Sirklene challenge?" asked Lord Hadrack.

"I am honored and humbled to do so."

"Aaron Beecroft, do you step forward to claim the position of King of Sommerhjem, having been chosen by right of having completed the Gylden Sirklene challenge?"

"I too am honored and humbled to do so."

"Will you, Lady Esmeralda, to the best of your ability, rule Sommerhjem with a firm, kind, and loving hand, placing the needs of the land of Sommerhjem and its folks foremost?"

"On my honor, I will."

"Will you, Aaron Beecroft, to the best of your ability, rule Sommerhjem with a firm, kind, and loving hand, placing the needs of the land of Sommerhjem and its folks foremost?"

"On my honor, I will."

"Then let it be so. I am honored as the chairman of the interim ruling council to present the new rulers of our land, Queen Esmeralda and King Aaron, and to turn the rule of Sommerhjem over to them."

It took a while amid all of the cheering and applauding for anyone to notice what was happening above us. When we did, a hush fell over the assembly. The quirrelit tree of golden light had risen even higher. It towered so high that its branches now spread out over the capital and beyond. As we became aware of the branches overhead, a light breeze flowed up from the harbor, carrying the scent of brine. The breeze turned into a brisk wind and began to stir the golden leaves of light from the branches, scattering them in all directions.

Some fell into the amphitheater and touched a folk here and there before fading away. I saw one fall and touch Master Clarisse. I was not surprised to see one land on our newly-declared king's shoulder and one fade away quickly in our new queen's hair. I was surprised to see one of the golden leaves of light on my sleeve and another one on Carz' back. I could not feel the leaf of light, but when it landed on me, I felt something shift inside of me.

When the last leaf of light fell from the golden quirrelit tree, the tree too began to fade. Not until we could no longer see it did conversation once again begin in the Well of Speaking. I heard a noise and turned to see the official-looking gentleman pounding his staff. When he had everyone's attention, he addressed Queen Esmeralda and King Aaron.

"Your Majesties, the Speakers Platform is now yours."

When the members of the now former interim ruling council stood to file off the Speakers Platform, Beezle, I guess I would now need to think of him as King Aaron, asked them to sit back down. He and Queen Esmeralda walked over and climbed the platform to address those assembled in the Well of Speaking.

"We are humbled and honored to be chosen as the rulers of Sommerhjem," stated Queen Esmeralda. "Please know we will work tirelessly to repair the damage done to our land over the long years since a ruler has been chosen by the Gylden Sirklene challenge. Judges will continue to hear petitions to right the wrongs many of you have suffered under Lord Klingflug's regency. Please be patient with us, for we wish to make thoughtful decisions for our land and our folks."

"In addition, we asked the members of the interim ruling council to remain seated behind us because we want them to continue on, not as a ruling council, but as advisors to the Crown. As in the past, when all of the voices of Sommerhjem were heard, so too will they be again," said King Aaron. "Word will be sent throughout the land inviting folks to come to us over the next few months to swear fidelity and bring any of their concerns to our attention. Know that one of our first concerns is to restore the balance in the treasury without overburdening folks with excessive taxes, starting with not having lavish balls and fetes to mark our being declared king and queen."

Regardless of whether Queen Esmeralda or our new king had anything more to say, they were interrupted by folks standing, applauding, and cheering. When the celebration once again settled down, the assembly was declared concluded. Before our new king and queen were escorted out of the Well of Speaking, Beezle stepped down from the Speakers Platform and approached those of us who had carried pieces of the oppgave ringe to the capital.

"I know all of you have put your lives on hold for a very long time. Queen Esmeralda and I would ask that you delay your leaving the capital for a few more days. We would like to meet with you day after next, if you would."

Chapter Fifty

The two days after the presentation of the new rulers of Sommerhjem in the Well of Speaking had been relaxing. In anticipation of leaving soon, all of us who had carried rings into the capital, along with those who were camping on the royal palace grounds, had begun the process of airing out our bedding, cleaning up our respective homewagons, wagons, and tents, and cleaning up errant debris we had left scattered about. Queen Esmeralda had sent word that we should take anything we might need from the royal stores to replenish our supplies.

During those two days I had time to get to know Nowles and Üba. Carz had taken Üba under his paw, which was good for the young hunting cat. I had a chance to look at some of the drawings Nowles had done for Yara. She had been quite correct in saying he was a gifted artist. I asked him what he hoped to do next, now that he had delivered his drawings to the royal library.

"I'd like to go on a walkabout. I'm of age," Nowles told me.

Being old enough in age to go on a walkabout was debatable. Being old enough to go on a walkabout after having spent time with the Huntress was not. I knew we needed to come up with a plan soon to get Üba and Nowles out of the capital with none the wiser. I thought it might be prudent to wait on the planning until after our meeting this afternoon with Queen Esmeralda and King Beezle. I still could not call him "King Aaron" no matter how hard I tried.

It was later than we had expected when Queen Esmeralda and King Beezle entered the small parlor where those of us who were accompanied by companion animals were gathered, including Nowles and Üba. I felt a bit sorry for Nowles, for he looked decidedly uncomfortable and a little worried.

"We apologize for being late. I am hopeful that once things settle down a bit, we will not be saddled with long-winded folks wasting the day. Seems everybody urgently needs our attention. We have declared the next two days meeting-free, much to the vexation of a number of folks. One, because there is a task that all of us in this room need to do together. Two, because there are a few other things that need to be arranged before all of you head out. And three, because we wanted to spend some time with all of you before you leave. Now, if you will follow us," said King Beezle.

I was surprised when we were led back down to the chamber with pillars. Even more surprising was the fact that, when we entered, the lanterns were already lit. After I walked into the chamber, I looked back and saw Nowles and Üba standing frozen in the doorway. Queen Esmeralda got his attention.

"You and Üba are needed here. Please enter the chamber and stand in front of the first pillar to the right of the door."

"But, but, all of these others carried pieces of the oppgave ringe to the capital. They are very important folks. I, I, I just happen to be lucky enough that Üba chooses to stay with me for now."

"You are just as important as these folks here. You and Üba have been called to help with a task this day," said Queen Esmeralda gently. "Now, please enter the chamber and stand in front of the pillar to the right of the door. You will notice that Üba is already on top of it. Thank you. Lom and Theora, would you please close the door to the chamber?"

As before, when Lom and Theora traced the outlines representing the two night wolves, several things happened at once. The outlines of the night wolves turned blue, a slight grinding noise could be heard, and from both sides of the opening of the chamber, stone doors swiftly slid out and closed off the chamber. Tala jumped off the pillar she had been sharing with Taarig and went to stand in front of the closed door. Theora moved to stand next to Tala.

Once the doors were closed and all of us were in place, Queen Esmeralda and King Beezle walked the labyrinth to the center of the chamber. They positioned themselves facing each other, toes touching the outside of the inlaid symbol of a quirrelit tree surrounded by a patterned border. King Beezle then turned and addressed us.

"If you would, one by one, starting with Nissa, please trace the outline of your companion animal on the pillar you stand before. Nowles, I do not think you will find an outline of a hunting cat on the pillar you stand before and Üba sits atop, but when it is your turn, try just placing your hand on the pillar."

One by one, we did as asked. As before, the outlines of our companion animals began to glow blue. When Nowles placed his hand on the pillar upon which Üba sat, the whole pillar glowed blue. A blue line flowed out from the base of the pillar Nowles touched. It continued to move along the path into the labyrinth, where it halted at the very center. Once it reached the middle of the labyrinth and touched the symbol of a quirrelit tree surrounded by a patterned border, that circular section of the floor began to rise up until it was a waist-high pillar.

Queen Esmeralda held her hand out to King Beezle. He reached in his pocket, drew out the oppgave ringe, and placed it in Queen Esmeralda's hand. She, in turn, placed the oppgave ringe on the top of the pillar. I watched in amazement as the oppgave ringe fell apart. Before that happened, I would have declared to anyone that those nine rings were fused together for all of time. I would have been wrong.

"Nissa, since you and Carz were the first to bring in pieces of the oppgave ringe to the capital, it seems only fitting that you be asked to carry one again. Would you and Carz enter the labyrinth, please?" requested Queen Esmeralda.

We did as requested.

"On behalf of the Crown, Nissa, would you serve the land of Sommerhjem once more by becoming the guardian of this piece of the oppgave ringe and, on your honor, protect it at all cost?" asked Queen Esmeralda.

"Yes, I would be honored," I said, as I took the piece of the oppgave ringe. King Beezle took a small golden pine spider silk pouch out of his pocket and handed it to me.

I left the labyrinth and took my place with Carz in front of the pillar with the hunting cat outline still glowing blue. Each of the other pairs who had carried pieces of the oppgave ringe to the capital, in turn, walked the labyrinth, accepted a piece of the oppgave ringe and a small golden pine spider silk pouch, and returned to stand by their pillar. The second to last to step forward were Nowles and Üba.

"On behalf of the Crown, Nowles, would you serve the land of

Sommerhjem by becoming the guardian of this piece of the oppgave ringe, and on your honor, protect it at all cost?" asked Queen Esmeralda.

Nowles looked more than overwhelmed and somewhat panicked.

"Lad, it is right that you take this piece of the oppgave ringe," said King Beezle, with just the right amount of dignity and gentleness. "While Nissa carried two pieces of the oppgave ringe because circumstances made that necessary, Master Clarisse has assured us that one piece per folk is the preferred method. You have been chosen to carry a piece of the oppgave ringe just as much as the others here. We ask that you guard it until such time as it is needed again, which we sincerely hope will be a long, long time from now."

"Yes, I would be honored," said Nowles, taking the piece of the oppgave ringe and the pouch of golden pine spider silk.

Lom was then called forward and received his piece of the oppgave ringe. When Queen Esmeralda picked up the last piece of the oppgave ringe, the pillar that had risen out of the floor smoothly descended, and the blue line retreated back out of the labyrinth, back to the pillar Nowles was in front of, and faded out. One by one, the glowing blue lines of each of the companion animals also faded out.

"Before we leave here where we cannot be overheard, we would speak with each of you. Greer, we would ask that you and your father continue your work to strengthen support for the Crown in your area. Yara, we would ask that you continue to be the royal librarian at large, specifically trying to gather the old books and scrolls, and also anything you can find concerning the time of King Griswold's daughter's reign."

Both Greer and Yara nodded in agreement.

"Besides finding what is written before it becomes lost, we also need to find out more about those ancient places scattered about Sommerhjem. Piper, we know you have a great interest in those places," said King Beezle. "Would you take on the task of trying to find out more about them?"

I saw the look of delight on Piper's face and knew that the king could not have asked a better boon from Piper.

"Nowles," King Beezle continued, "do you think you and Üba could travel with Piper and Jing for a while? Your artistic ability could come in handy in recording those ancient sites."

Now, Nowles had more of a stunned look on his face, but I could see that the idea held a great deal of appeal to him. He nodded a yes.

"Seeker Chance, as always, we are grateful for the tasks that the Order of Seekers does in searching out the old and lost knowledge. We would ask you to continue to do so. In addition, we would ask before you continue your journey that you have a conversation with Thorval Pedersen," requested Queen Esmeralda.

Now, that is interesting. I wonder what that is all about?

"Lom, we are well aware that you do not seek to become the next head royal palace gardener and want to continue your learning from Ealdred. We would ask that you might delay returning to Ealdred's home for a while longer. We need you, Theora, and Ealdred to spend some time in the small valley at the bottom of the royal palace garden to set it to rights and to help establish a home for the halekrets. The small valley will still open for the two of you, for a period of time. Would you both be willing to do so? I talked to Ealdred earlier, and he has said he would stay, if you both wished to," said Queen Esmeralda.

Lom and Theora both answered in the affirmative.

"Meryl, would you and Finn keep the Crown informed as to what is coming in on the tide where you live, and also what you observe and find while traveling?" asked King Beezle.

Meryl said she could not speak for Finn. She felt he would most probably be honored to be asked, and she could see the wisdom of having someone loyal to the Crown watching the sea.

"Nissa, there has been a long tradition of rovers listening and passing on information that the Crown might find of interest. Before you leave the capital, would you take the time to meet with Lady Celik and her son Elek?"

I answered in the affirmative. I knew that Da had been a member of Lady Celik's network of information gatherers. It would seem I was now to follow in my Da's footsteps.

We stayed only a little while longer in the chamber. I was the last one to leave and, as I stepped through the doorway, the door slid closed behind me. *How interesting,* I thought. *The door was open when we first came down here. Now that the new rulers have been chosen, and the oppgave ringe is in nine pieces again, the chamber has closed up.*

I spent about a week more in the capital meeting with Lady Celik and her son. During the week, one by one, those who had carried pieces of the oppgave ringe began to depart. It was hard to say goodbye to each and every one of them.

What surprised me most was one day after all of us had met in the chamber, Da came by to say he was going to be gone for a while. He was going to travel with Seeker Chance on a task for the Crown.

"What about Nana?" I asked.

"The royal herbalist and an herbalist named Siri have requested she work with them for a time. I'm going to leave the homewagon here and will be back to pick up both Nana and the homewagon when I return. I will miss you, daughter. I hope you will spend some time with Nana and me during the cold months."

I assured him I would. It was hard to say goodbye and watch him head up to the royal palace one last time. Finally, of those who were leaving, only Piper, Jing, Nowles, Üba, Carz, and I remained in the capital. We had decided that the easiest and simplest way to get Nowles and Üba out of the capital discreetly would be to have them travel out in my homewagon. We did not think anyone would think twice to see Piper and me travel out together, since it would be expected that we would both be heading south, Piper home to her family in the southern mountains and me to catch up with the other rovers moving from fair to fair.

The morning arrived when everything that needed to be done was done. I had packed up my homewagon, tucked away the stores, topped off the water barrel, and hitched up the cart. There was nothing left to do. Lom, Theora, Ealdred, Master Clarisse, Master Rollag, Journeyman Evan, Queen Esmeralda, and King Beezle came to see us off. It was harder than I thought it would be to say goodbye.

We left the capital without incident. It was good to be on the road again. It was a clear, sunny, blue sky day. There was a slight breeze that carried the scent of the sea and the smell of pine. As hard as it was to say farewell to the friends I had made over the last year, I was glad to be sitting on the driver's bench of my homewagon with Carz beside me, Nowles and Üba tucked away inside, and Piper riding astride her horse alongside. It felt so good to be traveling the royal road heading south. Who knew what adventures lay ahead down the road?

CPSIA information can be obtained
at www.ICGtesting.com
Printed in the USA
BVOW03*1055100417

480438BV00011B/3/P